THE RED WOLF

By

DAVID TINDELL

Cover art by Tanja G., www.premadecoverdesigns.com.
Formatting design by Amy Huntley,
www.theeyseforediting.com.

ISBN: 978-1535176842

To the Cold Warriors.
For decades, they held the line.
Most of them worked in the light,
some in the shadows.
When things got hot, they stepped into the breach.
And they were victorious.

During the Cold War, we lived in coded times
when it wasn't easy and there were
shades of gray and ambiguity.

John le Carré

Here's my strategy on the Cold War:
We win, they lose.

Ronald Reagan

CAST OF CHARACTERS

THE AMERICANS

Pallas Group:

JO ANN GEARY—Lt. Col., U.S. Air Force Special Operations, code name White Vixen.

KEITH JENNINGS—Major, U.S. Army Special Forces.

DENISE REINECKE—Major, U.S. Marine Corps, Diana Brigade veteran.

GERALD TELLER—Colonel, U.S. Marine Corps.

EDWARD ANASTAS—Lt. Cmdr., U.S. Navy.

WILL HARRISON—CIA Special Activities Division/Special Operations Group (SAD/SOG).

JOSEPH GEARY—Jo's father; Deputy Director of Operations, CIA.

JANELLE BOUDREAU—Assistant to the Chief of Staff for the senior senator from New Hampshire.

EDWARD FLANAGAN—National Security Advisor

ROGER PRESTON—Acting Director of Central Intelligence

THE SOVIETS

SERGEY GRECHKO—Colonel, Soviet Army *Spetsnaz;* code name *Krasniy Volk* (Red Wolf).

The Committee:

ARKADY VOLOSHIN—Major General, Soviet Air Force.

BORIS MELIKOV—General, Soviet Army.

VLADIMIR KLIMOV—Colonel General, Soviet Army.

VYACHESLAV BUTROVICH—Politburo member.

KONSTANTIN OBOLENSKY—General, Soviet Army GRU.

PAVEL DULTSEV—General, Soviet Army.

YEVGENY MALTSOV—Major, KGB; undercover intelligence operative, posing as Finnish businessman Lars Makkonen.

PROLOGUE

UKRAINIAN SSR,
SOVIET UNION
OCTOBER 1941

The man's hands were trembling so badly that he spilled half the vodka in the glass before slurping down the rest. A dribble of liquid ran down his chin into the whiskers that were already mostly white. Vasily knew the man was only thirty years old, but he looked almost twice that age.

"May I—have another, please, Comrade Captain?"

Vasily poured another three fingers of vodka into the glass. This time the man drank half of it without spilling, and when he set the glass down on the rough tabletop, his shakes had calmed somewhat. "All right, then, comrade," Vasily said, "tell me again what you saw."

The man took a deep breath, then wiped his mouth with the sleeve of his threadbare coat. "They came into the village at daybreak," he said, his voice a monotone. "Two cars, then three trucks. They came right to the commissar's house. You remember it, don't you, Vasily Aleksandrovich?"

"Yes, I do." Vasily could see it clearly in his mind's eye; it had been only six months since he'd last been to the village where he'd been born and raised. "Comrade Burlachenko's place, right?"

"That's right, Burlachenko, the fat one who—" The man stopped, looking up at Vasily with eyes that suddenly held fear and pleading. "I'm sorry, I meant no disrespect for the commissar."

"That's all right, Oleg Ivanovich, please continue," Vasily said. There was a time, not long ago, when a reference like that to a Commissar of the Party might result in harsh measures of re-education, but these were different times now, more desperate times. "Did you see their uniforms, the men who were in the cars and trucks?"

"Gray, like all of them. The officers had hats, but most of them had helmets. They broke down the commissar's door. I heard screams, and then they hauled the commissar and his wife and daughters outside. They were... they were still in their nightclothes."

"What were you doing that early on the street?" Vasily had to ask the question, for the benefit of the other officer in the room, although he knew the answer already. Many times he'd seen Oleg the milkman on his early rounds.

"I was beginning my morning deliveries. The commissar's house is always first. I was coming around the corner of the street with my cart, three buildings down. I don't think they saw me."

"What did they do with the commissar and his family?" Vasily asked, although he was already certain he knew. His chest tightened, but he had to find out as much as he could from the only witness they were likely to find. He doubted anybody else had escaped.

"They—they shot the commissar. In the head. One of the officers, with his pistol."

"And the women?"

Oleg tossed the rest of the vodka down and took a deep breath. "The commissar's wife, they shot her too. The two girls, they ripped their nightclothes off, and then—and then, four of the soldiers took them back inside the house..."

Vasily knew those girls. Antonina was fifteen or so, Veronika only, what, twelve? Thirteen? He turned away briefly, forcing himself to take a calming breath, then another. It was a moment before he could resume the questioning, although there wasn't much more to tell. Oleg ran back to his farmhouse on the outskirts of the village, leaving his cart in the street. In the barn he ignored the two cows and saddled his horse. She was an old mare but could still carry a rider even though she was accustomed to pulling the wagon. The shooting began just as Oleg started his desperate ride, waiting for a bullet to find his back.

For the first time since the milkman's arrival, Vasily's fellow officer, Filipov, spoke. "You did not stay to help your family escape?"

"He has no family," Vasily said. "His parents died years ago. His brother was in the Army in Finland, isn't that so, Oleg?"

"Yes, yes," the milkman said, his eyes flicking to Filipov and then quickly back to Vasily. "In his last letter, he said I should leave, head east, but..." Oleg stifled a sob. "I could not leave the village. It is all I have ever known." Desperate now, he looked up at Vasily again. "I had heard that there were partisans here," he said, his voice tinged with panic. "I knew you would want to know what happened, isn't that right, Vasily? I mean, Comrade Captain?"

Vasily reached across the table and patted the milkman on the arm. "You did well, Oleg," he said. "There was nothing you could've done by staying. You would have been shot, too." He stood. "You have shown great courage, Oleg. The information you have brought us is very valuable. Rest, now. You are safe here. I must talk with Lieutenant Filipov for a few minutes." A nod to the partisan at the door would serve to summon the woman, who would prepare food for Oleg, and a place to sleep.

"You will go to the village, won't you, Comrade Captain? You and your men will drive out those bastards, won't you?"

"Don't worry, Oleg. The Army has the force of all the people behind it. We shall prevail."

Outside the ramshackle house, Filipov lit a cigarette, offering one to Vasily, who declined. "What do you make of it?" the lieutenant asked.

"*Einsatzgruppen,* of course," Vasily said, his breath steaming into the night. "Probably *Sonderkommando* units." The dreaded paramilitary troops of the German SS were sweeping through every village right behind the *Wehrmacht* as the Red Army retreated. Sometimes they would shoot only a few people, but usually more. A lot more.

"They'll be coming here next," Filipov said. He and Vasily were the only two *Spetsnaz* troops in their platoon of partisan irregulars, working reconnaissance missions behind enemy lines. The Red Army had been on its heels ever since the German invasion this past summer, but at least now they were starting to get some things organized, inserting small teams here and there. Some were never heard from again, Vasily knew, and truth be told, he considered his own chances of surviving the war to be poor. But he had much to live for. Magda was back in Moscow, safe with her parents, and if he could ever get back, they would marry, and maybe someday raise a family. But he wondered whether that family, if it would ever exist, would be speaking Russian or German.

"We move out at dusk," Vasily said, looking at his watch. It was four in the afternoon. They would have to stay undercover in the village until nightfall. The *Luftwaffe* ruled the skies in daytime. It was a miracle, really, that Oleg the milkman had not been spotted by a plane and strafed into so much hamburger. Vasily had seen the havoc wrought by the Germans in their Stuka ground-attack planes.

"What of the villagers here?" Filipov asked.

Vasily looked back at him with hard eyes. "There is nothing we can do to protect them," he said. "Our mission is to find out what the Germans are doing. We must report back." They had no radio, so they would have to find their way back to Soviet lines, no easy task. Vasily figured the nearest friendly units might be fifty kilometers away, maybe more.

The men stood in silence for a few minutes, Filipov finishing his cigarette, Vasily deep in thought. He hated to leave without doing anything to help these villagers, not to mention the ones still alive—if any—back in his home village, from which Oleg had escaped. But he had his duty, and he had intelligence to report to his superiors.

Only twenty-six years old, Vasily Aleksandrovich

Grechko had seen much since joining the Army six years earlier. His dedication to the Party and aptitude for leadership quickly resulted in his elevation to the officer corps of a Red Army airborne brigade. Stalin had more paratroopers than the rest of the world's armies put together, and there was little doubt among the men they would be the vanguard of a Soviet assault into the heart of Europe. But in 1939 came the startling news that Stalin had agreed to a pact with Hitler, allowing for the division of Poland. Vasily's unit parachuted into eastern Poland in early September and he saw his first combat. A year later he was in Bessarabia, helping the Red Army wrest the province from Romania.

Then they waited and watched nervously as the Germans rolled to easy victories in western Europe. It was whispered that Stalin's grand vision was to have the Germans exhaust themselves against the British and French, giving the Red Army years of time to build up its strength for the inevitable conflict with Hitler's legions. The rumors must have been true, Vasily concluded, because the political commissars had begun to talk about the glorious days in the future when Soviet troops would walk the streets of Paris and Vienna. Berlin had not been mentioned.

But Vasily was not fooled. Even though he had grown up in a small village in Ukraine, he had a native intelligence that worked to his advantage in the Army, starting with his appointment to the Moscow Military School, and then his assignment to a parachute brigade. He learned quickly to keep his true thoughts to himself, developing the rare skill of being able to differentiate between political doublespeak and truly valuable information. Thus he was not at all surprised when the Wehrmacht launched itself into the Soviet Union in June. By then he had already begun his training with a new unit, loosely called *Voyska spetsialnogo naznacheniya,* or *Spetsnaz.* With his airborne training and combat experience, he advanced quickly and was given command of a partisan company. His familiarity with this part of Ukraine led to this mission.

"Do you think it is true, about Babi Yar?" Filipov asked.

"Probably," Vasily said. They'd already encountered enough refugees from Kiev to lend credence to the stories. On the face of it, Vasily could hardly believe it to be true. Just two weeks earlier, the Jews of Kiev had been rounded up by the Germans and taken to Babi Yar, a ravine northwest of the city, where they were forced to strip naked and then shot. As they fell into the pits, the next group had to lie down on top of the bodies. On and on it went, for two days.

"I heard twenty thousand," Filipov said.

Vasily knew it was more than that, maybe thirty to thirty-five thousand. "At least," he said. He also had heard that the massacre was the Germans' response to terror bombings carried out by Soviet NKVD units who had stayed behind in the occupied city.

But it was not just the Jews who were being rounded up by the Einsatzgruppen. Vasily didn't have much use for Jews, an attitude shared by many of his fellow Ukrainians, but he knew the Germans wouldn't stop there. The commissars said that Hitler intended to exterminate all Slavic peoples as well as the Jews, and in this case, Vasily felt that for once they were right.

"Bastards," Filipov said. "The Party will rally the people and we will drive them out."

"Yes, we will," Vasily said, but he did not have the blind faith of the younger man. He had seen too much. In some ways, he knew the Communists were no better than the Nazis, but this was an opinion he never dared share with anyone. What he knew to be true, though, was that the Party was the only thing holding the Soviet Union together. If it shattered, there would be no stopping the Germans. Their panzers would roll on, eastward all the way to the Urals and southward to the oil fields of the Caucasus, and in ten years these steppes and forests of his beloved Ukraine would have not a single human soul of Ukrainian or Russian descent. There would be Germans here, thousands of them, enjoying the *Lebensraum,* the "living space" promised to them by their beloved *Führer.*

The Party, for all its faults, was strong and disciplined, and those traits would be what would save his country, if it could be saved. Then, if he survived, Vasily would marry his beautiful Magda, and they would have a son, a boy who would grow into a strong and disciplined man, a soldier who would help the Party face the threats of the future, for there would always be threats.

"Gather the men," Vasily ordered. "Soon it will be time to go."

CHAPTER ONE

CAMP DAVID,
MARYLAND
JANUARY 1987

The first President of the United States Joseph Geary had met was Harry Truman. Geary had no trouble recalling the date: the sixth of June, 1945, and the place, a reception at the State Department headquarters. Geary recalled how nervous he'd been at twenty-five years of age, just a few years out of Yale and into his career at the Office of Strategic Services. On that night, the first anniversary of D-Day, Geary accompanied his department director to the reception, where everyone was surprised by Truman's arrival. Less than four months on the job after the tragic death of FDR, the former Missouri haberdasher impressed the young OSS operative with his folksy demeanor, behind which the perceptive agent sensed a stiff resolve. Geary had heard all the talk around Washington that Truman wasn't up to the job, was a political appointee by Roosevelt who had barely been on speaking terms with his vice president all the way back to the campaign the previous fall.

Like many others, Joe Geary wondered whether Truman had the right stuff, but after meeting him that night, he had no doubt. Over the course of the next several years, their paths would cross again. Geary also met Truman's successor, Dwight Eisenhower, and every president since then. Some he had respected professionally but not liked personally—Kennedy, for instance, a charismatic man whose philandering was something Geary simply could not approve of, and Nixon, who had a strong grasp of international affairs but simply was not a man you could warm up to. With others, it was the other way around.

But he had worked for all of them, first in OSS and then in its successor organization, the Central Intelligence Agency. His forty-plus years in the espionage business had led him to this last stop. As Deputy Director of Operations, he had been summoned to Camp David by no less than the current resident of the Oval Office, and not through intermediaries. The personal call earlier that day came to Geary's own secure phone, with the White House operator putting the call through. Once the requisite pops and clicks had sounded to give the electronic equivalent of an All Clear, Geary heard the famous voice, chatting for a few seconds, then asking him to come up to Camp David that evening for a talk. It was not a request that Geary or anyone else would have refused.

"The president will see you now," a man said. Geary knew him as the assistant chief of staff. The chief, Donald Regan, didn't normally accompany his boss to the official presidential retreat, named by Eisenhower in honor of his grandson. That was fine with Geary, who found Regan to be abrasive and overbearing. Ironically, both Regan and the president had served as lifeguards in their younger days. The word around CIA was that while the future president had spent his time saving people from drowning, his future chief of staff had spent his time watching out for kids pissing in the pool. Geary nodded at the man and went through the opened door.

There was only one person in the room, a man sitting on a leather couch near the crackling fireplace. He put down the book he'd been leafing through and rose, coming forward to greet his visitor. Once again, Geary was impressed by the president's physical size and ruddy complexion, belying his, what was it now, soon to be seventy-six years? "Joe, come in, nice to see you again," Ronald Reagan said, shaking hands with a strong grip. "How was the weather on the way up?" He motioned Geary to a chair near the couch.

"Not bad, sir, thank you." Geary had met Reagan shortly after his inauguration six years ago, had briefed him on several occasions, but always in the company of the Director of Central Intelligence. William Casey, though, was on medical leave now, fighting for his life from a hospital bed. His deputy, a political appointee who hadn't taken long to rub Geary the wrong way, was now running the agency. Why that man was not here now was puzzling. Casey had allowed his DDO a lot of room, and it hadn't taken the acting director long to signal that those days were ending.

"Get you anything?" the president asked. "It's after hours, so the bar's open."

"Thank you, sir. Scotch, neat."

"Good, good." The president motioned to the assistant chief, still standing in the open doorway. "Bill, tell Ed, Scotch neat for our guest, please. I'll keep him company."

While the president made small talk, Geary's ever-observant eyes took the measure of the man. Wearing a denim shirt, open at the neck, with khaki pants and loafers, Reagan looked more like a successful retired executive than a man still very much active in the world's toughest job. Geary knew of his exercise habits, his regular visits to the White House gym and his horseback riding and wood-chopping on the ranch out in California. That demanded Geary's respect. It was only recently, at his daughter's prodding, that Geary had started a regular exercise regimen again. Still, he looked like he was the older man, and not just because he was bald.

Geary was well aware of the stories about Reagan, how he was detached and incurious when it came to the details of shaping policy and managing his staff. There were plenty of people in the government, including some in the White House, who spoke of the president in disparaging terms. Geary had heard the occasional comments at cocktail parties, at meetings, even in foreign capitals from people who should've known better, or those who hadn't gotten over the fact that Reagan had demolished their candidates in two elections.

Geary heard a lot of stories in his job, but you couldn't discount the value of personal observation. He'd met with Reagan several times, and while he'd known presidents who had a better understanding of the details of one thing or another, none were better than Reagan at seeing the big picture. Geary remembered his meetings with Reagan's predecessor; although Geary liked him personally and greatly respected his Navy experience and strong religious faith, Jimmy Carter was truly one of those who not only couldn't see the forest for the trees, he couldn't see the trees for the leaves. In the end, Geary was sure, those contrasting perspectives were one reason Reagan had been sent to the White House and Carter had been sent back to his peanut farm in Georgia.

A steward came in with the drinks and served each of the men. "Thank you, Ed," the president said with a grin. The steward closed the door behind him on the way out. "Well, Joe, there's something I wanted to talk to you about, as you may have guessed."

Geary nodded. CIA had several things going on right now that Reagan might've been interested in discussing, but the DDO had tried not to anticipate the president's thoughts. That turned out to be a good thing.

"You did some good work helping me get ready for Reykjavik last fall," Reagan said, his mood instantly more serious. "I was ready for everything they threw at me over there."

"Thank you, sir," Geary said. His office had worked hard to assist Casey in putting together a full briefing for the president in advance of his meeting with the new General Secretary of the Communist Party of the Soviet Union, Mikhail Gorbachev. The result had been an agreement to reduce the two countries' nuclear arsenals. "It looks good for INF," he added. The Intermediate Range Nuclear Forces Treaty would hopefully be signed later this year. It was a significant breakthrough in Soviet-American relations.

"It looks good for a lot more than that," the president said. He took a sip of his drink, then gazed into the fire. His eyes turned back to Geary. "If we play our cards right, Joe, the Cold War could be over in a few years. Gorbachev wants that and so do I. He understands that the only way his country can survive is to move forward economically and politically."

"He's got a long way to go, sir," Geary said.

"That he does," Reagan said, nodding. "I have to tell you, Joe, I was impressed with the man when we met in Iceland. He has some good ideas but he's got a tough row to hoe over there. I wished him luck."

"He'll need it."

"I intend to keep the pressure on him, Joe, and I told him that. I'm going to Berlin this summer, and when I'm there I'm going right to that damn wall and I'll challenge him to tear it down. What do you think of that?"

Geary took a breath, turning it over. "That will take some guts, Mr. President," he said finally. "It's a little bit stronger than *'Ich bin ein Berliner.'*"

"Yes, well, Kennedy was there in the middle of this whole thing. We were still playing catch-up in many ways. Now, we're starting to see the light at the end of the tunnel. We can afford to be a little more aggressive, I think."

"It's not so much Gorbachev, it's the people who are running the Party," Geary said. "They're the ones who have the most to lose if democracy ever comes to Russia."

"Exactly. Gorbachev knows that. He's walking a real tightrope and we've got to keep him on it as long as we can." Reagan looked at Geary with a penetrating eye. "If he falls and the reactionaries take control, we've got some real trouble ahead. If they still had Andropov..."

"Fortunately for us, they don't," Geary said,

remembering the former KGB chief who had briefly headed the Soviet government upon Brezhnev's death a few years ago, before his own untimely demise. Did he detect a little twinkle in Reagan's eye?

"Yes, isn't it?" the president said. Reagan, of course, was one of the handful of people in the world who knew what had really happened to Yuri Andropov. Geary was another. But the less said about that, the better.

"How can I help, Mr. President?"

Reagan reached for a file on a side table, leafed through it briefly, and dropped it on the coffee table in front of Geary. The file had been sealed with red tape, was bordered in red and labeled TOP SECRET. "When I came back from Iceland, I had Bill Casey look into this situation for me. He found out a couple things and brought them to my attention. I got this report the other day and Bill recommended I talk to you about it. Even though he's in the hospital, we stay in touch. He thinks you're the man for this job."

"What job is that, sir?"

"Gorbachev is worried that some hard-liners over there are planning to move against him. He's not sure who they are, but he thinks they want to play it safe so it won't look like a full-scale coup. That would be dangerous. Who knows what would happen? He's worried that some of their satellites might react to unrest in Moscow by starting trouble of their own. Poland, especially."

Geary nodded. "The Poles might see it as their big chance. Others might follow suit—East Germany, Czechoslovakia..."

"If Gorbachev is taken out of the picture and their

empire starts breaking up, the hard-liners won't be able to hold it together without a real risk of bloodshed. If the Poles, the East Germans and the Czechs rise up, Moscow will have to send in the tanks, and if there's real resistance they risk NATO coming over the hill like the Seventh Cavalry."

Geary had his doubts about that. He was all too familiar with America's NATO allies. His concern must've shown on his face, because Reagan said, "I sense you're not really comfortable with that idea, Joe. If you're not, let's hear it."

"Very well, sir. With respect, Mr. President, would you order American troops into Eastern Europe? With or without NATO support?"

Reagan looked at him with a bit of a smile, but his eyes were narrow. "Well, now, Joe, I might not. Or I just might. We didn't do anything to help the Czechs in '68, or the Hungarians in '56. This time, we just might decide to help them. The American people didn't hire me to sit around. I think by now everybody understands that."

Geary saw the point. "Moscow wouldn't know for sure. This isn't '68 or '56."

Reagan raised an eyebrow and nodded. "That's right. Gorbachev knows how the game is played. He knows that whoever they are, they can't take that chance, so he thinks their idea will be to use one man, a very dangerous man it seems, to take him out."

Geary was only mildly surprised. "An assassination plot," he said. "A hard-liner steps in to save the country when its leader is killed."

"That's pretty much the gist of it," Reagan said. He pointed at the file on the coffee table. "Gorbachev told me he asked some of his key people who they might recommend to use in a mission to eliminate a European head of state. He said they all had one man at the top of the list. Highly-trained, operating independently of any control. They call him the Wolf." Reagan took a sip of his drink. "This Wolf fellow sounds like a pretty tough customer. Spetsnaz officer, two tours in Afghanistan. The *mujahedeen* were terrified of him. A crack shot, and he's an expert in hand-to-hand combat, some sort of martial art I've never heard of. Very tough customer indeed."

"The obvious question, Mr. President, is why doesn't Gorbachev just arrest this guy right now?"

"That's exactly what I asked him, and he said that he doesn't want to let these hard-liners, whoever they are, know he might be on to them. This particular agent has served the Soviet Union with distinction. Now, in Stalin's day there would have been no problem, Stalin would've given the word and the man would be gone. But times have changed over there. Gorbachev's not sure how deeply the KGB is involved in this, if they are at all. There are very few people he can trust right now, but evidently he feels he can trust me." Reagan leaned forward and set his drink down on the coffee table. "Joe, I want you to find this Wolf fellow and eliminate him before he gets to Gorbachev."

Geary looked down at the file. The enormity of the mission started to well up inside him. "Russia's a damn big country. To find one man, to stay a step ahead of the KGB, that's a pretty tall order."

"I know it is, Joe. But Gorbachev thinks it won't happen in Russia itself. His information is that the Wolf will try for him when he goes on a state visit to

Budapest in June. Take a look at the file and tell me what you think. I told him that we'll do everything we can."

"Very well, sir. Am I to report to the Acting Director on this?"

"No, I want you to report directly to me on this one. Casey doesn't trust Roger Preston. Took him on as a favor to a senator, thought better of it and was going to ease him out, but then Bill had his seizures and went to the hospital. And you don't report to Don Regan, either, just me. We need to keep this loop very closed. Bill trusts you, and so do I. You've done great work for your country. I know you've been thinking about retirement. I'm asking you for one last mission. I know there's a lot riding on this one, but I need a top man to oversee this operation and that's you."

"Thank you, Mr. President. I'll do the best I can."

Reagan smiled, nodding his approval. "I know you will. Now, I don't expect you to go after this fellow yourself. I thought this might be something you could have that new outfit take care of."

"We haven't formed it yet, sir, don't even have a name for it."

Reagan chuckled. "I'll leave that all up to you folks. Cap Weinberger tells me the whole thing is your idea anyway, is that right?"

Geary smiled. "It's been something we've been kicking around for a while, sir, in our shop and in the Pentagon as well. The new Special Operations Command is forming up soon, so a lot of ideas are floating around."

"You're too modest. I heard you're the main guy at Langley on this project. I have to tell you, the more I hear about it, the more I like it. Having an outfit like that will give me some flexibility, and that's something every president needs. The threats we face today are certainly serious enough, and who knows what we'll be facing tomorrow?" The president stood, and Geary followed suit.

"Well, Joe, I'm glad we had this little chat," the president said. "Are you heading back tonight? You're certainly welcome to bunk here. I've got plenty of room."

"Thank you, sir, but I really should be getting home. I have to be at my desk early in the morning. I want to get started on this right away."

"All right, good enough." Reagan walked him toward the door. "This new unit, I heard you're starting to put its leadership together. Would a certain Air Force officer of our mutual acquaintance be on the short list, by any chance?"

Geary returned his president's grin. "I've mentioned her name to a few people," he said. "She led the team that came out ahead in Operation COSMO a couple years back. I think she might have a shot."

Reagan's eyes widened, and he smiled even more broadly. "That's right, I remember hearing about that. I don't mind telling you, Joe, some of the boys over at the Pentagon are still pretty steamed about it. I'll have a word with Cap, make sure that her file doesn't somehow get lost before it gets to his desk."

"Thank you, Mr. President. I appreciate it. I just want her to have a fair shot. If there's someone better than her for the unit, so be it."

"Good, good. By the way, Maggie Thatcher asked me about her just the other day. They still think highly of her for helping them out in the Falklands." The president placed a brotherly hand on Joe's shoulder. "I know what it's like to be proud of a daughter, I've got two of 'em. From what I know about yours, she'll do well. Give her my best, will you?"

CHAPTER TWO

**HAMBURG,
WEST GERMANY
FEBRUARY 1987**

Every step she took made the assault on her senses more intense. Three weeks of this place hadn't made it any easier to deal with, but with any luck at all this would be the last night. She forced herself to stay focused and kept walking. Two blocks to go.

It was called the *Reeperbahn,* in the St. Pauli district of Hamburg, and even though Jo Ann Geary knew the English translation was "rope street," and had studied the history of the district and the city, none of that mattered now as she walked through the chilly, damp night. Just like every other night, she heard the techno-rock blaring from the clubs, the laughter and occasional scream coming from doors and alleyways. She smelled the pungent odor of marijuana smoke mixed with stale beer and what might be urine or worse, saw the garish flashing lights of the marquees and the more subtle red bulbs from the windows where the women preened. Her cover was convenient in that respect, as she could ignore the displays and not be afraid to let her irritation show. It was what any self-respecting and somewhat prudish North Korean would do.

Jo pushed the distractions aside and paid no attention to the catcalls from many of the men, and some of the women, who loitered around the club entrances and streetlamp poles. The mission came first, always, and tonight it would end, one way or another.

One more block.

She stepped off the curb to walk through the intersection, her stylish boot coming down on a soggy flyer advertising yet another sex club. Although she hardly moved her head at all, her eyes missed little, and the situational awareness she'd honed through years of training saved her once again. She stepped quickly back up onto the sidewalk as a canary-yellow Porsche roared through the stoplight, careening to the right around the corner with a blue and white police car only two seconds behind. Some of the pedestrians cheered the Porsche and gave the finger to the cops. Jo let them pass and kept going.

This was just another night in Hamburg's notorious red-light district, where all manner of transactions took place behind closed doors and sometimes out in the open. She passed the entrance to a club and, through the open doorway, caught a brief glimpse of naked flesh writhing on a small, poorly-lit stage. In that same club three weeks ago, she'd met her *Bundesnachrichtendienst* contact, sitting with the West German intelligence agent in the back row and trying to concentrate on his whispers as two overweight men staggered from the audience to join the two bored women already on stage.

But after tonight she could leave this all behind.

Half a block ahead she saw Li Meng outside the *bierhaus*, smoking a cigarette. The Chinese girl looked bored, and Jo wondered if she was already stoned. That was how Li Meng got through these nights, turning tricks in the back rooms of the tavern for twenty or thirty *Deutschmarks,* keeping maybe half for herself if the house was feeling generous. She'd arrived from Taiwan only two months ago. Jo wanted desperately to get her out of here, but the mission came first, and that was not to bring out one Chinese prostitute, but someone of far greater value.

That was a relative term, of course. What was the life of one Chinese hooker compared with a high-ranking officer in *Revolutionäre Zellen,* the Revolutionary Cells? To the BND Security Directorate, there was no comparison, which was why they'd sent Lieutenant Colonel Jo Ann Geary, on temporary detached duty from the U.S. Air Force's 1st Special Operations Wing, into the heart of the Reeperbahn to find Ralf Ohlendorf, one of the most wanted men in Germany. Two nights ago she'd found him, thanks to Li Meng, and tonight she was bringing him out.

***

For years the BND and the government's domestic counter-intelligence agency, *Bundesamt für Verfassungschutz,* had been hunting Ohlendorf. Reputed to be very high in the hierarchy of the RZ, he'd been responsible for terrorist attacks throughout the country and other European nations, including the 1981 bombing of the U.S. Army's V Corps headquarters in Frankfurt. Several agents from BND, BfV and foreign services had lost their lives attempting to find him.

The Germans had caught a break three weeks ago

when a woman from a North Korean trade delegation slipped away from her group in Bonn and into the empty seat of a beer hall booth occupied by a midlevel West German government bureaucrat. In her broken English she asked for political asylum, and the man had the presence of mind to notify BND immediately. What he didn't know, but which the woman quickly revealed to her new friends once she arrived at the safe house, was that she was an operative for MSS, the North Korean Ministry of State Security, and she'd been sent to make contact with a Revolutionary Cells group.

Things moved quickly. Desperate to exploit their opportunity but mindful that they had a limited window of time in which to act before MSS in Pyongyang discovered the truth, BND contacted its friends in the British MI6 and American CIA, asking if they knew of an operative who could impersonate this Korean woman for a short-term, dangerous mission. MI6 recommended an agent who had played a vital role in an operation during the Falklands War five years before, a woman who was very familiar to CIA as well. Thus it was that Jo Ann Geary, fluent in her mother's native language, found herself on a fast jet heading across the Atlantic.

***

"Hello, Li Meng," Jo said in Mandarin Chinese. "You need a jacket out here. It's cold."

"Hana Ru! I just came out for a smoke," the woman said, giving Jo a slight smile, but her eyes told the whole story. She was afraid. The man she knew only as Hans had taken a shine to her shortly after her arrival in the Reeperbahn, and Jo knew he had to be Ohlendorf from Li Meng's description of the tattoo on his back. BND had several good photos of the terrorist but the tattoo was the key. He could change his hair, grow a beard, even wear contacts to disguise his eye color, but he couldn't do anything about the ink, and only the women who shared his bed would see it.

"Let's go inside," Jo said, gently taking the young woman by the arm and leading her to the door. "I'm anxious to meet Hans."

"You have to talk to Konrad first." Li Meng led the way into the dark, smoky tavern. Rock music blared from a jukebox. In the dim lights Jo could see every type of person who cruised the streets in this district: punk rockers with wildly styled hair, slickly-dressed young men who could've been anything from accountants to pimps, muscle-bound gays, and everywhere scantily-clad women with garish makeup. A few of the men gave her the eye as she walked past. Jo had lost count of the propositions she'd brushed off in the past three weeks.

Li Meng led her to a corner booth where a man sat with two women, one white and blonde, the other of African descent. The man looked to be in his mid-forties, with slick-backed hair and a dark goatee that Jo felt certain was dyed. He glared first at Li Meng, then at Jo.

"You are persistent, I'll give you that," he said in German.

Jo answered in the same language. "As I said when we first met, I'm here to offer our help."

Konrad nodded to the empty space across the table, and Jo slid into the booth. To Li Meng, he said,

"Hans would like to see you." He nodded toward the back of the room. Li Meng blinked her eyes twice, then bowed slightly, glancing at Jo.

"I'll see you later," Jo said in Mandarin, trying to reassure her.

"Go powder your noses, girls," Konrad ordered. The blonde needed no encouragement, but the African girl lingered as she slid over his lap, pausing to grind her buttocks into his groin. "Not now," he said, slapping her on the hip. When she'd finally left, he shook his head. *"Schwarzerin.* That's all they think about."

"Thank you for agreeing to see me again," Jo said. Their first meeting had been two nights ago. Jo had slowly but efficiently worked her way through the district, dropping names supplied to her by BND, finally arriving at Konrad Schultz, suspected of being Ohlendorf's right-hand man.

"Your German is very good, *Fraulein* Ru." Schultz said. "I did not know they teach that in North Korea."

"My employers want to make sure we can converse in the native tongue of our fraternal socialist allies. Your language is elegant."

Schultz barked a laugh. "German is anything but elegant, Fraulein. It is a command language. You want elegance, go to Paris."

Jo forced a smile. "Perhaps on my next visit. Have you considered my offer?"

"Weapons we don't need," Schultz said, lowering his voice. "We can get all we want from our friends in the East." Jo knew that the East German security service, known as Stasi, had been running guns into the West for years, one of BfV's most vexing problems. "What we might need, though," Schultz continued, "is expertise in certain areas, such as, shall we say, in engineering?"

Jo nodded. “We can certainly provide assistance in that area,” she said, knowing that he meant demolitions work. “I myself have had some training in various forms of engineering.”

Schultz’s left eyebrow went up. “As it happens, we have a particular challenge in that area right now. Perhaps you can offer some assistance after all.”

She had to refrain from sounding too eager. “My superiors sent me here to make contact with your people and begin a relationship. We support your goals here in Europe.” She saw Schultz’s eyes narrowing slightly. “I would be most honored to lend whatever help I might be able to provide for your project. As a sign of our good faith.”

The German said nothing, and Jo knew it could go either way now. Then he said, “Since meeting you, I have been asking a few questions. We have friends in many places, some in position to know whether or not you are who you say you are.”

Jo had kept her hands in her lap, and now she shifted her position slightly so that her right hand was only a few inches from the top of her boot, where the *shuriken* was carefully concealed. Even though she was confident in her ability to defend herself with only her hands and feet, BND had suggested that having an extra weapon wouldn’t hurt, and the razor-sharp throwing star was a good one.

Schultz gave her a sly smile. “Your credentials are convincing,” he said. “My colleague would like to meet you and discuss these matters in more detail.”

“I am most pleased,” Jo said, bowing her head. She moved her hand back up to her lap.

“Let’s take a ride.”

CHAPTER THREE

HAMBURG,
WEST GERMANY
FEBRUARY 1987

Jo was blindfolded before the Audi pulled away from the curb. "Just a precaution," Schultz told her. Expecting at any moment to feel his hand on her thigh, Jo stayed focused on the task of counting the seconds before the car turned, then the direction. Fifteen before a left, another thirty and then a right. Five more turns over a span of four minutes. The car's speed had not gone above what was standard for urban driving in moderate traffic. Three stops along the way, and she heard the occasional honk of a horn, the growing blare and then fade of music. When they came to a stop, Jo knew they were still in the Reeperbahn, perhaps close to where they'd started out. Schultz had kept his hands to himself, but Jo was sure she'd have to deal with him later.

The door opened and a hand tugged at her arm. "Come out," a rough male voice commanded. When she stood, the blindfold was pulled away from behind her. They were behind a four-story building, and from the thumping music Jo knew it was another club. Schultz motioned her to follow him to a door. The man who'd pulled her from the car, who must've been their driver, was behind.

Her senses fully attuned to her surroundings, Jo allowed herself to feel *haragei,* an intuitive sense focused in her abdomen, the core of her being where her inner *ki* was based. Her years of training allowed her to focus without focusing, entering a state of *mushin,* "no mind." Her breathing would remain calm throughout what was to come, and she would be able to move swiftly and confidently without thought. "Be like water," she had been told by the intense, charismatic young *kung fu* instructor she'd trained with during her undergrad days in California. "Water can flow, it can crash." She'd learned much from her days with Bruce Lee, complementing the years of training she'd had before and since, preparing her for moments like these.

She was fully aware of the man behind her, his height and weight, even, to a degree, what he was feeling as his own ki radiated outward, undoubtedly without him being aware of it. He wanted to hurt her; he was good at hurting people, feeding on their pain.

Schultz was more disciplined, tougher, harder to read, but BND had prepared her with what they knew. He was a man of the knife, said to favor the traditional German dagger over the more nimble but shorter switchblade or butterfly. She would use the shuriken on him, but she'd have to make the first move. On the ring finger of her right hand was something she was saving for Ohlendorf.

Schultz knocked twice, hesitated, then another three knocks. A slot in the door at eye level opened and the German spoke a phrase, then stepped back. The door opened from inside, a tall blonde woman waiting. She greeted Schultz with a hug and sized up Jo Ann. "The Korean?" she asked him.

"Yes. Ralf is here?"

"Follow me."

***

They took her down a narrow flight of stairs into a musty, cold basement, then through a side door into the adjacent building. Music pulsed from above in this one, too, but it was slower, more muted, and her nose caught the scent of marijuana. A drug house, or perhaps a sex club. The blonde led them down a hallway. There was a circular staircase at the far end, which Jo noted carefully. The transmitter inside the Korean owl pendant she wore might not work below ground. Certainly the smaller backup in her left earring would not. She'd have to get to the street level to send the signal.

This was not their headquarters, only a meeting place, surely one of many. The terrorists were clever and a few could even be said to be brilliant, but most thought themselves much smarter than they actually were. Sooner or later they would be found; the West German intelligence services were big, efficient, and dedicated, and had access to resources far outstripping those of the terrorists. But it always came down to the agent in the field, gathering the information that would allow the police or military to move in, or more rarely making the hit herself. Tonight it would be up to Jo. All the skills she had learned from three decades of training were on call, some already in play. The layout of the basement warren of rooms was imprinted on her brain, updated at every step. Halfway down the hallway they came to a door and the blonde knocked twice, then three more times.

Inside was a simple desk with a man sitting behind it. She recognized him immediately as Ohlendorf. Forty-two years of age, unremarkable in appearance, Ohlendorf had been a leftist professor of economics at Heidelberg University before leaving ten years earlier to join the RZ, inspired by the group's participation in the hijacking of an Air France jetliner to Uganda in '76. Since then he'd risen steadily in the ranks. BND strongly suspected him to be a Stasi agent. That meant he had training in firearms and hand-to-hand combat, although those skills had likely degraded during his time in the West. Jo would be counting on that.

Ohlendorf rose from his chair. "Good evening, Fraulein Ru," he said. The blonde came around the desk to stand next to him. Schultz and the driver remained behind Jo, who was able to gauge their distance from her and the angles with surreptitious glances as she bowed toward the desk. The driver, to her right, was within range. Ohlendorf himself was wearing a leather jacket, unzipped, but when he'd stood up Jo saw the strap of a shoulder holster curling under his left arm. There was a door behind him to his left, slightly ajar.

"Good evening, sir," Jo said, bowing slightly. "I am honored to be in the presence of one of Germany's great revolutionary leaders. I bring you greetings from the Democratic People's Republic of Korea."

Ohlendorf remained standing. There were no other chairs in the room, which was to Jo's advantage, as it would be harder for her to move from a sitting position. "I regret that I do not have much time to devote to our meeting this evening," the German said. "I wanted to meet you and hear what you have to say. I will then discuss your proposal with my colleagues and we will decide on a course of action, perhaps leading to a more substantive discussion."

She knew her window of opportunity would be closing very quickly. She had to make them relax, if only a little, and then strike. "Of course," she said, smiling. "We stand ready to provide assistance to those engaged in the struggle against Western imperialism." She nodded to Schultz at her left. "*Herr* Schultz has told me that you are in need of someone with engineering skills. I would be most honored to offer my help."

Ohlendorf looked past her to Schultz. "You have told her about our plans?"

"Only that we may be looking for—"

Jo struck first at the driver, a side kick to his left knee. As large and no doubt as powerful as he was, his knee was still a fragile hinge, easily susceptible to serious, immobilizing injury. Jo's booted foot struck at nearly forty miles an hour with over half a ton of force. The driver screamed in pain as the knee buckled inward and he began toppling to his left.

Pulling back the leg slightly, Jo reached inside the top of the boot and pulled out the shuriken. The weapon was about eleven centimeters in diameter with four razor-sharp prongs. With her momentum continuing clockwise, Jo was able to plant the foot that had disabled the driver and deliver the shuriken in a backhand motion that sent the star swiftly across the small room. It embedded itself in Schultz's exposed neck, the force of the impact making him stagger backward two steps.

Jo's attention had already shifted to the two

Germans behind the desk, a flicker of movement having touched her peripheral vision as she threw the star. “Helga, *schiessen Sie die Weibsstück!*” Ohlendorf shouted, and even if Jo hadn’t known German, the sight of the Glock pistol in the blonde’s hand would’ve made his meaning clear.

Jo dropped to the floor as the gun fired. Helga’s aim was off. Instead of passing through the air where Jo had just been, the round drilled into the chest of the unfortunate Schultz, finishing the job started by the shuriken. Jo wasn’t about to give the blonde a chance to get off another shot. She put her shoulder into the front of the cheap wooden desk and shoved upward, pushing the desk into the Germans, drawing a grunt from Ohlendorf and an angry shriek from Helga. The blonde was causing more trouble than Jo anticipated, and the shot would bring even more. It was time to end this and get to her target.

Jo levered herself up and over the edge of the desk. Her left shoulder zinged a shot of pain down her arm; the collision with the desk might’ve damaged something inside. Ignoring the pain, she swung her legs around and kicked straight into the woman’s outstretched arms. The Glock clattered against the wall and down to the floor. Helga sagged into the corner, doubled over, but she wasn’t done yet. Snarling a curse, she came back at Jo, swinging wildly, untrained but still dangerous. Jo countered by coming inside the swing, blocking with her right arm and bringing her left elbow around and into the woman’s solar plexus. Completing the turn, Jo fired her right elbow up into the underside of the blonde’s jaw, snapping her head back as the jawbone cracked. Now she was done.

Jo snatched Helga's pistol and headed for the doorway behind the desk. Ohlendorf had darted through it as Jo made her move on his girlfriend. The light from the next room was dim. Glock at the ready, Jo hugged the wall and risked a quick glance. It was a bathroom, narrow with an open doorway on the other wall, and through it Jo saw Ohlendorf, stumbling over something on the floor. A woman screamed. Ohlendorf looked back, saw Jo and tugged a handgun from his shoulder holster. Jo fired two shots over his head. Regaining his balance, Ohlendorf took aim and Jo was about to squeeze off a killing shot when an odd-shaped object crashed into the side of the terrorist's head. The gun fell to the floor.

Less than twenty seconds had elapsed since Helga fired her shot, and Jo knew she couldn't count on many more before Ohlendorf's men reacted. Already she could hear a man shouting from somewhere else in the basement. She ran to the staggering terrorist, twisting the facing on her ring to deploy the needle. Pulling his left arm behind him and up into a painful chicken wing hold, she plunged the half-inch-long needle into the side of his neck. Ohlendorf gasped, and within three seconds he ceased to struggle, but stayed upright.

The room was small, poorly lit by a lamp on a nightstand next to a queen-sized bed. A nude woman lay amidst a rumple of sheets, red hair flowing over a pillow, eyes staring dully at Jo. Standing next to the bed with a ceramic ash tray in her hand was Li Meng.

"Hana Ru? Is that you?" The Chinese girl dropped the ash tray and clumsily tried to shield her breasts.

Jo nodded toward another door. "Where does that lead?"

"I... what?"

With one hand holding up the dazed Ohlendorf by the collar of his jacket, Jo took a step toward Li Meng and slapped her lightly. "Snap out of it! Put something on, we're getting out of here. What's through that door?"

Li Meng blinked, focused, then said, "A hallway, to stairs." She pulled a threadbare robe from a pile of clothes on the floor.

There was more shouting now and the sound of running feet. Jo pushed Ohlendorf ahead of her. The drug would keep him conscious but compliant. He tried to speak but his tongue refused to cooperate. Jo found his gun, another Glock, on the floor and stuck it in her waistband. At the doorway she glanced around. Nobody there, but that wouldn't last long. Men were coming, from the same direction she'd come when she entered the basement. To her right, the circular staircase was fifteen feet away.

Li Meng had shoved her feet into a pair of slippers and was cinching the robe's belt around her waist. "Go to the stairs," Jo commanded. "Hurry!" The Chinese girl brushed past her and ran.

Someone had burst into the meeting room. *"Ralf! Wo sind sie?"* a man shouted. Another man's voice: *"Dieter is todt!"* A shadow cut off some of the light coming into the connecting bathroom, and Jo fired two shots at the toilet tank. The ceramic shattered and water gushed out.

Jo shoved Ohlendorf ahead and down the hallway. "Up! Up those stairs!" she ordered. The German garbled something back at her but started climbing, tripping on the second step. *"Macht schnell!"* Jo yelled, and

Ohlendorf doubled his pace. Leftist he might be, but he was still a German and instinctively responded to orders.

As they neared the top, Jo clutched her pendant and pressed the button, sending out the alert signal. Looking past Ohlendorf, Jo saw Li Meng reach the small landing. She tried the knob of the closed door. The deep bass of rock music growled on the other side. "It's locked!" she wailed.

"Hold him up!" Jo said as Ohlendorf stumbled onto the landing. There wasn't room for three, so Jo had to stand on the top step of the stairs as she aimed at the doorknob. She would've preferred to try kicking the door, but not from this angle. She fired two rounds into the plate below the knob and the mechanism shattered. Li Meng put her shoulder to the door and it opened. The doorknob came out, clattering to the floor. "Go!" Jo yelled over the music.

Heavy curtains hung to the floor in front of them. They were somewhere behind a stage. Light leaked out through seams in the fabric and a guitar wailed a riff. From behind Jo could hear steps approaching the bottom of the staircase. A gun cracked and the round blasted splinters out of the door frame. *"Schiesst du nichts, Dummkopf!"* came from below. Jo knew they wouldn't fire on her again, fearful of hitting their leader, but she had no such concerns, so they'd be coming carefully. If they had any brains at all they'd be sending men around to the front of the theater to cut them off. She had to keep moving, had to get them to the street.

Jo saw an edge of a curtain and pulled it aside, shoving Ohlendorf through it. Red light bathed the stage. A naked man sat on a chair, a woman straddling him. Her stiletto heels were digging into the wooden floor as she ground her pelvis against his, but when she saw Ohlendorf and then Jo and the gun, she screamed. Trying to dismount, she toppled off him to her left, her globulous breasts heaving as she crashed to the stage. The man she'd been riding made a move to rise until he saw the business end of Jo's Glock pointed at him. "Don't move!" Jo said, and the man slumped back in the chair, hands covering what was left of his rapidly flagging erection.

She pushed Ohlendorf toward the stairs at stage left. Out in the audience she saw some figures moving toward the exit, others remaining in their seats. Li Meng skittered ahead of Jo and Ohlendorf to the stairs and stumbled down, regained her footing and ran up the aisle. Ohlendorf tripped on the first step and went down, Jo following, unable to keep him from falling and pulling her with him. It saved her life; two shots rang out from the rear of the stage.

Jo rolled off Ohlendorf, sighted on two men coming toward her and fired, hitting the first dead center in the chest, the second in the shoulder. The man staggered backward and his gun went off, the round hitting the naked man in his leg. Jo put the second terrorist down with two shots to his abdomen.

What was left of the audience was in full flight now, some yelling with panic. Three men were muscling through them from the entrance. Jo saw a red sign on the far wall. AUSGANG. "The side exit, Li Meng!" Jo yelled, pushing her captive ahead of her. The Chinese girl reached the door first and pushed on the handle. They rushed through and found themselves in a narrow alley. To their right, the street was fifteen yards away. Jo could hear sirens in the distance. “Get to the street,” she told Li Meng. “The police are on the way.”

“But you, Hana Ru?”

Ohlendorf had slumped to the ground. “We'll be right behind you,” Jo said. She saw a Dumpster along the outside wall of the building, ran behind it and shoved it forward, barricading the side door to the theater. Her shoulder zinged again. She was heading back to Ohlendorf when a shot from farther down the alley clanged off the Dumpster.

She dropped to one knee, bringing the Glock around, looking for the target. There, movement near a trash pile. She squeezed off two shots and then the hammer clicked on an empty chamber. Scuttling behind the Dumpster, she felt for the second gun she'd picked up downstairs, but it must've fallen from her waistband when she fell in the theater. Tamping down the fear, she looked around for another weapon. She had no more shuriken, only the now-empty Glock. Nothing else presented itself.

The man was good, moving silently. Jo saw him only as a dark shape gliding through the not-quite-as-dark shadows. A blade of light from the street faded to a stop just at the end of the Dumpster that now concealed her. He would have to come around it...

The movement was so swift she almost didn't catch it. Suddenly he was standing there, left leg in the light, and she caught the downward slant of his arms as he brought the pistol to bear in a two-handed grip. Jo tossed the Glock at him and rolled to her right as the man's pistol barked. Back on her feet, she went after his arms. *Fight the man, not the weapon,* her instructors had told her over and over. She grabbed his wrists and twisted up and around, pushing the gun upward and back on him.

To her surprise, he didn't fight the movement but flowed with it, allowing the gun to fall free as he relaxed his wrists and hands. He lashed out with a kick, catching Jo on her right thigh, and she felt a hand coming around her face, grabbing her jaw, twisting her heck, another hand pulling her arm around. She reacted instinctively, flowing with the movement herself, freeing her head and arm. His abdomen was exposed for a split second and she fired a punch into it. The man whoofed out a breath and collapsed around the punch, but not in the way Jo expected. He seemed almost to be absorbing the impact, and within two seconds he was attacking again.

Men were pounding on the inside of the door, but the Dumpster wouldn't budge. The sirens were getting closer. The man obviously meant to rescue Ohlendorf, and if Jo could hold on for another minute, her police and BND backup would be here, but now she wondered if she'd have that minute. This man fought her like nobody she'd ever faced, moving smoothly, almost without effort. It had been some time since she'd sparred against a kung fu stylist, but this was close to that. She had to reach deep back into her experience for help, and found it. She parried the man's elbow strike and landed a turning side kick. This was one he could not absorb. He crashed back against the Dumpster and for a brief moment, Jo saw his face. Blonde hair, somewhat Slavic features, with a small scar above the right eyebrow. He recovered his balance and looked toward the street. Flashing blue lights flooded the alley.

"Poka my ne vstretimsja snova, krasivaya," he said, and he was gone, back down the alley. Jo recognized the Russian: Until we meet again, beautiful.

Three men were at the entrance to the alley, pointing guns at her. Two of them were wearing police tactical gear, the third in civilian clothes. *"Hande hoch! Schnell!"* Hands up! Quickly!

Jo complied, saying, *"Reeper verdeckt!"* Cable Undercover, the code name of the operation.

"Authentifizieren!" the civilian demanded.

"Die Weisse Füchsin!" Jo shouted the authentication code. The White Vixen.

CHAPTER FOUR

RED ARMY PROVING GROUNDS, SIBERIAN MILITARY DISTRICT MARCH 1987

Major General of Aviation Arkady Voloshin never ceased to be amazed by the forests. How many thousands of square kilometers were covered by forest here in Siberia? He could find out, if he wished, merely by asking one of his aides to look it up, but the number was unimportant. A number could not do justice to the spectacle, especially for someone used to the wide steppes of Ukraine and western Russia.

"It takes your breath away, does it not, Arkady?"

Voloshin took in deep breath, the scent of pine almost overwhelming him. There was something else, too—it was clean, pure. So unlike the grimy air in the western cities that stank with pollution. "It does, and I then want to breathe in more of it," Voloshin said. He turned to the man next to him, General Boris Melikov. "Now I understand why you like serving out here, Boris. It is a man's world, is it not?"

"Indeed it is, my friend," Melikov answered with a proud grin. "Ever since my first trip here, before we were at Frunze, I longed for an assignment to Siberia. It is much like the forests of Byelorussia, where my father took me hunting and fishing, only many times better."

Voloshin had known Melikov for twenty years, since they'd met as students at M.V. Frunze Military Academy. They were different in many ways; Voloshin had grown up in Leningrad, a boy of the city who had gone into the Air Force, while Melikov was a child of Byelorussian farmers who almost naturally went to the Army. Yet they had much in common, not the least of which was the fact that their fathers had served in the Great Patriotic War together, tank officers in the same regiment that had smashed through the fascists' last line of defense into the rubble of Berlin. Both men were awarded the coveted Hero of the Soviet Union medal for valor in combat. After the war, they went back to their civilian lives but stayed in touch over the years. Voloshin always suspected that their fathers' influence helped the sons gain appointments to Frunze. That was contrary to the official policies of the Party, but it was also the way things often worked.

They were both in their winter greatcoats, although the sun was shining brightly on this day, a harbinger of springtime at last. According to Melikov, the winters were fierce out here. Voloshin had no reason to doubt him, but the beauty of the summer made up for it, and Melikov spent every spare moment hiking the woods and fishing the streams. Voloshin had joined him once for such an excursion and hoped to do it again. His current visit was for business. He rarely had time for pleasure anymore, except when he was in the cockpit of his MiG jet fighter. Perhaps, if their work succeeded, he would finally have time to come back here for pleasure once again.

If they did not succeed, though, things would be different. There would be no wide-open spaces in a *gulag,* even less in a grave.

Voloshin put that thought out of his mind, but he knew it would creep back. Such thoughts seemed to be occurring more frequently these days. He had to maintain discipline, stay focused. They were so close now, only a few months away. He sighed.

"I have a feeling I know your thoughts, Arkady."

"I was thinking that I would like to come back here sometime and go hiking with you again, Boris. But that all depends on certain things, doesn't it?"

"Indeed it does, my friend."

"Tell me again the reason for this particular exercise we are having here, Boris. Why the training here, in the wilderness? ZARNITSA will take place in an urban environment, after all."

"This is the result of a challenge, Arkady. General Klimov insisted that our mutual friend is not as proficient as we have made him out to be. So, the exercise."

Voloshin scoffed. "A waste of time and effort. *Krasniy Volk* is the best we have. There is no equal, not in the Soviet Union and certainly not in the West."

"I fully agree with you about his being the best *we* have. I am not so sure about what the West might have."

"They have James Bond, they have Superman, but those are men on movie screens, Boris. I am talking about real men who can go into the field and stop ours. I am confident in the abilities of Krasniy Volk."

Melikov nodded his head. "I have full confidence in him as well, but we should not discount the efficiency of the special forces troops within NATO. Particularly the American Navy SEALs and the British SAS."

"They are very good, yes, but they will not be going where our man will be going, is that not so?"

Melikov had to concede the point. “Very true, Arkady. In any event, Klimov is not yet convinced, and he carries much influence within our... organization, as you know. Therefore, we had to agree to this demonstration of our man’s abilities.”

Voloshin had to conceal his irritation. Their “organization” had no formal name, but its members often referred to it as “the Committee.” Innocuous and safe enough for conversation; nothing was ever written down on paper. For two years their security had held tight. Now they only needed a few more months of anonymity. Still, it was becoming increasingly difficult to hold it together, and this irritated Voloshin even more. With success nearly within their grasp, it should have been the opposite. Instead, tiny fissures were appearing, and Klimov was one of them.

“My perception is that only two or three others are with Klimov,” he said. “But they are a very important two or three.”

“Unfortunately true,” Melikov agreed. “If he backs out, everything falls apart, even if Krasniy Volk carries out his mission successfully. Klimov and his troops are the key to the second phase of the plan, and that is of equal importance to the first.”

There was no use debating it any longer. Melikov, ever the pragmatist, was right again. “I know,” Voloshin said. “All right, then. The exercise is tonight?”

“Actually, it got underway two days ago,” Melikov said. “He has five days, but tonight is perhaps the conclusion.”

Voloshin turned to his colleague. “‘Perhaps?’”

“Krasniy Volk decides when it concludes,” Melikov said. He gestured to the expanse of forest before them. “He is out there, now, somewhere.”

"What makes you think it will be tonight? You said he has a five-day window. There are still two days to go, after today."

Melikov checked his watch. "Klimov insisted on being here, perhaps to gloat. He is due in three hours."

"That was not scheduled. Krasniy Volk would not know this."

Melikov gave Voloshin a knowing look. "Klimov is underestimating him. That will prove to be a mistake, I think."

***

Colonel General Vladimir Klimov was a big man, nearly 190 centimeters tall, and he prided himself on keeping his large body just as fit as it had been when he'd played right defense on the Olympic hockey team that won gold at the '64 Winter Games. His hockey days had ended many years before, but Klimov stayed in shape nowadays with judo. Just a month ago he'd competed in a tournament in Volgograd; he lost in the quarterfinals, but it was a close match, and in the preliminary rounds he dominated his opponents, including that smartass KGB officer. What was his name again? Putinsky, or something like that. Supposedly had been awarded the title Master of Sport some years ago. The young whelp had put up a good struggle, Klimov had to give him that. A little too much attitude, but the fellow might amount to something. Klimov would have to keep an eye on him.

In the meantime, Klimov had his hands full with his official duties and of course with the Committee, which was taking more of his time as the days passed.

This trip out here to Siberia, for instance. Klimov had counted on getting in one more visit to his *dacha* on the Black Sea before getting down to business with the final planning and execution of ZARNITSA, but here he was. It wasn't the ends of the earth, but for a man at home in the towns and cities of western Russia it was close enough.

Well, it was his own fault. He just didn't quite believe this agent of theirs was as good as some other Committee members said he was. Yes, he'd read the man's service jacket, and it was impressive, but to carry out the mission they had planned for him, only three months away now, would require more than an impressive service jacket. It would require guts, determination and the ability to think on his feet. Klimov knew a thing or two about those traits. Nobody got to where he was without them.

It was only natural, only right, that he was the unofficial chairman of the Committee. Not only was he the highest-ranking military man in the group, he had the most outstanding record. He'd first caught the attention of Moscow while stationed in Cuba in 1962, when his unit captured a team of American commandos sent ashore in advance of the planned invasion. Kruschev's agreement with Kennedy had resulted in the U.S. team being quietly repatriated, but Klimov's role in the affair set his career on the path that had led to his current posting, a quarter-century later. As commander of the Moscow Military District, he was the most vital military officer on the Committee, and everybody else knew it.

He would just have to see about this Krasniy Volk fellow. His mission would be to penetrate a secure area and eliminate the target. That was easier said than done, Klimov had argued, so why not an exercise to test his abilities? Just to make things a little more interesting, Klimov had arranged for the exercise to include a company of KGB "Alpha" unit troops, specially trained counter-terrorism soldiers who were utterly ruthless. The Alpha unit was the last line of defense, so to speak, around this command post. Two companies of regular troops, Afghan War veterans from the 345th Guards Airborne Regiment, formed the outer ring. Six hundred of the toughest soldiers the Soviet Union could put in the field, all there to prevent one man from getting to this spot.

It was an impossible task. Not even the heroes of Western cinema could do it. Just the other night, Klimov had seen an American movie about a lone commando sent to Vietnam to rescue POWs, and he'd laughed out loud at the ineptitude of the Vietnamese and their so-called Soviet "advisers" who could not stop one over-muscled American. Well, Klimov thought now as he finished his steak, if Krasniy Volk failed, which he certainly would, perhaps the Committee could hire that Rambo fellow from the movie and send him on the ZARNITSA mission. He laughed again now at the very idea.

"A joke, Comrade General?" Voloshin asked.

"A funny moment from a film I saw recently," Klimov said. He took a sip of vodka and glanced at the younger man over the rim of his glass. Voloshin was an outstanding pilot and certainly deserved his rank, but he had a lot to learn. So did his friend Melikov. They were champions of Krasniy Volk, and when their champion failed this test, they and the rest of the

Committee would have to listen to Klimov when he talked about his alternate plan. There was a way to deal with their common problem without the risk of ZARNITSA. For now, though, he would enjoy himself for a few days as Krasniy Volk went down. He placed his knife and fork on the empty plate before him. "My compliments to your chef, Melikov. An excellent steak. Reindeer, you said?"

"Yes, Comrade General. I'm glad you enjoyed it."

One last sip of the vodka. "Comrades, I think I shall use the restroom, and then with your permission, Melikov, perhaps a little stroll in the night air and a smoke, if you don't mind?"

"Of course not, sir."

A few minutes later, Klimov left the small headquarters building and looked around. This base was not Melikov's regular command post; that was about fifty kilometers to the south. What had he said? Ah, yes, this was the northernmost outpost of his battalion. As such, it was rather small by comparison, but still large enough to house about fifty men. The few buildings were made of logs. It was more of a hunting lodge than a military post, but after all, they were over a thousand kilometers from their closest potential enemy, China. There was a wire fence around the perimeter, about two meters high, which Melikov had told him was there primarily to keep the wolves out. The wolves ruled this wilderness; man was the interloper here.

As he walked and lit a cigarette, Klimov reflected that in a few days' time there would be one less wolf he would have to be concerned with.

He drew in the smoke greedily. An American brand,

Marlboro. Unlike the vast majority of his countrymen, most of whom also smoked, he had access to Western cigarettes and did not have to tolerate the shitty domestic brands like *Trud.* He neared the western perimeter of the outpost, noting that the forest had been cut away for fifty meters surrounding the wire. At each corner was a guard tower. The closest one right now, which he thought was the southwest corner, was about seventy-five meters away. There was a half-moon out tonight, and it was getting cold. Presumably there was still snow in the higher elevations. Klimov's boots crunched the crusty dirt of the access road. He noted with approval that Melikov had removed all the natural grass from the ground within the outpost. Not only did that reduce the need for maintenance—soldiers should not waste their time as groundskeepers—but it was a security precaution, as any intruder would not have the advantage of a soft carpet of—

Something cold and hard touched the side of his neck. Klimov felt it press on his skin, ever so slightly, and he suddenly realized that it was a knife blade, only a few millimeters away from his carotid artery. What was—

An icy voice whispered in his ear, "Have I passed your test, Comrade General?"

CHAPTER FIVE

MCLEAN, VIRGINIA APRIL 1987

Her father's office looked almost the same as it had five years ago, but Jo noticed a few subtle differences. On the credenza was a different photo of her mother, one that must've been taken a few years earlier, just before Kim Nam-soon Geary began her last round of chemo. The long black hair was streaked with gray, and there were more wrinkles around the eyes than Jo remembered, but the eyes themselves still held the warmth and love Jo had known all her life. Even now, more than two years since Jo had said her final goodbye, she was still comforted by them, and by the sure knowledge that she would be with her mother again someday.

"I miss her, too," a deep voice behind her said.

"Appa!" Jo couldn't stop herself from jumping up from the chair and running into her father's arms. Even into adulthood, she called him by the Korean name for "daddy." Now she was a little girl again, and her father was comforting her once more. "Your secretary showed me in," she said.

"Sorry I was delayed." Joseph Geary held her at arm's length. "My daughter, the colonel."

"Lieutenant colonel, Appa. I might get my eagle in a few years, if I stay in."

"No question about it. Take a seat, honey." He sat down opposite her in the other chair that fronted his large desk.

The ring of hair around his bald crown was iron-gray now, but Jo was gratified to see that her father actually looked healthier than the last time she'd seen him, nearly a year ago. "You've been paying attention to my letters," she said with a smile.

He chuckled. "My daughter the lieutenant colonel, not only a fine officer in Uncle Sam's Air Force but also an expert on diet, nutrition and exercise."

She shared the laugh. "Not an expert, Appa. I just thought you could use some friendly advice."

"Well, it's excellent advice. I feel pretty good. Best I've felt in a few years. Bench-pressed my weight in the gym for the first time a few weeks ago. Not bad for an old fart like me."

That brought another smile. "You're not old."

"I'll be sixty-seven in a few months, young lady, and that is not exactly young. But I didn't ask you here to talk about my health."

"I didn't think so."

Her father smiled at her, but his eyes suddenly looked sad. He looked away briefly, then said, "JoJo, there's a new unit forming up pretty soon and your name came up."

The news gave Jo a thrill, tempered by her father's obvious hesitance. "That sounds interesting, Appa, but I can tell you're not excited about it."

Joseph forced a grin. "Well, any time my daughter is put in harm's way, I worry about it. But I'd rather have you doing something you love, even if it is dangerous sometimes." He reached over to his desk and picked up a file, flipped through it briefly, and handed it to Jo Ann. "This is a joint project with DOD and CIA."

The red-bordered file had one word: PALLAS. Inside were several typed pages and some organizational charts. Jo scanned them quickly and then looked at her father. "A new special operations group?"

"Yes," Joseph said, "named after the Greek Titan of warcraft. This is going to be an entirely new unit within Special Operations Command." Jo was more than familiar with the new command, which was due to be activated any day now. Air Force Special Operations was going to be folded into SOCOM, and Jo had assumed she'd eventually be assigned to a unit.

"And how did my name come up?" Jo asked.

"My office is coordinating with the Pentagon on this project and I was asked to recommend some people for leadership positions. I have several people over here in our Special Operations Group and listed their names after talking to them, but the only uniformed officer I thought about was you. And I've got to tell you, that little exercise you took part in at Bragg in '84 caught the attention of quite a few people."

Jo closed the file and handed it back to him. "I'm flattered."

"This unit will need good officers, JoJo, people with experience, and you have that in spades. The commanding officer billet is tentatively scheduled to be filled by an O-6 or its equivalent from my side of the fence. That's one step above your grade, but it's not set in stone. I can't nominate you for C.O. myself, but I intend to talk to some friends of mine and make a strong case for you. Based strictly on your merits, of course," he added with a proud grin.

Jo was taken aback. She had command experience but only in training units, not a field command. Women had been making great strides in the Air Force and other branches in the past decade or so, but it was still slower than she and many of her sisters would've preferred. "Thank you, Appa."

"It will be my pleasure. I'll be boosting my own people too, but the way I read the tea leaves, the Pentagon will insist on having a serving line officer in charge and the White House will probably go along with that. So we'll see. There's a meeting at SecDef's office tomorrow and I'd like you to accompany me. No final decisions will be made, but I'm given to understand one or two other people will be there who are in the running for the job."

"I'm already looking forward to it."

***

Jo spent the night at her father's house, a venerable home in a Falls Church gated community. Joseph had bought it four years earlier after a too-good-to-turn-down offer from a retiring colleague. It was much larger than the townhouse they'd owned for years, but he wanted to give his wife a large home to enjoy in their retirement. Six months after the move, her cancer was diagnosed. At least, Jo thought as she lay in bed in the guest room that night, her mother had been able to spend her last year in the home she'd always dreamed about. It wasn't the home Jo had grown up in; actually, there'd been several of those in four different countries, none of them particularly special. But she knew from her mother's letters that she had really enjoyed this last one.

Jo was used to sleeping in unfamiliar quarters, and this bedroom was certainly more comfortable that most of those she'd known, but she had some trouble nodding off. It was the excitement of tomorrow's meeting, yes, but it was also because she was in her parents' home, the last one her mother had lived in. So many memories, and it was almost as if her mother's spirit was still here. Finally, as she drifted off at last, she knew there would be one thing she'd have to do before the meeting. Something she'd put off for too long.

***

She declined her father's offer of a ride in his chauffeured CIA sedan the next morning, not just because he had to go to his office for a few hours before the eleven a.m. meeting, but because she had another mission to accomplish first. After a breakfast of her father's delicious scrambled eggs and bacon—low-fat turkey bacon, she noted with approval—she drove her rented Oldsmobile several blocks to the cemetery.

The grave was in a peaceful setting in the shade of a maple tree. This was only her third visit to the cemetery since the funeral, but Jo found it easily. Leaving the car on the narrow access road, she walked the twenty paces to the gravesite. Her black uniform pumps swished through the recently mowed grass, and the air had that musky aroma that heralds the beginning of spring.

It was not the right time of year for a proper Korean *charye* ceremony, to honor one's ancestors; not a holiday like *Chuseok,* the Korean version of Thanksgiving, or *Seollal,* the lunar New Year's Day, nor was it the anniversary of her mother's passing. If it were, Jo would have, once again, composed a proper ceremony as she had done one year after Kim's death. She vividly remembered being taught the ritual by her mother as a young girl, and they'd practiced it faithfully at least twice a year on the anniversaries of the deaths of Kim's parents, the grandparents Jo had never known.

But today there would be no special foods or wines, no native dress. At the grave, she pulled up a few crabgrass plants that had started to sprout. At least she would get to perform one ritual, the *beolcho.* After disposing of the weeds, she spread a towel on the grass to protect her knees and knelt down, bowing low. "Honored mother, I revere your memory," Jo whispered in Korean. "I miss you so."

Kim Nam-soon Geary had been raised a Buddhist by her parents in Seoul but she became a Christian shortly after marrying the tall, handsome American spy in 1948. Jo's own religious faith had been influenced not only by her parents but by all the cultures she'd grown up in and studied. Now, on a crisp early spring morning at her mother's grave, Jo fervently prayed that they would meet again. She offered her prayer to God above, convinced that her mother was at His side.

She missed her mother's counsel. Every step of Jo's path—college at Stanford, grad school at the Academy, every posting in the Air Force—Kim had been there for her, even if only at the end of a phone line or in words on a page. Jo remembered the night during the Diana training, when she thought she couldn't go on, opening the letter from home and reading, "I am so proud of you, daughter. My heart sings with joy, and your father's chest bursts with pride." Those words helped her persevere. Years later, after returning home from her fiancé's funeral, Kim had been there to hold her as she'd wept.

She knew Kim had always wanted grandchildren, but for Jo there was always duty. Her father had been responsible for that, she knew, although he'd never pressured her to take the path she'd chosen. There had always been a battle within Jo, between the desire to follow her father in service to her country, or to take her mother's path and settle down with a husband and children. She didn't know if she could do both. Jo knew some who'd tried, and even a few who'd succeeded, and if Ian had survived the Falklands she would've given it her best shot. Eventually, as Jo reached her mid-thirties, Kim must've known she would never hold a grandchild in her arms. Yet never once had she expressed disappointment in her daughter, only pride and that all-encompassing love.

Jo wondered now if the path she'd chosen was the right one. She would be thirty-seven in a few months. With her mother gone, Jo's desire to leave the Air Force, marry and have a family receded a little more every day. Sometimes she wondered if there still wasn't time to turn back. There was more to life than training, study, duty, wasn't there? Something told her now, as she raised her head and blinked away tears, that her time to choose her ultimate path was growing short.

CHAPTER SIX

UKRAINIAN SSR,
SOVIET UNION
APRIL 1987

If it wasn't one thing, it was another. Today it was the roof. Yesterday it had been the bathroom plumbing, the day before that... well, he had forgotten already, and he didn't care to spend time trying to remember. Whatever it had been, he had fixed it, and moved on to the next job.

Much like his life, reflected Sergey Vasilyevich Grechko as he worked on the roof. Last night's rain had revealed some leaks. He finished nailing the shingle over what he hoped was the last of them. Hanging the hammer back in his tool belt, he scuttled down the roof to the waiting ladder and carefully lowered himself to the ground. He liked to think he was as nimble as he had been twenty years earlier, but he was not kidding himself; he never did that. In his line of work, overestimating his abilities could prove fatal. Taking the ladder too quickly might result in a fall, and that might very well lead to a broken leg or worse. He could ill afford a disabling injury, not now, when there was much important work to do. As it was, his ribs still hurt from that Korean woman's kick.

He shook his head as he winced with the pain, and

the memory. The mission had been cursed from the beginning. He'd never had much respect for the West German terrorists to begin with and he had even less now. By the time the idiots had communicated with their Stasi contact, the pseudo-North Korean had gotten inside their security, which was laughable to begin with. It had been Grechko's bad fortune to be in East Berlin at the time, working with a Spetsnaz unit on a training exercise, when the order came from Moscow. He was to go to Hamburg and personally escort the clown Ohlendorf to the East. By the time he arrived, the Korean already had him. Grechko wondered who she was. Never had he encountered someone so skilled in hand-to-hand combat. It was a pity they had not been able to meet under more pleasant circumstances. He was always open to learning, especially from the only person in the world whom he had not defeated.

He had called it a draw, partly to salve his wounded pride, but also because he knew, after reviewing the fight in his mind, that neither one of them had been able to establish an advantage. The arrival of the police had caused him to prudently withdraw. The Stasi big shots had been pissed at the loss of Ohlendorf, but Grechko and his superiors cared little for what they thought. Had Grechko himself been captured, however, that would have been a calamity of the first order for KGB and many other men of high authority in Moscow.

The fact that she was a woman bothered him not a whit. Men of his father's generation would be appalled to think that a female could hold her own against a highly-trained man, this despite the experience of

Russian women ably filling combat roles in the Great Patriotic War. Grechko had traveled widely, though, and he knew that women, especially in the West, could perform virtually any task just as well as men, and sometimes better. So he was not at all surprised to have encountered a woman of her abilities. He sighed now as he contemplated it once more. Truly a waste; if they were on the same side, what might they be able to learn from each other, to accomplish together?

Grechko gazed back up the ladder to the roof, wondering when he would next have to make the climb. The dacha had been in his family for forty years, built by his father after the Great Patriotic War. Grechko would have liked to say that his father had built it with his own hands, but it would not be true. Many of the dachas in the region had been built by their owners, most of them veterans of the war as well, but the original Grechko cottage was erected by men from his father's home village, a gift for the man who helped free them from the fascists. At the time it was one simple room with a roof, no more than fifty meters square. Over the years it had been remodeled and expanded. Some of Grechko's earliest memories were of this place, helping his father with the carpentry and the plumbing. His mother and sister worked the vegetable garden. By the time Grechko had gone off to the service, the dacha was pretty close to the size and appearance it still had today.

A pity that his father had not been around to enjoy it much longer. Had Grechko been a religious man, he would have raged at a God who had brought his father through some of the worst combat of the century only to strike him down with the cancer just after turning fifty. When he had leave he would bring his mother here, but she was past seventy now and dementia had begun its pervasive invasion of her mind. She was better off staying at the rest home in Ternopil. His sister had not visited in years, ever since marrying a diplomat and heading off to the capitals of the decadent West. Her last letter had arrived two weeks ago, posted from Lisbon.

Grechko was putting his tools and the ladder away in the garage when he heard the vehicle. Instantly alert, he reached for the sidearm he wore constantly when he was out here. Inside the dacha itself were more weapons with enough ammunition to allow him to hold off a platoon of invaders. Glancing out the open door, he saw the car in the distance, winding through the forest. The fir trees obscured little. For years, Grechko had carefully trimmed them to allow for observation surprisingly far down the twisting, one-lane dirt road that meandered through the forest. Using the principles of camouflage he had learned over the years, Grechko had arranged his trimmings so that it would be unlikely anyone in the vehicle could see the dacha before Grechko saw them first, giving him a critical minute or two to assess the threat and take action.

This time, though, he recognized the car as a Volga, and attached to the front bumper was a red plate with a single gold star. So, it was Voloshin. Grechko had been wondering how long it would take before the general came to see him.

When the silver automobile left the tree line for the final thirty meters to the dacha, Grechko could confirm by sight that the general was driving, and he was alone. That was somewhat unusual; general officers in the Red Army almost never drove themselves anywhere, especially the many kilometers from the Kolomyia air base to the forest that sheltered Grechko's dacha here in the foothills of the Carpathians. It was, of course, a sign of the bourgeois to have a personal driver, something the high-ranking men of the Party, as well as the armed forces, conveniently ignored. But Voloshin was not a typical general officer, that much Grechko knew already.

The Volga came to a stop a respectable fifteen meters away and Voloshin got out. Except for the dark green Army field jacket, he was in civilian clothes: Western jeans, hiking boots, a dark red-and-black plaid shirt. The field jacket was devoid of insignia except for the single gold star on each lapel, matching the one on the field cap Voloshin held in his hand. "Good morning, Sergey Vasileyevich," Voloshin said, approaching and extending a hand.

"Good morning, General. To what do I owe the pleasure of this unannounced visit?" Grechko maintained eye contact throughout the handshake. Although his rank of colonel was below Voloshin's, this was Grechko's land, they were in mufti, and a salute was not necessary, at least in his view. Voloshin had made that clear by offering to shake hands. But in his greeting, Grechko had made it clear that he did not appreciate a surprise visit, even if the visitor was a general.

Voloshin, of course, picked up on this at once. "I would have called, but you have not yet seen fit to install a telephone here."

"I like my privacy. But, you are here. It was a long

drive for you. An early start, yes? Have you had breakfast?"

The general's smile, merely polite before, now grew wider with genuine warmth. "A long drive indeed, and no, I have not eaten."

"Neither have I. Come, join me."

"You do not subscribe to the old saying, then: 'Eat breakfast yourself, share lunch with a friend, give dinner to your enemy.'"

"Today, I make an exception."

***

Grechko had never seen a man eat *oladyi* like this before. "If you eat like this every morning, General, you will soon need new uniforms."

Voloshin finished off his last bite, sweeping the plate first to get the last drop of syrup. "I must compliment you, Sergey. You have added something to this recipe, yes? Not the traditional Ukrainian potato pancakes."

"I picked up some ideas on my last trip to America," Grechko said. He poured some tea for himself and his guest. "These are made of buttermilk. You like the syrup, yes?"

"It is exquisite. How is it made?"

"From the sap of maple trees. It is quite common in America. I brought this back from their province of Wisconsin. A pleasant place, even though it was settled by Germans and Poles, for the most part. But you did not drive all the way here just to enjoy my pancakes."

"No, I did not, although they were worth the trip."

"Join me in the sitting room, then."

The dacha's original single room was now used by Grechko for relaxing, reading, and entertaining the rare guest. The furniture was simple, by taste and necessity. Dachas were frequently robbed, although Grechko's heavy locks and sturdy doors, not to mention the bars that he put over the windows when he was gone, served as an effective deterrent. Also effective was Grechko's reputation. Ten years ago, before he had beefed up its security, the dacha had been broken into, but the thieves were sloppy. It was child's play for Grechko to track them down and punish them. The word quickly spread around the region that this particular dacha was to be avoided.

Still, Grechko was a man of simple needs when he was here, so his furnishings reflected that: comfortable, but not at all lavish. They were better, though, than what he remembered from his youth, particularly his bed, which was large and inviting, so unlike the roll-away bed he'd slept on as a boy.

Teacup in hand, Voloshin admired the photographs on the mantle of the fireplace. He nodded at one showing a group of soldiers. "Your father and his men?"

"Yes," Grechko said. "He is in the middle. That was his squad of Spetsnaz, after the liberation of his village."

"I drove through it on the way here. I saw the monument in the town square. Most impressive."

Grechko knew that most villages in the western Soviet Union had such monuments, dedicated to the men who had fought the Great Patriotic War against the fascists. That his father was one of them was his greatest source of pride. "He lost half his men driving the Nazis out, but they succeeded."

"I read about that mission," Voloshin said. "Your father personally took down the enemy commander and his guards, did he not?"

"He had help, but yes, he was there," Grechko said. He remembered the only time his father had spoken to him about it, the day before the son was to depart for his own service. They had shared a bottle of vodka together in this very room, a fire crackling in the hearth, as his father told the story, his voice breaking more than once as he recounted the courage and sacrifices of his comrades.

Voloshin stared at the photo silently for several seconds, then turned to face his host. "Sergey, your father believed strongly in our cause. We must have dedication equal to his, if we are to succeed."

Grechko stared at the tea in his cup. "There are no fascists in my village today, General. Who are we fighting?"

Voloshin sat on the small couch. "Our enemies today are much more subtle than the Germans ever were," he said. "They know they cannot defeat us on the field of battle. So, they try other means. They seek to destroy us from within, to make us doubt ourselves, our cause."

"And what is our cause? With respect, General, do not insult me by saying it is the same as the one my father and his comrades fought for. Your father, too. They fought to expel invaders from our country, invaders who were determined to wipe us from the face of the earth. The stakes were high. Everybody understood the consequences of defeat. It was not an option."

"The Party held the Union together against the

fascists. If the Party falls now, crumbles from within, what is to become of our country?"

Grechko set his cup on an end table next to a small framed picture of his sister. "Are we speaking now of the Soviet Union, or of Ukraine?"

"Both."

Grechko stared at the fireplace, where embers still glowed from the previous evening. He really should have stoked it again when he got up, but he felt it would warm up later. A little chill now was nothing, though. He had endured much, much worse. "You are a Russian, General, while I am Ukrainian. When we talk of 'our country,' we might be talking about different things."

Voloshin looked down at his teacup, then back at Grechko. "Let us speak freely, Sergey. We have built up trust between each other, have we not? We are military men. So, I tell you this in confidence. This might surprise you, but I do not fear a free and independent Ukraine. Perhaps someday it will be possible. But not yet."

Grechko laughed. "And this free and independent Ukraine, it will come about because I will assassinate the man who is trying to bring more freedom to the entire Soviet Union? That sounds like a contradiction to me, General."

He half-expected Voloshin to get angry, but instead the general merely smiled. "It does, doesn't it?" He took one more sip of tea and set the cup aside on another table. "Sergey Vasiliyevich, you know the political situation as well as I do. With his talk of *glasnost* and *perestroika,* Gorbachev is making a lot of very powerful people very nervous."

"What did they expect? The Politburo put him there, after Chernenko's death. Now they are surprised at what they got?" He shook his head in disgust. Politicians.

"Gorbachev is very skilled at what he does. Not everyone was supportive of his elevation to the leadership positions of the Party and the Union. Now those people are increasingly nervous about the path down which he is taking us."

Grechko looked at the general sharply. "And you are one of those nervous people?"

"I am concerned, but not necessarily because of that." He leaned forward, elbows on knees. "Along with a very few other trusted men on the Committee, I have been studying this situation for some time. We have come to the conclusion that a move against Gorbachev is inevitable. Within five years at the outside, probably sooner. And no, not the one we are actually planning, the one in which you have been asked to play such a prominent role."

"I'm listening."

"To force a change in government is a very delicate matter. This is not South America, where they happen as often as the change of seasons. Nor is this Africa, where some self-appointed generalissimo can gather a ragtag group of men with Kalashnikovs and storm the presidential palace. A civil war would tear our nation apart. The West might have to intervene, if only to make sure our nuclear weapons would not fall into the wrong hands. It could go very badly, very quickly. A catastrophe."

"It is best not to have such a thing, obviously."

Voloshin was clearly nervous, and he rose and

walked over to the mantle again. "You met General Klimov, out in Siberia."

"Yes. He did not seem very pleased to meet me, though."

That brought a grim smile. "As you know, Klimov commands the Moscow Military District. In many respects it is the most powerful command in the Red Army. It would not be unreasonable to say that no leader of the Soviet Union serves except at the behest of that one commander. With his troops he could take the Kremlin in a matter of hours. Then it would be up to outside commanders to decide if it was worth the risk to move against the city themselves."

Grechko knew that Voloshin was simplifying the matter to some extent. KGB had its tendrils everywhere and surely did not trust the Army. The intelligence service relied on its ability to detect potential threats to the government—which meant a threat to KGB—and deal with them before they could grow into something that would be too strong to take down. In many ways the Soviet Union was still a police state, not much changed from the days of Stalin and Kruschev. The Army had its tanks but the Party had its intelligence apparatus, which was designed to make sure those tanks only moved at the behest of the Party, and not against it. So far, it had worked quite well.

But Grechko also knew much about KGB since it was his nominal employer now and then, and he knew it was not infallible. The Army had its own intelligence service, the GRU, and while its official purpose was to find out everything there was to know about the military capabilities of potential foreign adversaries, it also kept a discreet eye on its civilian counterpart. So it might be possible for the Army, with GRU assistance, to move on the government. That was the case in every country, though. Grechko believed the reason the Red Army had never thrown out the politicians was the same reason why the Americans had never deposed theirs: loyalty to the nation. As inefficient and corrupt as the politicians could be, the military tended to give them a lot of latitude. There was much grumbling, of course, but the generals never seemed to think that the situation was bad enough to justify taking such an immense, irrevocable step.

Until now, evidently.

"Klimov does not like Gorbachev," Voloshin was saying, "and sees himself as the savior of the Soviet Union. I have become convinced in recent months that if we do not move now, Klimov will move on his own, or more likely in conjunction with other generals, to take over the government."

"You are saying, General, that you and your associates can control Klimov. I presume you have someone in mind to take over the leadership of the Party and the government when the man with the birthmark is no more?"

"We do," Voloshin said. "Someone who can be trusted to slow things down, build up our strength again, and when the time is right, make the appropriate reforms." He sat down again. "It pains me greatly to be involved in this, Sergey. Personally, I like Gorbachev. Quite frankly, some of his ideas are needed. The problem is, he is ten years ahead of his time. With that cowboy the Americans have in their White House, we cannot afford to show any weakness now."

"The actor?" Grechko laughed. "You are afraid of him? Tell me this is not so."

"I am afraid of no man," Voloshin said, "including you, Sergey." He stared hard at Grechko. "But you have not seen what I have seen. Our economy is precarious. The American defense buildup in the past few years has caused us to increase our own spending, and at the same time we are, in effect, encouraging our republics and our satellites in Europe to move further away from us. You know what is happening in the Baltic republics. Ever since that Latvian teenager, Lauska, was sent to a labor camp in '84 because he was involved in an underground independence movement, things have been shaky. You heard what happened in Riga last December when those students rioted after a rock concert. There have been many such incidents, mostly unreported in our news media, of course."

"Gorbachev has let the genie out of the bottle, General. Are you sure you can put it back inside?"

"We must try," Voloshin said. "If nothing is done, one of two things will happen. Klimov will find some new associates, and they will move on the Kremlin. Or, Gorbachev will continue along his present course and things will fall apart of their own accord. Either way it is a disaster for us. That is why we must move, now. I came here today to make sure you are with us, Sergey Vasiliyevich."

Grechko rose, stretched his back, and walked to a window. Voloshin's use of Grechko's patronymic, unusual among men of roughly the same age, emphasized the general's sincerity. Perhaps his desperation, also. It gave Grechko one more thing to consider.

Outside, springtime was slowly returning to the Ukrainian countryside. It had been so for centuries, long before Marx had come up with this idea called communism, before Lenin had brought it to Russia at the point of a gun. Grechko knew his country would be here long after everyone he knew now, including himself, was dead. The question was, would the Ukraine of the future be one of prosperity or despair? His father had fought for that future.

"Did you know, General, that my grandfather was a *kulak?*"

Without even looking at him, Grechko could sense Voloshin's unease. "No, I did not," the general said.

"My family, on my father's side, has Cossack blood," Grechko said. Outside, a rabbit hopped along the perimeter of the trees. He didn't see too many rabbits, especially since he no longer kept a garden, but also because of the many predators in the forest. It had taken hard, determined men to tame this wilderness hundreds of years ago, and from them had come the Cossacks. "My grandfather told me our people were important in the history of Ukraine. We resisted them all, General. The Poles and Lithuanians, the Austrians, finally the Russians. Eventually we accepted life under the tsars. My family became relatively wealthy. Then came Lenin and his Bolsheviks. Kulaks, peasants like my grandfather, he said, were bloodsuckers and vampires. When Stalin began to collectivize the farms, thousands of Ukrainians were sent to Siberia. Thousands more were killed."

"I have heard those stories," Voloshin said. Grechko wondered if the general was thinking of his own Russian family and whether his people had participated in the purges and forced starvation.

"My grandfather and his family escaped across the mountains to Romania," he said. "They avoided the worst of it. Finally they returned in 1935. Evidently things were not much better in Romania, and by then Stalin had turned his attention elsewhere. A few years later my father joined the Red Army." Grechko barked a harsh laugh. "How about that, General? My father chose to take up arms to protect the very regime that had so brutalized his country. Before he died, I asked him why he made that choice. He said, 'I did not want to be a farmer, and I wanted adventure.' He told me many times that he enjoyed the military life, and he knew that the fascists had to be resisted or all would be lost. Ukraine, Russia, everything. So he fought. He did not value his Ukrainian heritage as much as his own father did. But my grandfather told me all about what happened to us."

"That was a long time ago, Sergey," Voloshin said. "Times have changed."

"So, my father was Ukrainian, but my mother was Russian, a city girl from Moscow," Grechko continued, looking out at the trees as they moved slightly with the breeze. "She once told me a story. It was during the war. She was in Moscow, not yet married to my father. The Germans were within a few kilometers of the city. She was on a work detail, building tank defenses. She said it was a very frightening time."

Behind him, Voloshin said nothing. Grechko sighed, and continued. "One day, when they were at the depths of their despair, they were out working. In the distance she could hear the thunder of the artillery. That day it seemed closer than ever. The women were frightened. It was all women, the men were all at the front or, some said, many were preparing to move the government out of the city to the east, to the Urals. An armored limousine drove up and stopped. It was escorted by two military vehicles. The door of the limousine opened and a man emerged. It was Stalin. My mother said many of the women stopped working and stared. They were afraid they would be accused of not working hard enough, that the soldiers in the vehicles would open fire with their machine guns. But instead, Stalin looked at them, then held up a fist in triumph. 'We will not be defeated, comrades,' he said to them. Then he got back into the car and drove away. The women worked even harder. They knew Stalin was with them. And the tide turned."

Grechko turned away from the window. "You can now understand, General, that I have no illusions about Stalin, about the nation he helped to build and which our fathers fought to defend. He was a brutal man. But that day, my mother and her friends did not see the brutality. They saw strength and discipline. Our only hope, then and now."

"I understand how you feel, Sergey," Voloshin said. "There are few men in the Soviet Union as disciplined as you are. We need you. Are you with us?"

Grechko nodded. "I will do what needs to be done."

CHAPTER SEVEN

WASHINGTON, D.C.
APRIL 1987

Jo Ann never ceased to be amazed by the Pentagon, even after having served a nine-month tour there a few years before. During that time in the Air Force Office of Special Operations, she'd learned the building's massive numbers: over six and a half million square feet in size, home to more than thirty thousand employees every day, walking its more than seventeen miles of corridors. On sunny days many of them enjoyed the five-acre central plaza. Early in the Cold War it had been nicknamed "Ground Zero" on the assumption that one or more Soviet nuclear warheads would explode directly overhead in the opening salvo of World War III.

On this sunny day, Jo doubted very much that she or anyone else here would have to worry about that. As she walked toward the west entrance from the huge parking lot, she reflected that it was becoming increasingly unlikely that this structure, or anything else in the capital city, would ever be the target of an enemy attack. She kept up with the news, paying particular attention to East-West relations, and things seemed to be getting better. On the other hand, she also studied history, which showed that whenever a society successfully dealt with one external threat, another one seemed to take its place. That was one reason she continued to wear the uniform. Her country and its allies had faced down many threats before, some with her direct help, but she held no illusions about the future.

The Air Force offices were on the east side of the building. Jo thought it likely there would still be some people over there who served with her during her tour in '85, so hopefully she'd have time after the meeting to stop by and see who was around. She was almost at the west entrance when she heard the familiar sound of a helicopter coming in for a landing on the nearby pad.

She recognized it as a UH-1 Iroquois, painted in Army olive drab. A few seconds after it landed two officers jumped out and hustled her way, holding their caps on their heads against the rotor wash. The shorter man had a briefcase and wore a service cap, the taller man was empty-handed and sported a green beret. When he got closer she saw the shoulder patch on his green Class A jacket, then the striking gray eyes and lips curled into what could be a smirk or a sly grin, depending on your point of view. Jo had only seen it once before, on a memorable night more than two years ago, and her first impression hadn't been a favorable one. She thought about entering the building quickly but decided against it. She didn't want to give the impression she wanted to avoid him.

Jo struggled to get her emotions under control, seeking out her inner ki. She forced herself to remember that this particular officer had not been directly responsible for what had happened to her best friend on that night in North Carolina. But indirectly, oh yes indeed, he'd been in it right up to those gray eyes.

"Well, Major Geary," he said. His eyes caught the silver oak leaves on her service jacket. "Excuse me. Lieutenant Colonel Geary." He snapped off a salute. The man behind him, a first lieutenant, followed suit.

"As you were, gentlemen," Jo said, returning the salutes and noting the gold leaf on the taller man's jacket. They'd both moved up a grade since Bragg. "Major Jennings. We meet again."

"Under somewhat more pleasant circumstances this time," Jennings said. He stepped ahead of her and pulled the door open. "After you, ma'am."

"Thank you."

They checked through the security station, received their visitors' badges and entered the E Ring. Jennings stopped to look at the bustle of people, most of them in uniform, then said, "Well, Colonel, I have an appointment in–" He looked at his watch. "—about twenty minutes. Are you free for lunch?"

He had some nerve, Jo would give him that. "I'm afraid not, Major."

"Sorry to hear that. I was hoping we could talk about Fort Bragg. How long will you be in town? Maybe we could have dinner."

Jo forced herself to smile. He was pushing it. If anybody should have hard feelings about Bragg, it was her. "I'm having dinner with my father tonight."

She didn't miss the flicker of disappointment in his eyes, but he rallied. "Could we meet later, maybe, for a drink?"

She hesitated. What harm could it do? There were

still some questions she had about that night. She realized that in many ways, she still needed some closure. “All right.”

The smile was back. “Do you know Murphy’s Irish Pub, in Alexandria?”

“In Old Town? It’s been a few years, but I’m sure I can find it.”

“Great. Shall we say, nine o’clock?”

“I’ll see you there.” Even as she said it, she wondered why she was agreeing to what amounted to a date with a man she’d once fought and beaten in the field, a man who had nearly cheated her out of a hard-won victory that still rang hollow, all these months later. But in her fifteen years in the Air Force there’d been more than a few men, and some women, who had thrown roadblocks at her, and she had always tried to avoid looking in the rearview mirror once she got around them. None of those had ever been like this, but that didn’t matter, did it? The principle was the same.

The soldiers snapped off salutes. Jo returned them, even though saluting generally wasn’t required once you got inside the building, unless you happened to see the president. Jennings and the lieutenant headed off to the right. Jo watched them walk away, thinking back to that chilly night in the North Carolina woods years ago. Actually, it was two years, six months and three days ago, she remembered now. Not that long. She turned and walked off to the left.

***

The Secretary of Defense’s office complex had few of the trappings one might expect for one of the most powerful men in the country. The world, Jo corrected herself, stopping by the entryway to straighten her jacket. Casper Weinberger was in charge of the mightiest military force on the planet, and he was answerable only to one other man. She half-expected her father to be waiting on her out here, but then again, that wouldn't be appropriate, she reminded herself. Joseph was going to have to use all his well-honed people skills to convince the secretary and the other brass that Lieutenant Colonel Jo Ann Geary, who just happened to be his daughter, was the right officer to lead this new unit, but he would have to use those skills very carefully.

She made her way past two protective secretaries into a reception area, then to a conference room. Along the far wall a steward was putting the finishing touches to a table featuring coffee, soft drinks and the inevitable doughnuts. A bit late in the morning for that, Jo thought, but she wouldn't have been having one even if it was breakfast time. Three other men were in the room, one wearing colonel's eagles on his dark green Marine Corps jacket, the other two in civilian suits. One of them detached himself from the colonel and came over to greet her.

"Lieutenant Colonel Geary, I presume? Hello, I'm Brian Swantz, administrative assistant for Secretary Aldridge. He sends his regards and asks if you can stop by to say hello after the meeting."

Jo gladly shook Swantz's hand. It was nice to be recognized. Verne Orr had been Secretary of the Air Force during Jo's tour here, but obviously her work had made an impact. The current secretary, Edward Aldridge, had certainly reviewed her service jacket. "I'll be happy to," she said. "Are you here to represent the secretary?"

"Yes indeed," Swantz said. "We had a good selection of potential candidates to put forward for this job, but your jacket kept making it to the top of the stack. Congratulations."

"Thanks, but nothing's been decided yet." To be truthful, Jo doubted her chances were as good as Swantz might think them to be. She had experience both in administration and in the field, but she wasn't kidding herself. It was still a man's world in many ways, especially in the military. From what she'd heard, the CIA and other intelligence services were no different.

Two men in Navy blue entered the room, doffing their white service caps. Jo and Swantz rejoined the group so introductions could be made. The other civilian was Secretary Weinberger's chief of staff. The Marine colonel was Gerald Teller, a name Jo thought she should know, although she knew she'd never met him. A solid six-footer with high-and-tight sandy hair that was graying at the temples, Teller would not have been easy to forget. She filed it away for another part of her brain to work on while she met the sailors. Captain Richard McWilliams was tall and dark-haired with wire-rimmed glasses, looking more like an accountant than a naval officer, while Lieutenant Commander Edward Anastas was short and somewhat swarthy. Both wore the distinctive insignia of Navy Special Warfare, an eagle clutching a trident and flintlock pistol over an anchor, known within the SEALs as the "Budweiser."

"We have about ten minutes until the secretary arrives," the chief of staff said. "Army should be here any second."

"We'll keep things under control till they get here," Teller said.

"As usual, right, Jerry?" McWilliams asked with a laugh.

Teller grinned. He took a sip of coffee from a Styrofoam cup. "Dick and I have worked together a few times," he said to Jo. He extended a hand. "Pleased to meet you, Colonel."

"Likewise." The Marine's grip was firm but not excessive. This was a man who was used to command but who was also in command of himself. Jo liked him immediately. Among his service ribbon bars, Jo noticed the distinctive red-white-and-blue that designated the bearer had been awarded the Silver Star. A switch tripped in her memory. "I read an article recently in *Leatherneck* about Hill 488," she said. "You were there?"

Teller's gray eyes seemed to lose focus, but just for a split-second. "Yes," he said. "I was lucky enough to be one of those who made it out."

"I'd say skill had more to do with that than luck," Jo said. One of the most vicious small-unit battles of the Vietnam War, the June 1966 fight for Hill 488 was now part of Marine Corps lore. Sixteen Marines and their two Navy corpsmen, with help from close-air support, held off a battalion of North Vietnamese regulars for over twenty-four hours before they could be extracted. Toward the end much of the fighting was hand-to-hand. Teller was one of the dozen men who survived.

The Marine offered a tight grin. "Skill and one helluva tough staff sergeant to keep us together," he said. His eyes flicked to the Bronze Star ribbon bar that highlighted her own set, right next to one that wasn't American in origin. "I understand you've been involved in more than a few operations yourself, Colonel." He nodded toward her ribbon bars. "The George Cross. That was you down in Argentina with the Brits in '82, wasn't it?"

The man knew his medals. "Yes, and it's Jo." She was always surprised when someone told her they'd heard of her part in what was still supposed to be a top-secret chapter of the Falklands War. She tried not to think about it too much. She'd made it out alive, but someone very dear to her had not.

"Call me Jerry. I hope we'll be working together in this unit, Jo." He glanced at the door. "Ah, it appears the Army has come over the hill at last."

Two officers in Army green were entering the room. The one in the lead was a well-built black man wearing a green beret and colonel's eagles. Jo couldn't recall the face, although she thought she must've seen it somewhere. The other one, though, she knew very well.

"Colonel Geary, we meet again," Major Keith Jennings said. "I didn't expect to see you here."

CHAPTER EIGHT

MCLEAN,
VIRGINIA
APRIL 1987

"The secretary was very impressed with you, JoJo," her father said as he cut a piece from the New York strip steak on his plate.

"Probably not enough to give me command of the unit," Jo said. Her own steak was delicious, done just right. Her father had awakened the gas grill from its winter slumber and once again showed that while he had always been little more than helpless in a kitchen, out on the patio with his grill, he was king.

"I don't know about that," he said. His voice sounded upbeat, but his eyes couldn't hide the truth they both knew.

"Appa, let's be honest. There are three reasons why I won't be commanding."

"And they are?"

She put her knife down and held up a finger. "One: every other service had an officer there with higher rank than me. Two: the Army and Marine Corps officers have a lot more combat experience than I do. Three: all the rest of them have... well, they don't have breasts."

He chuckled as he forked a piece of baked potato

into his mouth. After a moment, he touched his napkin to his lips and looked her in the eye. “The reason the Air Force didn’t bring in a full bird colonel is because nobody in your unit has more field experience than you do. It’s always been the other services that have led the way in special operations, that’s no secret, but things are changing.”

“Not fast enough to give anybody in blue a real shot at something like this, especially if the person in blue is female.”

“Perhaps not,” he agreed. “As to rank, the secretary has already let it be known that he won’t automatically give command to the ranking officer. If he were to go strictly by the book, he’d have to give it to Carson, the Green Beret. Bird colonel, same as Teller, equivalent to McWilliams as a Navy captain, but more time in grade than either of them. Carson’s in line for a star in the next year or so. Plus, his combat experience is more extensive than theirs. Not by much, but probably by enough.”

“And then there’s the matter of anatomy.”

He grinned. “Well, in terms of gender, things are changing there, too, but—“

“I know: not fast enough.”

He finished off the last of his steak. “Look at it this way, JoJo. If you don’t get the C.O.’s job, you’re probably in line to be X.O. That would be a feather in your cap, and the Air Force’s.”

Executive officer. The thought had occurred to her during the meeting, which had been cordial but businesslike. Secretary Weinberger was well-organized and deftly steered things in the direction he wanted them to go. All of the operators had a healthy respect for each other's work, and to Jo's surprise there had been none of the subtle digs or even outright rudeness she'd sometimes seen at such meetings, when turf was being assigned and roles were being created. Careers often hinged on such things, and nobody got to this level in the military without thinking about his or her career. If you were close to pulling the pin, you wanted to go out with your last assignment in the books as a job done well. If you were eyeing a star, you needed to climb another rung or two and you sure didn't want to fall off the ladder.

She would just have to see. The secretary had promised they would have his decision in a week. The new commanding officer would be going right to work, and from what he'd said, the work would be more than just the administrative nuts and bolts involved in organizing a new unit. That meant a mission, and if something was in the wind, CIA probably knew about it...

"Appa, I understand that you can't disclose classified intelligence to me, but I got the feeling today that whoever winds up leading this unit will be putting a mission together pretty quickly. Am I reading the tea leaves incorrectly?"

Her father looked at her and smiled. "You're giving me that look again."

"What look is that?"

"The 'I-want-something-from-you' look that every daughter learns to give her father. You picked it up around age three."

She had to laugh. "Is it that obvious?"

"To me it is. I'm assuming when you're out in the field you're not quite as obvious."

She wadded up a napkin and tossed it at him. "Well?"

"There's always something going on, JoJo, you know that. But I can tell you that, yes, there will be work for you pretty soon."

"Important work, I hope?"

He dabbed a remnant of baked potato off his lower lip, then set the napkin down. "Is there any other kind?"

There was one more thing she'd been reluctant to bring up, but she couldn't hold it in any longer. "Appa, I have to ask you something."

He picked up on the change in her tone of voice. Setting his knife and fork aside, he dabbed at his lips and then leaned forward, elbows on the table. "Is it about the Iran-Contra thing?"

"Yes," she said, hating to admit it. The scandal had been all over the news for months. Reagan Administration officials had been selling arms to Iran and funneling the proceeds to the Contra rebels in Nicaragua, contrary to congressional mandates against such aid. The president had gone on television a month ago, admitting that in his efforts to use Iranian influence to free American hostages being held in the Middle East, and at the same time continue supporting the rebels fighting the Sandinistas, serious mistakes had been made. The CIA, involved on both fronts, was taking a beating in the media. Her father, as Deputy Director of Operations, had certainly been involved in the effort to destabilize the Sandinistas. "Is your job in jeopardy?"

"I don't think so, honey," Joseph said, suddenly looking very tired. "I could retire anytime I want. Frankly, I'm only staying on long enough to get Pallas

Group up and running, and see you through the first mission. I promised the president."

"I was surprised to hear of the DCI's resignation," Jo said. William Casey, the Director of Central Intelligence, had stepped down at the beginning of February, citing ill health. Jo well remembered the man who looked like a kindly grandfather but was in fact a sharp-as-a-tack spymaster. The meeting that began her involvement in EMINENCE, five years ago, had been held in Casey's office.

"I wasn't," Joseph said. "He really hasn't been in the best of health for some time. This thing didn't make him feel any better, that's for sure."

"What's going to happen now? Scuttlebutt has it that the president will have no choice but to appoint someone who'll be strictly by-the-book." Jo Ann knew all too well that office politics at Langley could be cutthroat, and periodically someone was brought in to ostensibly get the Agency back on the straight-and-narrow. In an organization that sometimes had to utilize unconventional methods to get the job done, that almost always led to firings and forced retirements. She desperately wanted her father to conclude his career with honor.

"You probably heard right," he said. Taking one final sip of wine, Joseph looked at her, and in his eyes she saw the steely resolve she remembered so well. "I don't want you worrying about me, honey. I'll be fine."

***

She treated herself to a bath and did her nails, then put on a short black skirt and an off-white chiffon blouse, the fruits of the trip she'd made to a trendy boutique after leaving the Pentagon, and slid her feet into a new pair of black pumps. A touch of eye shadow and lipstick, a deft spritz of perfume, and she was ready. For what, she wasn't completely sure, but what harm could it do to have a drink with a comrade-in-arms?

True, this particular comrade had once nearly cheated her out of a hard-earned triumph, but that had been a long time ago. She wondered if the subject of COSMO would come up tonight. She suspected it would, and it might be a fairly tense conversation. Then why was she making an effort to look good for a man she already didn't like? She had no answer for that one.

Downstairs, she looked for her father to tell him she was leaving. In his study she found a fire crackling in the hearth and a book waiting patiently beside his reading glasses on an end table next to his favorite chair. A tumbler with a few fingers of dark liquid and half-melted ice cubes sat next to the glasses. Jack Daniel's, her father's drink of choice. The book was *American Caesar,* a biography of Douglas MacArthur. Even as he approached retirement, Joseph Geary was still studying the lives of great men and women. "I want to know about leadership," he had once told his daughter. "How did they make decisions? How did they deal with failure? What separated them from the people they led?" It was a quest for knowledge his daughter had inherited.

She took a moment to gaze over the collection of framed photos on the mantle. Family shots. She smiled at seeing the face of her mother, even as her heart tightened. The Stanford graduation photo of Jo with her parents was prominently displayed. There were more on the wall across from the chair and reading lamp, and one of them caught her eye as her father entered the room.

"Going out?"

"I'm meeting someone for a drink in Alexandria," Jo said. She touched the photo. "I look terrible in this picture."

He peered at it and smiled. "You look great. Probably one of the few photos in existence of the Diana Brigade."

"The survivors, anyway, some of them," Jo said. Her memories drifted back over the years. How many now, ten? No, twelve. She was so young then. They all were. Fifty women plucked from the four branches and thrust into a cauldron of training and exercises that were designed with one purpose: to prove that women could not handle the stress of combat operations. Fourteen of them had made it. Jo was kneeling in the front row, third from the left, her utilities dirty and ragged just like everyone else's, her boonie hat askew, her M16 held proudly, stock in the dirt at her feet, and on her face was that tired but triumphant grin that was almost exactly the same as the grins of the other women.

"How many of them were with you on COSMO?" her father asked.

"Four." She looked up at him. "You gave the secretary that file, didn't you?"

"I didn't have to, JoJo. He knew about that, knew about EMINENCE, too. He doesn't miss much. That's why you were there today. That's why you'll be in the unit." He leaned over her and kissed her forehead. "I'm gonna turn in soon, honey." He gestured toward the MacArthur book. "I have to follow that old soldier through Korea before hitting the hay. Have a good time. What time does your flight leave tomorrow?"

"Ten a.m.," she said. She had to be at Anderson Air Force Base by nine; that pretty much precluded any late-night partying tonight. One drink and that would be it. She gave her father a smile. "Good night, Appa. I'll fix breakfast in the morning."

Her father smiled and headed to his chair. She touched the photo one last time, her fingertip on the smiling, dark-skinned woman kneeling next to her. "Kate," she whispered, and wiped away a tear.

CHAPTER NINE

FORT BRAGG,
NORTH CAROLINA
OCTOBER 1984

The near-half-moon was obscured by solid clouds, but through the infrared scope the ground rushing beneath the helicopter was rendered nearly as bright as noon under a green sun. There was no sign of their target, but Jo knew they couldn't be more than a couple kilometers away by now. Up ahead, the rolling, forested hills hid all manner of potential threats, but she was only interested in those with two legs. Next to her in the pilot's seat of the Black Hawk, Army Chief Warrant Officer Mary Benson was baring her teeth in a fierce grin. It was a damn good thing, Jo reflected, that Kate had recommended including a helo driver on the team, just in case.

"Can't be more than two klicks in front of us, Benson," Jo said over the intercom. "Set us down in that clearing at our ten o'clock."

"Roger that, Major." The pilot deftly pulled the bird into a turn and headed for the football field-sized gap in the trees.

"Kate, get 'em up back there," Jo ordered.

"We're set, Major. Give the word and we drop the lines." Jo could hear the excitement just barely being contained in her X.O.'s voice. They were all tired from two days in the field. The exercise started with the long march from the landing zone to the target, and then came rain that had made last night's camp a chore and a half, but Jo didn't feel tired now and she doubted any of the six other women in the helicopter were fatigued either. Pissed, yes indeed. They were well and truly upset, but they were focused. The prize was waiting for them, somewhere out in those trees. This time, they would not be denied.

Benson brought the helicopter into a hover about ten meters above the grass. Jo unbuckled her safety harness, but before removing her flight helmet she spoke into the intercom one last time. "You know what to do, Mary."

"You'll know when I find 'em," the chief warrant said. "We'll keep 'em occupied till you get there."

"Don't let Reinecke get too frisky with those guns," Jo warned. The M134 Gatling guns, one on each of the bird's weapons pylons, could throw out thousands of deadly 7.62mm rounds per minute. Jo didn't want to use them for what was technically not a live-fire exercise, but the situation had changed rather dramatically since the rules had been explained to them three days before.

"She's got a flair with 'em," Benson said. "Best get back there, Major."

In the cargo cabin, Jo saw her troopers still seated but ready to go. She held tight to the back of the co-pilot's seat as Benson brought the aircraft down toward the landing zone. With her intercom unplugged, Jo had to shout to make herself heard over the roar of the twin turboshaft engines. "You have the co-pilot seat, Denise!"

The lanky Marine captain flashed her a grin and started to climb past her into the cockpit. Jo tugged at her sleeve as she went by. “Be careful with those guns!”

“Oo-rah, Major,” Reinecke said with a nod.

From a jump seat next to the open starboard cargo door, Air Force Captain Katherine Simmons handed Jo her M16. Jo was already wearing her ALICE harness containing her extra ammo magazines—blank rounds for this exercise—as well as a pair of flash-bang grenades and other necessities. Her ruck was back at the camp, along with those of the other women on the assault team. They needed to stay light and move fast.

“Lines down!” Jo shouted. Four heavy-duty nylon lines were released, two on each side of the aircraft, anchored just inside the open doors. “Follow me!” She grabbed the nearest line and jumped.

***

“Right where we thought they’d be,” Kate whispered as she and Jo peered over the edge of the small ridge. Down in the narrow valley below was a line of figures moving steadily to the west. Through her binoculars Jo could make out fifteen shapes. Twelve would be the Special Forces A-Team, their rivals in this exercise. One more would be the umpire, and the two smaller ones in the middle were the two women from Jo’s team who’d been captured several hours earlier.

Operation COSMO had started out as a “capture-the-flag” exercise pitting the all-male Green Beret team against Jo’s group, comprised of a mix of Diana Brigade veterans and younger women who had applied for special operations training in their service branches. On the two-day hump to the target, an Opposing Force camp deep in the forests of Fort Bragg's huge operations area, Jo and her team had successfully foiled an ambush attempt by the A-Team, capturing two of the attacking troopers, but she'd lost two of her own in a counter-strike. Jo could live with that kind of exchange. What she couldn't live with was the fact that the Berets had gotten to the OPFOR compound four hours ahead of her and instead of assaulting the post to seize the flag, they'd had it handed to them by a cooperative officer without a shot being fired.

That same officer hadn't wanted to cooperate with Jo at all, which was why she hadn't bothered to get his permission to borrow his fully-loaded helicopter. Now they had rapidly overcome the A-Team's head start and the tables were about to be turned.

"Here comes Mary," Jo said. From the distance came the sound of helo rotors, and suddenly the Black Hawk roared over the tree line on the far side of the valley. "Pass the word, rear-guard element move now! Everybody else go on my signal."

Kate relayed the command down the line of troopers. To Jo's left, the umpire hugged the ground. "What are your intentions here, Major?" he asked.

Jo gave him a quick glance. Captain Barnes had been scrupulously fair all during the exercise, even backing Jo's play to take the OPFOR helo over the strong and profane objections of the post C.O. She knew that Barnes had seen action in Grenada a year ago. He could see right through a line of bull, so she didn't give him one. "My intentions are to get that flag, Captain, like I explained back at the OPFOR post."

"With a combat-loaded helicopter? The rules specifically call for no live fire on this exercise."

"That refers just to the arms me and my troopers can carry," Jo said.

"There's nothing in there about–"

Jo cut him off. "If you don't mind, Captain, I've got an assault to run." Down in the valley, the Gatlings of the Black Hawk roared. Jo saw the tracer rounds light up the ground fifty meters in front of the A-Team's point man. "Go! Go! Go!"

The rear-guard team of three troopers was already coming around behind the A-Team, which had halted its march at the appearance of the helicopter. Like the well-trained men they were, they'd gone to ground immediately, but the grass in this valley had been grazed by generations of deer and was less than a foot high. Jo saw the last two men in the file turn to face the threat from behind, but the rest were focused on the menacing helo to their front. Benson brought the bird in just twenty feet above the deck, and Reinecke stitched the ground with the Gatlings, expertly crossing the T. The Black Hawk pulled up well before the ridge line, executed a tight turn to the left and came in for another pass.

Jo saw all this as she and the three other women of the main assault team rushed down the hill and into the clearing. Jo came to a clump of three dead trees, scarred by some long-ago lightning strike, took a firing position from their cover and fired a five-round burst from her rifle. The men at the front of the Berets' line swung around to return fire, but then the Gatlings roared again as Benson made her second run across the T.

The umpire in the middle of the A-Team's line signaled three hits. Only two of the "enemy" had gotten off any shots at all, and Barnes, hustling down behind Jo, made no signal. "Lay down your weapons!" Jo shouted.

The helicopter turned around again and came back to the front of the formation, settling gently to the ground. Jo heard the engines spool down and the Black Hawk's spotlight flared to life, illuminating the Berets and their prisoners.

Just outside the cone of the spotlight, Jo gave another command. "I said, lay down your weapons!"

The cursing that followed was colorful, if unimaginative, Jo thought. She advanced into the light. "Come on, guys, can't you do better than 'Fuck you, bitch'?" With two of her women to her right, three more boxing in the men from their rear, and the Black Hawk facing them with its still-smoking Gatlings, Jo strode confidently to the third man in line. "Major Jennings, I'll take that flag, if you please."

The tall soldier flashed a grin that split his grease-painted face. "I don't think so," he said.

Another man approached from the line. "You've got three casualties here, Jennings," the umpire said. "Ed, any on your side?"

"Negative," Barnes replied.

The number two man in the line, eyes glaring with anger from under his boonie hat, stepped toward her, tall and broad-shouldered, his M4 like a toy in his big hands. "So far," he said.

"The rules of the exercise didn't say anything about using aircraft," Jennings said. He tried to make his voice hard and mean, but Jo sensed more amusement than anger.

"They didn't say we couldn't, either," Jo countered. "But I do recall that the objective is to *capture* the flag from the OPFOR, not to just have it handed over."

Jennings spread his hands. "He surrendered. What was I gonna do, say no?"

"Like hell," Kate said from Jo's right. "A post surrenders to you and you just walk away, no occupying force left behind? That don't sound like good Green Beanie work to me."

"What the fuck would you know about that, you zoomie cunt?" the big man said.

"You can kiss my ass, you cracker son–"

"Kate!" Jo said. She had rarely seen her friend this worked up, but the sergeant had used the one word guaranteed to instantly send any woman in uniform from zero to a hundred on the anger scale.

The big man shucked his pack and set his rifle down on it. "I don't think so, sweet thing. Don't wanna get stretch marks on my lips."

Jo took a step toward Kate as she pointed at Jennings. "Major, tell your man to stand down!"

Jennings took a step toward him. "Sergeant, that'll be–"

Kate rushed him, barely evading Jo's grasp. A hundred thirty pounds of barely-contained fury launched at the SF sergeant. He pivoted deftly, grabbed Kate's arms and tossed her ten feet in the air. Kate landed on her back with a sickening crunch and a scream of pain.

Jo rushed to her friend, lying prone in the light from the helo. Kneeling down, Jo could see the large rock underneath Kate's spine. "Medic!" Jo yelled. "Get a medic over here!"

One of the Berets and two of Jo's troopers rushed forward. "Step back, Major," Navy Lieutenant (j.g.) Carla Zenz said. She had been one of the two women captured. "Easy there, Kate," Zenz said, her voice calm, belying the tension Jo sensed from her.

"Hurts so bad..." Kate gasped, tears running down her face.

"Possible spinal injury," the Green Beret said. "Is there a stretcher board in that helo?" Zenz ran to the helicopter.

Tearing herself away from her friend, Jo looked at the sergeant. "You better damn well hope she recovers."

"Bitch came at me, or didn't you see that? *Ma'am,"* he added sarcastically.

Three strides brought Jo right up to him. "Major Jennings, I'm placing this man under arrest."

"Now, wait a minute," Jennings said, taking a step toward them.

"No slope's gonna take me anywhere," the sergeant growled, and his arm came back.

"Wrong answer," Jo said.

CHAPTER TEN

BUDAPEST,
HUNGARY
APRIL 1987

The view, Grechko had to admit, was spectacular. The wind picked up, causing him to tug his cap tighter. Spring had come to Hungary a few weeks before, but it could still get cold, even in midday.

He stood on the ramparts of the *Citadella,* the nineteenth century fortress atop Gellért Hill on the western side of the Danube. Across the river, the Pest half of the city stretched into the distance. Flat, crowded, so unlike hilly Buda here on the west bank. Grechko knew the history: Originally settled by the Celts, then used by the Romans as an outpost on their northern frontier, what became Budapest had been fought over many times throughout the centuries. The Habsburgs had thrown out the Turks in the seventeenth century and the Chain Bridge, below him and upriver to the left, linked the two halves in 1849. He would have to look at the bridge this evening, when it would be lit up to resemble the links of a chain over the river.

There had been fighting here even after the Habsburgs, Grechko knew, and more recently than the Great Patriotic War. Resting his hands on the cold stone of the Citadel's parapet, he looked down and to the left. Right down there, at the base of the stone wall, was where the tanks formed a skirmish line and began bombarding the insurgents across the Danube.

Operation WHIRLWIND, they called it. November 4, 1956, little more than thirty years ago now. Nearly three thousand Hungarians had died, most of them in those streets and buildings across the river. Soviet tanks roamed the streets of the city, firing indiscriminately at both civilian and military targets. Some seventy kilometers to the south, in a city then called Sztálinváros, the revolutionary leadership was overcome in a bold assault by Spetsnaz troops. A few days later the last resistance in the countryside collapsed, and the pro-Soviet government was restored to power.

It was fortunate, he thought now, that the list of Soviet casualties did not include the name of one Colonel Vasily Grechko, who had planned and led the decisive raid in Sztálinváros. His father lost some men in that operation, six out of the 699 Soviet soldiers who gave their lives to suppress their fraternal socialist allies. It was a pity, Grechko thought, that he didn't have time to visit that village, now called Dunaújváros, and walk in his father's footsteps.

He shook his head at the irony of it all. There was little doubt that had the Hungarian revolution succeeded back then, the rest of the Soviet satellites would've followed suit. Moscow would have responded with even more tanks, more death. The mighty Red Army that just a decade earlier had crushed the Germans would have shown little mercy to rebellious students and workers. His father had risked his life to prevent that. Now, the son was here, preparing to do the same. Vasily Grechko believed firmly in the Soviet Union and the righteousness of its cause. But what, really, did his son believe?

Grechko took a last look below and raised his eyes back to the Danube, flowing peacefully past him to the Black Sea over sixteen hundred kilometers away. Someday it would be nice to sail this river, he thought, on a yacht of some kind, or a cruise liner. Would it be possible to sail all the way from West Germany to the Black Sea? No, it would never be allowed. A pity. That type of thing would require a measure of freedom, would it not? Freedom for Hungary and all the nations through which the Danube flowed. His beloved Ukraine was not one of them, but if freedom came to nations like Hungary and Bulgaria and Romania, why not Ukraine? Yet here he was, planning a mission that would likely prevent that from ever happening.

"You appear deep in thought, comrade."

Grechko turned to the man next to him. The Ministry of Internal Affairs agent assigned as his guide was a pleasant enough fellow and spoke passable Russian, although of course Grechko did not trust him. He had no doubt that KGB had thoroughly penetrated the Hungarian security service, and this man—Andor Pataki, that was his name—might very well report this contact with a visiting Red Army officer. Despite Voloshin's assurance that Pataki was reliable, Grechko would reveal nothing of his true purpose here. When the time came for ZARNITSA, then he would have to see how far Pataki, and any other MIA operatives assigned to assist him, could be trusted. Not too far, he suspected. No, what he had to do would be as much a one-man operation as he could make it.

"The beauty of your city inspires deep thoughts, comrade," Grechko said with a smile. He could see in Pataki's eyes that he, too, was holding something back. It was the same with security officers the world over, but in this case, perhaps there was something else. Grechko had seen Pataki's file: age thirty-two, educated at Eötvös Loránd University in the city below, earning a degree in political science. After five years in the Hungarian Army he had been recruited into MIA. And somewhere along the way, if Voloshin was to be believed, Pataki had displayed enough pro-Soviet tendencies in his actions that the Committee had brought him in on the periphery of ZARNITSA.

The time was fast approaching when Grechko would, in fact, have to start trusting someone here, at least to a certain extent. It would not be possible for him to accomplish his mission without at least some help on the ground. He had worked with the security services of all Warsaw Pact nations, and he'd found most of their men, especially those trained in Moscow, to be fairly competent and efficient. Occasionally they delivered intelligence of real value to their superiors, who, of course, passed that intelligence on to KGB. But how would they perform when the shit hit the fan, as the Americans often said? Grechko knew the likely answer to that one: not very well. The Hungarian and Czech security services had not been very efficient in suppressing their own citizens' rebellions, had they? Now it was the Poles who were restive, along with those pesky Baltic republics. Grechko sighed. He knew from experience that sooner, rather than later, KGB would have to get more involved in those restive lands. If they went in too late, the tanks would not be far behind.

"Is there anything else you would like to see, comrade?" Pataki asked.

Grechko glanced at his watch. It was only mid-afternoon, but he wanted make his next visit before the site was overtaken by shadows. "Yes," he said. "Please take me to Heroes' Square."

Pataki nodded, and they walked toward the staircase. Grechko took one more look to the east, past Liberty Bridge to the mighty Danube as it flowed southward. How many bodies had been tossed into the river over the centuries? It occurred to him that the number was probably in the thousands. It also occurred to him that if he wasn't successful in his mission, if he didn't start focusing on his job, his body might be the next.

***

The Hungarians called it *Hösök tere*, Heroes' Square, and the Millenium Memorial was its only structure. Grechko had made a point of studying its history. In the center was a tall column upon which was a statue of the archangel Gabriel. He found it curious that this religious symbol was allowed to remain in a nominally atheistic nation, but then again, there were many religious sites in Russia, were there not? At the base of the column were seven statues, figures on horseback representing the Magyar chieftains who led their tribes into the Carpathian basin. Stretching out on both sides of the central column were colonnades.

"Tell me, comrade, about the statues on the colonnades," Grechko said.

"Certainly," Pataki said. "On the left, the inside statue on top is the symbol of War, a man driving a chariot using a snake as his whip. On the far end at the top, a man with a scythe and a woman sowing seed, representing Labor and Wealth. At the base, from the outside in..."

The Soviet agent kept listening but focused his attention on the surroundings, a trait he had developed over time and which had proven most useful. All of the seven figures at the base of the left colonnade, and the seven more on the right, represented heroes of Hungarian history. Interesting, to be sure, but irrelevant to his mission. What mattered most was that this structure would be the backdrop of an important event some two months from now, when a speech would be delivered here by the General Secretary of the Communist Party of the Soviet Union.

His target.

Could Grechko take him here? With a sniper rifle, it would be child's play. Well, maybe more difficult than that, but still something well within his skill set. KGB would be anticipating this, of course, and would have scouted all possible sniper nests within reasonable range. Troops would be stationed at each of them, and a politically-reliable officer or non-com would be in command at every location. As Pataki finished describing the monument, Grechko allowed his eyes to drift far to the left, and then back over the monument to the right. He had already observed the buildings to their rear during the walk here. He'd insisted on parking several blocks away and then walking down Népköztársaság Avenue to the square. To enjoy the day, he'd told his guide, but really to reconnoiter the area. How tall were the buildings? How difficult would it be to escape once he'd taken the shot? Side streets, alleys, everything had to be taken into account. Were the buildings easily accessible to someone who wished to quickly disappear? Offices, shops, apartments? A hundred things raced through his trained mind, and he catalogued them all carefully. Later in his hotel room he would go over a map, and perhaps he would return here for a more careful analysis.

Yet he felt certain that such analysis would conclude that a sniper shot would not be possible. This was not Dallas in 1963, when the inept American security services had allowed a lone rifleman to take what amounted to not just one or two but, incredibly, *three* nearly point-blank shots at their president. As poorly-trained as that man had been, and using a mail-order Italian carbine to boot, he had succeeded. Not without some help, Grechko knew, but he could count on no such assistance here in Budapest.

No, it would have to be done somewhere else. More up close and personal, which was his style anyway. The world was full of men who could shoot someone from long range. He had trained some of them himself, Spetsnaz snipers who had acquitted themselves well in Afghanistan. Along with them Grechko had sent more than a few of the mujahedeen to cavort with the virgins or whatever their false religion promised them. He had to smile at that. No, once his bullets had penetrated their hearts or their heads, they were dead. That was it. Just as it would be for him someday, but not for many years, he hoped.

"Is there anything else I can show you, comrade?" Pataki asked.

Grechko turned to him with a fraternal smile. "No, thank you, comrade. You have been most helpful. I think I shall return to my hotel. It has been a very interesting day, but perhaps a nap before dinner is in order."

He could see it in the Hungarian's eyes: he thinks me to be soft, another rich and connected Russian big shot who has nothing better to do than to come here and remind them who is in charge. Perhaps, though, Grechko was underestimating him. A friendly gesture might be in order. After all, he might need Pataki's assistance later.

"Of course, comrade," Pataki said. They turned to head back up Népköztársaság. Grechko made a point of ogling a beautiful blonde woman who walked past, and Pataki picked up on it. "If you are not busy later, after you have rested, might you be interested in a little... entertainment?"

The Ukrainian gave him a comradely grin. "Was I that obvious, my friend? Your women here are quite beautiful. I think I would like to get to know them a little better."

Pataki returned the grin. The look in his eyes had changed ever so subtly, but Grechko picked up on it. "I know just the place," the Hungarian said.

CHAPTER ELEVEN

ALEXANDRIA,
VIRGINIA
APRIL 1987

Jo parked her father's car on King Street, two blocks down from Murphy's. For a weeknight the streets were busy, but the mild weather probably had something to do with that. She'd visited the Old Town district occasionally during her Pentagon tour, but unlike some of her colleagues she'd never really explored the bar scene. There was something to be said for enjoying nightlife, but most of the time she was so tired after a day on duty and then a training session at her *dojang* that she just wanted to head home, fix a simple dinner and read.

There were several couples strolling the sidewalks, many hand in hand, and they seemed happy to be in each other's company. Jo saw one couple kiss and felt a pang of envy. She looked away as she walked past, but her peripheral vision caught the man's hand cupping his companion's rump. When was the last time a man had done that to her? In the five years since Ian's death…

She ripped her thoughts away from that path and forced them down another. It was the only way she could deal with it. Probably not the healthiest way, but it was her way and so far it had worked for her. Of course, whether or not any method of dealing with grief worked was in the mind of the beholder. Some would say she should have embraced it, allowed it to wash over her, so that she could come out the other side feeling cleansed, as one woman had once told her. She'd lost her husband in combat years before in Vietnam, and when Jo met her she was leading a grief counseling group at a Hurlburt Field, Jo's home base.

Marge had certainly meant well, Jo remembered now, and she was clearly disappointed when Jo stopped attending the sessions. She'd called a couple times and Jo finally agreed to meet her for lunch. At the time she found the woman's persistence irritating. Twelve years after Marge's husband was shot down, she had moved on with her life, raising their three children and remarrying. Maybe that was what bothered Jo the most. Having once had the intense love and happiness of a good marriage, Marge sought it out again and found it.

Jo, on the other hand, had not. She and Ian had talked about marriage just before he shipped out to the Falklands in that terrible spring of 1982. In the years since, Jo had not come close to falling in love again. She dated occasionally and had slept with two different men, both times more because she wanted the physical release of sex and not necessarily because she had strong feelings for them. They were nice guys and athletic enough to match her intensity, but although both wanted to pursue a relationship, she'd shut the door before they could get too close.

The entrance to Murphy's was three doors down. Why was she putting herself in this situation tonight?

She'd be surrounded by couples having a good time, enjoying each other. Likely many of them would go straight to bed when they got home. She should be back at her father's house, studying her languages or maybe sampling a volume from his library. Lord knew, she had precious little time with him anyway, and just being in his house gave Jo a sense of security. That thought brought a smile to her face. She'd been all over the world, had developed skills that made her, by any measure, one of the most lethal weapons on the planet, but here she was, feeling like the little girl who felt truly safe only near her father.

She slowed her pace, briefly considered turning back to the car, but then headed for the entrance. She could almost hear Kate's voice. *It'd be rude to stand him up, girl. Even if he is a conniving SOB.*

A cold breeze seemed to wash over her. Kate would be telling her a lot of things these days if it hadn't been for Jennings and his goon sergeant. But Jo might very well be working with Jennings, so perhaps it was time to clear the air, move forward. She paused in front of the door, steeled herself, and went inside.

Jo was surprised by the number of people here on a weeknight. Mostly couples, some groups, a few men who appeared to be alone. None of the women she saw were alone, though. Every one of them was either in a mixed group, with other women or alone with a man. She saw three men who appeared to be solo, and they saw her right away. Two of them flashed smiles at her. One gave her an I'm-too-cool-to-show-interest-in-you glance. Jennings wasn't one of them, though.

A shout of triumph and some yells of despair carried from around a corner past the bar. Jo took a few steps in that direction and a dart board with a bright red dart right on the bulls-eye came into view. Jennings had a big grin on his face and was accepting a bill from another man who didn't look nearly as pleased. The Army major folded the bill and slipped it into an inner pocket of his sport jacket. He saw Jo and waved. With a flip of his hand to the men around the dart board, he came over to meet her.

"Colonel, nice to see you," he said.

Jo had been prepared to dislike this man even more than she already did, but he looked different now than he had earlier in the day at the Pentagon, more relaxed and, she had to admit, more attractive. She caught herself smiling. "We're out of uniform, so how about first names?"

"Great. It's Keith," he said, extending his hand.

"Jo." His grip was firm but not overly so, and did he hold it just a little bit long? Then he released it and slid his hand to her elbow.

"How about a seat at the bar?"

"That sounds good," Jo said, allowing herself to be led to the ornate oak bar. Jennings picked out two empty stools with a couple on one side and a single man on the other.

Jo noticed how effortlessly Jennings moved, a man who was obviously in top physical condition and, more importantly, knew how to carry himself. That prompted a question: "Have you trained in martial arts?"

Jennings smiled. "Taekwondo and hapkido, *sam dan* in both. I don't really have to ask about your background, do I?"

"I've had... pretty extensive training," Jo said. She never bragged about her experience in the arts, unlike some people she'd encountered. Usually the bragging was done by those whose skills didn't live up to their hype.

"I could see that from our encounter at Bragg," Jennings said.

The bartender, a statuesque young blonde woman, approached with a friendly grin that spent a little less time on Jo than on Jennings. "Hi, guys, what can I get you?"

"I'll have a cosmopolitan," Jo said. "Finlandia vodka, if you have it."

"Sure thing," the woman said. "And for you?"

"I see you have Guinness on tap. I like it in a tall glass."

"Tall and long. My preference as well," she said, giving Jennings one more look before heading over to the taps. Jo tried to ignore her but couldn't.

Perhaps sensing her discomfort, Jennings shook his head, smiling. "Pretty lame line, if you ask me." He cleared his throat, suddenly turning serious. "Listen, I wanted to apologize for what happened at Bragg. I'm sorry I didn't reach out to you sooner."

Jo turned away, suddenly uncertain how to react. She sensed his sincerity, but her feelings about that night were something she'd carried with her for more than two years. She had never wanted any sort of revenge on Jennings or his men for what happened; nothing could ever make Kate whole again. But now that it was here, Jennings' apology hung in the air, and Jo wasn't sure what to do with it.

"Thank you," she finally said. She could accept his apology, but forgiveness might take a while. It was contrary to her faith, to her own principles, but some things were just very hard to deal with.

"How is Captain Simmons doing now?"

Jo took a breath, exhaled. "She's a paraplegic."

"I heard," Jennings said. The bartender arrived with their drinks. Jennings took a sip of his Guinness, licked his lips to catch a bit of foam, then said, "I checked up on her afterward. Went over to Walter Reed to see her, but they'd just transferred her somewhere."

"She went to a special hospital in Little Rock. She's from Arkansas, they felt her recovery would go better closer to family." Trying hard to hold her emotions in check, Jo took a sip of her drink. The vodka felt smooth going down.

"Have you seen her lately?"

"A few months ago," Jo said. "Her family invited me for Thanksgiving. She's doing about as well as one could expect." In fact, Kate had been as close to her old self then as Jo had seen her since the incident. Medically retired from the Air Force a year after Bragg, Kate had a job at a Veterans Administration hospital, working with disabled vets. "She's engaged to be married," Jo said. Why had she been reluctant to share that with Jennings?

"That's great!" he said. "Who's the lucky guy?"

"Her physical therapist. The wedding's in July." Jo couldn't suppress her smile, especially with the thought that she would be Kate's maid of honor.

"Well, let's toast the bride-to-be," Jennings said, raising his glass. "Please give her my best when you see her."

Jo's cosmopolitan was really quite good, and the name was ironic. "Operation COSMO," she said, deciding to get it out there. "Keith, you seem like a nice guy. Your service record must be first-rate or your colonel wouldn't have brought you to that meeting today. Why did you cheat that night?"

Jennings took a swig of beer and set the glass down on the bar, glancing at her, then back at the glass. For a moment Jo thought he wasn't going to answer, but then he looked at her again and said, "Going in, I had no intention of doing that. Three weeks earlier, my C.O. tells me my team has been chosen for a field exercise. Capture-the-flag, he says, against an all-female team. He ordered me to win, or I could expect my next posting to be somewhere very cold and very dull."

"Were you afraid we would beat you?"

His eyes flashed with what could've been arrogance, or maybe it was just pride. "Not in the slightest," he said. "Three days after getting the order I got your service jacket, or at least part of it. It was very impressive. There was a reference to that Diana project you'd been in. Scuttlebutt had it that a group of women had gone through a Q Course and made it out the other side, and you were the leader."

"It wasn't a real Q Course," Jo said. "The one you and your men went through was over a year long. They weren't willing to give us that much of a chance to prove ourselves, so they had us for three weeks. We were told it was very similar to your SFAS." Special Forces Assessment and Selection, a physical and psychological gauntlet that normally followed the Preparation and Conditioning phase, was designed to test the soldier's limits in the field. Many of the men who began the phase didn't finish. Some of Jo's women didn't, either.

"Did you do the Trek?"

"All thirty-two miles," Jo said. Even the memory of that infamous road march made her feet hurt.

"Damn," Jennings said. "How many in your unit graduated?"

"Fourteen out of fifty."

Jennings was visibly impressed. "That's a helluva ratio," he said, "about the same attrition rate as for men."

Jo lifted an eyebrow over the rim of her cocktail glass. "We were highly motivated," she said, and took a sip. "Kate was one the fourteen. She and three others from Diana joined me for COSMO. So your C.O. ordered you to win, but did he order you to break the rules, too?"

Jennings settled back on the stool, leaning into the ornately-carved spindled back. He looked away from her, sighed, and then said, "We got to the OPFOR compound ahead of schedule. We were highly motivated, too." He paused for another swallow of his beer. "I sent a two-man recon team to scout the target, and one of them reports back that I should get up there. So I hustle up to the perimeter and my other guy says, 'Check this out, Captain.' I look and damn if there isn't an officer with a big shit-eating grin on his face, carrying the flag and walking right toward us. So I go out there and he hands me the flag and says, 'Carry on, gentlemen,' salutes and goes back to the gate. I wasn't about to look a gift horse in the mouth so I told my team to saddle up and head for the exfil point. We knew we weren't that far ahead of you. What we didn't expect was that damn helo. That was a smart move on your part, Jo."

That was pretty much how Jo had expected things

had gone that night, and she had to be truthful with herself. There had always been the possibility that the game was rigged from the start. Some of the women on her team had talked about it as they geared up, but she had been too focused on the task at hand to consider it. "I made a mistake," Jo said. "I never figured something like that would happen."

"Well, you rectified that mistake pretty quickly," Jennings said. "You've been on enough ops to know that the other side cheats all the time. Sure as hell, in the work we're going to be doing together, it'll happen again."

"You're pretty confident you'll be selected?"

There was that cocky grin again. "I don't have any inside intel, but I like my colonel's chances for C.O. and that means I'll be his X.O."

Jo finished her drink and set the glass down on the bar. "We'll see," she said. "One last thing: what happened to your sergeant?"

Jennings laughed. "Zonker? I'm pleased to tell you that First Sergeant Zonkavich was busted in rank and found himself off my team. Of course, nothing I could do to him could measure up to the ass-kicking he got from you that night."

"It was... satisfying," Jo said, "but ultimately pointless. Kate's back wasn't healed by what I did."

"Unfortunately, no," Jennings agreed, "but you made a hell of an impression on the men, and word got around. I think it's safe to say that several of them started changing their attitudes towards women that night. In the long run you probably helped out more than a few wives and girlfriends, not to mention other women in uniform." He saluted her with his glass. "You helped out my team, ultimately. We all learned a hard lesson that night, and we were better off without Zonkavich. It was a mistake on my part to even put him on the team in the first place. He made it through Q Course with flying colors, great attitude, but something happened on one of his deployments. Wouldn't tell me about it, but it must've messed him up because that night he snapped. I got word later on that his wife had cheated on him. Sent him a picture of herself, in bed with the guy. An Air Force officer, as it turned out, and a black guy on top of it. Zonkavich's attitudes about race could be somewhat reactionary, you might say. Everybody on the team knew your lineup, so he knew your gal Kate was Air Force. When he saw that she was black, too, that must've put him over the edge." He drained the last of the Guinness. "I could use another, but I don't want to keep you too late."

It wasn't too late, and she found herself relaxing. "I'm good," she said. Her own drink was only half-gone, but maybe Blondie could freshen it up.

"Okay, then," Jennings said, signaling the bartender.

***

Before she knew it, the clock over the bar showed ten-thirty. Jennings caught her glancing that way. "Well, it's getting late," he said. "I've got an early call, and you probably do, too."

"Indeed I do," Jo said, reaching for her clutch.

"It's on me," Jennings said. He pulled a twenty-dollar bill from inside his jacket. "Actually, most of it's on the boys from the dart game." He added a ten from his wallet and set the bills on the bar, nodded at the bartender as she gave Jo a jealous look, and slid off the stool. "Can I walk you to your car?"

"Thank you," Jo said.

The man next to Jo was staring at her. He was in his forties, dressed a little too roughly for an upscale place like this, and there were two empty beer bottles in front of him on the bar, next to a five dollar bill and some change. A cigarette smoldered in an ash tray. "Have fun with your *do di,"* he said to Jennings. Jo felt her blood start to rise, but she forced it back.

They were two steps past him when Jennings asked, "What did he call you?"

"It's a Vietnamese insult," Jo said. Her knowledge of that language was very limited, but she'd picked up a few phrases.

"What's it mean?"

"Never mind, Keith. He's not worth the effort. Let's go." She walked toward the door, sensing that Jennings was following her, reluctantly. Behind them, the man laughed.

Outside, he took her arm. "Now tell me, what did that mean?"

"He called me 'the town bike.' As in, everybody rides you."

Jennings stopped in his tracks. "That son of a bitch! I'm gonna go back in there and–"

"Please, don't," Jo said, putting a hand on his upper arm. "He must've been over there. He probably didn't have a very good experience."

Jennings breathed in deeply, then exhaled, nostrils flaring as he calmed himself. "All right," he said. Then he winked at her. "Besides, all I was gonna do is tell him you could wipe the floor with him."

That drew a laugh from her. "Well, I rarely say no to a good workout, but not tonight."

"That's fine with me," Jennings laughed. "Now, that's not what I'd normally say to a gorgeous woman at this time of the evening."

The line. She'd been expecting it, but now after enjoying her time with the Army officer, she wasn't offended. In fact, she felt the tickle of pleasure any woman felt when an attractive man showed an interest in her. But this wasn't the time. "Keith, if we're going to be working together, we should keep it professional, don't you think?"

He nodded. "Yeah, I suppose so. But you know how it is, Jo. Eventually we won't be working together. Can I have a rain check?"

"I can't... make any promises in that regard," she said, perhaps a bit too formally.

Jennings seemed to sense he'd come close to something better left alone. "I understand," he said. "Now, let's get you to your car. I have a feeling the next few days will be pretty busy for both of us."

CHAPTER TWELVE

MACDILL AIR FORCE BASE, FLORIDA
APRIL 1987

"This is it?"

Jennings wasn't impressed with their new headquarters any more than Jo was, but the slapdash collection of offices was all they had received from the newborn Special Operations Command, activated only ten days earlier. Here at MacDill, the now-defunct U.S. Readiness Command was turning over its facilities to SOCOM. Pallas Group had been given a total of six small offices, a reception area and two slightly larger conference rooms. The desks were piled with old typewriters and blotters. Phones sat silently, and filing cabinets were shoved haphazardly against walls. The work detail that had brought in the supplies and furniture had departed only an hour ago, knocking off at eighteen hundred for evening chow. The shadows in the reception area had been banished when Jo flipped the light switch, revealing the fact that a great deal of work would have to be done before the new unit could call itself operational.

"We'll have to make do," Jo said, trying to hide her own disappointment. "It's only temporary, remember."

"Sure," the Army major said. "If I had a dollar for every time I've heard that one—"

"Then you'd have about half the money I'd have," another voice said behind them.

"Ten-HUT!" Jennings barked, snapping to attention. Jo followed suit, a second before Colonel Teller entered the room.

"At ease," the Marine veteran said. "I suppose my first order as C.O. of this outfit is that we can do away with the saluting and all that while we're here. In fact, we're going to be conducting ourselves more as civilians than as military when it comes to protocols."

"Congratulations, sir," Jo said, offering her hand.

"Thanks, Jo." Teller shook her hand, then Jennings'. "I've had this command about twenty-four hours and I'm behind already. Couldn't get a flight out of Quantico until this afternoon."

"Where do you want us to start, Colonel?" Jennings asked.

"Let's just look around and take stock of what we've got here. Tomorrow morning after chow and P.T. we'll get cracking on getting this organized."

"P.T., sir?"

Teller gave the soldier a stern look. "That's right, Major. In the Army you might know it as 'physical training.' Eat light and be ready to work. I think a mile run will be a good way to start things off." He turned to Jo. "I hear they've got a pretty good gym here, is that right, Jo?"

"Yes, sir. Nice equipment, mostly free weights, some Nautilus gear."

"We won't be paying much attention to candy-ass machines, people. We'll train for the kind of work we're going to be doing. They have a mat in there, don't they?"

"That's a roger, sir," Jo said, liking where this was going.

"Outstanding. Jo, one of your duties as my exec is to be in charge of the martial arts training for this outfit. I want every one of my people to be able to handle himself, or herself, if it comes to hand-to-hand in the field. In the kind of work we'll be doing, we won't be able to call in tanks or air strikes for support. Jo, I think you're the one to show us what to do. And I understand you've seen her in action, Keith?"

"Uh, yes, sir, I have," Jennings said. "I would agree with your assessment of the colonel's capabilities." He gave Jo sly look.

"All right, we'll put in about a half-hour in the gym after the run and then get to work here. I'm meeting with General Lindsay at 1400 tomorrow I'm sure he'll be giving me an idea of what he expects from us, short-term and long. Commander Anastas will be joining us sometime around 1300 when his flight gets in. I also have two other people coming in tomorrow to complete the staff."

"Who would they be, sir?" Jo asked.

"I'm bringing in a man from CIA's Special Activities Division, and a Marine Corps captain. Each of you is going to be in charge of dealing with your respective services, and in the case of our CIA asset, the civilian intelligence services. The general will be telling me how much latitude I'm going to be given in calling on those branches to give us what we need for our missions."

"Speaking of missions, sir," Jennings said, "any idea where we might see some action first?"

"No idea, Keith, but I wouldn't be surprised if I get something tomorrow. There always seems to be something in the pipeline in this line of work. Now, if we're done with our little coffee klatch here, folks, how about we take a look around and see about getting this place squared away?"

An hour later they emerged into the Florida evening. A warm breeze carried the smells and sounds of the air base: aviation fuel and diesel exhaust, rumbling jet engines, spinning helicopter rotors, occasionally a shout or a laugh. Jo knew them well, and even though she'd never spent much time here at MacDill, she was already starting to feel at home.

The blue Air Force Jeep that Jo had checked out of the motor pool that afternoon was dwarfed by the desert-tan, four-door vehicle parked next to it. It was the first HMMWV Jo had seen. Jennings whistled as he walked over to it and caressed its sloping lines. "How'd you manage to get hold of a Humvee, Colonel?"

"When I reported to the general's office, that's the vehicle they requisitioned for me. The second one on the base, from what I understand. The general's got the first."

"Hot damn," Jennings said, peering through the open window of the driver's door. "I hear these rigs can really move."

"Top speed is seventy per, unless she's fully loaded. I'm headed to the Officers' Club for a nightcap. Join me?" He looked back at Jo. "You too, of course, Jo."

"Thanks, but I think I'll turn in," she said. It had been a long day, and she still had a half-hour of German language study ahead of her.

"All right. See you outside the gym at oh-seven hundred." He pulled a key from his pocket and tossed it to Jennings. "You think you can handle this beast, Major?"

"Hell, yes." Jennings grinned broadly as he reached for the door handle. "See you in the morning, Jo."

"Good night, gentlemen." She watched them hop into the Humvee and in a few seconds the engine cranked, roared, then stalled.

"Crissakes, Jennings," she heard from inside, "this isn't a hot rod. Take it easy." The diesel caught again and smoothed out quickly as they sped off.

Men and their cars, Jo thought, looking forlornly at her lonely little Jeep. "I hope you know your way to the BOQ," she said. Her room at the Bachelor Officer's Quarters wasn't much, but it would do for now.

***

It took all morning and she had to skip lunch at the mess hall, but by mid-afternoon Jo had her office in a semblance of order. Munching on some granola chased by water, she leaned back against the wall near the door, surveying her new domain. Not as big as her office back at Hurlburt and definitely not as comfortable, not yet, but she still had to move her personal things over to this new base, not only for the office but for her quarters, whatever and wherever that would wind up being. Was it only a week ago she was at the Pentagon for the meeting at SecDef's office? Her calendar wasn't on the wall yet, but yes, a week and a day, actually.

Two days after her return to Hurlburt her new

orders had come in, transferring her to the unit known officially as the 85th Special Activities Group, assigned to be the executive officer under Colonel Teller. She immediately called her father, whose pride had no trouble coming through the phone line. An hour after that, Jennings called with his congratulations. Although disappointed that his own colonel hadn't gotten the top job, he was pleased to be on the team and looked forward to working with Jo. When she hung up, she thought how remarkable it was that her opinion of Jennings had changed so quickly in so short a time. Then again, she reflected, her first impression from Fort Bragg was decidedly negative, so he had nowhere to go but up.

The orders spurred a whirlwind of activity for Jo that showed no sign of letting up anytime soon. She had to wrap up her work on two projects at Hurlburt, brief her successor in the training unit, and start planning her move. The only time she'd taken in the last eight days for any kind of relaxation was the going-away party thrown for her by her colleagues. Focused as she was on the challenges ahead, Jo hadn't had much time to think about what she was leaving behind, but now she thought about the people she'd worked with, and what a close-knit team they'd become. Would this new unit bring her the same sense of fulfillment? That would largely be up to her. In the Air Force you went where they told you to go and made the best of it.

She heard a man's voice in the hallway. "Colonel Geary's office is the second one on the right, ma'am."

"Thank you, Airman," a woman answered, and heels clicked confidently on the tiled floor. A familiar face wearing a Marine Corps garrison cap leaned through the doorway. "I'm looking for the executive officer. You mean to tell me you're not running this place?"

"Denise!" Jo almost dropped her water bottle. She embraced her Diana Brigade comrade, standing on tip-toe to reach around the taller woman's shoulders.

The Marine officer stepped back, flashed the beaming smile Jo had seen turn men to putty and whipped a parade-ground-worthy salute. "Major Denise Reinecke, Marine Corps liaison, reporting for duty, ma'am."

Jo felt grubby in her blue Air Force utilities compared to the squared-away woman in front of her, but she returned the salute. "The colonel told me he was bringing in another Marine officer," she said, "but he didn't mention a name. Welcome to Pallas Group."

Denise looked around the office, which didn't take long. "Looks like I'm getting in on the ground floor."

"I think that saying we have a lot of work to do would be a serious understatement. Come on, I'll show you around. The colonel is meeting with the general. He should be here soon, and he'll be filling us in on what's on deck for us."

Denise patted the travel bag dangling from a shoulder strap. "I've got my utilities in here. Where can I change?"

"That would have to be the ladies' room."

"You mean the head? I know you zoomies are delicate folks, Colonel, but come on."

***

An hour later Jo was helping Denise move a file cabinet when Jennings stuck his head in the door.

"Colonel's back, ladies. Wants us in the main conference room."

Jo had given Denise fair warning that Jennings was in the Group, but the Marine captain's smile was forced when they were introduced. Over the next hour Jo had filled her in on what she and Jennings had talked about in Virginia. Now, as they were walking to the conference room, Denise was still trying to process it. "You went on a date with him?"

"Just two colleagues having a drink," Jo said, trying not to feel defensive. "I'm giving him the benefit of the doubt about it, Denise."

"Okay, but I gotta tell you, that night on the exercise I was real close to giving that puke sergeant a good hosing with my Gatlings."

Teller was in his Class-A Marine uniform, pulling files out of a bulging briefcase he'd set on the table. A man in casual civilian clothes occupied the chair to the colonel's left. The man stood when Jo, Jennings and Denise entered. About five-ten, brown hair, green eyes that had a veneer of suspicion, the unremarkable face had a small smile that Jo thought looked a little forced.

"All right, everybody," Teller began, "I want to introduce—wait, where's Anastas?"

"Right here, Colonel," the Navy lieutenant commander said as he came in. "Sorry, I was in the head." Jo had been re-introduced to the SEAL officer a couple hours earlier when he arrived at the headquarters.

"Very well. People, this is Will Harrison, CIA Special Activities Division." Names were exchanged along with handshakes. Jo couldn't get a read on Harrison, which was unusual for her, but not so unusual when it came to anyone from Langley, especially field operatives. The few she'd met had proven to be extremely competent but never completely comfortable around military personnel, even though some of them were ex-military themselves.

They seated themselves around the table as the colonel began passing out red-bordered files. "Like everything else we do here, this is to be considered Top Secret. These files are to be reviewed in this room and then given back to me for storage in my safe. As we get our protocols firmed up we'll decide how we're going to handle intel and other documents that are classified at lower levels."

The colonel placed his briefcase on the floor next to his chair at the head of the table and sat down. "I'd prefer to have a projector so we can display slides, but as we all know we're still ramping up around here. One of the things I discussed with the general this afternoon was basic staffing needs and so forth. I'll be working with his people to get us additional supplies, communications gear, whatever we feel we need. But don't expect much in the way of secretaries or errand boys running around here. We'll be getting a receptionist and that's about it."

Jo wasn't sure whether she liked the sound of that. She was used to an efficient, hard-working staff to handle the little things while she worked on larger projects for her unit. Anastas evidently felt the same way. "We'll have to make do without staff, Colonel?"

"This is a new kind of unit, Ed, and we'll be flying by the seat of our pants in some respects. SOCOM is just getting up and running. If you think things are disorganized here, you should see what's going on over at the general's office."

"Let's hope we don't have any wars breaking out anytime soon, then," Jennings said.

"Well, this is not a war, but we do have a mission," Teller said. "The code name is SNOW LEOPARD. Open your files, people."

Jo flipped the cover and looked at a grainy black-and-white photograph of a man, taken from some distance. He looked rather nondescript in some ways, but even with the substandard resolution, she sensed something about him, and it made her uncomfortable.

"That is the only photograph we have of a Soviet special operator who goes by the code name of KRASNIY VOLK."

Something clicked open in Jo's memory. "The Red Wolf," she translated. The photo wasn't good enough to show a scar above his eye, but she remembered the danger of that alley in Hamburg, the glimpse she'd gotten of the man who'd nearly killed her… She tried to prevent a shiver from running down her spine, and failed.

"You know him?" Denise asked her.

"We've met," Jo said.

Teller gave her a knowing look. He certainly had read about the Hamburg operation in Jo's service jacket. The colonel glanced at each person around the table, then said, "This individual is said to be the most dangerous man in the Soviet Union. In about six weeks he'll be in Budapest to assassinate Mikhail Gorbachev. Our mission is to stop him."

CHAPTER THIRTEEN

WASHINGTON, D.C.
MAY 1987

Janelle Boudreau had never really thought of herself as pretty. Oh, she had her moments—senior prom in high school, when she was a surprise choice for the court and everybody complimented her on her dress, her hair, her makeup. Even though it might've been a sympathy vote, the nerd had blossomed that evening, but in college at Dartmouth it was back to the books, the glasses and shapeless skirts, the jeans that never seemed to fit like they did on other girls.

Tonight, though, she was actually feeling attractive. She checked her mascara in the mirror one more time. "Phyllis, does this look right?"

Her roommate ducked her head through the bathroom doorway. "Perfect, J.B. It's that hunky Swede again tonight, right?"

"He's from Finland, but yes, he's a hunk," Janelle said, finishing with her lipstick and feeling the thrilling tingle down in her "business" that always seemed to show up when she thought of Lars. The new silk panties would be just perfect, not that she expected them to be on very long.

She was ready for a night out. The workdays were long in the office of the senior senator from New Hampshire, especially when you were the assistant to the chief of staff. It was rewarding work, though. Yes, her father had been instrumental in getting her the job, considering he was a major contributor to the senator's campaigns, but she'd proved herself since joining the office three years earlier. She'd worked her way up to her present job and that was all her doing, not Daddy's.

And there was more to come. Two weeks ago the chief had confided in her that he was going to resign in three months to go back home to Manchester to take over the family business, and she was going to be the senator's next chief. As a result, she was now being read in on some of the senator's more sensitive work. Some of it was mundane, but some was intriguing, like his work on the Select Committee on Intelligence. Yesterday, in fact, she'd been given her first chance to sit in on a committee meeting in the chief's stead, and a closed session to boot. She was still unsure about a lot of what was discussed, but she was a quick study and had made it a point to learn all she could about the committee's work. It was a dizzying array of acronyms and code names, but it was starting to make sense, tying in with snippets of conversations she'd heard and documents she'd seen around the office. Much of it had to do with the Russians, like yesterday's session. There had been a lot of discussion about Gorbachev, and some of the exchanges were sharp, sarcastic, even rude. The senator in particular had been very skeptical of the report about a plot against the Soviet leader.

But tonight she would not think about work. Tonight she would think about her tall, handsome Finn, and hopefully she would do more than just think about him.

***

Janelle shrieked with ecstasy, her legs gripping him like a vise, and she shuddered as the orgasm washed through her. Lars held himself back, teasing her, and then he pushed himself deep inside and let it go, adding a groan for her benefit. She pulled him close, purring into his ear, and for the first time he heard her use the word “love.”

He sighed, making it seem like a physical release rather than emotional, and they kissed. He wished she hadn’t said that. It always made things more difficult. He rolled off her damp body and faked a satisfied laugh. Putting the word out of his mind, he considered her nudity. The job had its fringe benefits, that was for sure. She was not the most attractive woman he had ever bedded–she could afford to lose a couple kilos, and her face was a tad plain–but what she lacked in physical charms she made up for with enthusiasm. There was certainly something to be said for that.

“Would you share a joint with me?” he asked.

“Love to,” she said, cuddling close to him. He prepared the cigarette, using the special blend of ingredients he’d been given for the occasion. Lighting it with a Bic, he gulped in a puff and exhaled without ingesting any of the smoke, then handed the joint to her. Janelle took a healthy drag, held it in, and then exhaled with a slight cough. “Sorry,” she said, handing it back.

"That's all right," he said. It was only a matter of time now.

An hour later she drifted off into what he knew would be a deep sleep. He was far from sleepy. What she had just told him was more than interesting; in fact, it had the potential to provide him with a ticket out of this place. He slipped silently from the bed, picked up his silk robe from a chair and padded barefoot into the next room, shutting the door behind him.

The door was more than a physical barrier, it was a transition point. On the bedroom side he was Lars Makkonen, executive vice president of Paasio Incorporated, an import-export firm based in Helsinki with an office in New York which he allegedly managed. Makkonen made frequent trips to Washington for the purpose of meeting trade representatives from other countries and lobbying members of Congress. It was on this current visit that he had met the luscious little American morsel known as Janelle Boudreau.

On this side of the door he was Major Yevgeny Maltsov of the KGB's First Chief Directorate. Thirty-six years old, Maltsov had been recruited by KGB from the Soviet Air Force in 1973 and had proven to be an adept student, quickly establishing himself as a first-rate field operative. His blonde good looks, a gift from his Estonian mother, combined with his chiseled physique to make him extremely attractive to women and also certain men, a trait his KGB superiors duly noted. Thus it was that Maltsov became one of KGB's most efficient practitioners of the "honey trap," the sexual seduction of targeted persons for the purposes of extracting intelligence. In the past fifteen years or so,

KGB had been utilizing male agents for its honey trap operations more frequently, especially in Western Europe and America, as the women in those nations became more sexually liberated, politically active and professionally ambitious.

Maltsov poured himself two fingers of vodka and sat back in the cushioned chair behind his desk. The apartment, lavish by Soviet standards, was ostensibly maintained by his company for its employees' use in Washington. Maltsov had been here for three weeks now and was getting bored. This was his fourth assignment in the capital city of his nation's greatest enemy, and while the work was interesting, the women were not nearly as glamorous as those he'd found in places like London and Rome. Perhaps now he could return to Europe. It would all depend on how long his superiors wanted him to stay here. If they judged that the Boudreau woman could provide them with more information, he would find himself returning more frequently than he might like.

Well, it could be worse, he thought. If another agent, based in the Soviet Embassy, had not been at the cocktail party at the French Embassy last month and overheard that senator's chief of staff talking about Janelle's imminent promotion, Maltsov would've found himself back in Moscow for his mandatory three weeks of "consultations," training sessions that were actually designed to gauge his continuing reliability and loyalty to the State. He was certainly not ready to go back, so he'd been pleased when this assignment came his way. He had always been taught that the decadent West was doomed, destined to fall under the boot of the New Soviet Man and the cause of socialism. Privately, he had his doubts about that, but in the meantime it was really a pretty nice place to live.

To business, then. Maltsov finished his drink and reached for a notepad. Using a one-time cipher, he composed a carefully worded message that he would leave in a dead drop tomorrow morning precisely at nine. Eight hours later he would return and find instructions directing him to a meeting at one of four different rendezvous points, where he would make his report to his handler. What would be done with the information was not his concern. The only thing that mattered was what the information would mean for his career. If the intel was judged valuable, he might just have to stay here awhile longer and continue bedding the rather chubby but energetic American woman. Perhaps it would be valuable enough to result in him being rewarded with Rome, or maybe Istanbul. Now, that was certainly interesting. He'd heard many tales about Turkish women. Perhaps tomorrow, after making his drop, he would visit that shop, the one featuring exotic varieties of pornography. Surely they would have some items from the Middle East.

What was it that Russian comedian said? Maltsov had just seen him the other night on television, and now he chuckled at the memory of the man's hilarious act. Ah, yes: "What a country." He took another sip of his vodka. In some ways he would be sorry to leave.

CHAPTER FOURTEEN

**MACDILL AIR FORCE BASE,
FLORIDA
MAY 1987**

Jo Ann was on the mat finishing her post-workout stretching when the tall man finally approached her. She'd seen him at the gym several times, usually with one or two other men, all in their early twenties. Uniforms were seldom seen in the weight room and never on the mat, so she had no idea what rank he might be, although his youth and casual attitude pointed at being enlisted. Rank was rarely observed here anyway, although officers tended to work out together and enlisted men and women kept company with their own as well. She hadn't seen a lot of fraternization between officers and enlisted, but today was evidently going to be her day.

"Hi there," the man said. On the other side of the room, two other men were watching while pretending not to. His crew, no doubt.

"Hello," Jo said. It only took her a few seconds to size him up. About six-three and in decent shape, he moved easily and probably considered himself a ladies' man. Jo had seen him hitting on other women in the gym, without much apparent success. He was wearing dark blue sweat pants and a gray University of Minnesota tee shirt with the sleeves cut off.

"You work out a lot?" he asked. Dirty blonde hair, green eyes, but the sleeveless tee revealed upper arms that weren't as toned as he probably thought they were, and there was a bit of a belly pressing against the bottom front of the shirt.

"Now and then," she said, nimbly getting to her feet. Heavy rain had canceled Pallas Group's usual morning run, and this was one of the two days a week they did not have training here on the mat, so Jo had decided to hit the gym after leaving the office and before heading to the officers' mess for dinner. Colonel Teller had said he would be joining her, but he must've been held up.

Jo certainly wasn't interested in starting anything with this airman, but didn't want to be rude. She grabbed her towel and ran it over the back of her neck. Too late, she realized this raised her shirt an extra inch or two, and today she'd made the unfortunate choice to wear her only cutoff tee. The airman's eyes didn't miss a thing. "Nice abs," he said.

"Thank you," she said, trying to think of a way to make a graceful exit.

"I've seen you doing some karate stuff here. I was wondering if you might be interested in working out."

He certainly hadn't seen her training any of the group, or he would've known what she did was much more than "karate stuff." He'd seen her working against the heavy bag, though, like this evening. "Thanks, but I really have to be going," she said.

"Oh, come on, just a few minutes. My name's Matt, by the way. And you are…?"

"Jo Ann," she said, resisting the temptation to state her full name with rank.

He gestured to where his friends were waiting. "My buddies over there, they were wondering how a pretty little thing like you might fare in a little throw-down with me. I did some boxing smokers back home."

She couldn't resist. "Oh, really? What's a smoker?"

His chest expanded by at least an inch. "Well, it's boxing, unsanctioned boxing, you might say. Up in Minnesota, where I'm from."

She nodded at his shirt. "You went to school there?"

"Well, ah, for a while," he said. "Then I joined up. But yeah, go Gophers!"

"Ah, yes, a rodent."

"Hey, now–"

The Minnesotan's two buddies came over to the edge of the mat. "Hey, Matt, you gonna spar with the babe or what?"

"Matt," Jo said, looking up at him with eyes wide.

"Yeah?"

"Just don't hurt me, okay?"

He smiled. "Oh, don't you worry your pretty little head about that," he said, and started dancing around the mat, boxer-style, throwing some shadow punches. "Hey, Gary, toss us those gloves over there." One of the men took two pairs of boxing gloves from a shelf and flipped them into the ring. Matt caught his pair and put them on, but Jo picked up the smaller pair and tossed them back.

"No gloves, honey?" His eyes were shining.

"Too heavy," she said, relaxing her body, her breathing under control, watching him circle her. She really didn't want to do this, so she'd end it quickly, and relatively painlessly for him. "Okay, Matt, give me your best shot."

"All right, here it comes–"

His looping roundhouse punch might've caused serious harm to Jo's head had it been there, but she ducked underneath the swing and landed a roundhouse kick to his exposed midsection. Even though she'd only struck with about half her power, he woofed as he doubled over. Stepping close to him, she took the extended right arm, turned her hip against his and executed a judo throw that sent him crashing to the mat. The airman's two buddies whooped in delight.

He staggered to his feet, shook his head and came back at her, only now he was angry. He was being humiliated in front of his friends and didn't like it, Jo knew, but now he was allowing his emotions to take over, a bad mistake. He threw a one-two combination that Jo deflected by blocking his gloved hands. There were any number of ways she could disable him now, but she didn't want to take it that far, so she drove a side kick into his chest.

How to end it? He was seriously pissed now, and wanted to hurt her. Maybe it was time to try something she'd been working on lately. Again he came at her, more cautiously now, but she lowered her hands to draw a punch and he threw another roundhouse, unable to pass up the tantalizing target. Again she ducked, stepped inside and tossed him again. This time she crashed down on top of him, driving an elbow into his midsection. She shifted position, grabbed his limp right arm and leaned back on the mat, her legs locking the arm as she cranked back on it, bending it backwards over her powerful thigh.

He yelled in pain, and she said, "Time to tap out, Matt." Instead, he pulled at her legs with his free hand,

and she cranked a little harder. "Tap out!" Gasping, he slapped the mat twice. She released him and glided easily to her feet.

At the edge of the mat, the airman's two buddies had yielded to Colonel Teller, wearing chinos and a Marine Corps sweatshirt. "I believe you've actually worked up a sweat, Colonel Geary," he said.

"Just getting in a little workout, sir."

"Well, if you're done with your little patty-cake session with that gentleman, we have work to do. I'm calling the exec staff for a short meeting at the office before dinner. Get your gear and I'll drive you over."

***

Back at the office, Teller led the way into the conference room, where Jennings sat going through a red-bordered file. Will Harrison, the CIA liaison, was opposite the Green Beret. Both men started to rise but the colonel said, "As you were," and took his seat at the head of the table. Jo made a decision and sat next to Harrison, who nodded a greeting with the closest thing to a warm smile Jo had seen on him. In the four meetings they'd attended together she'd heard him say maybe a dozen words, and outside the office he kept to himself. Perhaps his reticence was due to the fact that everyone else in Pallas was active military. Sitting next to him might give him a subtle hint that he was one of the group, civilian or not.

"Will anyone else be joining us, sir?" she asked.

"Not this time, Jo." He turned to Harrison. "Will, I assume that's what you brought us from Langley?"

"Yes, sir." The agent gestured to the file. "It's not a lot, unfortunately."

Jennings slid the file across the table to Jo. "You've got that right. Colonel, we deploy for SNOW LEOPARD in less than thirty days, we have next to nothing on the target, and none of us have ever been to Budapest."

"I have," Harrison said.

"All right, one of us, then," Jennings said. "The city will be crawling with KGB and Hungarian security. We have to get there, which is no easy task in the first place, then find one guy and take him out before the hit on his target. I have to tell you, sir, this doesn't sound good to me."

Teller nodded, sitting back in his chair. "I know, Keith. Doesn't sound too great to me either, but that's our mission. Pallas Group was put together for jobs like this. We'll have all the support we need from CIA, NSA, and NATO intelligence services. But yes, we're the ones going in."

Jennings sat back, shaking his head. Jo had her misgivings about the mission as well, but her experience in covert operations had taught her that nothing was ever easy in this business when you went into the field. "I've been to Budapest as well," she said, recalling her few days there five years earlier in the company of an East German double agent who would've killed her later if Jo hadn't gotten him first.

"I wasn't aware of that," Teller said.

"Operation EMINENCE, sir," she said. "It was just long enough to meet my contact and assume my cover identity before flying to Argentina. As far as actually operating there, though, I wouldn't say my experience in the city counts for much." The most dangerous part had been in the ladies' room at the airport, with a very nervous Larisa Kocharian Schröder in the locked stall next to hers. Jo remembered her fear as she dropped the half-opened lipstick on the floor, the contact signal for Larisa. Jo expected the door to her stall to be smashed in by security troops, but then the other lipstick dropped to the floor, and the exchange of clothing and carry-on bags went off without a hitch. Jo had never asked what had happened to the Armenian woman. Hopefully she was living quietly and safely somewhere in the West. The man she'd married had not made it out of Buenos Aires alive.

"But it's something, anyway," the colonel said. "Jo, you're the only one here who's had contact with the Wolf. I know you mentioned it before, but let's go over it again."

Jo recounted her fight with the Soviet agent in the dark Hamburg alley three months earlier. When she described how the Wolf had nearly defeated her, she saw Jennings' eyes widen slightly.

"A tough customer," the Army major said.

"The toughest I've ever faced," Jo agreed.

"Well, that's why he's been tasked with the mission we're going to stop," Teller said. "Keith, you've operated behind the Curtain, haven't you?"

"Yes, sir, three times. Twice to Czechoslovakia, once to East Germany."

"Jo, when you were there, you were impersonating an Armenian, so that's your cover again. How's your Russian?"

She quickly considered that. "It needs to be brushed up, sir."

"Then start brushing. I know Keith is fluent in German, and from what I understand, German is taught in Hungarian schools, right, Will?"

The CIA agent nodded. "Every Hungarian student has two foreign languages by the time they get through high school. One of them is usually German. In college they pick up one or two more."

"You three will be going in," Teller said. "Keith, your cover is an East German journalist. Jo is a writer on assignment from a magazine in Armenia. Will has one he's used successfully before."

"What would that be?" Jennings asked.

"Austrian journalist," he said. The way he said it, his demeanor, somehow didn't click with Jo. She'd held off so far, but now she knew that later in the evening she'd have to make a phone call.

***

"I'm surprised at you, JoJo," her father said. The secure phone line made his voice sound slightly hollow. "I didn't personally select Harrison for the unit, but I reviewed his file. He's done good work for us, not just in Europe but in Central America."

Jo sat back in the chair behind her desk. The office was quiet. She'd come back alone after dinner at the officers' club, saying she had some paperwork to finish up. Fibbing about that to the colonel wasn't easy, and now she felt even worse. She could hear the anger in her father's voice, rare but undeniable. "I'm sorry, Appa. It's just... well, I just don't have a good feeling about him."

"Have you made an effort to get to know him?"

"Not really, but–"

"Good Christ, Jo! Pallas Group isn't a Scout troop, it's a specialized covert action unit and you have some serious work to do. We need serious, well-trained people to do it and you're one of them, and so is Will Harrison."

She apologized again. This had truly been a bad idea. She heard her father sigh on the other end. "Are you all right, Appa?"

There was silence, then, "Director Casey died today."

Jo was shocked. She hadn't watched the news in days, hadn't picked up a paper, largely because she knew the Iran-Contra hearings had begun. With her father's career possibly in jeopardy, she'd found it hard to focus on her own work the past few weeks. Now, her sense of worry increased. "I'm so sorry," she said. "I know you were close to him." Appointed to his post in 1979 by Casey's predecessor, Admiral Stansfield Turner, Joseph had worked closely with Casey since the new director came to CIA under Reagan in '81.

"The last few months have been tough, but he's free from his pain now. As for the rest of us, I suppose what happens on the Hill in the next few weeks will tell the tale."

"Is there anything I can do?"

"Yes," he said, and the old, steely discipline was back. "Get to know Harrison. You can trust him. He probably doesn't know he can trust you. A lot of our people who worked in El Salvador and Nicaragua are feeling kind of nervous these days. And one more thing."

"Yes?"

"The most important thing. Get to Budapest and stop that bastard. If he succeeds, we'll have a lot more trouble than anything that might come out of these damn hearings."

CHAPTER FIFTEEN

**KUBINKA AIR BASE,
MOSCOW OBLAST
MAY 1987**

"I call the meeting to order," General Voloshin said. He looked around the table, doing another head count. Including himself, five men were present. Only one was missing. "Has General Klimov sent word to anyone about being late?"

"I received a telephone call from him just as I was departing my office," one of the two civilians said. Dressed in his usual attire, an impeccably tailored three-piece suit, the slightly-built, balding man looked like a college professor, which in fact he had been before being elevated to the Politburo by Gorbachev three years ago.

"What did he say, Comrade Butrovich?" General Melikov asked. Voloshin saw the look in his friend's eyes. Butrovich was one of those they suspected of being allied with Klimov. The other was the uniformed man sitting next to him, Dultsev, the commanding officer of 7th Guards Rocket Division.

"He asked me to inform the Committee that he may not be able to attend, due to pressing business at his headquarters."

"Well, if he is not here by now, we shall assume his

business was indeed pressing," Voloshin said. "Comrades, the purpose of this meeting is to discuss the security of Operation ZARNITSA. General Obolensky, I give you the floor."

The GRU general cleared his throat. He had no files, no documents to share; the Committee never put anything on paper. Voloshin wished once again that he could at least doodle on a pad in front of him. "Our comrades in KGB have a very reliable agent in Washington who has obtained some interesting information," Obolensky said. "The American Senate committee that oversees their intelligence services was told by a CIA official that they have become aware of a possible plot against the General Secretary."

"There are always plots," Melikov said. "The question is, do they know about ZARNITSA?"

"That is not entirely clear, at least according to the information I have," Obolensky said.

"If what I learned was the extent of KGB's knowledge, then I would say, it is possible."

"What makes you think it is possible?" Dultsev asked.

"The agent's source said she overheard the words 'imminent threat.'"

"That could mean anything, or nothing at all," Voloshin said, wishing he was really as confident as he fought to appear. "The Americans are excitable. They often see threats where there are none."

"Indeed," Butrovich agreed. "Is it not true their CIA often lies to Congress? They overstate the threat from us, for example, in order to obtain increased funding."

"If that is the case here, they are likely wasting their time," Oblensky said. "The CIA is under intense pressure because of the scandal involving how they funded their counter-revolutionaries in Nicaragua. They could be, as the Americans say, whistling in the dark."

"Perhaps," Voloshin said, "but then the question becomes, how is KGB interpreting the whistle?"

"Their reaction will depend on how much specific information they have," Melikov said. "If it is just a vague reference to a possible plot against the General Secretary, they do not have much to go on. They would increase security around him and be on the lookout for signs of such a plot, even more than they usually are."

"Could they persuade him to cancel the Budapest trip?" Butrovich asked. "If they do, then ZARNITSA must be called off. We could not possibly strike within the Soviet Union itself."

Voloshin wondered if Butrovich's concern was sincere or whether he was simply playing Klimov's game. If the operation was derailed, the absent general would surely advance his own plan, doubtless designed to result with himself in the General Secretary's chair. The Committee's current intention was to replace Gorbachev with what amounted to a junta, at least until a consensus could be reached among the remaining members of the Politburo about a successor who would lead the nation in the direction the Committee desired.

Voloshin had to be careful here. He could not afford to alienate Butrovich and Dultsev. It was a dilemma, to be sure; he did not trust Klimov, but they needed his troops to secure the capital if the plan was to succeed. "The trip is still six weeks away," he said. "Comrade Gorbachev has placed a high priority on this visit. He feels he must respond to the Americans, who are putting pressure on NATO to be more aggressive. Their president is going to Berlin the week before. It is said he is going to issue a direct challenge to Gorbachev when he is there."

Butrovich snorted. "That old fool? Why should we care what he says?"

Obolensky shook his head. "Do not underestimate his influence, Comrade Academician. The American people love him, despite his current political troubles. The NATO nations respect him. They know he would support them fully in any conflict with the Warsaw Pact. Therefore, they are not as afraid of us as they used to be."

"Indeed, they are not," Melikov said. "Look what they have done just since Reagan took power. They ejected our Cuban fraternal socialist allies from Grenada. They have halted our initiatives in Central America. Even the British have regained their confidence, with their success in the Falkland Islands. Meanwhile, what about us? We have had all those setbacks, and our effort in Afghanistan is a joke, thanks in large part to the American CIA arming the mujahedeen."

"That will come back to haunt them," Butrovich said. "The Muslims cannot be trusted. Everybody knows that. Look at how much trouble we have had with the Arabs. We give them billions of rubles' worth of equipment and training, then they reject our advice on how to use it and wind up crushed by the Zionists, again and again."

"Comrades, let us return to the matter at hand," Voloshin said. The discussion went on for another twenty minutes. Finally, he decided there had been enough talk. "Comrades, I have heard nothing here that should cause us to change our plans. I propose that we continue with ZARNITSA as scheduled."

Around the table, heads nodded, although nobody appeared terribly relaxed. As the operation approached its climax, it was only natural for the pressure on the Committee's members to grow. This latest development only added to the pressure. The Air Force general surveyed the faces of the men before him. Would any of them crack? He doubted it. They were all in too deep now. Even if one of them betrayed the Committee to KGB, that man would go down with the rest of them. It would be the torture chambers in the basement of the Lubyanka for sure, followed by a firing squad. After the basement, execution would be an act of mercy.

"I think we all agree with General Voloshin's recommendation," Butrovich said. "The situation becomes more critical every day. What happened in Moscow two days ago should remind us of the need for action." Heads nodded again. Within the Kremlin there was a great deal of concern about the unsanctioned demonstration held by *Pamyat,* a so-called "national patriotic Orthodox Christian movement." Ostensibly called to protest the construction of a war memorial on Poklonnaya Hill, many in the Politburo felt it was really a test to see how the government would react. Militia troops had contained the demonstration without firing a shot, and Boris Yeltsin, First Secretary of the Moscow City Committee, had persuaded the group to disperse after a two-hour meeting.

"As a precaution, I suggest we tell our asset to be extra vigilant," Butrovich said. "It is only six weeks before the action. Perhaps he should disappear until then."

"An excellent idea, comrade," Voloshin said. "I will pass the word to him as soon as I can."

***

They came for him in the middle of the night, as he knew they would. Grechko had arrived at his dacha the previous morning, planning for a two-day stay, perhaps three, during which he could use the peace and quiet to complete his planning for the operation. The peace and quiet was interrupted late in the afternoon by the sound of a motorcycle, then a tentative knock on his door. One rap, then two, then one again.

After confirming through the peephole that only one person was outside, Grechko opened the door to his visitor, a man from the village. In his late twenties, dressed like the peasant he was, Dima held his hat in his hand as he looked up at the taller Spetsnaz officer. Ten years ago, he had been one of the three hooligans who had burglarized Grechko's dacha. Dima was the only one who begged for mercy when Grechko caught up with them. The other two had not been so smart. Since then, the reformed young man had served as Grechko's eyes and ears in the village.

"Yes, Dima?"

"Comrade, I came from the village as soon as I could. There are men in the village, I think they are KGB."

Grechko allowed him inside, shutting the door behind him. How many? Were they in uniform?"

"One car, a large Zil, with two in civilian clothing, two in uniform. They looked like the Army, but they had the blue piping you told me to watch for. They are KGB, yes?"

"You are correct, my friend," Grechko said. Undoubtedly they were from the Ninth Chief Directorate, elite paramilitary soldiers trained in counter-insurgency and other lethal tasks. They were not men to be trifled with, and there would be only one reason why they would be in his village, barely ten kilometers away from the dacha.

"What do you want me to do, comrade?"

Grechko reached into his pocket and put a wad of bills into Dima's hand, along with a key. "Take this, return to your family, and say nothing."

The peasant looked at the money. "This is much too generous, I cannot–"

Grechko closed the man's hand around the money, then clapped him on the shoulder. "Dima, you must take this and help your family. I will be going away for a while. I'm not sure when I will return. I'd like you to keep watch on this place for me. I can count on you, can't I?"

Dima stood at attention, clicking his heels together, but his upper lip trembled. "Yes, comrade. I will care for it as I would my own home."

Grechko suppressed a sigh. Twice a year he followed a specific set of protocols, informing a trusted associate in Moscow he was still alive. If a reporting date went by without contact, his associate had a series of instructions to follow. One of them was delivering title of this property to Dima. Now, as he showed the man out the door, he had a feeling those instructions might just have to be followed in a few months.

Well, perhaps, he thought some six hours later, perhaps not. From his carefully concealed perch in the forest, he watched them come. Three cars, stopping well down the only road in, and eight men spreading out. From what he could see through his special night-vision optics, six appeared to be in battle dress, armed with submachine guns. The two in civilian clothes held pistols.

Dima's warning had given Grechko plenty of time to consider his options. None of them were particularly appealing. He thought of leaving immediately, but something held him back. Maybe he had been wrong, maybe the KGB men were in the village for some other reason. Even as he thought of that, he knew he was kidding himself, but still he would not flee, not until he was sure. Now, as he saw in the approaching men the certainty that the dacha would be lost to him forever, he had to fight back a brief but intense feeling of sadness. Could he possibly be getting sentimental as he aged? Evidently so. After all, the dacha was the last tangible link he held to his father, other than the few photographs and military decorations he'd preserved in his various safe houses. Over the years, anticipating this very eventuality, he'd prepared three such places, one in Leningrad, another in Poland and the third in Romania. Aside from them and his apartment in Moscow, where he kept nothing of any real value, what he had in the pack at the base of the tree five meters below held everything he would need to bring from this life into whatever life awaited him after ZARNITSA.

He had concluded Voloshin was right about the

necessity of the operation, but the general was a fool to trust Klimov, who was well-known to be a gambling man. The stories of his visits to Monte Carlo were legendary within the Spetsnaz community, since he often used operators as bodyguards when he went abroad for entertainment. Grechko made it even money that Klimov would turn on the Committee and make a play for leadership of the Party and Union himself. All he needed would be an ally within KGB. Now the evidence of that was coming down the road, and as he watched them, four men broke off and melted into the woods, two on each side of the road.

Curious, though, that Klimov would move against him now, well before ZARNITSA. It would have been easier to wait until Grechko carried out the mission, but maybe not. It could be that Klimov had his own operation in mind, and he needed to eliminate the Committee's most dangerous asset first. Yes, that made sense. If the Committee decided the noble general had gone rogue, they might just designate him as Grechko's next target. And to be sure, Klimov had not forgotten what happened on his recent visit to Siberia.

In any event, it was time to go. The Spetsnaz officer slowly lowered himself from his perch, hardly making a sound as his boots touched the ground. He knew this forest like the back of his hand, having explored it thoroughly as a boy, and his skills as a woodsman had never left him. He'd practiced them all over the world, from Siberia to Vietnam, Nicaragua to Angola. He'd even ventured out into the wilds of the American West, on horseback no less. But that had been for pleasure. This was business of the most serious kind.

He could easily have hunted each of the KGB men advancing on his dacha, killed them all and made his escape, but it was not necessary. Although it might buy him some time, such slaughter would only enrage KGB and thus seriously inhibit his ability to get out of the country and carry out his mission. And truthfully he had nothing against any of these men, whoever they were. So Grechko set out silently at an angle away from their direction of advance. He estimated it would take him only thirty minutes to get to the side road where he had parked his vehicle, and from there it was an hour's drive to the Polish frontier. The border guards would be on alert once KGB discovered he'd slipped their noose, but he knew places where he could cross without too much trouble. Best not to tarry, though.

He'd gone less than a hundred meters when he heard the snap of a twig. Instantly he froze, all his senses alert. Even at night in the forest, his vision was surprisingly sharp, so much so he did not need the optical device now in his pack. He waited, then he saw the darker shape moving against the background, no more than ten meters ahead, crossing his path. A bear? No, he sniffed the air and caught the scent of human sweat.

He cursed himself for his carelessness. KGB had brought in more than the men he had seen. Another squad was advancing on the dacha from this direction. How many? He couldn't tell. Surely, though, this man was at the nearer end of the skirmish line. More would be beyond him.

Grechko intended to wait and let the man pass, then slip behind him and keep going. But now the man stopped, swiveling his head slowly side to side, and then he took a tentative step closer. Oh, he was good, this one. Not quite good enough, though. Grechko stifled a sigh. Now he would have to do something about this man. Slowly he drew his favorite combat knife, a Kizlyar Voron-3. Its 16.5-centimeter blade had tasted human flesh on five continents. Waiting until the soldier walked carefully past him, Grechko moved as silent as a cat, but his strike was much more deadly.

CHAPTER SIXTEEN

**BOSTON,
MASSACHUSETTS
MAY 1987**

"Mr. Makkonen, it is good to see you," the stocky man said, raising his cocktail glass in salute. The Russian accent clung to his English like a warm mitten. Maltsov detected a hint of the Pomor dialect, from the Murmansk area of the extreme northwestern Soviet Union. He remembered it well from his time in the Air Force. He'd spent a very long winter at a base up there, with occasional warm nights supplied by local girls more than willing to entertain a dashing officer.

Maltsov tuned out the chatter of the party around him. "Mister... Yakov, is it?" This man could be the contact he'd been ordered to make. The coded message he'd found at the dead drop yesterday had surprised him. Going to a reception on the Harvard University campus was just about the last thing he expected to be doing on a Saturday evening. Phyllis had been very disappointed when he broke their date.

"Yes, yes. I work for Comrade Minister Zaitsev." Yakov nodded at the tall, ice-blonde woman who was chatting with the university chancellor.

Maltsov knew the Minister of Culture was a former

pole vaulter, a silver medalist in some past Olympics. Not too long in the past, he thought, noting the firm tone of her calves below her dress. He forced himself to focus his attention on Yakov. "Tell me, Comrade Makkonen," Yakov said, "are you familiar with the work of Leonid Nosyrev?"

"Yes, somewhat. He has a new film out, does he not? *Laughter and Grief by the Barents Sea,* I believe."

"By the White Sea," Yakov corrected. The signal was confirmed. Yakov nodded and took the younger man gently by the elbow, leading him toward a quiet spot in the room. "Comrade," he said in Russian, "I am to tell you that you must leave the United States immediately."

"But... why?"

Yakov smiled, but Maltsov could see the hardness in his eyes. "Your American girlfriend has betrayed you, comrade. Evidently there was something about your pillow talk that made her suspicious. According to our sources, you have been under FBI surveillance for several days. They were going to arrest you tonight when you took her back to your apartment."

Maltsov's veins turned to rivers of ice. It took all of his discipline to avoid showing more than the barest hint of concern. "Unfortunately, you do not have diplomatic immunity," Yakov said. "You must leave the country before you are caught. I assume you exercised caution on your trip here?"

"Of course," Maltsov said. During his drive to the airport in Richmond he had executed the countermeasures he'd been taught years ago by KGB, following what the Americans called SDRs, surveillance detection routes, so by the time he was deep into

Virginia he was reasonably certain he was not being followed. But of course one could never be sure, especially when one's techniques were a bit rusty.

Yakov reached into an inside pocket of his suit jacket and withdrew some folded papers. "Your flight is set for nine o'clock in the morning."

"Why could I not have been told this yesterday? I could've been on a plane out of Washington."

Yakov laughed heartily, as if he'd just been told a joke. "They were watching the Washington airports, you idiot! That is why we had you drive to Richmond first and fly from there. It will not take them long to start watching all the airports on the East Coast. It might already be too late."

Maltsov took a deep breath. What he had always feared had come to pass, but the shock was starting to wear off. He had to think about this. Now that his real identity was known to the FBI, it would soon be known to all the Western intelligence services. Returning to the Soviet Union meant he would never be allowed to go abroad again. That was not a pleasant thought. He had prepared a contingency plan for this eventuality, but it was not something he could discuss with Comrade Yakov. "I understand," he said. "I presume I am not to return to my hotel this evening?"

"That is correct. In those papers is the address of a safe house we have in the Dorchester section of this city. There is a car outside waiting for you. Your driver's name is Pyotr. He knows the city. Give him the address and he will take you there. In the morning he will drive you to Logan International. Also in those papers is your new passport. You will fly to Stockholm and from there to Moscow."

Maltsov sighed. He had to show the proper balance between disappointment and loyalty, but his mind was already sorting through his options. “Very well. Thank you, comrade.”

Yakov nodded, smiling broadly. Anyone watching would think the two men had just concluded a friendly chat, but the KGB agent’s eyes were anything but friendly. “Oh, and comrade, there are to be no deviations from this plan. Do we understand each other?”

“Perfectly. *Do svidanya.*”

***

“Well, if we had to do a training exercise, I’m glad it was here,” Jennings said. “I’ve never been to Boston. How about you?”

“Once, years ago,” Jo said. She noted the time on the wall clock. “Six o’clock. Where’s Will? Maybe we could find a quiet place for dinner.”

“He stepped out with the colonel.” Jennings stood up and stretched. “Good thing I brought my walking shoes today.”

Jo knew how he felt. They must’ve put on several miles, and some of downtown Boston’s sidewalks weren’t in the best of shape, although the cobblestones they occasionally encountered were charming.

Overall, the exercise had gone well. The debrief that just concluded, conducted by Colonel Teller and a CIA official from the Directorate of Operations, had given the three Pallas field operatives high marks. It certainly helped that all of them had past experience operating in European urban centers. The exercise consisted primarily of surveillance tasks, with local FBI agents acting as their targets. Boston had been chosen because its quirky downtown more closely resembled an old European city than anything else they could find stateside on short notice.

"They threw a few curve balls at us," Jo said, "but I think it turned out well."

"Speaking of curve balls, the Red Sox are in town," Jennings said. "I'm thinking of staying over and going to the game tomorrow before heading back to the base. Ever been to Fenway?"

Jo glanced at the Army major. Was he asking her out on a date, or was it just one colleague to another? She was tempted; baseball had always intrigued her, but she didn't consider herself a big fan. Certainly not like her father, who knew the history of the New York Yankees almost by heart. Well, why not? "I guess that–"

She was interrupted by the colonel's arrival. "Jo, Greg, come with me."

They followed the Marine officer into the hallway. "What's up, Colonel?" Jennings asked.

"New intel just came in about a target we need to take down."

"Where at, sir?"

Teller looked over his shoulder at Jo. "Right here in Boston." He made a quick left into an office. Will Harrison and the CIA agent from DDO were there along with another man and a woman. Teller made the introductions. "Lieutenant Colonel Geary, Major Jennings, this is Stacy King, Special Agent in Charge for the FBI Boston office, and her assistant, Agent Timothy Santine."

Hands were quickly offered and shaken. King was

Jo's height, about ten years older with blonde hair showing a few streaks of gray. She was all business. "Let's get right to it," she said, pointing a remote control at a TV set on a nearby table. A photo flickered to life, showing a blonde, good-looking man sitting at a bar with a woman who had obviously worked hard to make herself more attractive than she actually was.

"I apologize for the short notice, but we have a rapidly developing situation here," King said. "The man you see in this photo goes by the name of Lars Makkonen, supposedly a Finnish national who frequently travels to D.C. to lobby Congress on behalf of his company." She clicked through five more photos, each showing the man with the woman, some inside the bar, others as they were leaving and getting into a car. "The woman is a staffer for a senator who sits on the Intelligence Committee. These were taken three nights ago in D.C. Normally he takes her to his apartment, but this time he didn't. When he called her last night to break their date for tonight, we knew he'd be in the wind very soon."

"Unfortunately, our surveillance team lost him as he drove west out of D.C. into Maryland," Santine said, "but a few hours ago we got a lead from Richmond. He'd flown out of Richmond International late last night and arrived in Boston around dawn."

"I'm guessing her position on that committee is not a coincidence," Jo said.

"Very true, Colonel Geary," King said. "We took a routine look at Mr. Makkonen about a year ago, but he was cleared by Finnish security, thanks to a KGB mole, as it turns out. The Russians had built a very thorough legend for Makkonen in Helsinki, but when we told the

Finns about our renewed interest in him, they rolled up the mole and it led to this." Another click, and a standard Soviet military ID photo was displayed. "We now have reason to believe Makkonen is actually this man."

It was definitely the same man, younger, his hair somewhat shorter. Jo recognized the uniform. "Soviet Air Force," she said.

"Formerly of the Air Force," Santine said. "His real name is Maltsov. According to the Finns, he works for KGB."

"And after what his girlfriend told us, we're pretty sure of it," King said.

"So what do you need us for?" Jennings asked, drawing a look from Teller.

"He's still here in Boston," King said. "Our guess is that he plans to fly out of here very soon, but we can't be sure. It's possible he could leave by train or car and head somewhere else in New England or make a run for Canada. We have orders to pick him up tonight, but there's a problem."

"From what Special Agent King tells me," Teller said, "our friend Major Maltsov has gotten himself to a safe house in an area here in Boston that's somewhat politically sensitive."

"What does that mean?" Jo asked.

King looked at her. "It means that we can't go in there with a full SWAT team and storm the place. He's in Dorchester, which has a large minority population. The police raided a drug house in that neighborhood just last week. Four civilians were killed. The place is a powder keg and another raid this soon might just set it off."

"The civilians were all drug suspects, armed to the teeth and resisting arrest" Harrison said, "but that evidently didn't matter."

"This city has had more than its share of racial problems, some of them fairly recent," King said. "We need a covert action team to go in there and take him. We don't have time to bring in one of our special units from D.C. or New York. We caught a break with you people already here. If, that is, you're willing to work with us on this operation."

"We're in," Teller said. "When do we move?"

King glanced at her watch. "Three hours."

"Then we'd better get to work."

CHAPTER SEVENTEEN

BOSTON, MASSACHUSETTS
MAY 1987

There was a definite chill in the air. Everyone could feel it, and it wasn't just the temperature, a relatively mild fifty-five degrees. Jo pulled the collar of her jacket tighter and wished she was wearing jeans instead of a short skirt. Down the street, dimly illuminated by the flickering, yellow fluorescent street lamp, the target house waited, squat and foreboding. At one time, maybe half a century before in Depression-era Boston, it had been a new home for someone, perhaps a doctor's family or a lawyer's.

Not now. In daylight, Jo was sure she would've seen peeling dark red paint, a ratty excuse for a yard, torn screens on some of the windows. Near the cracked cement walkup steps a rusting bicycle with banana handlebars leaned against the wall.

A tinny voice whispered in her earpiece. "Vixen, are you in position?"

"Roger that, Badger," she said. The button microphone on her collar transmitted the words back to Teller in the command vehicle a block away. The technology was still new, similar to what Jo had used during her Hamburg mission with the West German

BND, and it had limited range, but it was working fine at the moment. The men on the team had all chosen code names based on their college alma maters. Teller had attended Wisconsin, Jennings went to Penn State and Harrison to Michigan State. Jo had kept the one she'd used since her mission to South America five years ago.

"You're on, Vixen," Teller said.

"On the move. Keep the channel open." She made sure her hair covered her earpiece and took a calming breath to steady herself.

She crossed the street and headed toward the house, pausing twice to check for traffic. There were only a few cars on the move, an occasional Cadillac with flashy rims contrasting with the more typical sedans and compacts, featureless except for the degree of rust and disrepair that varied by car. Most of them had stereo speakers thundering the rhythmic, aggressive music Jo had learned was called hip-hop. Pedestrians were even less numerous, and all of them avoided the house Jo was heading for now.

The team had discussed means of accessing the safe house where the Russian was reportedly stashed. Without knowing for sure, they couldn't afford to force their way in and thus alert the real safe house if this one turned out to be the wrong one. The boldest option was the one Jo suggested. Boston's Chinatown was near the north end of the Dorchester district, about a fifteen-minute drive from the target. King had confirmed that it was not at all unknown for Asians to come down to Dorchester to score drugs. It was risky, but nothing they would be doing this night was without risk.

Jo hopped onto the sidewalk, avoiding a broken liquor bottle in the gutter. Her low heels clacked on the pavement, echoing off the dark faces of the houses. On one porch, three teenage boys, all black, eyed her carefully. “Yo, chinkerbell!” one of them yelled at her, drawing laughter from the other two. Jo looked at them, feigning fear, and kept moving. Three doors down was the target. If they followed her, things could go south quickly. They stayed on their stoop.

Jo was certain that the majority of people in this neighborhood were law-abiding citizens, but the sun had gone down and those people were almost all indoors now, or heading that way. She had no choice but to view everyone she encountered as a potential threat. Somewhere out there in the darkness, Jennings and Harrison were employing more stealthy means to get into position.

“At the target,” she said, stopping to peer up at the numbers, playing the part of the nervous newcomer. She didn’t feel good going in unarmed, but they’d decided it had to be risked. She could hardly claim to be a nervous yuppie looking for a drug score if she was found to be carrying a gun. She climbed up the three steps and pressed the doorbell. From inside, she heard a buzz over the music.

Nothing happened. She buzzed again, knowing her instructions called for her to leave if nobody answered within three minutes. Back down the street, the teens on the stoop stood up and looked her way.

Jo saw the peephole in the door go dark, then heard the unlatching of two locks. The door opened a few inches until it was stopped by a chain. A black woman stared out at her. “What you want, girl?”

"I—I'm looking for a little help," she said, offering a scared smile. "I heard you could maybe help me out."

"Who tol' you that?"

"Lee Kwon, at the Lotus Club," she said, giving the name of a notorious drug lord that King had obtained from the Boston police.

"Why don't he help you?"

"He wasn't there tonight." She looked back at the teens, who were sauntering up the street, now just one house away. "Look, I don't want any trouble. Just some blow, you know?"

A man's face appeared above the woman's. "Maybe we can help you out, mama-san," he said, grinning a gap-toothed smile. "Let her in, Carla."

The living room, if it could be called that, was dimly lit and smelled of marijuana and beer. A large TV squatted silently in the corner, images of an NBA game flickering on the screen. Soul music soothed from speakers on either side of the TV. The only furniture was a sofa and an easy chair, along with a coffee table covered with magazines, ash trays and beer bottles. A skinny black man with dreadlocks sprawled in the chair, dragging on the largest joint Jo had ever seen. He grinned at her and said, "Chinkerbell, you wan' some ganja? Bes' shit you ever had, gar-on-tee."

On the couch, a buxom black woman and a skinny white girl stared at her. The blonde's eyes were vacant, but the black woman's were filled with suspicion. Aside from the coffee table, the room was surprisingly clean. Carla sashayed through the room and into the adjacent dining room and kitchen. "You check her out good, Dwight," she said over her shoulder.

"Get them arms up, mama-san," the man at the

doorway said. After she complied he ran his hands down her sides and then her front, squeezing her breasts. “Oh, you packin’, mama-san, but not a rod.”

“Dat’s what you got, mon,” the man in the chair said. “You gonna give dis girl what she want?”

“Maybe,” Dwight said, giving her breasts one last feel. “Depends on what she got to offer.”

“I can pay,” Jo said. “I have money.”

“Oh, don’t worry, mama-san, I give you a fair price. Maybe we can agree on something that’ll get you a discount,” he said.

The black woman stood up from the couch, large bosom swaying in her tube top. “No man o’ mine gonna fuck no skanky chink bitch,” she said indignantly. “Give her to Whitey upstairs. Professor say, keep him happy till mornin’. He be done wit’ Angela by now.”

“You shut up!” Dwight growled. “The professor ain’t here now.”

In Jo’s earpiece, a voice whispered, “In position.”

In the kitchen, a large, very white man wearing a dark suit moved across the room toward a microwave oven on the counter. Not their target, but enough confirmation for Jo.

“So, mama-san,” Dwight said, putting his hands on her shoulders, massaging them with anticipation, “we’ll do some business. You make my friend upstairs happy, I’ll knock off, say, ten percent. You make me happy, I’ll go another fifteen. What you got to say about that?”

Jo turned to face him, smiling up at him, measuring the angles. “Just one word: execute.”

Dwight’s eyes narrowed, then went wide as Jo’s knee drove up into his groin. From behind she sensed movement. With a glance over her right shoulder she fired a back kick that caught the black woman in the ribcage right under her breasts, driving her back on top of the blonde. They tumbled off the couch onto the floor.

From the chair, the Jamaican moved with surprising quickness. He wasn't as stoned as he appeared to be. Jo saw the knife flash as it came around in an arc. As she moved, Jo heard the back door crashing open and the rapid pop-pop of Tasers. Carla's scream was quickly muffled, followed by two heavy thumps. Jo ducked under the sweep of the knife, reached up to grab the Jamaican's wrist and elbow and twisted the arm violently behind him. He yelled in pain, cut short when a man dressed completely in black stepped into the room and knocked him unconscious with the butt of a handgun. Under the camo paint she recognized the face of Jennings.

Jo pointed to the nearby staircase. "Upstairs." She took the Glock handgun Jennings pulled from a holster at the small of his back and took the stairs two at a time.

"I've got your six," Jennings said. Into his collar mic he said, "Main floor is clear. Spartan has it secured. Target is on the second floor. Vixen and I are moving up."

"Double-time it, Lion," Teller said. "We don't want to let the natives get too restless. We're sixty seconds away."

"Roger that, Badger."

***

Maltsov heard the commotion downstairs and knew immediately that the Americans had come for him. Fortunately, he had finished with Angela a few minutes before and had just returned from the cramped bathroom down the hall. He took a deep breath, sat down in the chair next to the rickety dresser and began pulling on his socks.

"What's going on?" Angela said sleepily. She moved one dark leg out from under the sheet, wiggling her toes. For the first time, Maltsov noticed the nails were painted pink.

"I suggest you get dressed, dear heart. Your countrymen have arrived."

"What? Who do you mean?"

Maltsov gave her a sad grin. For a political science major at a university as prestigious as Boston College—or was it Boston University?—she was surprisingly naïve. He knew as soon as he'd met her, an hour before, that she had drugged herself somehow before being driven over here from her campus. He appreciated the professor's efforts for the cause of world socialism, though. Whatever drug she had taken, it had not inhibited her in bed.

But that was over now. Maltsov had decided he would not attempt to escape or resist if the American security forces invaded the house, as it was apparent they were now doing. He finished tying his shoes, straightened the collar of his shirt and sat back in the chair. He felt surprisingly calm, even relieved. This hadn't been part of his plan, but maybe it would be better. Certainly easier.

The door crashed open and two figures filled the doorway, the smaller one pointing a gun at Angela on the bed, the taller one aiming right at Maltsov. "Freeze, comrade," the taller one said in a voice that brooked no argument. Maltsov raised his hands.

Angela screamed, clutching the sheet to her breasts as she scurried up to the headboard. The smaller figure, a woman, took a step toward her and leveled the gun at Angela's face. "Be quiet!" she ordered, and the coed's next shriek quickly retreated into a whimper.

"I am unarmed," Maltsov said.

The woman took another step into the bedroom and the light from the small bedside table lamp revealed an amazing pair of legs. Maltsov followed them up to the short black skirt, the stylish dark red jacket and the Asian face draped with long black hair. The handgun she pointed at Angela was held in a very professional grip. She looked over at Maltsov and then back to Angela and motioned to the girl in the bed. "On your feet," she said, adding a movement with the gun.

"I'm not... I'm naked," Angela said, pulling the sheet closer.

"Stand up very slowly and put your hands behind your head," the Asian woman ordered. Angela complied, a scared, childlike look on her face. Maltsov had assumed she was at least twenty-one, but perhaps she was younger. She had mentioned to him that she and the professor were intimate. One more piece of information the Americans might be interested in. They would probably be more interested in the professor's efforts on behalf of KGB, but if they knew about Angela, they might be able to double him. He was a married man, Maltsov had heard, and both his marriage and his prestigious post at the university would be jeopardized by news of an affair with a student.

The man, dressed entirely in black and his face

camouflaged, followed the woman and expertly frisked Maltsov as the woman trained her weapon on him, flicking her eyes back and forth quickly between him and the trembling Angela. Whoever she was, the Asian woman was highly trained. She had not allowed Angela to begin dressing herself, where she might have been able to bring a concealed weapon into play. These were professionals, not to be trifled with.

The man stepped back and trained his weapon on Maltsov, allowing the woman to aim hers back at Angela. She nodded at the clothing lying next to the bed and said, “Put your underwear and shirt back on.” Angela quickly complied. “Okay, let’s go. You first, honey. Lion, escort the guest of honor.”

Down on the first floor, another black-clad man was standing guard over the two women and the Jamaican, who had been trussed up with plastic restraints. The man Maltsov knew as Dwight was hog-tied with his wrists connected to his ankles. Evidently he’d offered some resistance, as one eye was puffy and swelling. The black woman and the blonde were cuffed together, back to back. The black-clad man was peeking through a curtain that covered the picture window. “What’s the situation outside, Spartan?” the Asian woman asked.

“Not good,” the man at the window said. “We’ve got a dozen people, maybe more, on the street and the sidewalk. They know something’s going down.”

“Any local police?”

“Not a peep from Boston’s finest. Mother Hen told us we’d be on our own. She wasn’t kidding.” He gestured at a backpack on the couch. “Your gear’s in there, Vixen.”

"Thanks." She flipped open the flap and pulled out a pair of black fatigue pants along with a long-sleeved black shirt and a watch cap. Digging toward the bottom, she withdrew the last items, black socks and sneakers with Velcro straps. Maltsov watched her kick her pumps off with evident relish. She slipped off her skirt, and in spite of his situation Maltsov couldn't help noticing that her black panties did little to conceal a splendid *krupu.* Off came her red jacket, but her black undershirt stayed on, quickly covered by a long-sleeved black shirt. She gathered her long hair and covered it with a black baseball cap. In seconds she was suited up, a remarkable transformation from attractive if somewhat trashy woman to no-nonsense warrior, with a very appropriate code name to boot. The KGB agent's opinion of her went up another notch.

She touched something in her right ear. "Building is secure, Badger. We have the package, ready for exfil, and a crowd of about a dozen or more outside in front." She listened intently for a few seconds, then said, "We'll go out the back way and come down the alley. On our way now."

"It's about a hundred meters to Badger's position," Lion said.

"Let's move out." Vixen led the way through the kitchen, stepping over the unfortunate Pyotr, now bound and unconscious. Carla was manacled to a kitchen chair, duct tape covering her mouth. She glared at them with hatred, but the tape muffled her shouts.

They reached the back door and Vixen turned to Maltsov. *"Chto takoe vash rang i rod vojsk?"* she asked. What is your rank and branch of service?

Maltsov was impressed yet again. "Major, First Chief Directorate, Committee for State Security," he replied in English. "I will tell you nothing more until I am safe and we have an agreement."

"Fair enough, Major. We'll get you there, but you have to cooperate with us. Our orders are to bring you in alive, if possible. I emphasize those last two words. Do we understand each other?"

Maltsov knew very well they would kill him if he tried to escape now. "We do," he said. With his hands manacled in front of him, he could still do some damage if he so chose, but his KGB hand-to-hand combat training was well in the past and would not take him very far against three well-trained, armed and highly motivated operatives. Discretion was truly the better part of valor for him now.

"Good. I'm sure you know that if we're overrun by these people they'll take note of your skin color and won't bother asking about your political affiliation. It's in your best interest to stay close to us." As if to emphasize her point, she held up her handgun and ratcheted a round into its chamber.

Maltsov nodded. He had no illusions in that regard. The *Negry* he was likely to encounter outside were far removed from those he'd seen at the Harvard cocktail party earlier. A political commissar back home would say it was yet another indication of the inherent unfairness of capitalism. Even as the thought entered his brain, Maltsov had to stifle a laugh. This was not exactly a theoretical exercise now, was it?

"Moving out," Vixen said to her unseen controller, waiting somewhere out there in the sinister darkness. After turning off the kitchen light, she opened the back door and led the way down the cement steps to the back yard.

Maltsov could hear the sound of the crowd growing out in the front yard of the house. Where were the sirens? Were the police so afraid that they refused to intervene here? No, he knew that American police were largely quite fearless in that regard, if usually prudent. This "Mother Hen" the man code-named Spartan had referred to must be the team's control officer and had withheld police support to avoid unnecessarily inciting the locals. A smart move.

The woman moved almost without sound down the alley, the men following at a trot. What light there was barely allowed them to avoid parked vehicles and overflowing trash cans. Maltsov stumbled once and was immediately caught by the arm from behind. "Stay on your feet, Ivan," Lion said, and Maltsov felt the business end of a gun in the small of his back. He kept running.

The safe house—not so safe after all, he thought—was about fifty meters behind them when he heard shouts. Risking a glance over his shoulder, he saw figures coming from the yard into the alley and giving chase.

Lion had seen them too. "Vixen, hostiles on our six, fifty meters back."

He heard the woman give an order but couldn't make it out. Lion heard her clearly through his earpiece, though. "Roger that. One G60 coming up." Maltsov knew what that meant. He kept his eyes trained on the end of the alley up ahead and saw a vehicle pulling to a stop across the entrance. Three seconds later a loud bang heralded a flash like a thousand light bulbs going on at once. The shouting from behind turned to yells of pain and anger. They would be unharmed except perhaps for some perforated eardrums. More importantly, their night vision would be destroyed for several minutes.

They were at the vehicle, a large one the Americans called an SUV. The passenger side rear door swung open and Vixen held it for him. “Inside!” Maltsov dove through the space, almost cracking his skull on the frame of the doorway. The opposite door opened and the operative known as Spartan entered. The man who’d thrown the grenade jammed him from the passenger side, with Vixen in front of him. Doors slammed shut and the vehicle’s engine roared as the rear wheels caught on some gravel before tearing into the pavement with a scream of rubber. The man at the wheel handled it effortlessly. Vixen was next to him in the passenger seat. She turned around to him and pulled off her ball cap, allowing her raven hair to come free.

“Welcome to the rest of your life, Major,” she said. He saw a grin of triumph trying to get to the surface.

She was just about the most exotic woman Maltsov had ever seen, even more so because now she represented something he’d always yearned to achieve: freedom. He realized it was within his grasp, or as close to it as the Americans would allow.

He sat back in the seat. It would be enough.

CHAPTER EIGHTEEN

**TAMPA,
FLORIDA
MAY 1987**

Jo had found an apartment in the Ballast Point neighborhood of South Tampa, just a few minutes from the base. On the second floor of the building, the apartment featured a balcony with a nice view of neighboring Hillsborough Bay to the east. Leaning against the railing with the early afternoon sun washing over her, she felt a pang of regret that she hadn't had too much time to spend here since moving in. It was another glorious day, weather-wise, although she knew that in another few weeks the humidity would start climbing, adding another level of challenge to their morning P.T.

The colonel had given her and the rest of the Boston team the day off after their redeye flight landed near dawn of the morning after the assault on the Dorchester safe house. Jo put the time to good use, fixing herself a light breakfast and then hitting the hay. Although she'd slept some on the flight, she suddenly found herself so tired that she could barely crawl into bed.

A solid eight hours' sleep and fifteen minutes of yoga had done the trick. She took a sip of tea as she went over the events of the mission. All in all, she thought, it had gone well, although she could count on the colonel pointing out some areas for improvement when they went through the debriefing. But that wouldn't be till tomorrow morning. For now, the rest of this day was hers.

As she contemplated a man and woman jogging through the park, Jo wondered idly what she might do today. Well, there was laundry, for one thing, and her usual solo training and language study. The Russian was coming along nicely; she'd actually had a rather fluent conversation with the captured KGB agent before the FBI took him away to another safe house.

But maybe tonight she should just relax. Get her chores done, go through the Russian material she received weekly from the base's intelligence office, and then maybe dinner somewhere and a movie. The Russian studies would be interesting; over eight thousand daily newspapers were published in the Soviet Union in some sixty languages, and SOCOM had access to a great many of them, some only a few days old. She had dailies from Leningrad and Moscow to peruse, along with the latest editions of *Pravda* and *Krasnaya Zvezda*, from the Ministry of Defense. Her latest packet even included a paper printed in Korean, *Lenin Kichi,* published in the republic of Kazakhstan. When she'd asked about it, she found, to her great surprise, that the Soviet republics of central Asia had a fairly large population of ethnic Koreans, who referred to themselves as the *Koryo-saram.* Certainly she wasn't the only one who had noticed that, so it was likely she'd one day be tasked for a mission there.

But that was something to think about later. What

about today? Maybe a movie. She'd have to check the Tampa paper. Something light, maybe a comedy. She could use a laugh.

She was leaving the movie theater and still regretting ever having gone inside when she saw Will Harrison standing out on the sidewalk, hands in the pockets of his jacket. He had a smile on his face, one more genuine than the few she'd seen on him at the base.

"Hey, Will, this is a surprise," she said. She was glad to see him, but also wondered how he had just happened to be outside the theater she'd been in.

"I'll bet you're thinking that this was one of the worst movies you've ever seen," he said.

"How did you know that?"

He glanced up at the marquee. "I saw Roger Ebert's review in the paper the other day. He said *Ishtar* is, quote, 'a truly dreadful film.' Was he right?"

She laughed. "Yes, he was. I wish I'd read that first, it would've saved me some time and money. The popcorn was good, anyway."

"Well, at least there's that," he said. "I'll save my ticket money for the next Arnold film."

"Arnold Schwarzenegger? You're a fan?"

"Big time. His next one's coming out in a few weeks. *Predator*, Arnie takes on a space alien in the jungle."

Jo rolled her eyes. "I like his films, but come on, an alien?"

"Well, maybe it'll work." He hesitated, then said, "I

know a nice bar a couple blocks away. Can I buy you a drink?"

It had been over a week since Jo's father had told her she should get to know Harrison better. Maybe now was the time. "All right, sure."

***

Jo took a sip of her cosmopolitan and took in the scene inside the lounge. Over on a small stage at the end of the room a jazz combo was tuning up. Several couples were occupying tables or space along the bar. Most of them had short haircuts and were easily identified as military personnel, thus the threat level was low. She'd long ago trained herself in situational awareness, to the point where it was now second nature. She glanced at Will and saw he'd been doing the same thing. He caught her eye and winked. "I think we're okay here," he said with a small grin.

That drew a laugh from her, and she got the conversational ball rolling with a gentle question about his background. "I'm a Yooper," he said, and when he saw her quizzical expression he added, "Escanaba, in the Upper Peninsula of Michigan." He explained how he'd gotten a wrestling scholarship to Michigan State and one day made a snap decision to join CIA after talking to an on-campus recruiter.

"How long have you been in SAD?" she asked. Jo had worked with Special Activities Division operatives a few times over the years, but never in a long-term group like Pallas.

"Five years," he said. "I was one of the rare birds who came in without previous military experience."

Jo knew the great majority of agents within SAD's Special Operations Group came into the Agency from the special operations commands of the various military branches. Twice before she'd been approached by CIA with offers to come over and work their side of the fence, but she'd always resisted. Eventually she'd retire from the Air Force, and who knew where her path would lead then? She had fifteen years in, and five more would give her enough to seriously consider a move. She'd only be forty-two.

Will certainly must have shown CIA something special to get invited into SAD/SOG. Yet he was just about the most unpretentious man she'd known in a long time. Military people, especially men, tended to have a swagger about them. The smart ones, like the colonel and, to a lesser extent Jennings, kept it under control. Others weren't quite that circumspect, and sometimes that got them into trouble.

"Married?" she asked. "Children?"

Will looked down at his drink, then shook his head. When he looked back at her, his eyes seemed distant. "I got married in college," he said. "She was a student like me. Track team. Thought she was pregnant. She wasn't, but we married anyway. A mistake. The divorce was final just before we graduated."

"I'm sorry," she said.

"Nothing to be sorry about," he said, forcing a smile. "We should've just lived together. Would've saved us some money in the end, if nothing else. Youthful exuberance sometimes overrules good sense, wouldn't you agree?"

"Yes, it often does," she said, downing the last of

her drink. She knew where this was going, but before she could change the subject, he asked about her own background.

"And how about you, Jo? I'm betting you kept your youthful exuberance pretty much under control."

"There were one or two occasions when I didn't," she said. She signaled the waitress for another drink. "I met a guy at Stanford. Nice guy, political science major, but he got active in the antiwar movement and I was Air Force ROTC, so that was something he just couldn't get past."

This piqued his interest. "Did you try to get past it?"

She shrugged her shoulder. "I made an effort. But then he and his buddies showed up at my unit's honors ceremony and started throwing balloons with fake blood at us. That sort of made up my mind." It sounded silly now, seventeen years later, but at the time she had been mortified. The image of her father's new suit spattered with red dye would never leave her, but Joseph had kept his dignity while campus police hauled her boyfriend and the other protesters away. A few years later she'd run into a classmate who told her the incredible news that Jimmy Davis, California surfer dude turned antiwar activist, was actually suspected to be a Soviet agent, and he'd vanished. The FBI had started investigating him right after the incident. Jo had always suspected her father might have had a word with someone to get that ball rolling.

Will took a few kernels of popcorn from the bowl on the table, chewed in silence, then said, "I read the EMINENCE file. You did some great work down in Argentina."

"I wasn't aware particular mission files were being passed around the group," she said with some defensiveness. She'd been given short bios of each other Pallas member, but nothing about their specific operations.

"Forgive me," he said, "but when I was asked to volunteer for this outfit, I wanted to know who I'd be working with. That operation is going to be legendary in the Agency one of these days, Jo. And you being the DDO's daughter makes it even more interesting, you have to admit. So I called in a favor from a friend of mine and took a look at the file. The redacted version, of course. It'll be some time before the full version is released, if it ever is."

She didn't know what to say about that. In some way it felt like her privacy had been violated, but in another way she was pleased that a colleague, and a very experienced one at that, was impressed. Jo wondered how much was in there about Ian. She thought about asking Will, but before she could ask the question, he answered it.

"Colonel Masters was mentioned, of course. I did some checking about him when I saw the name."

Jo could hardly believe it. This was really carrying things too far. She was ready to stand up and leave when Will said, "It was the same guy I knew."

"You... you knew Ian?"

"Yes, I worked with him on a mission in Belize, 1980. I was liaising with MI6 and the local intelligence shop to stop a gun-running operation the Cubans were using to funnel arms to the guerillas in El Salvador. We needed some muscle and we got a platoon of Royal Marines. Ian was their commanding officer, and a damn good one he was. Thanks to him and his guys, we were successful."

She looked away, taking a deep breath. Her lower lip trembled slightly. She felt Will's hand touching hers on the table. "I'm sorry, I didn't mean to upset you," he said gently.

The chaos and terror of that terrible night came rushing back at her: the assault on the Argentine air base, Ian taking a bullet in his side, the desperate run to the beach and the firefight as they waited for the boats from the submarine. The enemy soldier ready to plunge his knife into her chest. The round from Ian's pistol that ended the Argentine's life and saved hers. "It's all right," she said, using a napkin to dab an eye. "Ian and I were... very close."

"I kind of thought you were."

Her second drink arrived and she took a gulp, pushing the memories back to that little corner of her memory where they belonged. She was quiet, and Will said nothing for a full minute. Then, "I'm really not sure why I do this, Jo. This work we do. I'm still trying to figure it out. May I ask you a question?"

"Sure."

"Why do you do it?"

That was unexpected. In truth, she'd been thinking about that more often lately, and doing some reading on the subject. Why, indeed? "My mother was Korean," she said. "After she died in '84, I found some letters she'd received years before, from an uncle in Seoul. He told her they were descended from the Hwarang. You might think of them as Korea's version of the Japanese samurai."

"Really?"

“They flourished in the Silla dynasty, starting in the sixth century A.D. They had what came to be known as ‘Five Commandments for Secular Life’: Loyalty to one’s lord or nation; love and respect your parents and teachers; trust among friends; never retreat in battle; never take a life without just cause.”

“Impressive,” Will said. “And you’re descended from them?”

“Yes,” she said. “My mother had told me something about them when I was a child. My uncle's letter prompted me to learn more. When I studied their commandments, it fit in perfectly with how I feel about what I do. The Hwarang protected the innocent, and when we put on the uniform today, that’s what we do.”

Will smiled, raising his glass. “Well, I decided to join this outfit because I wanted to work with real warriors. I think I made the right choice.”

***

Later, lying in bed, she thought about the evening. She’d enjoyed Will’s company very much, especially because he had not made a pass at her. He was a very good dancer, which didn’t surprise her since she’d already seen how well he handled himself on the training mat. He offered to walk her home, but she graciously declined and he didn’t push it.

There was only one thing about the evening that bothered her. She hadn’t asked Will how he’d known she was inside the theater. Now she wished she had. Somehow she felt that she wouldn’t like the answer.

CHAPTER NINETEEN

**BRATISLAVA,
CZECHOSLOVAKIA
MAY 1987**

Grechko was not comfortable in small spaces. He supposed it was a touch of claustrophobia, but up here on the sixth floor of St. Michael's Tower he had a magnificent view of Bratislava's Old Town, in particular Michalská Street below. That made up for the close quarters of the small room that led onto the balcony. He checked his watch. The general was overdue.

In the twelve days since he had abandoned his dacha in Ukraine, Grechko had been on the move, never spending more than two nights in the same place. After crossing the border into Poland he'd relaxed somewhat for the next hundred and twenty kilometers to his safe house in the city of Rzeszów. Everything was in order at his apartment in a nondescript, workingman's section of the city. He'd allowed himself to unwind for two days, going out only for provisions the first night.

He quickly discovered that life as a fugitive did not appeal to him. Although he had no direct evidence that KGB was actively hunting him, he had little doubt but that his former colleagues had alerted their subordinate agencies in the Warsaw Pact to be on the lookout for him. There was a time when he would have been very worried about that in Poland; its security agency, *Służba Bezpieczeństwa,* was once one of the most feared and respected in Eastern Europe. As recently as 1984, the SB had kidnapped, beaten and murdered a Catholic priest who had been working with the Solidarity movement. The public uproar forced the government to rein in the SB, and it hadn't taken Grechko long to sense things were different here now. The police presence on the streets was notably less obvious compared to his last visit just two years earlier.

He could not afford to take chances, though, so he'd been forced to take appropriate steps. Fortunately he was experienced in such things, having traveled fairly widely in the West without ever coming into direct contact with police or security agents. He had to be more cautious here, of course, for unlike their counterparts in the West, these countries allowed their internal security forces to be much more vigorous, as they didn't really have to pay much attention to things like constitutional rights. As long as he obeyed traffic laws and kept a low profile, he could go virtually anywhere in the NATO nations and non-aligned countries without much trouble. Even in Asian countries, where his Caucasian features were not among the majority, he had rarely experienced any difficulties.

Not so now. First in Poland and now in Czechoslovakia he drove the main highways and thoroughfares as little as possible, avoiding the random checkpoints that the police often used. He traveled only during the daylight hours, when traffic was more plentiful.

To avoid renting cars he traded his own on the black market in Poland, then traded the new one for another similarly nondescript vehicle after crossing the Czech border. He stayed at small inns in rural villages or rented rooms in city tenements where few questions were asked.

Altering his appearance was critical. He never wore the same clothing two days in a row, always wearing a hat in public and sunglasses except on very cloudy days. He'd darkened his hair and grew a short beard which he also colored. When he walked in public he affected a slight slouch. Fortunately the weather had been cool, allowing him to wear jackets which he switched daily, always a size too big to help conceal him even more.

It was starting to wear on him, and there were still some weeks to go before the mission in Budapest. Security around the General Secretary was bound to be tight, which he had anticipated, but it was possible that it would now be tightened even further if KGB suspected Grechko was on the hunt for Gorbachev. He had managed his funds carefully but eventually he would run out of money, especially if he had to go to ground even longer after the mission. Thus, he had sent a message to Voloshin through their secure communications channel asking for a meeting here in Bratislava.

If the general did not show, Grechko would know that he had been compromised. Although he did not doubt Voloshin's faith in the cause for which he had enlisted the help of the Spetsnaz veteran, he also did not doubt that Voloshin would eventually tell everything he knew if KGB took him to their basement in the Lubyanka. If that happened, it would only be a matter of time before they came for Grechko with a determination that would greatly exceed what he had experienced in Ukraine.

But if Voloshin did arrive on time, then perhaps, just perhaps, the mission could go forward.

***

The general looked at his watch. Nearly ten a.m., and it was still ten minutes by foot to Michalská Street. Would Grechko give him those extra few minutes? Voloshin cursed himself for not declining the invitation from the Czech Air Force general to join him for morning physical training and then breakfast at the officers club. The general, however, was anxious to show his hospitality to the visiting Soviet officer. Just days ago the Czechs had been roundly embarrassed when they were unable to intercept a civilian engineer who had escaped to West Germany in a homemade ultralight aircraft. This general's unit was not responsible for the failure, but he was not about to waste his chance to impress Voloshin.

But even though he was now running late, Voloshin couldn't afford to hurry. As it was, his uniform attracted unwanted attention from several pedestrians. Although his flight jacket was mostly unadorned of insignia, the few that were in evidence, along with his service cap, left little doubt as to where he was from and, more importantly to these people, what he represented. More than a few Czechs scowled at him, and one young man hawked and spat near his boots.

Voloshin had always liked Czechoslovakia for its

charming architecture and picturesque country villages, but the Czechs had rarely returned his affection. Perhaps it was only his imagination, but it appeared to be worse now. Really, though, what could he expect? Less than twenty years ago his nation's tanks had rolled through this very city, helping to crush the "Prague Spring." Czech blood had been spilled, perhaps on this very street. The people had long memories.

It was eight minutes after the hour when he found the confectionary shop Grechko had designated for the rendezvous. Inside, Voloshin was almost overcome by the delectable scents. Returning to his task, he loitered near the display cases and finally selected a *koláče,* carrying it outside in a small paper sack while resisting the temptation to take a bite, even as his stomach growled. Lingering outside the shop, he wondered how long he should wait for the Spetsnaz operative to make contact.

A full minute went by. Voloshin decided to stroll back down the street, away from the tower at the north end. Concluding that he might as well have a snack, he opened the bag and was startled to see a small folded piece of paper inside, on top of the pastry. He kept his hand inside the bag, pretending to rummage for something, and unfolded the paper.

Alley behind Primate's Palace, 1030.

***

"You are late, General," the voice said from the shadows. Voloshin did his best to conceal his surprise. He thought he had been fully aware of everything in the alley, but once again Krasniy Volk had proven himself. Voloshin stopped and turned away, fishing in his jacket pocket for a pack of cigarettes. He rarely smoked, but now it seemed like a good idea. At the very least it would give a random observer a reason for his decision to walk down the alley.

"I was unavoidably detained at the base," Voloshin said. He had to quickly take command of this situation. He was, after all, this man's de facto commanding officer. If there was one thing Voloshin had learned in all his years of service in his nation's armed forces, it was that an officer had to exert his authority at all times, or else the men under him would never give him their respect and obedience. "I am pleased that you were able to avoid our KGB colleagues in Ukraine," he said, taking a puff and fighting the urge to cough.

"You, of course, knew nothing about that in advance," Grechko said.

"That is true. One of my comrades on the Committee made some discreet inquiries. A KGB undercover operative in America learned that their CIA has at least some indication of a possible move against our mutual friend. Thus, KGB wanted to question you to see if you knew anybody who might be inclined to participate in such a thing."

Grechko offered a soft chuckle. "So it is that they sent two squads of Ninth Chief Directorate men through my forest during the night. Just to knock on my door and have a comradely chat."

"I am somewhat skeptical as well, my friend. But I have no reason to believe ZARNITSA has been compromised. If it was, I would surely be under arrest, would I not?"

"Perhaps. It is also possible that they have already turned you, and now they have sent you here to draw me out."

Voloshin did not have to see into the darkness to know that Grechko probably had a weapon out right now, likely a knife. He fought to remain calm, taking another drag on the cigarette. "That is possible, but not true. You will have to accept my word on that, Sergey Vasileyevich."

There were a few seconds of silence. Voloshin looked to his left toward the end of the alley where a man and woman strolled past on the sidewalk without looking toward him. To his right at the other end, a solitary man stood looking at the street. The man's head started to turn toward the alley.

Voloshin felt a hand grab the collar of his jacket and pull him back toward the wall, out of the light. "Make no sound, General," Grechko said softly. "He is a Czech internal security agent."

"Has he made you?" Voloshin whispered.

"No," Grechko said. "But I made him earlier this morning. Probably a routine day for him, but it would become a special day if he were to see a Soviet officer engaged in suspicious activity."

The man peered down the alley and appeared ready to take a step toward them, but then he stopped and pulled a device out of his pocket. A small radio transmitter/receiver. The Czech held it to his ear, spoke a few words that Voloshin couldn't make out, then took three quick steps past the alley entrance and was gone from view. Voloshin could not suppress his sigh of relief. He turned to face Grechko, close enough now to make out the man's features. "We do not have much time," Voloshin said. "He may be back. We should go somewhere else where we can talk privately."

"We stay here," Grechko said. "You are an excellent pilot, Comrade General, but as a spymaster you have much to learn. You come to a clandestine meeting with an operative in the field, and you are in uniform? You will draw attention, and I cannot be seen with you. KGB may have you under surveillance."

"I don't think they do," Voloshin said, knowing immediately it was foolish to say so.

"Do *not* underestimate them," Grechko said harshly. "If I had done that I would be in the Lubyanka right now. Did you bring what I requested?"

The general dug into a pocket and pulled out a wad of bills. "I have twenty-five thousand American dollars for you. This amount should prove sufficient."

Without counting them, Grechko took the bills and stuffed them into his own pocket. Voloshin knew that Grechko would use the money on the black market, where American dollars were prized. If he made his way to the West after the mission, they would be even more valuable, although they wouldn't last long. If he knew Grechko, though, the operative already had that contingency well in hand.

"You still have almost a month before completing the mission," Voloshin said. "I know this is stressful for you. Will you be able to hold out that long?"

"It is nothing new for me, Comrade General. Do not be concerned."

"I have to be concerned, Sergey Vasilyevich. If you are taken, they will break you, and that will lead them to me." He could not see Grechko's eyes very well, but he sensed that they narrowed.

"Don't worry about that," Grechko said. "They will not take me. Not alive, anyway."

"I did not mean that the way it sounded, my friend. We are all in this together, you know. One break in the chain will lead to each of us, eventually."

"Then you should make sure your colleagues on the Committee remain stalwart in their dedication to ZARNITSA and this brave new world into which you will lead our country. Or should I say, brave *old* world?"

"What do you mean by that?"

"When I was in America I saw one of their old television programs, about a masked vigilante in their Old West. 'Return with us now to those thrilling days of yesteryear,' the announcer said. Very apt, is it not?"

Voloshin was angered, not only at being challenged by Grechko but because he knew the man was more right than not. "If you are talking about Stalin, my friend, you are much mistaken. Those days are gone forever, and good riddance to them. We will move our country into the twenty-first century, not take us back in time to the mid-twentieth. And we will do it with order and discipline, not the chaos that our mutual friend is spreading." He spread his hands in a sign of appeal. "Our fathers have told us about the Great Patriotic War, how united our country was. We had purpose, we had order, and ultimately we had victory. Would it not be a great achievement to instill that spirit in our country once more?"

"That was different," Grechko snapped. "It was war. The fascists meant to kill most of us and enslave the rest. Our very survival was at stake. But I will not debate this with you, Comrade General. You are an educated man. When you walk these streets here, do you see the people looking at you with smiles? They hate us, and for good reason. 'Sixty-eight was not that long ago."

Voloshin bristled at that. "Your own relative was instrumental in that operation, comrade." Andrei Antonovich Grechko, who had led 1st Guards Army in the war and rose to the rank of Marshal of the Soviet Union, was Minister of Defense during the Prague Spring and drew up the orders for half a million Soviet and allied troops to crush the liberal regime of Alexander Dubček.

"A cousin of my grandfather," Grechko said. "I never knew him. In any event, he is dead and we are here. We will restrict our future contact to the message system we have established. If I do not get a response at the appointed time, or if it is there but contains any of our pre-arranged stress code words, I will abort the mission and you will not see or hear of me again." In the dim light, Voloshin could see the assassin grinning. "Do not be concerned about me having retribution upon you, my friend. If everything goes to *dermo*, watching out for me will be the least of your problems."

"When you get to Budapest, will you be working with your MIA contact?"

"Under the circumstances, that might not be very wise, don't you think?"

Voloshin saw the logic of that. But without any kind of support in Hungary, Grechko's chances of successfully executing ZARNITSA were, he estimated, less than fifty-fifty. "You can trust Pataki. Otherwise you will be on your own, then, my friend."

"I have done it before," Grechko said, "and in places with more hostile conditions than I am liable to find among our fraternal socialist allies in Hungary. Do what you can to keep KGB off my back. I will decide whether or not Pataki can be trusted. One way or another, I will handle the mission."

Voloshin extended his hand. He had come to have a great deal of respect for this man, even a sort of affection. "Good luck, Sergey Vasilyevich. When this is all over, contact me. We will have a place for a man such as you."

Grechko's handshake was firm but brief. "If you are successful, Comrade General, I rather think you will need men like me more than ever."

CHAPTER TWENTY

TAMPA, FLORIDA MAY 1987

Memorial Day meant only a half-day of training and planning for Pallas Group at MacDill. The colonel ordered the office closed at noon and told everyone to take the rest of the day off. Jo didn't need any convincing. Although her Russian was coming along better than she'd dared hope, she didn't want to look at another Cyrillic letter for at least twenty-four hours.

Morning P.T. had been canceled so the group could attend the Memorial Day service on the base. Missing the morning run, Jo had mentioned to Jennings that she intended to get in a mile or so when she got back to her apartment. She was straightening the books on her office bookcase shelf when the Special Forces major knocked on the open door.

"Still planning that run this afternoon?" he asked.

"Yes," she said. "There's a nice running path in a park near my apartment."

"Care for some company? I'd be happy to buy us lunch after the run."

She looked up at the tall Army officer. Since that night in Virginia more than a month earlier, Jennings had not offered to get together socially, even for a beer after office hours. Two or three times, she'd seen him at the officers' club with a shapely, blonde Air Force lieutenant. There'd been a tickle of jealousy on the first occasion, but since then Jo had just considered the possible security problems of a Pallas member getting involved in a romantic relationship. Teller had cautioned them all about extracurricular activities. But, she knew, boys would be boys. For that matter, girls would be girls, too.

Jo was tempted to ask if the Meg Ryan lookalike was busy, but she resisted. Instead, she said, "Sure, but instead of lunch, how about I fix us a couple smoothies after the run?"

"What's a smoothie?"

***

They met at Ballast Point Park and stretched out before the run. To their right, Hillsborough Bay was dotted with pleasure boats, many of them stately craft that sailed out of the yacht club at the north end of the bay, adjacent to the airport. Families and couples were out for a stroll, enjoying the spring day. Jo reflected that they were also enjoying the freedom of living in America. The people she would be among very soon had little concept of that.

Jennings was in great shape. She had to give him that, unable to keep herself from giving him the once-over. He wore a gray Penn State tee shirt with cutoff sleeves, navy blue nylon shorts and a pair of electric-blue running shoes. "Asics, just got 'em," he told her. "Fresh out of the box. They have this new gel cushion."

By comparison, Jo's pair of well-worn Nikes looked hopelessly outdated. But, the red sports bra she wore, revealing plenty of midriff above her black shorts, ensured that Jennings wouldn't be paying attention to her shoes.

"Two klicks up along Bayshore and then back?" he asked.

"Sounds good."

She was hard-pressed to keep up his pace, sensing that every time she drew even with him, he added just a tad more speed. Soon they topped off at a good stride, matching what they did on the base. In minutes Jo was perspiring, but it felt good. There was enough shade from the palm trees along the boulevard to ward off fears of sunburn.

Two kilometers would bring them to the intersection with West Bayview Avenue. Two hundred meters before that, Jo noticed a car parked along West Knights, a dark blue Volkswagen Jetta, facing the bay. She recognized the face of the man at the wheel.

"Don't look right at it, but catch the blue Jetta near the corner, facing this way," she said to Jennings.

"Got it," he said. They jogged past the intersection. Jo knew better than to risk a glance backward, but she knew the car would still be there, at least long enough to see if they would turn around in the next few blocks. "What do you want to do about him?" Jennings asked.

"We'll continue on to West Bayview," she said. "You cut west on Bayview and come back around him. I'll turn around and head south down Bayshore."

"He'll notice you're alone."

She glanced down and saw her nipples showing through the wet fabric of the bra. Ordinarily that would have caused her to cover up, but not today. "He might, but I think he'll be distracted just long enough for you to surprise him."

Jennings glanced down at her. "Oh. Right."

They came to the intersection. Jo knew that a building at the corner would screen them momentarily from anyone watching two blocks to the south. "Okay, break off," she said. Jennings shot across the northbound lane and the boulevard and kicked it into high gear to get across the southbound lane just behind a bus. Jo slowed to a walk, caught her breath, crossed over to the southbound lane and headed back, slowing her pace a bit to give the SF major more time.

When she got to the next street, West Tambay, she could see the Jetta in its parking spot, its occupant still behind the wheel. Glancing to her right, she caught a gray-and-blue form streaking across the street and disappearing between buildings. She hoped Jennings could find a clear path to the next street.

Slowing again, she approached the intersection with West Knights, just in time to see the Jetta pulling into traffic. The car turned right and headed down Bayshore. But before the turn, she'd clearly seen the face of the driver.

Jennings was running toward the intersection from further down West Tambay, but he slowed as he approached the corner. Jo joined him as he bent over, hands on knees, breathing heavily. "I saw him pull out," he said when he'd caught his breath.

"I got a good look at him," Jo said. "It was Harrison, all right."

Jennings stood and looked south down Bayshore. The Jetta was long gone. "What the hell was he doing here?"

"This isn't the first time he's been watching me," Jo said. She told him about the night she'd come out of the theater to see Harrison waiting for her. "Have you seen him anywhere besides the base?"

"Not that I can recall," Jennings said. "I don't even know where he lives." He looked at Jo. "Could it be he's just interested in you? And I mean *interested* as in getting-into-the-sack interested."

"That's possible," she said, "but I didn't get that vibe from him when we were having a drink after the movie."

"Well, I don't like it," Jennings said. "I think we should take it to the colonel."

Jo shook her head. "Keith, if he's hanging around me because he's just... well, that's not really the colonel's business."

"Yes, it is," Keith said. "We're about to deploy on a highly sensitive, potentially dangerous mission. If he's just acting like a moonstruck kid, that's bad enough. But if there's something more to this, that's even worse. I'm not going into the field with a guy like that."

Jo thought that over, forcing herself to look at it objectively. Jennings was right. "Okay. But I don't want to talk to Will first. If this was any other situation, I'd ask him what's going on, privately. But this is different."

"Damn right it is. Staff meeting tomorrow morning after P.T. All the cards go on the table."

***

He hated the view. It was a beautiful spring day, but Edward Flanagan's perspective from this side of the White House wasn't nearly as good as it was from the opposite side. Facing south made all the difference, and not just for the view. The boss's office was on that side, and the offices nearest to his were reserved for his closest aides, including the chief of staff. When you looked out a window from that side, you saw the Rose Garden in all its glory, especially at this time of year. You could see the president's helicopter, Marine One, landing and then taking off, and sometimes that helicopter would have you on board.

Marine One never landed on the North Lawn. Nothing much happened on this side. At least, outside the walls. Inside, even on a holiday, things were happening all the time.

The phone on the National Security Advisor's desk buzzed, and the light that flashed was for his private line, the one that was not routed through the White House switchboard. Less than six months in this job and he still got a thrill when that line lit up, because whoever was on the other end always had very important information for him, or was calling in response to his request, ready to receive his orders.

He picked up the receiver, punched the button, and said, "Flanagan."

"This is Preston."

"Roger, how are things at Langley today?" the NSA asked the Acting Director of Central Intelligence.

"Not good. Our man in Tampa thinks they made him."

Flanagan sat down at his desk. "Define 'they,' please."

"Two of the operatives, Jennings and Geary."

"Is he sure?"

"Not completely," Preston said, "but he anticipates

something will happen tomorrow. Probably in the morning. There's a staff meeting down there."

The NSA picked up a pencil and began doodling on a pad. It was something he did to help him deal with tension, an old habit from college. Lately he'd been doing it a lot. "Was he careless?"

There was a sigh on the other end. "He says no, but I'm not sure. To tell you the truth, I don't think his heart's in it. I think he really wants to be on the team, go on the mission."

The pencil snapped. "For Christ's sake! I thought you said we could rely on him!"

The voice at the other end hardened. "I said he was really our only choice. He would be reliable, but only to a point."

Flanagan forced himself to calm down. "So now he's at that point, is that it?"

"Evidently."

The NSA found another pencil in the middle drawer and began tapping it on the pad.

"What do you suggest we do?" the ADCI finally asked.

"I'm thinking about it."

"Well, you'd better think fast. Webster's coming in tomorrow and he's going to start cleaning house."

Flanagan knew all about William Webster, who was leaving his post as Director of the FBI after nine years to take over at Langley. Preston had been serving as Acting Director since Casey stepped down in December. Less than twenty-four hours from now he would go back to being Deputy Director, and his influence would decline precipitously, at least in the area Flanagan wanted him to influence.

"You still don't know what he'll say about Pallas Group?" the NSA asked.

"We haven't discussed it. In any event, it's being run out of Weinberger's office. The DCI has a say in it, but not the final say. That's from your boss, you'll recall."

"You don't have to remind me," Flanagan said, nearly cracking the second pencil. Since taking over this office from the disgraced John Poindexter he'd been trying his damnedest to rein in the cowboys running around the Pentagon and Langley. Unfortunately, that was proving difficult to do, primarily because the man he worked for thought he was a cowboy himself.

"Geary's going to be a problem," the ADCI said.

"The girl?" Flanagan had seen photos of her. Very nice indeed, reminding him a lot of one of the more exotic hooch maids he'd had in Vietnam. She'd done very well at keeping his plumbing clean.

"No, her father," Preston said. "He's been a prime supporter of Pallas, as you know. The word is that SNOW LEOPARD was given to him personally by RAWHIDE."

Christ, he hated that code name for the president. Just another cowboy thing. Why couldn't it have been something more dignified? Like his predecessor's, DEACON. But that was just one more reason why men like Flanagan were needed to save this administration from itself. "I'll work on that from this end. When do they deploy?"

"In three weeks. Right after RAWHIDE gets back from Berlin."

The NSA flipped a page on his desktop calendar.

"You have to get Webster to kill the mission no later than... call it the tenth of June. He's not going to Berlin, is he?"

"No, but you are."

"I know. You have to work on him and try to get him to show Geary the door. Without Geary to muck things up, we can lean on Weinberger." He sat back in his chair, his confidence rising again. "We can stay in touch from Germany if we have to. It would be better if we could get it done before the trip. The closer we get to their deployment, the harder it will be. Once they get over there, it may well be impossible."

There was a moment of silence on the line, and then Preston said, "Perhaps we should reconsider our direction here."

The NSA immediately knew where this was going, but he asked the question anyway. "What do you mean?"

"Would it be such a bad thing if SNOW LEOPARD succeeds?"

"Look, I don't give a rat's ass about the guy with the birthmark. His whole place is going to fall down anyway, whether he's around or not. If he's not it just might take a little longer. My concern is this outfit. If they pull off this mission, they'll get another one, and it'll only be a matter of time before they're sent someplace they shouldn't go." That's how this whole damned Nicaragua thing had started. RAWHIDE's heart was in the right place, Flanagan had to give him that; the president certainly couldn't allow the Cubans and Soviets to set up client states in Central America, but he'd put some loose cannons in charge of the operation and now here they were, with Congress falling all over themselves holding hearings and the Democrats thinking they just might have a shot in '88. The NSA sighed, then reverted back to the collegial, we're-all-friends-here tone that had always served him so well. "Roger, you know what's going on. We're trying to keep our nuts out of the fire over here. I don't need another fire to pop up when this one burns out. We have to stick together on this, or we're all going to be looking for work in a couple years."

"All right. I'm with you. You know that, don't you?"

The NSA relaxed a little. He looked around the office. If he played his cards right, pretty soon he might have one of those offices facing the South Lawn. If not in this administration, then in the next. If he could get RAWHIDE through this boondoggle, then his vice president, TIMBERWOLF, was a shoo-in for his own term, and he would need someone to fill one of those favored offices. But the NSA absolutely could not tolerate any shenanigans that would bring on another scandal. Poindexter had not survived this one. Flanagan was determined to survive. He always had. Others had fallen away, stumbling or quitting or dying, but he survived.

"I know that, Roger. Don't worry. When the time comes I'll remember who my friends are."

CHAPTER TWENTY-ONE

MACDILL AIR FORCE BASE,
FLORIDA
MAY 1987

During her drive to the base the next morning, Jo wondered how the vibe in the group would be at P.T. After their run the previous day, she'd treated Jennings to his first-ever smoothie and they'd talked about Harrison. They agreed to bring it up when the SNOW LEOPARD team met the next morning following the regular staff meeting. As upset as he was, Jennings agreed to keep a lid on it till then.

Harrison had been his usual quiet self before the run, nodding greetings to both Jo and Jennings along with everyone else. When they got inside the gym and onto the mat, Jo saw the major edging over toward the CIA officer, hoping to get paired with him in the drills.

That was something Jo wanted to avoid, so she decided to head Jennings off at the pass. "Okay, people, it's boy-girl today." With a nod, she motioned Denise Reinecke, the Marine Corps major, to pair up with Jennings, while Jo chose Harrison. Jennings gave her a look, but she ignored it. The SF major quickly had other things to think about, as Reinecke easily parried his first strike and took him to the mat with an efficient hip toss.

The class went well. In the women's locker room after the workout, Jo thought again about the dynamic between Harrison and Jennings. It had been almost a month since they started working in the unit, yet she'd never seen the two men spending any time together other than what was strictly required in the office or on the mat. They went to the base's firing ranges separately. Jo almost always did her shooting with Denise, who had proven to be a definite asset to Pallas in a very short time. Jo could easily see her becoming an effective field officer.

But now, with SNOW LEOPARD only a few weeks away, Jo was seriously concerned about the ability of the mission team to work together in what would surely be a hostile, dangerous environment. Today would be crucial. Harrison was scheduled to conduct a class on urban tradecraft and operating in a Warsaw Pact capital. Their lives might depend on getting this right. She had no desire to spend any time in a Soviet gulag.

Jo sat on a bench to pull her boots on. She rather liked going to work every day in mufti. Today she'd chosen a new pair of Calvin Klein jeans to go with a cream-colored top and a new pair of gray, low-topped boots. Denise had been giving her some fashion tips, and Jo still had a ways to go. Right now the Marine major was standing at the small vanity counter, touching up her makeup in the mirror, wearing nothing but a pair of leopard-print panties. Jo had to appreciate a body like that. Three inches taller than Jo, Denise had the build of an Olympic athlete, and in fact had been a hurdler on the Naval Academy women's track team. She'd held her own against Jennings in the drills.

"Say, Jo," Reinecke said, "what's up with Keith this morning?"

"What do you mean?" Jo asked, hoisting the strap of her gym bag over her shoulder.

"He seemed preoccupied. I asked him out to dinner tonight and he just said he'd get back to me." She put her hands on her hips and stared at the mirror. Jo could read her mind: How could any man not say yes to this?

Sexual tension in the unit was the last thing Pallas needed right now, on top of everything else. "I don't know, Denise," Jo said, "I'm not sure if it's a good idea to date within the office."

"It's just two colleagues having dinner, Jo," she said, and gave Jo a sly grin. "Don't worry. My dad told me, 'Don't get your meat where you get your bread.'" Seeing Jo's awkward expression, she laughed. "My dad's a Marine too. He tends to be rather blunt."

***

Colonel Teller efficiently dispensed with the few items on the morning's agenda. Jo could sense he was aware that something was not right. After a half-hour, he said, "All right, that's it for the regular morning brief. Except for the mission team, everybody's dismissed." He nodded to Anastas, the Navy lieutenant commander. "Ed, I want you to stay for this, too."

"Aye aye, sir," Anastas said, sitting down again. Denise was the last person out of the room, carefully closing the door behind her with a quick look at Jo. Perceptive as always, the Marine surely knew something was going on.

Teller leaned back in his chair, but he was not relaxed. "All right, what the hell's going on here? I've sat in warmer rooms in Alaska in January."

"We have a problem," Jo said. She and Jennings had talked briefly during the run about how to get this out in the open. She was senior, so she'd offered to bring it up. With a glance to her right at Harrison, who returned it evenly, she related the events of the previous day, adding her encounter with the CIA officer a few nights earlier outside the movie theater. She didn't mention how she'd shared a drink with him that night.

"You want to tell us what's going on, Will?" Teller asked. Jennings sat with his arms crossed, frowning across the table at Harrison. At the far end, Anastas looked worried.

Jo was hoping Harrison would claim both incidents were merely coincidence, but his demeanor confirmed they weren't. Looking straight back at Teller, he said, "Colonel, I'm sorry, but I'm under orders."

Teller gave him a look that Jo was certain had cowed many a Marine. "Bet your ass you are. My orders. This is my outfit until General Lindsay says otherwise. So, let's have it. Or, you can leave now, and I'll have you cut loose back to Langley before lunchtime. Your choice."

Harrison fidgeted ever so slightly, then sighed. "I can probably kiss my CIA career goodbye, but what the hell." He looked at Jo. "My orders come from higher up than the DDO."

She felt a twinge of relief. As the Deputy Director of Operations, her father oversaw Harrison's unit, Special Activities Division/Special Operations Group. It had occurred to her that maybe Joseph had instructed Harrison to keep a discreet eye on her, but she could hardly imagine him being that worried.

"What exactly *are* your orders?" Jennings asked. "And who gave them?"

"The day before I came down here I was summoned to the ADCI's office. I expected Jo's father to be there, because he's DDO, after all, but it was just the Acting Director. My boss had already told me I'd gotten the Pallas billet, of course, and I assumed the ADCI just wanted to wish me luck, but he had something else in mind."

"Which was?" Jo asked.

Harrison looked at her, then back at the colonel. "I was instructed to run light surveillance on Pallas Group senior members off base, and keep him informed of our activities and plans. I was to report to him personally."

Jo could see a dark cloud forming on Teller's brow. "How often do you report?" the colonel asked.

"I was told to call in weekly," Harrison said, "but I've only made two reports in the five weeks we've been down here, and neither of them had much to say."

Jennings' eyebrows raised. "Only two?"

Harrison looked the SF major straight in the eye. "That's right, Major. I've been putting them off. I never liked the idea of being a snitch and I like it even less now that I've had a chance to work with all of you." He paused, looking at each of them. "When I first heard about this outfit spinning up, I decided I really wanted to be a part of it. I told ADCI that and said I didn't want to jeopardize my position. He told me not to worry about it. But I do worry about it." He paused again, then said,

"Look, I'm sorry. I know I'm history now, but I want Pallas Group to succeed. I like working with all of you. This outfit has a chance to make a real difference."

Harrison's words hung in the air. Finally, Jo said, "Why do you think they wanted you to do this, Will?"

"'They'?" Jennings said.

"Nobody at Langley ever does anything without clearing it with someone higher up," Jo said. "Trust me on that one. If the Acting Director was telling Will to report back to him on what we're doing, he's reporting to someone higher up the food chain."

Anastas spoke for the first time since he'd taken his seat again. "Who's higher than the head of the CIA?"

"The White House," Teller said. "The DCI sits on the National Security Council, which is chaired by the president."

That brought another pause to the room. Jo finally said, "I can't imagine the president doing this. He was the one who gave my father SNOW LEOPARD."

"He's not," Teller said. "Someone else on the NSC is pulling ADCI's chain on this one."

"Who? Who else is on the NSC anyway?" Jennings asked.

"By statute, the vice president and the secretaries of State, Defense and Energy," Jo said. She and her father had talked about the NSC's work more than once.

Jennings again: "Anybody else?"

"Besides the DCI, or the acting DCI in this case, the Attorney General normally sits in," the colonel said. "Throw in the White House chief of staff and the National Security Advisor, and the Chairman of the Joint Chiefs."

"One or more of those gave ADCI the idea," Jennings said. He looked at Harrison. "Any ideas on that?"

"My money's on the NSA," the CIA officer said. "He just came on board a few months ago, and the word around SAD/SOG is that he and the ADCI are pretty chummy."

"Did Preston actually say anything about that when you met with him?" Teller asked, using the ADCI's name for the first time.

"No," Harrison said, "but he used the word *we* a few times. As in, 'We need to keep an eye on things pretty closely these days, Will.'"

"The Iran-Contra hearings," Jo said. Things were starting to add up for her, and she could see the men were doing their arithmetic, too.

"Fucking politicians," Jennings said. "Can't leave well enough alone." Anastas and Harrison nodded their agreement.

"All right," Teller said, "I hate politics as much as any of you do, but we've all been around the block enough times to know that we can't really get away from it, except maybe when we're in the field. So we've got some pretty critical eyes on us. We shouldn't be surprised at that."

"So what do we do now, Colonel?" Anastas asked.

"We do what we're being paid to do. We have a mission and we deploy pretty damn soon."

"Without Will?" Jo asked. She didn't like the idea of a teammate spying on them, but she sensed Harrison was still one of the good guys.

"I don't want to be going into a deployment and have to worry about watching my back," Jennings said.

Another pause. Jo said, "Maybe we can use this to our advantage."

"How so?" the colonel asked.

"Let Will tell them things aren't going well down here. In fact, we might have to bag the mission entirely. We keep the fiction going right up until we're in the air heading to Europe. By the time we get on the ground over there, it'll be too late for them to recall us."

"They can abort the mission whenever they want," Jennings said.

"Not really," Teller said. "Once we get the 'go' order, only SOCOM can call us back, and Lindsay answers to the Joint Chiefs. I know Admiral Crowe, and he won't give that order unless he gets it directly from SecDef, who would get it right from the president. I think we're in good shape once we get in the air."

The colonel looked around the room. "That means Will stays on board," he said. "Keith, Jo, you have a say in this. If you say no, Will's out and we read Ed into the mission. It'll make things a little tougher for you over there."

Jo didn't hesitate. "I want him along. Will has more experience behind the Curtain than all of us put together. Plus he can run interference with our CIA contacts over there."

Teller looked at Jennings. "Keith?"

Jennings stared at Harrison, then said, "Okay."

Harrison slumped back in his seat and exhaled. "Thanks, guys. I won't let you down."

"If you do," Jennings said, "you'd better hope we're in different cells in the gulag."

CHAPTER TWENTY-TWO

GYÖR, HUNGARY
JUNE 1987

On the surface, a handball match appeared to be an unusual place for intelligence officers to meet, but in this western Hungarian city handball was king. Tonight the match was between the local women's club, Györi Glaboplast ETO, and the visitors from Debrecen. Grechko had found a seat toward the top of the bleachers, with no other spectators within several meters. Soon after the match began, he was joined by Pataki, the MIA officer he'd met in Budapest during his reconnaissance mission. How long ago was that? It seemed ages, yet it was barely more than a month. Before departing the capital, Grechko had told Pataki about the signal to be used in the event Grechko wanted another meeting, and now here they were.

The Hungarian seemed to be entirely too interested in the action on the court. "I did not know you were such a fan," Grechko remarked once guarded pleasantries had been exchanged, followed by Pataki's suppressed yell of encouragement as a red-clad Debrecen player made a spectacular play.

"It is practically our national sport," Pataki said.

"Our women took bronze at the '76 Olympics, the first time women's handball was in the Games."

"What about 1980?" Grechko asked, although he already suspected the answer.

Pataki frowned. "We did not medal in Moscow. And in '84, of course, we boycotted the Los Angeles games, along with our fraternal socialist allies." He snorted. "Except for the Yugoslavs, and they wound up winning the gold."

"Someday the men in Belgrade will need help from *their* fraternal socialist allies, and then where will they be?" Grechko said. He gestured toward the court. "They are certainly athletic," he said. He appreciated athletes for their dedication and willingness to sacrifice. In his youth he had played ice hockey, like so many Soviet boys, but he'd especially liked kickboxing. Even today he followed the sport, although his last match was more than fifteen years in the past. He'd been keeping an eye on a strapping young lad from Kiev named Klitschko, Lately, though, he'd been a bit too preoccupied to follow sport.

His first order of business this evening was to re-establish the sense of comradeship he'd begun with the younger man in Budapest. "And these women are attractive," he added with a chuckle. "They would prove a challenge in bed, would they not?"

"A challenge indeed, as I have heard that most of them are lesbians," Pataki said. "But I don't think we are here to discuss the sexual proclivities of our women handballers, my friend, as interesting as that might be." He paused as the crowd roared in approval of a goal by the home team. "What can I do for you, comrade?"

This was the point where Grechko had to make a leap of faith. Perhaps "faith" was not the correct word, in a nominally atheistic society, but that's what it was, to be sure. Before they parted in Bratislava, Voloshin told him that Pataki could be trusted. Now that would be tested.

"Comrade, I am told that you are one of the bright young stars of your service. Therefore I am going to assume you are politically astute as well as professionally competent."

Pataki hesitated, then said, "I pay attention to things, comrade. In my profession that is necessary." He glanced at the Ukrainian. "I suspect it is in yours as well."

Grechko nodded. "I am also informed that you can be trusted to assist me with a matter that requires a considerable degree of circumspection."

"My superior passed the message to me, along with instructions to assist you in whatever way I can. How may I be of service?"

"Tell me, what is your opinion of General Secretary Gorbachev?"

The Hungarian was quiet as the crowd roared again. Three rows in front of them, two young men exchanged what the West knew as a "high five." On the court, two of the green-clad Győr players hugged to celebrate a fine defensive play.

"Some say he is a man of vision," Pataki said carefully. "Others are not so sure."

"And what group do you see yourself in?"

Another silence, then, "The latter."

Grechko nodded, making his decision. "What I am about to tell you is most secret. To reveal anything about our conversation, or any subsequent activities we might engage in as a result, could very well bring on the most serious consequences." He looked at the younger man. "Do you understand what I am saying?"

Pataki answered the look with one of his own. "Perfectly, comrade."

***

The night club, according to Pataki, was known as one of Györ's most Westernized establishments. Grechko found the atmosphere uncomfortably loud, with blaring German techno-rock and flashing lights. In America they would have called it a "disco," which he had visited on his earlier visits to the land of his greatest enemy. He hadn't liked them, either, but had to concede they were fruitful sources of potential assets. The people who frequented them were almost uniformly young, idealistic, impressionable. That was true everywhere, Grechko had discovered, and he had every reason to believe it would be the same here in Hungary.

It was Pataki who had suggested this club after hearing what Grechko wanted to do. "The place you're referring to," the MIA agent had said, "is about halfway between here and Budapest. Many who work there live in this city, especially those who work during the summer tourist season. We have a good chance of finding one or two of them at this place."

Now, he and the Hungarian sat at a small table along the back wall. As usual, Grechko had taken a seat giving him a view of the entrance, and he also knew where the back exit was, beyond the lavatories.

Although he thought his chances of arrest at the hands of KGB were considerably less here in Hungary than they had been in Poland, he was not inclined to take chances.

Pataki gestured toward a group of young women dancing on the wood floor, multicolored lights flashing above them. "Those four," he said. "Two are from the Glaboplast team. I saw their team jackets when they came in."

Grechko had seen them as well. "And the other two?"

"Students, I believe, probably at the engineering school here. It is possible one or both might work at the place in question, or at least know someone who does."

The Soviet agent nodded his agreement. "I will leave you to make the approach, comrade," he said. "I noticed a bar down the block. I will wait for you there."

Pataki gave him a sly smile. "Based on what I saw in Budapest, I would say your ability to impress these ladies would be the equal of mine, if not superior."

"Different place, different atmosphere and certainly different women," Grechko said. "You are younger than I am, my friend, and you know this city and its people." He rose. "I'll see you at the bar."

***

It was an hour later that Pataki entered the bar with two young women. Grechko had assumed that his first possibilities hadn't panned out, and indeed these two women had not been among the group of four they'd initially targeted. Grechko also noticed that the women were already somewhat inebriated.

"Erich, look what I have found!" Pataki announced in German. The girls giggled, and the taller of the two, a blonde, slid into the booth next to Grechko. Pataki and the brunette took the seat across from them.

For this phase of the operation Grechko had chosen a "legend" that had often served him well, that of an officer in the East German Air Force, the *Luftstreitkräfte.* He was fluent in German and with this identity, backed up by his expertly—and illegally—crafted credentials, he was able to maintain a degree of his natural military bearing, adding a bit of verbal and physical swagger common to fighter pilots. Pataki, also fluent in the language, was now playing the role of his second cousin, escorting his older relative during his leave in Hungary.

"Hi!" the blonde said, squeezing Grechko's arm. "Georg says you are a pilot. What kind of planes do you fly?"

"Lately, the Su-22 fighter-bomber," Grechko said. "Can I buy you ladies a drink?"

"Sure!" the blonde said. "I'm Anna, and this is my friend Greta."

Grechko signaled the waitress. "Four beers, please. Soproni, if you have it."

"You know your Hungarian beers, Erich," Anna said. She squeezed his arm again. "My, you have a strong arm."

"My cousin needs a lot of strength to fly those fighter planes," Pataki said helpfully.

"Is that right?" Greta asked, green eyes wide.

Grechko shrugged. "The Sukhoi, she is hard to control sometimes, you know. A firm hand is needed."

"I hope you won't be too firm with me," Anna said.

***

Grechko stared up at the ceiling of the hotel room. A stain around the light fixture spoke of the establishment's degree of dedication to proper maintenance. But, he had to admit, the bed was comfortable and the sheets were a cut above the typical light-sandpaper grade that he'd put up with on his earlier, and thankfully infrequent, visits to Russian hotels. The ever-resourceful Pataki had suggested this place, further burnishing his standing in Grechko's eyes.

From the tiny bathroom came the sound of a toilet flushing. The door opened, revealing Anna standing nude, running a brush through her hair in front of the mirror over the vanity. Satisfied, she walked back to the bed, showing a control of her equilibrium Grechko would not have expected, considering the amount of alcohol she'd consumed. Well, he thought, perhaps her orgasm had burned some of that off.

She crawled back onto the bed and lay next to him on her stomach, brushing her hand lightly over his chest, down over his abdomen and lower still, teasing him with a delicate touch. "I have heard that pilots are known for their... what's the word?"

"Ausdauer," he said. Endurance.

"That's the one," she said. "Staying power." Her fingers continued their dance.

A second time at bat, as the Americans would say, was certainly not out of the question. But first, there was business. "You have a wonderful figure," he said. "The horseback riding, I suppose?"

"Yes. I like to ride," she said, eyebrows raising briefly.

"This horse farm you work at, it is a large place?" He already knew the answer to that, having done his research.

"Bodor Major is one of the biggest in the country," she said. "Over a hundred hectares, and lots of horses. Do you ride?"

"Of course," Grechko said. "My ancestors were Prussian, known for their horsemanship. They were bourgeoisie, to be sure," he said sternly. "It is good that the workers rose up to overthrow them and their corrupt system."

"Yeah, right," she said. "Marx and Engels, rah-rah. You want to talk politics?"

"Not if you have something else in mind," he said.

She smiled, bent down and kissed him where it felt best. In her young but skilled hand, he was growing hard again. "Maybe you could come out and visit me there," she said, pausing to lick him. "I could show you a good ride."

"You already have," he said.

She laughed. "I meant a horse ride. Men! You Germans are no different than Hungarians."

"We are much more disciplined," Grechko said. He pulled her up by the shoulders and she helped by throwing her leg across him. Bringing her head close, he kissed her deeply. Against his chest, he felt her nipples harden.

"I would like to go riding with you," he said as he lifted his hips and pushed hers down. She sighed deeply as he slid inside her.

"My big German pilot," she said, starting to grind against him.

"When can I come visit you?" he asked.

She propped herself up with her arms, freeing her breasts for his attention. "Maybe next weekend," she said. "After that we have a special guest. No other visitors."

"Really?" They were starting to get into the rhythm now. He tweaked her nipples, bringing a gasp.

"Yes. The Russian, Gorbachev, he is coming to our farm for a special show."

"That must be exciting." She was exquisitely tight around him, and he forced himself to concentrate.

"And I am to be in the show," she said, pushing herself down on him to the hilt. "It is a great honor." Her hips started moving again, ever so slightly, and he loosened his grip, encouraging her to take command. "I will be doing a special performance," she breathed. "Oh!" She increased her pace.

He pulled her down to him and thrust deeply, bringing another gasp from her as he thought, So will I.

CHAPTER TWENTY-THREE

MCLEAN,
VIRGINIA
JUNE 12, 1987

"Mr. Gorbachev, open this gate!"

The crowd roared, and American flags waved by hundreds. At the podium, flanked by a reviewing stand fronted with black, red and orange bunting, Ronald Reagan paused and looked out over the huge throng. Behind him stood the twelve massive Doric gray pillars of the Brandenburg Gate, just as they had for almost exactly two hundred years, with the gold quadriga on top, a four-horse chariot driven by Eirene, the goddess of peace. Behind the gate was East Berlin, home to over a million and a quarter people, many of whom were hunkered down next to radios or television sets in their homes, listening to a broadcast that only a few years before would have meant imprisonment for those listeners, and still might.

Unseen by most of the crowd, two large panes of bulletproof glass stood guard between the speaker and possible snipers in East Berlin. The chance of such an event were small, but there was no sense in tempting fate.

"Mr. Gorbachev, tear down this wall!"

The energy of the crowd could almost be felt from the television screen, even though the scene it depicted was five thousand miles away. In virtually every conference room at CIA, in both the Original and New Headquarters buildings, TV screens carried the color image from Berlin. The groups of viewers ranged from three or four people to dozens. Conversation during the speech was muted, at most, emerging only when the speaker paused for the crowd's cheers. The overwhelming majority of comments by the viewers were favorable. Some raised questions about how this would play in certain capitals. Speculation about that was all over the spectrum.

In one particular office, it was not. The man behind the desk aimed a remote control at the TV and muted the volume, then pressed a button on his desktop intercom. "Sarah, please contact DDO Geary, let him know I'd like to see him as soon as he's available." A glance at the clock on the wall led to an additional request. "Tell him I'd like him here by ten o'clock at the latest."

A minute later, the intercom buzzed. "Mr. Preston, DDO Geary says he'll be here at ten."

"Very well. When he arrives, tell him to come right in, and hold my calls."

***

"A most impressive speech," the tall German next to Flanagan said. On the dais, the president was shaking hands and receiving congratulations from the assembled VIPs. First in line was Helmut Kohl, Chancellor of the Federal Republic.

The National Security Advisor had struggled to control his own emotions during the speech. He'd read an advance draft, had gone over it with the president and his other advisers, although the NSA's advice, careful as it was, had gone largely unheeded. He'd cautioned against needless provocations, but had been overruled.

"Sometimes it's not wise to goad the bear," Flanagan said, "especially when you're close to his den."

The German looked down at Flanagan with a look that might have been pity, contempt, or both. What was his name again? Schultz, Schmidt, whatever. He was the chairman of the *Bundessicherheitsrat,* the Federal Security Council of West Germany, and thus Flanagan's counterpart. "Perhaps, Herr Flanagan," Schultz or Schmidt said, "but the bear in question is old and sick. That is the time to goad him, is it not, when he is at his weakest?"

"It may also be the time when he's most desperate," Flanagan countered, suddenly tired of this German, of this entire country, and he'd only arrived here the day before when Air Force One touched down after its flight from Rome. At least Italy had been pleasant. The food was certainly much better. After eight days of it, though, he'd been forced to loosen his belt a notch this morning. The German, on the other hand, looked like he could've stepped right out of an old SS recruiting poster as the symbol of Aryan supremacy.

"Well, we shall see," the German said. "It appears the party is breaking up." On the dais, Kohl was escorting the president toward the stairs. Flanagan wondered if the two leaders would work the crowd.

Secret Service agents were right on the mark, waiting at the foot of the stairs. Doubtless there were several agents from *Bundeskriminalamt,* the Federal Criminal Police, on hand as well, over and above those guarding Kohl and the other German big shots. Flanagan doubted there would be any trouble.

No, if there was trouble, it would not be here in West Berlin, or in Bonn, where they were heading next. The jet was warming up at Tempelhof right now. Flanagan glanced at his watch. If Preston was on the ball, he should be giving the word to Geary right about now. If the word didn't get delivered, the trouble Flanagan feared would be taking place a week from now in another old European capital about four hundred miles away.

***

The door swung open after a quick double knock. The Deputy Director of Operations stuck his bald head in and asked, "You wanted to see me, Mr. Preston?"

The Deputy Director of Central Intelligence didn't miss the ever-so-delicate emphasis on the last two words. From day one he'd let it be known that he was never to be addressed by his first name, even by his most immediate subordinates. They were, after all, *subordinates,* and this was not a country club, despite what some people thought. "Yes, Joe, come on in, have a seat."

He waited until Geary had made himself comfortable, or as comfortable as the leather chair in front of Preston's desk would allow. That was another one of his changes. The chairs he'd inherited had been far too cozy. They'd been replaced the day after his arrival. Geary was tall enough to make this one even more cramped.

Preston began with the most obvious question. "Did you catch the speech?"

"Yes, of course," Geary answered. "He dropped a verbal bomb on them, didn't he?"

The DDCI sat back in his chair, which was very comfortable. "I rather wish he hadn't," he said.

"Why not?"

Damn, but he was obstinate. One of the first things Preston had wanted to do upon becoming Acting Director was show Geary the door. Oh, it would've been done respectfully, of course, a retirement with a nice goodbye party, maybe a gold watch, something like that. But one thing Preston had learned in his climb up the bureaucratic ladder in this town was how to read the way the winds were blowing, and he'd quickly divined that Geary was touched by a warm breeze emanating from 1600 Pennsylvania. There were ways around that, though. Now that he was no longer Acting Director, he had to be even more careful. The new Director had been a long-time FBI man and tended to side with the veterans here at CIA, and Preston was not in that group. Geary most certainly was.

"Things are at a delicate stage over in AE right now," Preston said.

"You mean the Soviet Union?"

"Why, yes, of course."

Geary's lips turned up at the corners ever so slightly. "The digraph we use now is PD."

Preston forced himself to smile. "My mistake," he said, unable to conceal a degree of tension. "Anyway,

I'm not sure we should be rocking that boat. Their skipper is rocking it enough all by himself."

"Well, it's not as if they didn't know this was coming," Geary said. "I expect that tomorrow's *Pravda* won't have anything nice to say about the speech, but I doubt if anyone in the Kremlin was surprised by the rhetoric."

"Perhaps not," Preston said, "but I think the worst thing we could do right now is anything that would make things worse over there. Words are bad enough. When we ratchet up the rhetoric, they get jumpy over there. It was right about the time of the 'Evil Empire' speech that they got Operation RYAN up and running, wasn't it?" There, that ought to impress Geary. Even though Preston had been an undersecretary at the State Department back then, he'd done his homework. Of course that had been at Flanagan's "request," but that was beside the point.

"RYAN was an intelligence collection effort that Andropov got started in '81," Geary said. "They were concerned that we might launch a surprise attack. They cranked it up a few notches after we did some naval exercises off their coasts, just to test their readiness."

"Naval exercises?" This was something Preston had not heard before.

Geary nodded. "The biggest was in '81. We put USS *Eisenhower* in the middle of a fleet of eighty-three ships. Ours, the Brits, Canadians and Norwegians, sailed them right through the GIUK Gap and they never saw us coming."

Preston had to scramble through his memory and just in time he remembered that GIUK stood for

Greenland-Iceland-United Kingdom. "Very provocative," he managed to say.

Another nod. "We went after them on their Pacific coast, too, and on their Arctic coast, which they didn't think possible. The Pacific exercises in '83 really rattled them. The CNO told Congress, now what did he say..." Geary stared at the ceiling, then said, "Oh, yeah. 'They're as naked as a jaybird there and they know it.'"

"We were lucky they didn't fire a missile at one of those ships," Preston said, trying to conceal his agitation.

"Both sides have been doing this type of brinksmanship for nearly forty years now," Geary said. "As I'm sure you know," he added dryly.

"Well, perhaps it's time we stop taking such unnecessary chances." Geary's eyes narrowed. He'd been around the block a few times, Preston knew, and was nobody's fool. Better to just put it out there. "Joe, it's a very delicate time over there and we can't afford to be unnecessarily belligerent. This SNOW LEOPARD mission has to be stopped."

Geary's eyes went wide. "I beg your pardon?"

Preston picked up a sheet of paper from his desk, glanced at it and then handed it to the DDO. "Our liaison to SOCOM, what's his name, Phillips?" In fact, Preston knew the man's name very well. In the past month he'd had two very private meetings with the assistant deputy DDO. Relatively new to CIA, Phillips was an up-and-coming, bright young man who nevertheless had made some poor decisions in his choice of friends, decisions that Preston had made clear he was willing to forget about in exchange for Phillips' cooperation in certain areas. As liaison between CIA and the new special ops command down in Florida, he was privy to some very critical information, which Preston was now privy to as well. "I want him to present that to the general down there, today. I'm pulling the plug on this operation, effective immediately."

Geary sat up a little straighter. "This is signed by the National Security Advisor."

Preston knew he was gambling now, but he had to play his cards. "Yes, I received that from the NSA just this morning, faxed from Air Force One."

"What does Director Webster have to say about this?"

Preston had to be very careful here. He wasn't sure what type of relationship, if any, existed between Webster and Geary. He didn't think they'd had any private meetings since Webster had assumed the directorship sixteen days ago, but he couldn't be sure. What he was about to do was a big gamble, but the stakes were high. "The director is in Japan right now, as you know. In his absence, I'm in charge here, and I've received no order from him that exempts decisions about Pallas Group from my authority." Technically, that was true. It was also true that Preston had not yet brought up Pallas in any of his discussions with Webster. The man had a lot on his plate, after all.

Geary eyed him carefully, and Preston had to focus on keeping his breathing steady. This was certainly different than the arguments over trade policy he'd engaged in over at State. Finally, Geary spoke. "With respect, sir, you don't have the authority to abort this mission and neither does the National Security Advisor. Pallas Group is under the command of SOCOM, which is run out of the Pentagon and SecDef's office." He spread his hands. "CIA does not have jurisdiction over that unit. I couldn't tell them what to do even if I wanted to, which I don't."

Preston didn't miss the visible toughening of Geary's body language with that last sentence. Well, two could play the tough-guy game. "I have my orders, Geary, and now so do you. Get that to Phillips and pull the plug. Today."

"Are you out of your mind?"

"Excuse me?"

"You heard me. Let me say this again: You *do not* have that authority. I don't know what kind of dumb-ass games you and Flanagan are playing, but if the two of you want SNOW LEOPARD put on ice, you'll have to get that word from someone else."

"Like who?"

Geary rose and gestured toward the TV set. "Like the guy who just gave that speech," he said. He turned and walked to the door.

Preston was on his feet now, too. Leaning on his desk, he said, "You walk out that door before I give you leave, mister, and you might as well keep walking!"

Geary paused with his hand on the doorknob. Turning back to Preston, he smiled. "Hey, I could be sitting on my veranda on St. Thomas having a mai tai by tomorrow afternoon and it wouldn't bother me a bit, you pompous ass, so if you're going to threaten me, you might want to come up with something better. You're in the big leagues now, in case you haven't noticed." He slammed the door behind him on the way out.

CHAPTER TWENTY-FOUR

MACDILL AIR FORCE BASE, FLORIDA
JUNE 15, 1987

"Any final questions?"

Teller looked at each of the three people around the table. Only two months ago Geary, Jennings and Harrison had been virtual strangers, known to each other, if at all, only by reputation. Now they were a team.

The Marine colonel had played quarterback at Wisconsin back in what now seemed like the Dark Ages, when men had short hair and women wore bras, Ike was in the White House and things were a lot simpler. In those days Teller was part of a team and loved the feeling of camaraderie, of working together and striving toward a goal, so after graduation he'd traded in his cardinal-and-white jersey for Marine Corps khaki. Things got more complicated in his country and his life, but the essence of the warrior stayed the same. Over the years he'd learned how to be one and how to help create one. These people had come to him as accomplished warriors in their own right, and in a very short time he'd molded them into a brand-new team. Damn, he was proud of them.

It hadn't taken a whole lot of molding, though.

Polishing, perhaps that was a better word. Now they were about to embark on a mission that might end badly for one or even all of them. In other words, it was another day at the office for Uncle Sam's finest.

Jennings tapped the paper on top of the pages in his file. "Colonel, is this staggered travel schedule really necessary?"

"I can take that one, Colonel," Harrison said. When Jennings looked at the CIA operative, Teller didn't miss the hint of suspicion. Progress had been made since the showdown over Harrison's activities on behalf of the NSA, but Teller knew that only the mission would ultimately show if the two men could work together smoothly. This wouldn't be the first time a team would go into the field without complete confidence in each other, and that was a situation he would rather avoid. He'd seen it in 'Nam more than once, and those teams were usually the ones that incurred the most casualties. He would've preferred another two weeks of training here to let the men forge more of a bond, but they were out of time. He nodded at Harrison.

"Operational security," Harrison said. "The less we're seen together, the better."

"I get why we split up, but why can't we do that when we get to Europe?" Jennings asked.

"An additional precaution," Harrison said. "If we show up in Amsterdam or Frankfurt on the same flight, we're easier to spot."

"If someone's watching," Jennings said.

"We can't take the chance that they won't be," Teller said. "Each of you has to establish your legend first with your travel schedule. You'll all be coming into Hungary from your supposed country of origin." He glanced down at the itinerary. "Jo has the toughest road. Tomorrow morning out of Miami to Rome, overnight there, then to Belgrade and Budapest, arriving late afternoon Wednesday. You won't have much time to shake off the jet lag." Teller didn't like the schedule, but the longer his people were behind the Curtain the riskier it would be for them. He looked at the Korean-American Air Force officer. "Get as much rest as you can, Jo, and bring some reading material," he said.

She smiled. "Some books in Russian, some in German," she said. "Hopefully the flights will have some interesting movies."

"Maybe on the Alitalia flight to Rome," Teller said. "You fly Aeroflot the rest of the way." That brought smiles from everyone. They all knew about the Soviet airline, infamous for its inefficiency and poor service. But if anybody could handle that, it would be Geary. The colonel had been wearing the uniform for more than a quarter-century and he'd never met anybody, male or female, who could match her self-discipline. That file on her op in Argentina had been one hell of a read, especially the remarks from the Brits. She'd do all right on this one.

He looked back at the paper. "Will, you go out an hour later, to JFK in New York and then across the pond to Amsterdam and then Vienna. Keith, Miami direct to London, then to Stockholm and East Berlin. Each of you overnights and then on to Budapest. You're there about twelve hours ahead of Jo, so make good use of your time. Establish your contact and get to the safe house." Teller fretted about that part. CIA was supposed to provide one of their people for in-country support, initially to get the team to a safe house, make sure they were supplied for the mission and then stand by for exfiltration if the primary exfil plan went bad. Just to be on the safe side, he'd had Geary make a call to her father earlier in the day.

"You're all set for your trip, Colonel?" Harrison asked. Teller considered him for a moment. Harrison had been true to his word, feeding bogus reports to Langley, just two since their little showdown a couple weeks ago, but they must've been good enough to keep the heat turned down because they'd not gotten an order to abort the mission. All they needed was another twelve hours or so and they'd be in the air. SOCOM could still pull the plug, but the colonel knew that would be unlikely once they left the States. Still, he was concerned.

"From here to Andrews and then direct to Ramstein," he said. He'd be on military flights all the way, from base to base until arriving in West Germany. He'd monitor the mission from Patch Barracks in Stuttgart, using the facilities of Special Operations Command, Europe. "SOCEUR will have everything I'll need to keep an eye on you," he said.

"Except backup," Jennings said.

"We'll have some from our CIA station at the embassy in Budapest," Harrison said. "Director Geary has assured us of that."

"Well, if we're out in the field somewhere and need exfil, there won't be any choppers coming in to get us," Jennings said.

"I thought you Green Beret guys were trained to live off the land for a while," Jo said.That drew a grin from Teller. The popular theme among the Marines was that anybody who wasn't a Marine was a candy-ass, even Green Beanies, but he knew from experience in Vietnam and elsewhere that was far from the truth. There was nothing wrong with a little good-natured ribbing, though, and Geary's dry humor was usually just what the doctor ordered. From the way Jennings smiled and shook his head, he knew this was one of those times. Kudos to the zoomie.

"Let's just hope it doesn't come to that," Jennings said. "If we have to hump it overland all the way to Austria, I don't know if you two will be able to keep up."

"Okay, kiddies, let's wrap this up," Teller said. He glanced at the clock on the wall. "It's better than four hours from here to Miami. You're sure you want to drive it? The motor pool has your car ready, but I could whistle up some air to get you down there."

"Travel security starts now, Colonel," Harrison said. "We can take one vehicle down there but when we hit town we split up to different hotels. Cabs to the airport in the morning."

"All right, then you'd better get moving," Teller said. He rose, and everybody else came to their feet as well. "Try to stay out of trouble till you get there. Happy hunting."

***

It was Bermuda again. The beach stretched out before her, endless white sands, the surf lapping up around her feet. She dug her toes eagerly into the wet sand and threw her head back, soaking in the warm sun. The breeze caressed her bare breasts.

Ian was there, as always, with his cocky British

smile, the broad shoulders and back trained to peak performance by the Special Boat Squadron and arms that could pound out a hundred pushups or hold her tenderly. “You look terrific,” he said. “I want you, Jo. Now.”

She went to him, into his arms. “The war will come soon,” he whispered, holding her close. “I won’t come back.”

The tears came again, and now she was on another beach, much farther south, at night with Ian next to her, a bullet in his side, and men coming for them. One leveled a rifle.

BANG!

She awoke with a start, orienting herself in a split-second, and sat up in the back seat. From beneath her she felt the unnatural thumping. “What happened?” she asked.

Jennings fought the wheel and quickly regained control. “Flat tire,” he said, steering the car toward the shoulder. In the passenger seat, Harrison shook his head and loosed a curse. “Lights up ahead,” Jennings said. “I don’t think I can make it there.”

“Don’t try,” Harrison said. “We’ll change the tire here.”

Jo checked her watch as the car shuddered to a stop. Seven-thirty, two and a half hours since leaving the base. “Any idea where we are?” she asked.

“Just east of Nowhere, South Florida,” Jennings said. “Another two hours to Miami.” He unbuckled his seat belt, checked the side mirror and waited as an eighteen-wheeler roared past. “Hope the spare’s good.”

Harrison and Jo joined him on the shoulder. The right rear tire was the culprit. Jennings opened the trunk and in a minute had removed their luggage and pulled out the spare and the jack. “Shit. It’s one of those new doughnuts,” he said. “Terrific. We can’t make it to Miami with this damn thing. How far to the next town?”

“Twenty miles,” Harrison said, clicking on a flashlight. “Let’s hope they have an all-night garage.”

“It’s not that late,” Jo said. “Good thing we started out when we did, even if it meant skipping dinner.”

Harrison was looking down the road. “About a mile to that place,” he said. “Looks like a roadhouse. Maybe they have burgers.”

“I’ll check it out,” Jo said. The evening was warm but not too humid. The walk would do her good. She needed to put the dream away.

“You okay?” Harrison asked. “You were mumbling something back there.”

“Hold the light, for crissakes,” Jennings said as he popped the hubcap and began his assault on the lug nuts.

***

The first sign of potential trouble was the half-dozen motorcycles in the gravel parking lot, along with four pickup trucks, all of them with Confederate-flag bumper stickers or window decals, most of them more than one. But a neon sign in the window did say BURGE S, and Jo assumed that at one time there’d been an R in there.

Everything about the place told her she should turn around and head back to the car, help the guys with the tire and ride with them to the next town, but she was here and now she felt the urge to use the bathroom. There was also the slight possibility that they might actually have something decent to eat inside. She opened the door and the muffled music turned into full-bore Hank Williams Jr. The smell of smoke and stale beer was right on Hank's heels, along with the aroma of fried food. Her stomach roiled, a combination of hunger and revulsion. It had been years since she'd had a hamburger, but she supposed she could deal with the grease tonight if that's all they had.

Four men in jeans, sleeveless shirts and bandanas surrounded a pool table. At the bar, four other men sat on stools, two dressed like the pool players, two others wearing ball caps. Jo counted two occupied booths along the far wall, each with a young man and woman in residence. The bartender was filling a glass from a beer tap, and a chubby waitress banged out of the double doors at the end of the bar with two plates of food, heading for the booths. Of the fourteen pairs of eyes in the room, all but two focused immediately on the newcomer.

First things first. Past the bar next to the kitchen was an entryway to what Jo assumed was the location of the restrooms. As she began walking, the pool game resumed but most of the eyes in the place didn't leave her. Senses alive, she took in the surroundings, noting the rear exit to the left of the kitchen doors, down another hallway. Some of the men had tattoos on their upper arms, and she saw what appeared to be crudely applied prison ink on some of their hands. Two of the men sitting at the bar and at least two of the pool players had slender bulges in their pockets that most likely indicated knives. In the booths, the two women now looked at her and the looks weren't friendly. One last impression registered as she reached the entrance to the ladies' room: all the people in the place, except for her, were Caucasian.

Much to her relief, the rest room was actually fairly clean. She made sure to wet a paper towel and wipe the ring on the toilet, then dry it with another towel. Completing her business, she washed her hands and took care to dry them completely. The only weapons she might be able to deploy out there were cue sticks and it wouldn't do to have slippery hands.

Neither Jennings nor Harrison were in the bar. She considered leaving but when her stomach rumbled again, she decided to at least have a look at the menu, then report back to the men. Besides, her parents had always told her that to simply use a business's restroom without buying something was rude.

She chose one of the four empty booths along the wall past the pool table, at right angles from the four booths on the kitchen side. The location put the pool table between her and both exits, but the fact that these four were empty gave her fewer immediate threats to consider. Sliding a plastic-covered two-sided menu from behind the napkin dispenser, she had a sudden longing for the day when she would be able to sit down in a restaurant without having to think tactically.

The waitress appeared. "Howdy," she said in a friendly Southern drawl. "What can I getcha?"

"Just a glass of water for now," Jo said, returning the smile. "I have two friends outside, and we might be ordering some food before we move on."

"That'd be right fine," she said. "Special tonight's

chicken-fried steak. Jimmy's own home-style gravy, mashed potatoes, four-ninety-five for the plate."

Her stomach did another roll. "Thanks."

"Be back in a sec' with your water."

It took about fifteen, but the waitress brought back a tall glass with ice. "Just wave when you want to order," she said, then turned and sashayed back to the bar. Hank had turned the jukebox over to Reba McEntire, who was warbling something about her husband up in Massachusetts.

It took Jo only another few seconds to scan the menu. Fried, fried and more fried. Well, it would have to do. Where were the guys? It was taking much too long to change that tire.

"Eight ball in the corner," one of the pool players said, and when he sank the shot he hooted in triumph. "Another five-spot goes to a good home, Joe Bob. Wanna donate another one?"

"I'm done, Pete. Hey, ask the lady there."

Pete swaggered around the table and approached her, chalking up his cue. "Hey, sugar, how 'bout it? They shoot pool in Tokyo, don't they?"

"I'm sure they do," Jo said, "but no, thank you." She took a sip of the water. Everything would depend on what Pete and his buddies did next.

"Maybe she ain't a Jap, Pete," another one of the bikers said. "One o' them Viet-nam-ese, maybe?"

"Hope not," Joe Bob said, an edge in his voice. "My brother got killed fightin' them gooks." He took two determined steps over to stand near Pete. "So, you from Hanoi, are you?"

So, it would be like this. She sighed as anger flared inside her. All these years of protecting this country and she had to put up with this racist clown? Collecting herself, she began sliding into mushin, tapping back the anger. “Actually, gentlemen,” she said, “my mother was from Korea. Her country survived because of the heroism of Americans, like my father.” She set the menu aside and slid out of the booth. They could find a place to eat in the next town while the tire was being fixed.

“Well, I ‘preciate that, even if ol’ Joe Bob don’t,” Pete said. “Whyn’t you an’ me just have ourselves a dance?”

“No thanks,” Jo said. She took a step to go past him, but he put a meaty hand on her shoulder.

“We ain’t had that dance yet, sugar. Sit your pretty little ass back down while Joe Bob here picks out a good slow–”

“I’ll lead,” Jo said. She reached for the hand with her right, cupping it and bending the fingers back. With her left she guided Pete’s elbow back and then around and up, shoving his hand toward his armpit. The big man gasped and did exactly what Jo expected, trying to bend forward to relieve the pressure. She guided him a little more and bent him backward instead. Disoriented, surprised and off-balance, Pete would now go where she wanted him to go.

“Hey!” Joe Bob stepped forward and brought his cue stick up. Jo maneuvered Pete around and slammed him belly-first into the pool table. His cue stick bounced back and Jo grabbed it in the air. Releasing Pete’s hand and its now-dislocated fingers, she brought the stick around and parried Joe Bob’s awkward strike, retaliating with a sharp jab into his solar plexus with the base end of the stick, then an uppercut strike into the chin. Joe Bob careened back against the table and collapsed to the floor.

The men who had been watching the pool game stopped their advance as Jo whipped the stick around and into a ready position, as she had thousands of times with her *bo* in the dojo. She could now deal with either of them if they attacked with their own sticks, but if anybody brought out a knife or, worse, a handgun, all bets were off. Defending against a knife or gun might involve using lethal force, and that would mean the police would get involved. Their mission would be over. For three tense seconds the men hesitated. None of the men at the bar or in booths moved, but they were all watching her.

The outside door opened and Jennings stepped in, followed closely by Harrison. They took in the scene and Jennings asked, “You okay, Jo? Sorry it took so long, we lost a couple lug nuts.”

“Hey, man, we don’t want no trouble,” one of the bikers said, backing away from the pool table with his hands raised. On the floor, Pete sat massaging his hand, grimacing in pain. Joe Bob was out cold; he’d hit his head on the floor.

“You folks want some food, it’s on the house,” the bartender said.

“We’ll pass, thank you,” Jo said. She set her stick on the table and stepped around Pete, who eyed her with a mix of fear and bewilderment.

One of the men at the bar clapped and said, “Shit fire, I never seen anything like that. Right outta a Bruce Lee movie.”

“He was my teacher,” Jo said. She headed to the door. To Jennings she said, “Let’s go get that tire fixed.”

CHAPTER TWENTY-FIVE

WASHINGTON, D.C.
JUNE 15, 1987

Flanagan sat back in his chair and massaged his temples, trying to work out the last of the jet lag. The return flight from Bonn had landed two days ago, but unlike RAWHIDE, Flanagan and the rest of the peons didn't have the luxury of a bedroom on board. Even though his seat was as comfortable as one he'd find in first class of the world's best airline, he'd slept fitfully.

He spent part of the trip back with the reporters, continuing his quest to cultivate a select handful. Fortunately a couple of the ones he'd targeted were on the press list this time. Flanagan knew he didn't have the gift that some of his colleagues had; there were people in this building who had reporters eating out of their hand after ten minutes. The president himself was first among equals in that regard. Still, the National Security Advisor had been able to win over two of them, a columnist from the *Washington Post* and a correspondent from CBS News. Neither of them were on the first string with their respective organizations, but they were better than nothing. The *Post* writer, Arnold Sanders, had proven particularly useful in Flanagan's bid to move U.S. foreign policy in a new, post-Iran-Contra direction.

All it took, really, was a tidbit here and there, some of them really no more than inferences or rumors he'd picked up in the West Wing and which had proven to be completely vacuous. But like every media personality he'd ever met, they lapped it all up and Sanders was no exception. Every newspaper reporter fancied himself the next Woodward or Bernstein, every TV personality wanted to be the next Rather or Donaldson. He'd found the women in the media to be particularly aggressive. He'd heard stories that certain of them were more than willing to get between the sheets with a source, but Flanagan wondered if that was more locker-room braggadocio than fact. In any event, he had not yet had a reporter take it that far with him. There were two or three he found intriguing in that respect, but he'd wait for them to make the first move.

At the moment he was more concerned with Preston over at CIA. His report of the disastrous meeting with Geary had not been well received by the NSA. In fact, Flanagan thought it entirely possible that Preston's days at Langley were numbered. It would not be out of the question for Geary to complain to Webster about the DDCI, and Webster could very well make a move that would not be one Flanagan wanted. Worse yet, Webster had RAWHIDE's ear. Flanagan would have to proceed very carefully; if he were linked to Preston, they might go down together.

Preston's latest news was even more discouraging. The SNOW LEOPARD team had gone dark as of mid-day yesterday. The last report from Harrison, three days earlier, indicated there was a rising level of distrust and even confusion in Pallas Group about the mission to Hungary. But Flanagan was beginning to wonder about that. If the team was now off the radar, that could mean they were being deployed on schedule. And that would mean Harrison's reports might have been bogus all along. Had the man been playing Preston? Flanagan could not discount the possibility.

Harrison could not be counted on, that was now clear, but fortunately, Flanagan had a backup plan. That was one thing he'd learned early on: don't put all your cards on the table unless you have an unbeatable hand. SOCOM had proven to be an extraordinarily tightly-run operation in an amazingly short span of time. The NSA grudgingly concluded that the people down at MacDill really knew their business. Good for the country, but not very good for him. Well, he had that one final card to play, a risky one to be sure, but it appeared it might prove necessary to play it.

From what he'd learned in Europe, he was convinced his course was correct. The West Germans, naïve as always, were optimistic about the course of the relationship between NATO and the Soviet Union. All the West had to do to win the Cold War was sit tight, they said, and let events in Moscow play themselves out. In fact, they were already starting to talk about the challenges that would come when the two Germanys were reunited. Flanagan wasn't so sure that was a wise course for future American policy. A reunified Germany would quickly become an even bigger economic and political powerhouse on the Continent than the Federal Republic already was, and that could only mean a further diminution of American influence. And had anybody thought of what would replace communism in Russia if the Soviet Union fell?

That was only one of the problems that could be complicated by this blasted Pallas Group. It was only a matter of time before they got into something they shouldn't, and then the shit storm would be even worse than Iran-Contra.

One problem at a time, he thought, checking his daily agenda once again. Every item on it was trivial, even mundane. This was not going to be one of the days he enjoyed, a day when he could shape events rather than simply help manage them. Some days were like that, though, like it or not. He reached for the top file from his IN box.

The private line on his phone buzzed. "Flanagan."

"Ed, this is Arnie," the voice said. The NSA quickly tamped down the irritation of having a reporter address him by his first name. After all, he'd given Sanders permission.

"Arnie, good to hear from you. Got over your jet lag yet?"

"Pretty much. How about you?"

"I hit the gym pretty hard yesterday, so I'm good," Flanagan lied. He hadn't seen the inside of a gym since his college days.

Sanders chuckled, almost as if he knew. "Great. Say, I picked up something from one of our stringers this morning. Thought you might find it interesting, considering what we discussed on the plane the other day."

That caused Flanagan's interest level to perk up. "Is that so?"

"Our guy from the *Miami Herald* got it from their

guy at the Fort Myers paper, who got it off the police blotter. Seems last night a gang member was brought into the emergency room at a local hospital with a bad concussion."

"Gang member?"

"Biker gang. Apparently there's an outfit down there that's a pretty rough bunch. Anyway, the guy told the docs that he'd been assaulted by an Asian woman in a bar. The docs told the cops, but the biker didn't want to say anything more about it. That's as far as it went with the cops, but I made a phone call to the hospital. Talked to an E.R. nurse who said the biker's buddy had been in there too, with several dislocated fingers, and his story was that this babe took him and his buddy out in no time at all. These are not small guys we're talking about here. It got my attention because you mentioned that one of the people in that outfit you're interested in is an Asian woman. I think you used the words, 'a woman with uncommon skill.'"

"Yes, exactly," Flanagan said, sitting up straighter. "Where did this happen?"

"A roadhouse about two hours west of Miami."

"Interesting."

"What would that gal be doing down there, do you think? Some sort of training exercise that these clowns stumbled into?"

"Could be, Arnie, could be. But don't quote me on this. In fact, if I were you I wouldn't print anything about it."

"I hadn't thought of it in terms of a story, Ed. Just wanted to run it by you."

It was a good tip, but Flanagan was finding the conversation increasingly irritating. He partially covered the mouthpiece with his hand and said, "Okay, I'll be right there." Then into the phone, "Gotta go, the boss just sent for me. Might be something left over from Germany."

"Is that right? Well, I'd appreciate a call when you have the time."

"I'll get back to you." He clicked off the call and took a moment to collect his thoughts. The Pallas team was on the move. It was time to play that last card. He punched the button for his private line, took a moment to collect his thoughts, and then tapped out a number.

***

Roger Preston put the phone down and sat back, allowing his eyes to roam around his office. He'd been doing that a lot the past couple days, in fact after every phone call. Fortunately, none of them had included the words, "The director would like to see you in his office." But he felt more and more certain that it was only a matter of time. His self-preservation instincts, which had served him so well at State, didn't seem to be working here in this building. How could that be? A bureaucracy was a bureaucracy, wasn't it? Things should be pretty much the same everywhere.

But that didn't seem to be the case here at Langley. Over at Foggy Bottom, where diplomacy was king and negotiation was coin of its realm, he had learned how to get along in order to get where he wanted to go. Here, though, they played the game differently. He'd talked about that with a former colleague over drinks one night a few months back. This fellow had worked at both places but in the reverse of Preston, and he said there were significant differences. The gist of it was, at State they played a modern variation of what the British used to call the Great Game. At Langley, it wasn't a game.

CIA played for keeps. Lives were at stake, and the daily decisions made over here might result in Americans being thrown into prison, or worse, over there. That was something Preston had noticed almost immediately after coming over to CIA from State. There, it was almost like every day was another theoretical exercise. A chess game, as many of his colleagues had called it. The chess master had to be willing to sacrifice a few pieces, mostly pawns, in order to protect his own king and force the opponent into a position where the victor could, in essence, dictate terms. At CIA, Preston found out quickly that many of those pawns now worked for him and they all had names, many of them spouses and children waiting for them to come home, and it was the job of Preston and the other people on the upper floors to do everything possible to ensure exactly that, as long as the mission was accomplished.

He reached behind him and unlocked the file cabinet in his credenza. The file he was looking for was thin, with only two pieces of paper. He pulled it out, hesitated a moment, then opened it.

It is with great regret that I offer my sincere condolences for your loss...

Twice during his tenure as Acting Director, Preston had to write such letters to the families of operatives killed while on duty. The two men were lost due to training accidents, but that didn't make the letters any easier to write. In fact, the task was the most difficult thing he'd ever had to do. If those men had been sacrificed while on a mission he had authorized, the difficulty would've been several orders of magnitude higher, he knew. Ed Flanagan never had to write such letters. Yes, as National Security Advisor he had to counsel the president on matters of war and peace, and his counsel might actually influence the man in the Oval Office to send Americans into battle, but Flanagan would never have to write the letters when the flag-covered caskets came home. And that made all the difference. He put the file back in the cabinet, locked it and sat back in his chair.

How had he let it to come to this? How had he allowed his wagon to be hitched to that of a man like Flanagan? Still thinking of what he'd heard on the phone call, Preston forced himself to consider the path he'd taken to this point. Well, for one thing, Flanagan seemed to be the kind of man Preston fancied himself to be but had never quite become: a man with a plan, willing to take risks and step on a few toes in order to achieve his goal. For Flanagan that goal was power and influence, and Preston had been around Washington long enough to know that while the NSA was already in a position that provided him with those very things, he might very well be able to attain even more. Two years from now, barring a calamity even more serious than the current Iran-Contra fiasco, the vice president would be moving up to occupy the Oval Office and Flanagan would likely be his chief of staff. And Flanagan had made it clear to Preston that if–no, *when* that happened, he would remember his friends.

Preston had truly enjoyed his time at State and wouldn't mind going back there. Maybe not as secretary, for he understood he didn't have the political connections to be considered for that role, but perhaps as deputy. There was also the possibility that he could stay here at Langley and move back into the director's office he'd recently occupied as caretaker, because Webster would surely resign after the next election. Both possibilities were intriguing to Preston and he knew deep down that he would need help to get one or the other—help from a man like Edward Flanagan.

Right now, though, there was a fork in Roger Preston's path. One direction led to that bright future, and the other to... what? What was the worst that could happen? If he defied Flanagan now, refused to carry out his "suggestion," Preston would likely be out of a job within a few weeks. At the very least, he would continue to muddle through the rest of his time here at CIA and, when Webster left, the new director would come in and almost certainly choose his own deputy. Sooner or later, Preston would find himself looking for a job. The good news was, there would always be a job waiting for a man like him, a former government insider. That job would likely pay considerably more than he was making now. But the bad news was that the power and influence would be virtually gone. Was he ready to give that up?

He swiveled his chair around and looked at the photos on the credenza. The largest one was of his wife, another of his two kids, but his favorite was the only black-and-white one, showing him with his mother. It was taken on his graduation day at Columbia, almost thirty years ago now. Such a great smile she'd had, this one filled with pride and love for her only child on his big day. His eyes filled and he blinked furiously, forcing himself to turn away.

Preston did not consider himself to be a bad man by any means. Until now, he had never faced a decision here at CIA, and certainly not at State, which he knew could place careers and even lives at stake for what were essentially reasons important only to himself. His mother, God rest her soul, would have called that acting selfishly. His father, consumed as he was by his climb up the corporate ladder, would have told him to do what he had to do to get ahead. He'd relied on his father's influence as a wealthy alumnus to get into Columbia, on his father's influence as a campaign donor to get into the State Department, and now he was relying on the influence of another man more powerful than him to advance further up the ladder. Was that a bad thing? Some men were meant to be followers, not leaders, after all.

The DDCI shut off the memory of his mother and picked up his phone.

CHAPTER TWENTY-SIX

ROME, ITALY
JUNE 16, 1987

The woman behind the hotel's front desk was young, gorgeous and eager to please. Jo Ann Geary didn't feel anything like that after ten hours in an airliner, but she forced herself to smile. *"Buona sera, signorina. Parli inglese?"*

"Yes," the young woman answered. "But your Italian is very good."

"It's also very limited," Jo said. "I have a reservation." She handed over her fake American passport and a credit card. The receptionist took them and tapped on her computer keyboard.

"Yes, Miss Curtis, we have you down for one room, queen bed." She printed out an invoice. "Sign here please." In another minute the check-in was complete. It would be the second and last time she would use the identity of Elizabeth Curtis, an employee of PaineWebber. She'd first used this legend checking in at Miami International early that morning. Or was it yesterday morning? Despite having slept a few hours on the flight, she was still feeling a bit foggy. She needed to get some exercise.

"Do you have a pool here?" She searched her Italian vocabulary. *"Avete una piscina?"*

"Si, signora," the receptionist said, "but it closes in one hour."

"That's fine, thank you."

***

By the time Jo got into the water it was nine-thirty p.m. local time and she was alone. Rome was six hours ahead of U.S. Eastern Time and she would be in this time zone for the remainder of the mission. Another day and she'd be acclimated. She'd lost count of her intercontinental flights, and she thought that by now she should be getting used to this, but on the other hand she was getting older. Maybe she just didn't have the staying power she'd had a dozen years ago.

As Jo swam her laps she thought about that. A part of her refused to accept the possibility that at thirty-six—well, thirty-seven in two more months—she was past her physical prime. There were, of course, any number of ways to measure that, none of them really definitive. Her annual physicals had always produced top-tier results, and she knew from her training that she could handle herself in combat with any other woman and most men. And really, did anything else count?

Well, yes, there was one thing, something she tried not to think about too often. Objectively, Jo knew that with continued discipline in her lifestyle she could maintain her maximum level of fitness for at least another fifteen to twenty years, but there was one organ that would remain on its own immutable timetable. When menopause began, she would no longer be able to have children.

She reached the end of the pool's ten-meter length, did a flip turn and headed back to the shallow end, turning onto her back. Overhead, the room's fluorescent lights glared down at her. An idle question occurred to her: if left on, how long before they would burn out? Jo had no idea. How old would she be when menopause began? Forty-five, forty-six? She'd never read anything about whether a woman could extend her reproductive life. Maybe, subconsciously, she'd been afraid to check. But even if she could, would she really want to have a baby that late in life? She would be a senior citizen when that child graduated high school.

No, if she were to have a baby, it would have to be pretty soon. She'd heard that women becoming pregnant in their late thirties had greater risk of problems, both for themselves and the child. And then there was the fairly significant question of who the father would be. Jo had known a couple women, both Air Force officers in fact, who had resigned their commissions in order to have a family, both choosing artificial insemination. Could she go that route?

Two more laps. Jo tried to put it out of her mind. Why was she even thinking about that now, with the mission underway? She had to stay focused. At the deep end she was about to go into her final flip turn when she caught movement back toward the pool room entrance. She made the turn and stayed under as she launched off the wall. Releasing a slow stream of bubbles, she kicked down toward the pool's bottom, which was now rising quickly from its six-foot maximum at the deep end. Tilting her head up, she tried to discern any more movement beyond the shallow end.

There. Something coming toward the table nearest the steps that led from the pool's floor to the surface. Touching the bottom step, Jo turned, still below the surface, and kicked back to the deep end. It was probably nothing to worry about, some late-arriving guest wanting a rejuvenating dip, just like her. But there was no reason not to play it safe. She would be in a tough spot no matter where she was if he started shooting, but she remembered the first rule of self-defense: don't be there. Or at least, don't be too close.

Her lungs were starting to burn as she reached the bottom of the ladder at the deep end. Climbing out here would expose her back to the person at the shallow end, so she broke the surface with only her head. Her eyes quickly focused on the table where she'd left her towel folded on the seat of a chair. The other chair was occupied by a man in a business suit, and another man stood near the entrance. Everything about them said "Agency." Neither one of them reached inside his jacket for a weapon.

The seated man smiled. "Colonel Geary," he said, in English with an American accent. "We've been waiting for you. Did you enjoy your swim?"

"I'm not quite done yet," she said. She pushed off the wall and was at the steps with five strong strokes. She stepped out of the pool and saw the man's eyes widen slightly with appreciation as he took in her bikini-clad figure. "Now, I'm done," she said, walking over to the table and picking up her towel, along with the throwing star hidden in the fold. Palming the weapon, she began to towel herself dry. "I'm assuming you have a name."

The man stood up. "I'm with the embassy," he said.

"My credentials." He carefully held open his jacket and slowly reached inside, producing a wallet, which he flipped open. Jo saw the State Department ID card and matching photo.

"What can I do for you, Mr. Brown?"

"My partner and I have orders to escort you to the embassy. We'll accompany you back to your room so you can get dressed."

"I had a long flight and it's late," she said. "Why should I come with you?"

"I was told you'd recognize the phrase, 'water buffalo.'"

The abort code. Jo felt an immediate crush of disappointment, but pushed it aside. She fastened the towel around her waist and carefully tucked the throwing star into the fold. "I'll need confirmation of that from your superiors," she said.

"Don't worry, they work late, too."

***

Jo had already set her watch to Central European Time and it was on the dot of ten p.m. when she walked through the hotel lobby with Brown and his nameless partner. She'd left her single suitcase behind, but kept the shuriken hidden. Brown's credential had looked legitimate, he knew the abort code and procedure now was to go to the nearest American embassy, but it still didn't feel quite right. She'd learned the hard way to trust her instincts.

In the hotel parking lot, Brown went to the driver's door of a nondescript Fiat while his partner held open the front passenger door for her, then got in the back seat behind her. Within minutes they were on a highway, heading west into the city proper on A91. Jo had taken this highway before and knew it was about a half-hour drive to the embassy, the road turning quickly from a highway into a city street.

She soon saw the ancient Colosseum, brightly lit tonight, in the distance to their left, and closer on their right the Basilica of St. John Lateran. But instead of following Via Merulana to the north-northwest and deeper into the city to the embassy, Brown turned right onto a side street, then left onto a narrower street that was almost an alley. He pulled to a stop in front of a two-story residential building.

"Bathroom stop?" Jo asked.

"This is where we get out, Colonel," Brown said. Behind her, the other agent got out of the car and opened her door.

"I'll take a wild guess and say that this isn't the embassy," she said as she unbuckled her seat belt. The street was lined with trees and poorly lit, with no other traffic at the moment and no pedestrians.

"Our instructions were to bring you here. Sorry for the confusion."

Jo took a step out of the car and felt the other man's hand on her right elbow. "I don't like being confused," she said. It took fewer than three seconds for her to break the man's grip, lever him to the ground and rip his gun out of his concealed hip holster. She pointed it at Brown. "Now let's clear this up," she said.

With the front of the car between them, Brown couldn't see his partner lying flat on the street, left arm pinned behind him in a chicken wing and held there by Jo's knee, but he could see the business end of the gun pointed at his chest. He slowly held up his hands. “Take it easy, Colonel,” he said.

“Take out your sidearm, Mr. Brown. Very good. Now I want you to hold it out by the barrel and walk around the front of the car.”

The agent did as ordered. Underneath her, his partner cursed and squirmed, causing Jo to move her knee upward slightly along his back, ratcheting up the pain in his shoulder. “Now, set the weapon on the hood of the car and walk backwards to the driver’s door. Get inside and put your hands on the wheel, ten and two. And don’t bother with the seat belt.”

When Brown had complied, Jo let the other man get up slowly and told him to walk ten paces down the street, keeping his hands on his head. Jo held one gun on him and kept the other on Brown through the open front passenger window as she slid into the front seat. “Okay, let’s go to the embassy,” she said. “For real this time.”

“What about him?”

“He’ll find his way back.”

***

The U.S. Embassy was on Via Vittorio Veneto, across from Palazzo Margherita. The Marine at the guard post accepted Brown’s credentials with a careful look at Jo, who had put one of the pistols in the car’s glove box and was holding the other on Brown, concealed by a newspaper that had been left in the back seat. She had no intention of using the gun, especially once they reached the embassy grounds, but it wouldn’t hurt to keep Brown thinking, just in case he had ideas about slipping the guard a distress code. The guard waved them through the gate without comment.

Within five minutes they were outside the office of the Chief of Station, who had retired to his apartment within the compound earlier in the evening. Twenty minutes later a middle-aged man marched into the small waiting area, dressed in a rumpled white shirt, casual pants and scuffed, black shoes. He was also wearing a scowl. “Brown, what the hell is going on?”

The agent stood. “Sorry to disturb you, sir, but we have a problem.”

The chief saw Jo and his eyes narrowed. “If this is who I think it is, yeah, we’ve got a big one.”

Jo stood as well. “Good evening, Chief. Might I suggest we step into your office?”

“Okay,” the chief said once Brown closed the door behind them. He stood behind his desk, leaning forward with his hands on the back of his chair. A name plate on the desk told visitors that the office was occupied by FRED BLAKE, CULTURAL AFFAIRS DEPUTY, one of the standard covers for a CIA station chief. Jo had met a few chiefs in her time, all of them highly competent, well-organized and disciplined. None of them liked surprises, either, and this man was obviously no different. He glared at Brown. “Where’s Davis?”

“Uh, he’s–’

“Mr. Blake, I’m Lieutenant Colonel Jo Ann Geary, Air Force Special Operations. You’ll forgive me if I don’t show you my credentials. My purpose here in Italy is highly confidential.” Jo and her team had been ordered never to identify themselves as Pallas Group members except to those cleared to know, and this Fred Blake certainly wasn't on that list. "Mr. Brown and his partner came to my hotel and said they were ordered to escort me to the embassy. Imagine my surprise when we wound up on a side street some distance from here instead."

"And how, then, did you wind up here? Brown?"

"Well, sir, she–"

Jo interrupted again. "I presume that was a safe house where they were to keep me incommunicado," Jo said. "I persuaded the gentlemen that it would be better to bring me here instead." She produced Brown's handgun and gave it back to the embarrassed agent.

Blake's eyes twinkled and he couldn't suppress a hint of a grin. "Your reputation preceded you, Colonel," he said. "I cautioned Brown and Davis to be careful. Evidently they didn't take me as seriously as they should have. Why don't we sit down? Not you, Brown. You and I will talk in the morning."

When they were alone, Blake's mood softened slightly. "Okay, Colonel, I don't know how you got the drop on those bozos but I assume it would make for a pretty good story for another day. Right now we have a problem. Did Brown manage to give you the code phrase before you, ah, took charge of the situation?"

"Yes, he did. And if we'd come here right away, there wouldn't have been any problems. That would've been in line with my mission protocols."

"I wasn't aware of that, sorry. I got the word from Langley earlier this evening and was told to have you taken to a safe house and held there until further notice."

"May I ask who gave you that order?"

Blake hesitated, then said, "Officially, I'm not supposed to tell you that, but I have a feeling this whole thing is rapidly turning into what I used to call a 'goat rope' when I was in the Navy. I would imagine you have something similar in the Air Force."

Jo returned his smile. "We certainly do, Chief. But I think I can clear this up with one phone call. Could you provide me with a secure line back to the States?"

"Under the circumstances, that's the least we can do."

CHAPTER TWENTY-SEVEN

LONDON,
UNITED KINGDOM
JUNE 16, 1987

Jennings sensed something was wrong the moment he stepped into the terminal at Heathrow. It wasn't just that he was tired from the nine-hour flight; he'd napped for a couple hours and managed to do some stretching in the rear of the cabin, just enough to get loosened up and shake off some of the cobwebs. No, he'd been in enough foreign airports to know when things were right, and when they weren't.

By the time he got to the baggage carousel, he thought he might've been overreacting. Then he saw a man sitting on a chair glance at him over the top of a newspaper and flick his eyes back down. Everybody else in the terminal looked like the usual harried, tired travelers he'd seen a hundred times. He retrieved his small bag and made his way to the cab stand. If he was planning on shaking any surveillance by making a cleaning run to the hotel, this would be the place for his first overt move. He joined the line waiting for cabs and kneeled down to tie his shoe, using the movement to mask his glance back into the terminal through the glass door. Was that the same guy with the paper?

Jennings couldn't be sure from this angle, but he did see another cab swinging around to the curb in front of the one that had just parked. Pushing his way past an Asian woman with a quick "Beg your pardon," he slid into the cab a split-second after its previous occupant stepped out. Fifteen minutes later he was entering the hotel lobby.

"Bruce Parker. I have a reservation." The dark-skinned woman behind the front desk, probably Pakistani, smiled at him. Just then his stomach growled, and she smiled wider. For God's sake, he thought, it was his usual perfect timing. "Sorry," he said, deciding to make the most of it. "I suppose I should ask you to recommend a pub where I can get a late dinner."

"Certainly, sir. The Fat Badger, four blocks down. Take a right out the front door."

Jennings couldn't suppress a chuckle. He'd have to tell his Wisconsin-born colonel about this one when he got back to MacDill. "Thanks," he said, retrieving his false credit card and room key.

The shower felt great and so did the change of clothes. As he checked himself in the mirror one last time, he caught himself wondering if the Pakistani gal was getting off work any time soon. "Stow that, Major," he muttered. "You're on duty." He left the room and headed back out into the night, taking note of the three people in the lobby as he walked through: Two men, one woman, none with faces he remembered from the airport.

The night air was crisp and had the usual dirty taste of a city but with something just a little different. His last time in London had been in '85, on a weekend leave during a training cycle with 21st Special Air Services. He remembered that assignment with affection. What a great bunch of mates that squadron had been. Their weekend in the city was almost as memorable as the training. Well, hell, it was a lot more memorable; there weren't any women with them in the field, but in London there had been more than a few.

Thinking of those women made him think of Jo. He glanced at his watch. She'd be in Rome by now, no doubt safely curled up in bed with yet another foreign-language novel or history book. He shook his head, smiling. He'd never met anyone like her before. His few previous interactions with Air Force Special Ops people had not been too memorable, but she was one of a kind, and he suspected that would've been the case whatever branch of service she'd chosen.

Damn, but she'd been something that night at the bar in Virginia. Not just the way she looked, the way she dressed, but the way she carried herself. The evening hadn't ended quite the way he'd hoped, but that was probably for the best, he thought now. Although the image of the exotic lieutenant colonel in bed was more than tantalizing, he knew that getting involved like that now would only make their professional relationship more difficult than it needed to be. She'd been right about that.

But they wouldn't be in the same unit forever, so who knew what might happen down the road? You never knew what might be—

The car that drove past him went through a pool of light from a streetlamp and the face behind the wheel was visible for a split-second, long enough for Jennings to place it with one of the men who'd been in the hotel lobby. He watched the car continue on up the street, past the pub, then take a right down a side street. Probably nothing, but he didn't believe in coincidences. A half block later he was at the pub's front door.

Inside it was smoky, on the dark side, fairly quiet. It was a weeknight, after all, and this was in a relatively upscale part of the city. Like most pubs, this one didn't have a TV screen, always tough for an American to get used to. He found a small table and took a seat facing the door. The waitress sauntered over and asked, "What'll it be, mate?"

"Let's see... Oh yeah, I remember this from my last time here. Do you have Old Speckled Hen?"

The girl, a blonde in her early twenties, smiled a little more widely. "That we do, Yank. A pint?

"Yes, and are you still serving food?"

"A'course. Fish and chips the special tonight, with mushy peas. Three quid."

He'd changed twenty U.S. dollars for pounds at the airport, enough for just such an occasion. "That'll do."

A minute later she was back with his beer. "Food will be up in a couple minutes. In town for a while?"

She was lingering, and he knew the look. "Just overnight. Heading out tomorrow," he said. He'd almost added "to the Continent."

"Right. My name's Jane. Be back in a minute." Another smile and she walked over to a nearby table to wait on the couple there, her well-formed derriere filling out her jeans nicely.

A man came in alone and took a seat at an empty table across the room. Jennings thought he might've been another traveler like himself, just here for a nightcap and maybe a late dinner. Or, maybe not. Jane approached him and when she took his order, he saw her eyebrows raise, just as they had when she'd heard Jennings' American accent.

If there were just two of them, the guy in the car would be parked outside to pick up the tail when Jennings left. Or, he might be covering the side or back, depending on where the exit was. Jennings looked around casually as he sipped his beer. The back exit, he saw now, was past the restrooms, which were marked with a sign that said LOO.

Jane brought his plate of food to him. The aroma was wonderful, and he realized he was hungrier than he thought. Come to think of it, Jane was looking pretty wonderful, too. He'd drained two-thirds of his beer. This stuff was stronger than he remembered.

"There you be," she said. "Get you another pint?"

"Not quite yet," he said. "I'll let you know."

"Hope so," she said. She hesitated, then said, "By the way, I get off at eleven."

He smiled back at her. "I'll keep that in mind." Still looking at her, he slid his eyes toward the American. The man was looking at him, then turned quickly away as he caught the movement of Jennings' head.

While he ate he considered how this could be played. If they were Agency, they might just be here to keep an eye on him, an extra security precaution, but he doubted that. Something else was going on. He thought of Harrison, who should've been in Amsterdam by now. The SF major hoped the spook had enough sense to stay out of the red light district.

He tried a forkful of the mushy peas. Not bad. Didn't look very tantalizing but not bad at all. Across the bar, the American was sipping his beer and looking at a newspaper. Jennings could hardly believe the poor tradecraft. No reasonable person would try to read something in this low light. His senses perked up another notch when a woman walked in from the street. She was wearing a long leather coat and a floppy hat, but he still recognized her as the woman from the hotel lobby. She took a seat two tables down from the guy.

Jennings still had a piece of fish and a few chips in the basket, not to mention more than half the peas in their bowl, but it was time to go. Not too obviously, though. Jane walked past him toward another table, and in the two seconds she was between him and the Agency guy, Jennings took a five-pound note out of his jacket pocket and slid it onto the table.

On her way back to the bar, Jane smiled at him. "Ready for that pint, now?"

"Let you know after I visit the loo," he said.

"Back there. Gent's on the left," she said, pointing.

Without looking back he couldn't tell if he was obscured from the American man's view, but he thought he might have at least some cover. He went into the restroom and took a moment to relieve himself—nerves, he knew. No matter how much experience he gained, there were always nerves to contend with.

Coming back through the door, he turned immediately left toward the rear entrance, rather than right and back to the main room of the pub. The back door creaked as he swung it open, then the screen door's hinge gave a rusty crack as he pushed through. If those people really were Agency, they would be onto him now. Stepping into the alley, he turned left and walked quickly past a Dumpster and assorted piles of smelly trash. Something skittered away from him, and he caught a glimpse of a long, hairless tail.

If he was going to make it back to his hotel, he would have to double back somehow. Emerging from the alley, he took a right and walked a half-block to the next corner. Another right should point him in the correct direction, but when he looked around the corner he saw headlights coming toward him. He ran across the street, hoping the lights wouldn't catch him too clearly, and kept going down the next block. From behind he heard the growl of an approaching car. The streetlamps here weren't quite as efficient as they might've been in New York, making it easy for him to stay clear of their light, but he'd have to keep moving or his pursuers, whoever they were, would be on him.

There was another alley and he turned into it quickly. Immediately he saw two things that told him he'd made a mistake. The first was the wall about ten paces down, blocking any exit in that direction. The second was a pair of men, one of them holding a woman from behind, his hand over her mouth. The other man was going through her purse. A third man lay unconscious on the grimy pavement.

The woman saw Jennings and struggled harder, eyes wide, pleading. The man holding her saw Jennings as well. "Shite! We got comp'ny, Frankie."

The man rifling the purse, shorter and whiter than his comrade, turned around. "You best be movin' on, mate. Nothin' here concernin' you."

Jennings shoved the people pursuing him to the back of his mind. If he kept moving he might still lose them, but now that wasn't an option. He had his mission and to complete that he had to stay operational, but his Special Forces heritage kicked in. The SF motto, *De oppresso liber,* was something he and every other Green Beret took very seriously. To free the oppressed. He could no more leave these men to their work than he could stop breathing.

"Let her go," he said.

Frankie's eyes narrowed and he grinned. "A Yank, are you? Well, you ain't a copper, that's for sure. Not your town, not your country, Yank. Piss off."

Jennings took a step forward and slipped his right hand into his jacket pocket. He didn't have anything there except his room key, but they didn't know that. "Let her go and nobody gets hurt, boys. I won't tell you again."

"Wills, you stick the bird if this Nancy boy don't leave us be," Frankie said.

The man holding the woman reached with his free hand into a pants pocket and pulled out a switch knife, the blade snicking into place as he held it up. "Hate to cut this bird, Nancy boy, but I will if–"

Jennings flipped the heavy room key at Wills's face, then brought his right hand around and grabbed a handful of Frankie's greasy hair, pulling down hard as he brought his right knee up. The man's face crashed into the knee and he bounced off with a muffled yelp, falling back against the stack of trash bags along the wall.

The thug with the knife had brought it up to try blocking the incoming key, but missed. The key slapped into his forehead and he stepped back, loosening his hold on the woman, who squirmed free. "Run!" Jennings yelled.

“My husband!” she said, but instead of kneeling down to check him, she froze. Jennings pushed past her and went for Wills.

“Stay back, Yank, or I’ll cut you open.”

“Oh, no you won’t,” Jennings said, stepping inside the man’s arm as he started to bring the knife around in a slashing motion. Catching the wrist, Jennings drove his elbow in the man’s face, cartilage crunching as the nose splattered. Using both hands now, Jennings twisted the arm and brought it down hard on his knee, breaking the elbow. The knife flew away as Wills dropped to the ground with a scream.

The woman had helped her husband to a sitting position. She looked back at Jennings with a mix of fear and gratitude. “Th... thanks,” she said.

The SF major grabbed her husband’s other arm and hefted him to his feet. He had a nasty bump on his left temple. “Get him to a hospital,” Jennings said to the woman. She didn’t need to be told twice. Grabbing her purse, she stumbled out of the alley to the left, supporting her husband. She spotted something and raised her arm, and as they disappeared Jennings heard her yell for help.

A car pulled to a stop in front of the alley, headlights pointing toward the fleeing couple. A man stepped out of the front passenger seat. “Major Jennings, you need to come with us,” the man said.

Although the light was poor, Jennings knew it was the American from the bar. He’d seen the other man at the wheel as the dome light came on. Jennings was still feeling the adrenaline surge from the confrontation and didn’t really feel like going anywhere, except back to his hotel. “Who the hell are you?”

"We're friends," the man said. "You need to come with us back to the embassy."

"And why should I do that? Can't a guy get a beer in this town without getting hassled?"

"The police are on their way, Major, and you don't want to be answering their questions. I just have two words for you: water buffalo."

Jennings could think of only two more words: *Oh, shit.*

CHAPTER TWENTY-EIGHT

WASHINGTON, D.C.
JUNE 17, 1987

Joseph Geary arrived ten minutes early for his appointment, only because traffic had been light coming in from Langley and the meeting he'd just finished there had ended earlier than expected. Too nervous to sit in the secretary's outer office, he stepped into the adjacent Cabinet Room. The only other occupant was a steward, filling the large jar of jelly beans that sat in the center of the long oval table, directly across from the president's seat in the middle on the east side. At the far end, niches holding busts of Washington and Franklin flanked the fireplace. Those were recent additions, Geary noted, remembering the doorways that used to be there. The room looked a lot better than it had when he'd made his first visit. When was that, anyway? Fall of '62? Yes, that was it, during the Missile Crisis. He'd accompanied the DCI, John McCone, and when he'd heard Kennedy and his men talking about invading Cuba, sinking Soviet submarines and launching a pre-emptive nuclear strike, it was the first time in Geary's life that he felt truly terrified. Geary was on the team that put together the president's intelligence briefings, so he knew all about where the missiles were, where the submarines lurked, and what Soviet installations were targeted. But hearing the president actually talking about them, weighing his options and wondering aloud about whether or not to launch first suddenly made everything Geary had been working on seem very real. His job was analysis and presenting facts. The man chairing the meeting that day was the one who had to consider those facts and make the tough calls. That was where the buck truly stopped.

Kruschev had pushed the young president right to the brink, but JFK had not backed down. A history major at Princeton, Geary knew that there were tipping points, when things could go one way or the other. That week nearly a quarter century ago had been one of them. Kennedy had risked everything to stand up to the Soviets, and he'd prevailed. Reagan's decision to save Gorbachev from assassination might just be another one. But right now there was a man in the West Wing who would soon be doing his best to convince the president that his decision was the wrong one.

Geary was glad he'd gotten here early. The extra minutes gave him a final opportunity to calm himself down. He'd come very close to physically assaulting Preston, as close to snapping as he'd ever been in his career. It had just been the two of them with Webster in the DCI's office, and Preston's wheedling and evasions finally became too much. Geary must've looked like he was about to spring out of his chair and go for Preston's throat, because Webster gave him one of those looks that could not be misunderstood, a look that said *I'll handle this.* And handle it he did. Preston was cleaning out his desk right now. Geary had been given the task of informing the president about Preston's actions, and about whom he had really been working for.

The president's secretary appeared in the doorway behind him. "The president said you can go right in, sir. He's wrapping up another call, but he's expecting you."

"Thank you," Geary said, unable for the life of him to remember the lady's name. It was the fatigue and the stress, and it was only ten in the morning. Of course if he'd had a good night's sleep the night before... Taking a moment to compose himself, he walked into her office and pushed the inner door open.

Ronald Reagan sat at his desk, holding the telephone to his left ear as he jotted something on a pad. He looked up as Geary entered and motioned him to come in. "No, Trent, I won't be considering someone else. Bork's the best man for the job." Reagan looked up at Geary and shook his head slightly. "Well, you just tell your people to calm down and we'll work across the aisle and get it done.... Good, keep me posted." He put the phone back in its cradle with what Geary thought was a little extra emphasis. "Have a seat, Joe," Reagan said, nodding to the chair on his right. "I'll tell you, dealing with Congress is like herding cats. But you've testified in enough hearings to know that, I'm sure."

Geary took the seat. "I really don't envy you that part of your job, sir."

The president sat back in his chair. "Somebody's got to do it, I suppose. Justice Powell hasn't even officially retired yet and already they're telling me the man I want to put on the Court won't pass muster. Well, we'll see about that." He tossed his pen on the desk and raised an eyebrow.

Geary knew that was his cue. "Thank you for taking the time to see me, Mr. President."

"Always happy to talk to you, Joe. Are your people over there now?"

Geary looked at the red plaque sitting on the corner of the desk, deliberately facing the president's visitors. IT CAN BE DONE, in gold letters. The wooden desk, Geary knew, was built from timbers salvaged from HMS *Resolute* and presented to Rutherford Hayes by Queen Victoria in 1880. Geary hoped he would be resolute through the next few minutes.

"Yes, Mr. President, they are, but there's been a problem."

Frowning, the president plucked a jelly bean from the jar he always kept handy. "I have a feeling I'll need something a little bit stronger than one of these," he said, "but it'll have to do for now."

***

Twenty minutes later, Geary stood in the Roosevelt Room, staring at the portrait over the mantel. In it, Theodore Roosevelt, who had used this room as his office eighty years before, sat on a rearing horse, wearing his tailor-made khaki Rough Rider uniform. What conversations had been held right here between that man and the men who worked for him? Geary imagined that there had been more than a few contentious discussions here during TR's time. A modern version of one was going on in the Oval Office just across the hall right now.

Geary knew he should have been on his way back to Langley by now, but something had made him stay. He wanted to know what the result of that conversation would be, and he wanted to know it right away. One of the men in that office had put three Americans in an unnecessary jam and their mission in serious jeopardy, a mission Joseph Geary believed was vital to the national security of the United States.

And one of those Americans was his daughter.

The door to the right of the mantel was open, but from where he stood Geary couldn't see across the hallway to the Oval. He stepped around the door to the south wall and took in the portrait of Franklin Roosevelt. Someday, Geary supposed, a Democrat would be elected and then FDR would be over the mantel again. By then Geary would be retired. His veranda on St. Thomas was calling him, a little more loudly every day. Some days, like today, he could almost feel the warmth of the Caribbean sun.

The Oval Office door opened and Edward Flanagan stepped out. He saw Geary across the hallway and his eyes narrowed. Geary returned the stare, telling himself he would not back down, not now. So much would depend on what had happened inside that office.

Flanagan seemed to gather himself, then stepped across the hallway and into the room, closing the door behind him. "Do you have any idea of what you've done?" he asked, biting off the words.

Geary stared down at the shorter man. "I reported to the president about complications in a mission he ordered. You and Preston were those complications. Director Webster has taken care of one of them, and I assume the president has now taken care of the other one."

Flanagan lifted his chin and his nostrils flared. For a moment Geary thought the man might throw a punch. Instead, Flanagan looked away, then back at Geary. "You'll hear it soon enough. The president has accepted my resignation. I'll be out of here by the end of the week. I would imagine you're not sorry about that."

The DDO allowed a slight grin to touch his lips. "I would imagine you're right. But I have a feeling you'll land on your feet. There's probably more than one think tank out there that will welcome you with open arms."

There was a tense moment of silence, and then Flanagan said, "You do realize, don't you, that if your team is successful it will probably cause serious problems down the road for this country?"

"If I believed that, I would have advised the president against it. He came to me with a problem and asked me to fix it. Ultimately I work for him, and I told him I would do my best. That team in Europe is our best shot. Our only shot."

Flanagan's only response was to shake his head and look away in disgust. "Suppose they fail," he said, looking back at Geary. "Suppose Gorbachev is shot and one of your people is captured. Do you have any idea of the trouble that will cause? Do you have any concept of it at all? I was in Vietnam, you know, and no mission ever goes exactly as planned."

Geary couldn't suppress the grin anymore. "Yeah, you were in Vietnam, Flanagan, and the closest you ever came to a mission was spending four days at an artillery fire support base."

"I have a Purple Heart from my service, mister!"

This time Geary laughed out loud. "Perforated eardrum. You got too close to a howitzer and forgot to put your earplugs in. From what I heard you were one of the biggest REMF's the Army had ever seen in country." He could see the NSA didn't like being reminded about that part of his not-so-sterling military career. Well, no officer ever wanted to be known as a Rear Echelon Mother Fucker. Geary had met a few of those during his own CIA service over there, particularly during his still-classified work in the Phoenix Program.

"You'll regret that, Geary."

The DDO took a small step toward Flanagan, who stepped back involuntarily. "You go right ahead and write your op-ed piece for the *Post*. See if anybody gives a rat's ass." He turned to the door.

"Your daughter might care when I drop her name to a reporter I know."

In his forty years in the CIA, Joseph Geary had been face-to-face with Soviet assassins. He'd jousted verbally with combative, naïve Congressmen, ignored snide remarks at cocktail parties, resisted pulling the trigger on a Viet Cong prisoner who laughed when he admitted slitting the throats of a village chief and his four children. But none of those people had ever put his daughter in danger. Before he could stop himself, his right hand was around Flanagan's throat.

There was a knock at the door, and Geary released his grip. Flanagan fell back, gagging. The DDO looked at him and said, "If you ever do that, you and I will have another conversation, and it won't be quite this friendly." He opened the door and pushed his way past a startled young woman, causing her to drop her file of papers on the floor.

CHAPTER TWENTY-NINE

CSÁSZÁR,
HUNGARY
JUNE 17, 1987

Grechko saw Pataki walk down the sidewalk past the market, check for traffic—really unnecessary, as there were very few autos in this small town—and cross over to the park. The Spetsnaz operative had been observing the park for the past half-hour from various locations and was reasonably sure they were free of any surveillance. Pataki, in fact, had assured him that his MIA colleagues were focusing their efforts now on Budapest and would not be coming to Bodor Major, the nearby horse farm, until the next day. It was then they would probably do a cursory sweep through this village.

It never hurt to be prudent, though, and so Grechko remained on alert. By now it was almost second nature for him. He felt more relaxed than he had been since that last day at his dacha in Ukraine. The evening with the young Hungarian woman a week ago had helped him release some tension, as had their subsequent afternoon at the horse farm on Saturday. The riding had been invigorating, more than he imagined it could be, and Anna's athleticism in bed that evening only enhanced his good mood. After seeing the farm itself and hearing her describe the details of Gorbachev's visit—amazingly, she had totally disregarded her employer's instructions to remain silent about them—Grechko was more confident than ever about the success of his mission.

Just to be on the safe side, as the Americans would say, he'd made a quick visit to Belgrade on Sunday, a four-hour drive from Budapest. He'd debated the trip in his mind for several days, finally deciding that allowing himself to be seen in Yugoslavia would throw KGB off his trail. While in Belgrade he'd looked up an old contact in SDB, the Yugoslav security service, confiding in him that he was spending a few days in the capital before heading to Greece. Grechko knew the man would report the contact to his superiors and from there KGB would get the word their man was heading south.

The safe house Pataki had provided in Budapest was more than adequate, and from that base Grechko was able to surreptitiously observe many of the early preparations for the arrival of his target. The MIA agent supplied him with a classified copy of the Soviet leader's itinerary, which only reassured Grechko that his decision to complete the operation at the horse farm was his only viable option. Security would be tight in Budapest, but after careful consideration he decided it would be worth the risk to spend the day in the Hungarian capital when Gorbachev was there. He would leave the city after the speech at Heroes Square, scheduled for mid-afternoon, allowing plenty of time for the drive west to the village near the horse farm. Gorbachev would arrive there in late morning of the following day, and after his tour would have lunch and then be entertained by the horse show before returning to Budapest and the flight back to Moscow.

The flight he would never take.

The Hungarian agent crossed the street and walked into the park. Grechko sighed. He knew what had to be done now, and in a way it saddened him. A sign of sentimentality in his old age, perhaps? No, it was merely practical. Pataki had been useful, indeed vital, but could not be completely trusted. Nobody could be completely trusted.

"Good morning, comrade," Pataki said as he joined Grechko on the bench. "You look well."

"Thank you," Grechko said. "It is a beautiful day."

Pataki grinned. "Something tells me you were able to see the fair maid Anna again."

"Indeed," the Ukrainian replied. "Comrade, I have reached a decision about the mission."

"Yes?"

"The horse farm is out. My survey a few days ago convinced me that it would be too formidable of a problem for us to solve."

Grechko watched Pataki closely for any reaction, but the Hungarian merely nodded. "I see," he said. "Of course I defer to your judgment on this matter, comrade. Is it to be Heroes Square, then?"

"No, that is even worse," Grechko said. "But the airport is a different matter."

Pataki turned in surprise. "The airport? But security there is bound to be very tight, will it not?"

Grechko shook his head and allowed a tight smile to play across his lips. "Upon his arrival, yes. His departure, probably not so much. After all, the danger will have passed. The obvious places in Budapest are the Technical University, which he visits after his luncheon meeting with your General Secretary, and then the square. After the speech, he has more meetings and then the symphony in the evening."

Pataki sighed slightly. "The airport, then," he said, "when they have relaxed, because he will be just about on the plane for home."

"Actually, I will wait until he is on the plane."

This time Pataki's head snapped around. "What?"

"When his plane is lifting off, comrade, you and I will be at that end of the runway, with two American Stinger missiles. I will take the first shot, you the second."

Grechko didn't miss the movement of Pataki's Adam's apple. "You... you have these weapons, comrade?"

"Yes." Of course he did not, but Pataki would never know that. "Our target will be an Ilyushin Il-62. The Stinger is very effective against it."

"You know this from Afghanistan, I presume?"

"No," Grechko said, and played his ace card. "Do you recall the crash of that Ilyushin in Warsaw, just last month?"

"Yes, of course. A terrible accident. Nearly two hundred dead."

Grechko looked at him. "It was no accident. The fire in the engine was caused by a Stinger missile fired by Polish counterrevolutionaries. KGB and Polish intelligence strongly suspect the Solidarity movement was behind it, with the assistance of the American CIA."

It was a lie, of course. The airliner had almost certainly been downed by a mechanical failure in one of its engines, causing a fire. The idiots at the airport in Modlin had denied the pilot's desperate plea for permission to land there, and so he had turned around and tried for a return to Warsaw.

"My God," Pataki said. After a moment, he asked, "Do they have anyone under arrest?"

"Not yet," Grechko said, "but I expect some movement in the case very soon."

"I see," the Hungarian said, turning his head again to stare straight ahead. Then he nodded. "It has... elegance, I suppose. The KGB will think the Americans are behind this, too."

"That is the idea," Grechko said. "After all, the Americans and their cowboy president cannot be trusted. He has agents everywhere."

***

For the next half-hour they discussed the airport plan. Grechko was familiar with the facility, having overseen a joint training exercise there a few years earlier involving Soviet and Hungarian commandos. KGB fully expected more trouble from Muslim separatists out of the southern republics and wanted to be prepared. Having spent some time in places like Chechnya, Grechko was certain that when the Muslims in those lands inevitably rose up, actions a little more vigorous than storming a hijacked airliner would be necessary.

He thought about that now as he bade Pataki goodbye with a nod and a handshake. While his eyes automatically tracked a car that came down the road and drove slowly past the park, his brain continued to work the problem, this time in a more abstract form. An interesting question, to be sure: what would be the result of this mission's success? Would the Committee be able to rule the nation, as Voloshin and his colleagues evidently believed they could? Well, it would not be the first time Russia would come under the dominion of an iron-fisted dictatorship, and probably also not the last. And Grechko had little doubt that Voloshin would quickly determine that an iron fist was necessary.

Grechko walked briskly out of the park and crossed the street, heading farther into the village toward the inn where he had rented a room. The proprietress, a woman who had been widowed when her police officer husband was killed in a hunting accident three years before, had hinted broadly in her decent German that Grechko could have the room for free if he was willing to share her bed. Grechko considered her Rubenesque curves and the thin mustache on her upper lip, compared her with the lithe Anna, and graciously declined her offer.

He entered the front room of the inn and saw two men sitting at a table, holding mugs of beer. The merry widow had recently begun serving meals and drinks in the front room to supplement her income, an effort that apparently was having mixed results. Grechko immediately assessed the threat potential of the men and dismissed them. Both were well into their sixties, probably veterans of the Great Patriotic War, based on the frayed garrison cap one of them wore. He did not recognize the pin on the left front of the cap, though, and the men were speaking in their native Magyar. Grechko nodded at them and sat at an empty table. Perhaps it wasn't too early for lunch.

"Guten morgen, Herr Bauer," the innkeeper said, coming out from the back room, eyes sparkling as she saw him. The eyes rolled up and to the right briefly as she thought, then said, *"Wollen Sie mittagessen haben?"*

"Yes, thank you, lunch would be fine," Grechko replied. "And what have we today?"

"Goulash! My mother, her, ah... *Rezept!"*

He couldn't hide his smile at the woman's pride over her mother's recipe. "That sounds delicious," he said. Less than ten minutes later, his first spoonful of the stew confirmed that it was very tasty indeed. Accompanied by a thick slice of buttered bread and a schooner of beer, the lunch was one of the best he'd had in weeks. *Frau* Herczog beamed at him from across the serving counter.

At the other table, the two old veterans were becoming more animated. Grechko's ears perked up when he heard one of them say "Gorbachev" with clear disdain. He tuned in more carefully, and when he heard the term *"kibaszott oroszok,"* he knew they were talking about Russians in general, and not kindly.

Grechko used the last of his bread to swab out the remainder of the goulash, then stood and carried the bowl and spoon over to his hostess. "Another beer, Herr Bauer?" she asked hopefully.

"No, thank you," he said, handing her the empty schooner. "Tell me, those two gentlemen, they are veterans, yes?"

"Oh, *ja,* from the war. They live here in town. They come here quite often and tell their stories. Same stories, over and over."

Grechko saw the man with the cap pantomiming a

machine gun, saying something that included the word *Ukrajna,* and then rattling off a poor rendition of a heavy-caliber weapon on full auto. From the way he held his hands Grechko assumed the man had been in a tank crew.

"They fought for the Hungarian army?" he asked the innkeeper, already suspecting the answer.

"Yes, they were both with, *ach,* I do not know the German, but in Magyar it is *Kárpát Csoport.* They were in Russia."

It was then he remembered what unit the pin on the man's cap represented. His father had showed one just like it to him when he was about ten, and told him the story of how his brother, little Sergey's uncle, had been killed fighting the invading Hungarians and Germans. His uncle's unit had been defending a Ukrainian farmhouse and were cut down by a trio of Hungarian light tanks using machine guns. The Hungarians were part of the Carpathian Group, an elite strike force.

Just like the one this old *ublyudok* had just demonstrated, Grechko thought, bile rising in his throat. At the table, the two men laughed and raised their schooners. *"Általános Miklós,"* the old tanker said, and they clinked their beer schooners together. Grechko recognized the name. He'd found it during his research into his uncle's and father's war service. Major General Béla Miklós, the first commander of the Carpathian Group's mechanized units, was awarded the Knight's Cross by Hitler late in 1941 for his exemplary service on the Eastern Front.

Killing Ukrainians.

The veterans dropped some paper *forint* currency

on the table, waved at Frau Herczog and exited through the inn's front door, the machine-gunner slapping the back of his comrade as they left, still laughing.

Grechko knew he should not let this upset him. The war had been over for more than forty years, and the Hungarians lost. Ever since then, they had been a client state of the Soviet Union, although not a willing one. Their uprising in 1956 had been crushed by Soviet troops, including Grechko's own father. You'd think that by now they would have learned their lesson, but no. The young ones, like Anna, did not seem to care. The old ones, like these two veterans, still remembered killing Russians and Ukrainians with fondness—memories they would not have dared to recall aloud had they known who the man eating goulash really was.

Grechko remembered something he had read, about some other place, maybe in some other time. *The regime will make people afraid of it, but not make them believe in it.* It was clear these Hungarians, along with the Czechs and Poles he had encountered in the past few weeks, did not believe in the regime that ruled their lives. But did they fear it, anymore? Evidently not.

It is time, he thought, for that to change.

CHAPTER THIRTY

BUDAPEST,
HUNGARY
JUNE 18, 1987

Jo knocked at the door, saw the peephole go dark on the other side, and heard the rattle of a chain and the clack of a deadbolt. The door creaked open and Jennings filled the doorway, smiling. "What's the password?" he asked.

"Wise guy," Jo said as she slipped past him.

"That's not the password," the SF major said as he closed and locked the door. "But this time I'll look the other way."

She was tired and a little tense and certainly not in a joking mood, but she forced herself to take it in the spirit in which it was given. Seeing Harrison relaxing on a threadbare couch in the small living room of the apartment released some of her tension. Everybody had made it. "Will, glad to see you're here," she said.

"It was touch and go in Vienna," the CIA agent said. "Greg had some problems in London. How about you?"

She nodded as she sat in the room's only padded chair, feeling the springs poke at her bottom through the faux leather. The local CIA station had not gone to any great expense with this place. She could hardly wait to feel the sheets on her bed. Assuming she had a bed, of course. The plan was for her to sleep back at her hotel that night, but that could change. "I had to call Langley from Rome," she said. "Have we heard from the colonel?"

Jennings took a seat on the couch next to Harrison, and Jo was gratified to see there was no obvious tension between the two men. They'd both been in Budapest for half a day already; maybe they'd had a chance to talk things over.

"The local spooks had this for us when we got here," Jennings said. He pulled a flimsy sheet of paper out of his shirt pocket and handed it to Jo.

061887 1835Z

AUTHENTICATOR: FOXTROT DELTA ECHO 321

MESSAGE FOLLOWS:

WATER BUFFALO IS DOWN. SNOW LEOPARD RULES. ENJOY THE SHOPPING.

BADGER

MESSAGE ENDS

"Well, we're still on," Jo said. She handed the flimsy back to Jennings. "The colonel must feel confident that our covers weren't blown."

Taking the message, Jennings said, "It's edible, but I'm not that hungry." He rose and went into the bathroom, crumpled the message and dropped it in the toilet, pulling the chain and producing a loud gurgling flush that would make an American plumber cringe. "Gotta love the workmanship here," he said as he rejoined them in the living room.

"What did you learn on your recon?" Jo asked.

"If the Wolf is going to make the hit here, it'll have

to be Heroes Square," Harrison said. "Our people at the embassy got the itinerary from one of their sources. It's pretty straightforward, but the only time G will be out in the open is at the square for his speech tomorrow afternoon." As an added security precaution, they had agreed to use Gorbachev's initial instead of his name. "He'll be touring a university earlier in the afternoon, but security is bound to be pretty tight. The Hungarians will be keeping the campus locked down while he's there. After the speech he won't be out in public again till he attends the symphony that night following a state dinner. And they won't be doing the state dinner like we do at the White House. Very private, pretty short, really. The word is he really enjoys the symphony and wanted to see Budapest's finest even if it means a late night for him."

Jo nodded. Everything they knew about their adversary, and it wasn't much, indicated he would not make an overt strike. "We can assume he's an expert marksman, but I still don't think he'll go for a long-range shot at the square," she said.

Jennings agreed. "KGB and the Hungarians will have all the possible sniper hides covered for about a two-mile radius around the square," he said. "The boys and girls at our embassy have been noticing a lot of activity here the past few days. More of a uniformed presence, as I'm sure you saw coming in."

She nodded again. Soldiers bearing submachine guns were common at Eastern European airports, but this time she noticed more than the usual number. Her passport had been scrutinized carefully at customs and she was questioned by a Russian-speaking officer who had been called over to the desk by the stern woman in the chair. She knew her responses were flawless and textured with the requisite Armenian accent. They let her pass. She was pretty sure she hadn't been followed as she took a cab to her hotel, but it was hard to tell if there was any surveillance of her when she left the hotel for a meandering walk through the downtown district and a stop for a quick supper at a small restaurant. She was supposedly here as a journalist, and so had to act like one, interested in her surroundings but not as much as a tourist might be. Armed soldiers were on every street corner. With darkness falling she was able to be a little more active in her efforts to lose anybody on her tail as she made her way to the safe house. The half-raised blinds in the middle window of the second-floor apartment had told her the place was secure.

"What's the estimated crowd at the speech?" she asked

"Could be around a hundred thousand," Harrison said.

Jo felt a rush of despair, but fought against it. "I know what you're thinking," Jennings said. "Three people trying to find one guy among a hundred thousand. Not exactly the greatest odds."

"No, but maybe we can make them a little more favorable," she said. "We need to know about his route to the square, how long he'll be in the open, how close he'll get to the crowd. Will, what do our friends at the embassy have for us?"

Harrison picked up a file that had been lying on the rickety coffee table. "Not a lot. Let's hope it's enough."

***

Two hours later, Jo stepped out into the Hungarian night. Jennings and Harrison would be following shortly, on their way back to their own hotels. It had been decided early on in the mission planning that staying at the safe house would be too risky, in spite of its name. Security agents might be keeping an eye on hotels, seeing which guests made it back to their rooms overnight and which didn't. Jo didn't think that too likely but there was no use taking unnecessary chances this late in the game.

Jo never considered the odds for or against success in any mission. The very nature of their work ensured that the other side would have almost all the advantages. Her team's only edge was that Budapest was a big city and the local police and government security people, even augmented by the large Soviet contingent that was undoubtedly here, were vastly outnumbered. But the security forces made up for that by being well-organized, with instant communications and the ability to go anywhere they wanted, anytime. Plus they had all the guns, Jo reminded herself. Almost all; the Wolf would have one, probably two. Against that, the three Americans each had a handgun, hidden back at the safe house now, to be retrieved in the morning before they moved into position.

The issue of weapons had been hotly debated back at MacDill. To be caught over here in possession of a firearm, especially now in this city, would mean imprisonment at the very least, probably combined with interrogation techniques that would be anything but pleasant. Jo knew if she was captured, repatriation would be only a faint hope. Did they still execute spies over here? She had no intention of finding out. Despite the added risk, the decision had been made to arm the team once they arrived in Budapest. Each of them were skilled in the use of handguns, and their chances of taking out the Wolf were greatly improved if they didn't have to rely only on knives, or their own hands and feet.

The night air was cool on her cheeks as she made her way back to her hotel, taking a roundabout route designed to help her detect any surveillance. It was just past ten o'clock but people were still out and about, although not so many as would be found in a city on the other side of the Curtain. The streets of Paris or Amsterdam would be busier, louder, more relaxed. Here, Jo felt the discomfort she always felt in Eastern Europe, a sense of... repression. How much of it was just in her mind, though? Certainly this was not even close to what she'd felt on her missions to China, and nothing at all like that time in North Korea. No, the days she'd spent in the Hermit Kingdom, just about a year ago now, were four of the most harrowing of her life. Budapest, even with its own unique dangers, was a walk in the park by comparison.

Several men eyed her as they passed, even some of those who were with women of their own. Jo was used to that by now, automatically analyzing each man who noticed her, and the women too, as to their potential threat level. There were disadvantages for being an attractive woman in her line of work, but she'd found that there were important pluses about it, too. Men were much more likely to volunteer information to a woman who was attractive. Many, she'd found, were almost eager to boast about who, and what, they knew. There were always a few who could resist her charms, though, and they were the most dangerous adversaries of all.

She crossed a street to avoid two large men who were walking toward her on the sidewalk. A boat horn hooted from the Danube, only a few blocks away. Would the Chain Bridge be lit tonight? She'd heard of its beauty, but actually seeing it would have to wait for another trip. She stepped up on the curb and brushed past a young man and woman, holding hands, the woman giggling as the man whispered something in her ear. Another four steps brought her to an intersection. Her hotel was another four blocks ahead, but Jo turned left, tossing a quick glance over her shoulder. The two men who had been on the other side of the street were now crossing over to her side and were heading her way. Had she been made?

Jo's senses were on full alert now, but she could not yet allow herself to slip into mushin, as comfortable as that was. She still needed to have all her wits about her, could not afford to just react. Now she had to think, but not panic. A restaurant was ten steps away, and she maintained her unhurried pace as she approached. Outside the door a sign listed the menu, and she stopped to look at it. It was printed in Magyar, of course, but also in German. She had no interest in the night's special, though. She shot a glance to her left, back down the street, and saw the two men just coming around the corner. One continued across the street with the light as his partner stopped at a public telephone, briefly turning his back to her.

Jo made a decision and pulled open the door of the restaurant. Inside it was dimly lit, and the spicy aromas from the kitchen caused her stomach to tighten. A smiling young woman waited at the maître d' stand. She spoke a greeting in Magyar.

Jo replied in German. *"Sprechen Sie Deutsch?"*

"Ja, Ein fur Abendessen?"

She had no interest in dining, but she did have a strong interest in finding the rear entrance. "My husband will be joining me shortly," she fibbed. "May I use your ladies' room while I wait?

"Of course. It's in the back."

"Thank you." She made her way through the restaurant, where about half the tables were occupied. A few men's heads turned her way, none of them causing a blip in her automatic threat analysis. She saw the restroom entrance but no rear exit, which would never pass muster in an American establishment.

A waitress came through another door with two plates of food. Jo waited till she had passed and then went through the door into the kitchen. A man in a white chef's hat looked her way, eyes widening slightly as he stirred a large pot of soup. Jo smiled and said in German, "Who knew his wife would show up? Where's the back door?" He nodded toward the rear.

Moments later the chilly night air enveloped her again. Allowing a moment to let her eyes to adjust to the darkness, Jo collected herself and made a decision. If those two men were indeed shadowing her, they could only have known her from the hotel or seen her exit the safe house. If the safe house was under surveillance, they were all in danger right now. But if they'd started at the hotel, lost her earlier and just picked her up again, it might be just routine surveillance of a foreign national, even though that foreign national was apparently a Soviet citizen.

She exited the alley, got her bearings quickly and headed toward the hotel. She took the most direct route, using the turns to check for anybody trailing her, but nobody stood out, nothing resembling the two men she'd seen earlier. Maybe her restaurant dodge had worked.

The moment she turned a final corner and saw one of the men standing at the main entrance to her hotel, she knew it hadn't. She maintained her pace, calming herself. There was still a chance the man wasn't a security officer at all, and if he was, maybe he was interested in somebody else. She walked past without looking directly at him and was about to turn for the main door when she felt a hand on her arm.

"Izvinitye, tovarisch. Moment, pozhaluysta?" Excuse me, comrade. A moment, please?

Jo replied in Russian. "What can I do for you, comrade?"

"You are out for an evening stroll, yes?"

A Hungarian officer would've been much more reluctant to confront a Soviet citizen, so this man was KGB. She would have to play this carefully. "It is a beautiful city, but now I am ready to retire for the evening."

"Your papers, please."

Jo produced her forged Soviet internal passport, with the special leaflet that allowed travel to other Eastern Bloc countries like Hungary. The KGB agent stepped closer to an outdoor light on the building, flipping the passport's pages. The man looked at her. "I do not see an entry visa," he said.

"One is not required, comrade," Jo said. "Hungary is a Comecon member." The Council for Mutual

Economic Assistance, founded by the Soviets in 1949, included every Warsaw Pact country plus other socialist nations such as Cuba. Soviet citizens were allowed to travel with relative freedom within the bloc.

"So it is," he said. He flipped another page. "You were a beautiful teenager, Comrade Kocharian," he said. "How old were you when the photo was taken? Thirteen?"

"Sixteen, comrade, and the second photo was taken when I was twenty-five, as required by law." If she was still doing this at forty-five, another photo would have to be added.

The KGB officer nodded. "Your home in Yerevan, is it close to the Pambak?"

Jo shook her head. "I'm afraid you have your cities confused, comrade. The Pambak is in Kirovakan. Our river in Yerevan is the Hrazdan, and my flat is about a half-kilometer away. Have you ever been there?"

The agent was clearly uncomfortable now. "No," he said.

Jo smiled at him. "You must visit," she said. "I will show you the statue of Mother Armenia. You know, the one that replaced the big statue of Stalin."

His eyes narrowed, and she immediately regretted goading him with the Stalin statue. He tapped the passport on his thumb, then handed the passport back to her. "Enjoy your stay in Budapest, comrade."

CHAPTER THIRTY-ONE

BUDAPEST,
HUNGARY
JUNE 19, 1987

Jo heard the Russian voice through her earpiece. *"Stavropol' dvizhetsya. Tridsat' minut na ploschad."* She reached up and adjusted her black beret with three fingers, giving the signal to Jennings and Harrison that G was on the move, thirty minutes out from Heroes Square. KGB was using the General Secretary's place of birth—Stavropol, a city in the Caucasus— as his code name, which CIA's Budapest Station had anticipated. They had also been right on the money with the radio frequency, programmed into the German-made transistor radio that Jo carried. If she pressed a small button on the earpiece or a similar one on the radio itself, now hidden in her jacket pocket, the frequency would switch immediately to Kossuth Rádió, the official Hungarian government station.

She stood near the main entrance to the square, at the end of Népköztársaság Avenue. Jennings and Harrison were both within a hundred feet of her, but now they would be moving to the southeast along Dósza György Avenue, which paralleled the square. The

Soviet motorcade would be approaching from that direction. The Pallas team didn't have access to the exact route, but their study of the city map the night before had left little doubt. After leaving the Technical University on the west side of the Danube, the motorcade would proceed to the Liberty Bridge and cross the river. Twenty minutes later, maybe quicker because the thoroughfares would have been cleared of traffic, the police motorcycles and the four limousines would turn left off Thököly Avenue onto Dósza György.

The team had arrived at the square early enough to get a good idea of the security setup. They could already see the traffic barriers that would funnel the motorcade onto the southeast side of the square. A large podium had been erected just in front of the ornamental iron chain that protected a cenotaph honoring the heroes who had given Hungary its independence. Behind the cenotaph rose the huge column topped by a statue of the archangel Gabriel. Jo thought it ironic that the leader of the nation which had held Hungary in virtual bondage for forty years would choose this particular spot for his speech. The limousines would stop along the southeast side of the square, and G would have a walk of less than a hundred feet to the podium. A barrier had been placed along the length of the walk, and Jo estimated the crowd would be no closer than twenty feet to the dignitaries. The entire back half of the square had been cordoned off. In the open half, the crowd already numbered in the thousands, with more people coming down Népköztársaság and Dósza György.

But it didn't appear the crowd would be as large as they had heard. Many Hungarians had evidently decided to stay away in protest, or perhaps watch the speech on television. Jo had counted three different trucks bearing the logo of M1, the state TV of Hungary. One of them was located near the motorcade's planned entrance to the square.

If the Wolf was going to strike here, it would be when his target exited his limo and made his way to the podium, or perhaps on the return walk. There was a small chance G would stop on the way back to mingle with the crowd, as he had on previous visits to the Baltic states, but those hadn't turned out so well. The crowd today didn't look any more welcoming than those had been, so Jo and the team thought it likely the guest of honor wouldn't waste any time heading back to his limo.

Jennings had already found his way to a prime location near the entrance, right near a TV truck. Harrison would be circling around to the edge of the square to cover the street, just in case their target made his play as the limos were turning into the square. Jo was coming from the central part of the square, giving the Americans the chance to fix the chokepoints within an invisible triangle. If the Wolf was here today, they'd find him in that triangle.

***

Grechko was still a block away from Heroes Square when he saw the students, a few stragglers who were walking quickly to where their comrades had already gathered. Some were carrying signs, and the uniformed police did nothing but watch them walk past. He knew his target's timetable, thanks to Pataki, and there was still a half-hour to go before the motorcade's arrival. Several thousand people had already gathered in the square, some of them holding signs as well. Not nearly as many as he'd seen in demonstrations in the West, but for an East Bloc nation this was a worrisome number. Frequently the government would encourage signs that ridiculed the West, and on May Day in Moscow he had seen many that celebrated heroes of the Great Patriotic War. State television would show these as examples of how the Soviet people did indeed have freedom of expression, although Grechko doubted whether anyone in the West really believed that, except for the truly naïve few who might be found on university campuses.

This was different, though, and Grechko definitely sensed the mood of the crowd. It was not friendly. He saw one woman, in her seventies if she was a day, carrying a sign with the photo of a young man, and below the photo was the year 1956, boldly printed in red. She looked determined as she stood there, even defiant. Grechko knew without asking that the young man in the photo was her son, and he'd been killed in the Soviet invasion. She'd been waiting to carry that sign for thirty-one years, and today was the day.

In the growing restlessness of the crowd, Grechko also sensed something else: an opportunity. He had underestimated the Hungarians. The leader of the nation that had oppressed and bullied theirs for decades was going to appear right in front of a monument to their ancient heroes, and these people were going to show him that they would no longer be intimidated. The police, and the many MIA and KGB agents in plain clothes who were undoubtedly mingling with the crowd, would certainly be on high alert, but they would also have to contend with a great many potential threats, many more than they were used to dealing with. In such a situation, his odds of completing his mission right here and now were greater than he anticipated they would be. He might not have to wait till the next day. He had to be ready. If an opportunity presented itself, he might very well have to take advantage of it.

Grechko's weapon already had a silencer attached, and he considered removing it. The sound of the shots would galvanize the crowd, perhaps causing panic. The police would react quickly, but maybe they would overreact. In the ensuing chaos he would have a good chance of making a clean getaway. Probably a better chance than he would have the next day, on the more controlled and much less populous grounds of the horse farm. His plan for the farm was very good, he knew that, but this might be even better. The downside of using an unsilenced weapon was that the sound of the shots—he would fire three times—could very well focus immediate attention on him. He decided to leave the silencer on. Chances were great that once the target went down, one or more of his security detail would begin firing wildly into the crowd, creating the panic that would cover Grechko's escape.

He would just have to evaluate the situation as it presented itself. To that end, he began working his way toward the southeast corner of the square, where the motorcade would arrive. If he was to have a chance, it would be there.

***

Jennings had found a spot close to a TV truck near the motorcade entrance. It had been nearly twenty minutes since Jo's signal, so he knew the limousines could appear any moment now. Next to him was a gaggle of students, several carrying signs. More were on the other side of the motorcade route created by the barriers. Compared to protest signs seen in the West, these were pretty mild, at least those that were printed in Russian. He had a working knowledge of that language but nothing at all of the Hungarians' native Magyar, a notoriously difficult tongue. But the Russian signs were critical of this event's guest of honor and his country, so he assumed the ones in Magyar were no different. G would not be facing a friendly crowd.

The Special Forces major took a moment to consider the political implications. If the Russians were hoping to provide a propaganda counterpoint to Reagan's visit to Berlin the week before, they were going to fail miserably. The question would be, what impact would this have in the West? M1's signal could be seen in Austria, where NATO intelligence agencies would record the broadcast and analyze it carefully. Undoubtedly some of it, if not all, would be picked up by commercial stations in the West as well. Some of the more clever students had anticipated this and carried signs with no words, only with imagery that would need no translation. Prominent among these were the Soviet hammer and sickle paired with the Nazi swastika.

They had balls, Jennings had to give them that. It wasn't too long ago that the forerunners of these kids had been cut down in these streets like wheat on a collective farm at harvest time. There were no tanks today, though, no heavy weapons at all. The soldiers with their Kalashnikovs could do some damage, of course, but Jennings sensed they weren't going to be inclined to use those weapons. Unless the students got aggressive, and Jennings had seen enough demonstrations to know that it never took much of a spark to light a fire. G would have a heavily-armed security detachment that would think nothing of taking out some Hungarian students if they presented a serious threat.

One well-trained man, though, might be able to get through.

His senses on full alert, Jennings carefully surveyed the crowd through his sunglasses. They had only a rough idea of the Wolf's appearance, and from Jo's near-fatal encounter with him in Hamburg they'd been able to deduce his approximate height and weight. They calculated he'd be anywhere from five-ten to six-three, solidly built but not too distinctive, and on a chilly day like today he'd be wearing a coat, probably a hat as well.

Jennings was watching a pair of blonde female students, each carrying signs printed in Russian, when he caught a movement toward the fringe of their immediate group. Without moving his head, he shifted his eyes to his left. There, the guy with the newsboy cap, like so many men were wearing today, but this character was different. His mode of dress showed he was trying to look nondescript but Jennings knew a trained man when he saw one. The giveaways were very subtle, but they were all over this guy. It was the way he moved, how he didn't show the same emotions as the rest of the crowd, how he seemed calm amidst the growing excitement. It was him, all right.

Jennings reached up and adjusted his glasses, giving the signal to Harrison and Jo, if they were able to catch it, that he had eyes on the target. He would repeat the signal twice more in the next minute. The TV truck was to his left, and he'd lose sight of the Wolf if he went behind it. At that moment a cameraman and a guy with a sound boom, who had been at the front of the truck closest to Jennings, took their gear back toward the entrance to the square. Jennings took the opportunity and walked right behind them. The crowd was behind the barrier about twenty meters away. In the distance he heard the brief whoop of a siren. The motorcade was coming past the last intersection.

***

Grechko saw the lead motorcycles slowing as they came down Dósza György, preparing to turn into the square. Behind the six motorcycles were four armored Zil limousines. Grechko knew that his target would be in the second one. They were sloppy; unlike American presidential motorcades, which had at least ten vehicles and sometimes many more, these fools did not have high-powered sport-utility vehicles filled with heavily-armed security troops. Even though Pataki had not been able to provide an exact roster of persons within the Zils, Grechko knew that the first limo would hold six KGB agents at the most, who would form the target's flying wedge of security on foot. The second limo would have the target and whatever Hungarian big shot was coming along for the ride, plus aides for both men, and one more security agent next to the driver. The third vehicle would have another four or five security agents and the fourth would contain a medical team. Three Budapest police cars brought up the rear. That was how KGB had been running its motorcades for years and they weren't going to change now.

The key factor now was what side of the vehicle the target would emerge from. Grechko was betting it was the driver's side, facing the square. The target was well aware of the power of television, so he would get out that side, ready to wave to the crowd and the cameras. There would be a span of no more than three seconds between his emergence from the limo and his enclosure by the lead vehicle's security team. Grechko could empty his Makarov's entire ten-round magazine in that time. He would need only one, but would fire two more to make sure. He slid his right hand into the deep pocket of his jacket where the weapon waited, its silencer still attached.

The motorcycles were pulling into the square when Grechko looked back at the TV truck, almost directly opposite him now, and saw the man with the sunglasses, looking right at him. The man was reaching into his own jacket pocket and instantly Grechko knew that he had been made.

CHAPTER THIRTY-TWO

BUDAPEST,
HUNGARY
JUNE 19, 1987

Will Harrison was standing at the southeast corner of Heroes Square when he saw Jennings give the eyes-on signal. Following his partner's gaze, Harrison scanned the several dozen people immediately across the entranceway the limos were about to enter. It took him only four seconds to sort them out and lock onto the man Jennings had seen.

At first glance he didn't look like much. Average height and build, average clothing, but then he saw the same signs he knew the SF major had seen. Even though the man was not moving very much, he was not allowing the crowd to control his movements. He was fluid, smooth. His facial expression didn't change like those around him as the people became aware of the approaching motorcade. He had the brim of his cap pulled down just a little too low. Most of all, he kept his right hand in his jacket pocket. Every other man was moving his hands in and out of his pockets, but not this guy.

Harrison looked to his left and saw Jo, still about

thirty meters away, walking steadily toward them but not at a hurried pace. The last thing they wanted now was to draw attention from their target or the police. But just as he thought this, the target began to move, and he wasn't moving to his left, getting into better position for a shot at G when the limos rolled to a stop, but to his right, toward the edge of the square. The target must've realized Jennings had spotted him.

If the target made it out of the square, they'd lose him. He could head southeast down Dósza György and turn into a side street, losing himself in the warren of apartment buildings and shops. If he headed in the other direction, he could get to the intersection with Népköztársaság and go down into the subway, or walk down the boulevard amidst the crowds. No, he had to be stopped here, now.

Walking next to a young student couple as they moved toward the square, Harrison reached into his right jacket pocket and clutched his silenced pistol. He would wait until he was abreast of the target and shoot through the jacket into the man's side. The wound would be fatal, but not instantly so. Harrison could continue walking as if nothing had happened and once he was in the midst of the crowd within the square, he could make his way back to the safe house as they'd planned. He felt a brief thrill; he was going to take out the Wolf, not Jennings, the cocky Green Beret, and not Jo, the human weapon.

They were only fifteen meters apart now and the gap was closing quickly. It looked like the target would come right by him, allowing Harrison to stay with his students, making his attack less obvious. Twenty meters beyond the target, Jennings was sliding along the traffic barriers set up on the southeast side of the motorcade entrance to the square.

Eight meters. Harrison kept his eyes straight ahead, using his peripheral vision to track the target. He resisted the impulse to speed up his own pace. Let it happen, just as they had in training. He kept his breathing under control, just as Jo had counseled them so many times on the mat back at MacDill.

Five meters. He kept his right hand in his jacket pocket, bringing his left up to blow in it, but with his right he positioned the pistol.

Two meters, one meter, and as he brought the pistol up slightly within the pocket, the target's right hand shot out and connected with Harrison's right forearm, just below the elbow. The move was so fast the CIA operative had barely registered it at all, but the pain was instantaneous and overwhelming. His entire forearm and hand went numb, and he couldn't suppress a gasp. It was as if a jet of fire raced up through his bicep. He became light-headed, lost his focus, stumbled. The students looked at him with bewildered expressions.

Harrison recovered his balance, his mind screaming at him over the blazing pain: *Stay focused. Don't draw their attention. Focus!* He had to stop walking, forced himself to breathe deeply. He couldn't pull his hand out of the pocket. To his left he saw a uniformed policeman about ten meters away, looking at him, his head tilting slightly. Harrison knew that his actions had tipped off the cop. If he was detained now, with the gun, it was all over. The cop started walking toward him. Harrison felt the urge to flee, to run for all he was worth, but his brain somehow couldn't connect to his legs.

Someone gripped his left arm and he heard a familiar laugh. *"Heinrich! Da bist du ja!"*

It was Jo. She'd said, "There you are!" Why was she speaking German? Her cover was a woman from Armenia, she should be speaking Russian, but—

The cop was near them now. *"Jól van, uram?"* From Harrison's slight knowledge of Magyar, he thought the cop was asking him how he was doing.

"Excuse us, officer," Jo said in German, giving the cop her most dazzling smile, "we're just here on holiday, and my boyfriend has had a little too much to drink. Already!"

The cop gave him a stern look, then nodded at Jo. "You take him away," he said in halting German. "Too much here."

"Yes, isn't it exciting, comrade?" Jo pulled Harrison by the arm. Thank God his legs were moving. "Thank you, officer. Come on, Heinrich, you need to sit down."

Jo led them out of the square just as the lead motorcycles rolled into the southeast corner entrance. The pain was starting to lessen rapidly, but his right arm was still numb. For a panicky moment he thought it might be permanently damaged. Jo seemed to sense his fear. "He hit you on the *kote* pressure point," she said in English. "It'll come back in an hour or so."

The target was walking briskly down Dósza György. "He's getting away," Harrison said.

"He won't. Greg's on his tail."

"We need to help him."

"You're out of commission until this thing wears off," Jo said, as they double-timed it across the street. "Get to the subway and back to the safe house."

"But–"

"That's an order, Will."

***

Jennings saw Jo leading Harrison away from the square. What the hell happened to him? The SF major had taken his eyes off the target for only a split second as a TV crewman bumped into him at the back of the van, just as the Wolf was approaching the CIA operative. Then Harrison was stumbling like he'd been stabbed, but Jennings saw no sign of a wound.

The target was walking briskly down Dósza György on the opposite side as the last of the motorcade's limos glided into the square's access street. The trailing police cars pulled up to the curb, flanking the entrance. Jennings walked in front of the lead cruiser, a small Russian-made Lada that wouldn't have lasted twenty minutes in an American city, and crossed the street. Glancing quickly to his right, he saw Jo standing with Harrison near the metro station at the end of Népköztársaság. She touched him on his right arm and then started walking down the sidewalk toward Jennings.

The Wolf turned right on the first intersecting street, Délibáb Avenue, and kept moving. Jennings had to make yet another snap decision: wait for Jo to catch up to him, or follow the target now. He knew there really wasn't much choice, and started walking quickly toward the corner. Behind him there was a murmur in the crowd, a rising tide of sound that didn't include cheers of welcome.

Like most of the streets in this part of the city, Délibáb was lined with trees and ornate old buildings, not yet sullied by Soviet-style utilitarianism. But right now Jennings was more concerned about what building the Wolf might try to enter in order to evade any possible surveillance.

He didn't have to wait long. Forty yards down the street, the target crossed over to the southeast side and kept going, pushing through a low iron gate and into the courtyard of what appeared to be an apartment building.

Jennings didn't have much choice here, either. Trotting across to the same side, he hustled to the edge of the building's property, just in time to see the Wolf open the elaborate front doors and step inside. Glancing back over his shoulder, Jennings saw Jo turn the corner and step up her pace as she saw him. He nodded toward the building and vaulted over the low stone wall. He landed softly and withdrew his Beretta 92 from his shoulder holster, the silencer already attached.

The courtyard, shaded by the maidenhair trees and carpeted by sparse grass, was empty. Jennings ran to the entry and took the six stairs in two steps. Both of the doors had windows, and he could see nobody in the foyer. He pushed the left door open, its hinges grating, and slipped inside. Ahead of him was a short hallway to the right of a staircase, one door on the right of the hallway, an elevator at the end. Had the Wolf gone into the apartment? Jennings doubted it; a few days' worth of newspapers littered the floor in front of the door, so it would almost certainly be locked and the target hadn't had time to pick it.

From above he heard the sound of footsteps on the staircase. Weapon at the ready, Jennings started up toward the first landing, twelve steps away.

***

Grechko heard the door open one floor below and knew the man who had followed him from the square was coming inside. Was he KGB? MIA? It made no difference. Unless Grechko could gain entry to one of these apartments or find the rear entrance, he would have to confront the man and deal with him.

He cursed himself for his decision to come to the square today. Yes, it had seemed like a good idea when he knew the motorcade was on its way, presenting him with an opportunity, but in hindsight he had been foolish even to entertain the thought of taking out his target here. And now he had been spotted by a security agent and was in danger of being captured or killed. Neither prospect held much appeal for him.

He stepped onto the second floor and looked quickly around. A row of apartment doors lined the outer wall, closed and silent, a few of them with newspapers on the floor before them, like the door on the first floor. He heard no obvious signs of occupation. Quickly he decided that his best option was to follow the hallway around to the back of the building. Most of these apartment complexes had front and rear stairwells.

There was a slight creaking of wood from below. Oh, this one was good, Grechko concluded. He was being careful. He knew where his quarry was. Undoubtedly he already had his weapon at the ready. Grechko considered waiting to see the man come around the stairs at the landing and taking his shot there, but again he decided that it would be better to escape without leaving a dead or wounded man behind him to raise the alarm in the city. Instead, he walked quickly to his left for ten meters and followed the hallway, making another turn to the left at the corner.

The stretch that greeted him was a good twenty meters long and had apartment doors on the right side. From down the hall came the sound of a television, mixed with music from a radio. Somebody was home today in at least two of the flats. He began walking down the hallway. His second step produced a loud wooden creak as the floor sagged slightly underneath his shoe.

***

Jennings heard the sound as he stepped onto the second floor, hugging the wall. He knew it was from the hallway around to his left and took a chance, crouching low and swinging around the corner with his gun trained straight ahead. Nobody there, but he heard another creak as the Wolf picked up his pace. Grabbing one of the rolled-up newspapers from the floor, Jennings raced to the corner of the hallway and tossed the paper ahead of him. From down the hall came two muffled pops and the newspaper exploded, with both rounds embedding themselves into the wall in small clouds of plaster.

The bits of shredded paper were still floating downward as Jennings dove to the floor, rolled and fired two shots down the hallway. "State security!" he shouted in Russian. "Drop your weapon!"

The man was ten meters down the hall, standing with his left hand clutching his right bicep. Jennings motioned with his own weapon and the Wolf crouched down and set his pistol on the floor, then stood back up.

Jennings carefully got to his feet, keeping his

weapon trained on the Russian's center mass, and walked slowly toward him. Their orders were to capture the Wolf if possible, kill him if necessary. Someone higher up the food chain had decided it would be worth the risk to bring him in for interrogation. The boys at the embassy were probably wetting themselves at the thought. Jennings knew he could pop him right now and be done with it, and who would ever know? But an order was an order, and he'd already winged this guy. The prospect of capturing the most dangerous man in the Soviet arsenal was right in front of him, only a few meters away. Backup right now would've been nice, but for the next minute or so until Jo arrived, it was his show.

"Very slowly now, back away from the gun," he ordered as he advanced on the Russian. The man took a step backward, then another. "Very good. Now, put your hands behind your head."

"I cannot move my arm," the man said, and Jennings was impressed by how calm his voice was. He tried to see if there was blood seeping between the man's fingers, but the fabric of the coat was dark to begin with. Still, a wound serious enough to debilitate the arm should've been bleeding enough to show.

Jennings had plastic zip cuffs in his jacket pocket. Cuffing this character was going to be tricky, but they'd trained for this, usually with two people, but he could do it alone. "Turn around," he ordered. The man complied, still holding his right arm. Jennings took another step closer. "Spread your arms."

The end of Jennings' silencer was within three feet of the target's back. As the Wolf held out his left hand, Jennings saw there was no blood on the fingers, and an alarm bell started ringing in the back of the SF major's brain just as the Russian twisted his body and fell to the floor, to the right of Jennings' line of fire. Before he could react the Russian's feet shot up and scissored Jennings' forearm. Pain shot through his arm in both directions and he couldn't maintain his grip on the pistol.

***

Grechko swung his right leg as the man staggered back with a yell. He connected with the back of the man's knee and he went down. He was not KGB, of that Grechko was certain, not with that accent. A westerner, probably a NATO agent. Very well, he could be killed without arousing undue suspicion. The Spetsnaz operative reached back for his own gun, and when he brought it back around, his enemy, much to Grechko's surprise, was coming at him, his right arm dangling uselessly, forearm bent slightly where Grechko's kick had broken the ulna. The westerner leaped and slapped Grechko's gun aside, following through with a backfist strike to the head.

The blow connected but Grechko had turned his head instinctively and received only a fraction of its intended power. Maintaining breathing control, Grechko exhaled to rid himself of the immediate pain from the strike and continued moving, rolling out from under the man as he brought a leg up for a solid kick to the chest. Grechko aimed for the throat but came in too low. The man was stunned nevertheless, collapsing onto the floor with a groan. Grechko brought his weapon around as he rose quickly to his feet. Below him, the man coughed and looked up, eyes wide with the awareness that his life was about to end.

"Sie sind nicht russich," Grechko said. *"Sind Sie deutscher?"* He switched to English. "Or perhaps you are British. MI6?"

"Go fuck yourself."

"Well, an American. Tell me, who sent you?"

The man on the floor didn't reply. Grechko sighed, but before he could pull the trigger he heard a spitting sound from down the hallway and the unmistakable buzz of a nine-millimeter round passing inches from his head, followed by a female voice in Russian. "Drop your weapon or you die!"

He looked to the end of the hallway and could not believe his eyes. Could it be? Yes, there was no doubt. It was the Asian woman from the alley in Hamburg.

Grechko stepped back from the prone American. If they were working together, doubtless she was American as well. He put aside the obvious question of why the Americans would send operatives after him and rapidly considered his options. There were not many, but one revealed itself at that moment as one of the apartment doors opened and a little girl leaned out. Behind her came the shrill cry of a woman.

Grechko saw the Asian woman's eyes flick toward the girl and he didn't hesitate. He brought his weapon up and fired toward the child, deliberately missing her by mere centimeters, causing her to cry out in alarm as he bolted away down the hallway, firing wildly over his shoulder. He expected to feel the impact of bullets in his back, but none came and he turned the corner. Ahead of him was the staircase to the back of the building, and he knew he had made his escape.

CHAPTER THIRTY-THREE

BUDAPEST, HUNGARY JUNE 19, 1987

Harrison was waiting for them at the safe house when Jo and Jennings came through the door. The SF major collapsed on the couch, his face white, sweat beading on his forehead as he clutched his right forearm.

"What the hell happened?" Harrison asked as he closed and locked the door.

"His encounter with the Wolf didn't go so well," Jo said. She stepped into the bathroom and grabbed a towel. "Is there any ice in the refrigerator?"

"I think there might be some cubes," Harrison said. He went to Jennings on the couch and gestured to the arm. "Is it broken?"

"Hell yes, it's broken!" Jennings sucked in his breath as he struggled to remove his jacket. Harrison helped him, then rolled up Jennings' sleeve, took the towel containing the ice cubes from Jo and placed it gently on his forearm.

"Hold your arm in place, high on your chest above the heart," Harrison said. Jennings winced as he complied.

Jo filled the CIA agent in on the events in the apartment building. Harrison unconsciously rubbed his own elbow as Jo related what Jennings had said about the fight. "Sounds like a helluva gun disarm technique," Harrison said.

"I got too close to him," Jennings said. "Should've tapped him right away."

"I stopped at a phone booth and alerted the embassy," Jo said. "We need to get you medical treatment." She'd used the code word that indicated a non-life-threatening medical emergency, which would alert the CIA station chief to their situation. They'd been assured during the mission planning that such an alert would get embassy personnel to the safe house within thirty minutes.

"The embassy has a fully staffed clinic," Harrison said. "How long since your call?"

Jo checked her watch. "Fifteen minutes. I called from the first booth I saw after we exited the metro."

"Were you followed?"

"I don't think so," Jo said, "but I can't be sure. I had to take the most direct route here."

Harrison looked grim as he flexed his right arm. "We stopped him at the square, but that means he'll go for the shot at the horse farm tomorrow. And now we're down to two people."

"How's your arm?" Jo asked.

"It's sore, but there's no serious damage. I'll be good to go tomorrow."

Jennings had been following the conversation. "So will I."

"You most certainly will not be," Jo said. "At the very least you'll be in an air cast and a sling."

Jennings struggled to sit up, wincing in pain. "I'll be–"

"Lie back down on that couch, Major," Jo said. "That's an order."

"You're lucky all he did was break your arm," Harrison said. "If Jo hadn't showed up, you'd be dead."

Jennings' eyes blazed in spite of his pain. "Well, where the hell were you? I saw what happened in the square. He took you out with one simple nerve punch. Don't those clowns at The Farm teach you people self-defense?"

Harrison's fists balled. "You want a matched set, Keith?"

Jo stepped between them before he could take a step toward the prone soldier. "That's enough! Will, sit down." She looked down at Jennings. "As for you, Major, try to keep calm until the embassy team gets here."

Harrison sighed as he sat in the chair, then said, "I'll send word back with them that we need to recon this horse farm as best we can. They can send over a packet later tonight, maybe with a briefer who knows the place. They might have to tap into one or two of their local assets."

"The more people who know about us being here, the greater potential for a leak," Jo said.

"I know, but we really don't have much choice at this point. We had our shot at the Wolf today and we blew it."

"Speaking of shots," Jennings said, "why didn't you drill the son of a bitch, Jo?"

Jo sat down in the only empty chair and shook her head. "His shot at the girl distracted me. I've never seen anybody move that fast before and still shoot so accurately. By the time I reacquired the target, he was running down the hallway and firing back at me. I ducked and rolled, came back up and he was around the corner and gone. I couldn't pursue because I heard sirens. We had to get out of there before the police showed up." They'd made it out of the building's rear exit just seconds ahead of the police.

Jennings shook his head, then wiped his brow with a sleeve. "What a clusterfuck," he said. "We had three swings at him and missed every time."

"Yes," Jo said, "but we're not out of the game yet."

Harrison excused himself and went into the bathroom, closing the door behind him. Jennings fiddled with his cold pack, then stared at the ceiling. Finally, he said, "Damn."

Jo got up and went over to the couch, sitting beside him. "Don't blame yourself, Keith," she said.

"I had him, Jo. I had the bastard dead to rights. Good as he is, he's not Superman. I could've double-tapped him and we'd be on the way to the airport right now."

She placed a hand on his shoulder. "We have our orders," Jo reminded him. "You did the right thing."

He looked at her and his eyes were hard, despite the pain. "If you have a shot tomorrow, Jo, take it. Don't screw around with this guy. If he gets away, he might be coming after our people next." He reached across with his left hand and grasped hers. "Take the damn shot, okay?"

"He won't be getting away, I promise."

***

Dusk was descending on the city as she left the safe house and made her way to the rendezvous with the Hungarian contact. She immediately sensed that the city felt different. Jo had often thought that cities had their own spirits, and tonight, Budapest's was not as tense as it had been ten hours before. This time she took a roundabout route, watching for possible surveillance. The police presence on the streets was dramatically different than it had been during the day. The people who were out and about seemed more relaxed, too.

At the square, she had felt their frustration, their resentment. But, fortunately, it had not boiled over. There were no incidents. Jo had seen a replay of the event on TV. Gorbachev arrived, walked briskly from his limousine to the podium, was introduced to polite applause, and gave his speech virtually without interruption. The Soviet leader talked about "seeking different roads to the future," and "the compelling necessity of the principle of freedom of choice." Jo had seen bewilderment on the faces of many Hungarians in the crowd. This was not what they had expected. Twenty minutes after he began, Gorbachev concluded his address by thanking his hosts and the people of Hungary for their hospitality, and exited the podium to applause, even some cheers.

The briefer from the embassy arrived at eight o'clock, but he wasn't able to tell them much about the horse farm. Everyone agreed it was the only logical place left for the Wolf to make his move. It would be the only time during the whole day when G would be out in the open, even remotely accessible to the Hungarian public. The agent provided forged press credentials for Jo and Harrison. "These should get you in," he said, "but we don't have his exact itinerary there. We have a contact in Hungarian security who knows the drill for tomorrow. He'll meet you tonight at nine o'clock. The recognition signal is 'bunny hop.'" The agent handed Jo a slip of paper with an address.

***

The pub was just off Vaci Street, the trendiest location in downtown Budapest, or at least as trendy as things got in a communist capital, Jo thought as she took note of the three couples around tables on the outdoor patio that crowded the sidewalk. The Hungarians had so much potential, and it could only be unleashed by freedom. Maybe that would happen now. From the time Pallas had been tasked with this mission, Jo hadn't really given much thought to the politics of the situation, but Gorbachev's speech had impressed upon her that she was now in the midst of history.

That history would take a sharp turn to the right, though, if they failed in their mission and the Wolf succeeded in his. After that, it might not be too much longer before the tanks were rolling through these streets again.

Jo went inside and found an empty table in a corner. A waitress appeared, asked a question in Magyar, and when Jo responded in German, the young blonde woman switched effortlessly to that language. Jo ordered a beer. A minute later, the waitress was back with a mug of brew that had a light orange color. Jo gave it a taste. "Like citrus," she said.

"It's called a Bunny Hop." The waitress checked her watch. "My shift is over in five minutes," she said. "I'll join you for a nightcap."

A few minutes later the waitress slid into a chair across from Jo, her own beer in hand. "I was told to expect a man," Jo said.

"Perhaps whoever told you just made an assumption. My name is Anna." The blonde took a sip of her beer.

"How long have you been in MIA?"

"Ten years," she said. "I'm older than I look," she added with a smile. "It is, how do you Americans say it? Handy. Especially when dealing with KGB. They are very good, professional, but they are still men, if you catch my drift."

"Such as a certain agent of our mutual concern?"

"He is not officially KGB anymore," the waitress said. "Believe me, they look for him even as you do."

"And you are not looking for him?" Jo asked. "What is Hungarian security's interest?"

"We seek mutually beneficial cooperation with our fraternal socialist allies," Anna said, with just a touch of sarcasm. "At the same time, there are certain elements within our government who would wish him success. They have managed to provide him with direct support here through an MIA agent. This man we know about, and he will be dealt with later. My own immediate superiors, however, do not want to see our guest from Moscow assassinated, most certainly not on our own soil. It is a tightrope that we must walk, you see. When we learned that this rogue was in our country, we were told to observe only, and not to inform KGB. They already assume he is here anyway."

Jo could appreciate the Hungarians' delicate position. "In my country, we have had some experience in dealing with contrary political factions, even within our own agency."

"Indeed," the MIA agent said. She took a healthy drink from her mug. "So it is that we made a discreet inquiry with our American counterparts, asking if they might provide us with some assistance in dealing with this problem. We were informed of your presence in our country, and your purpose. We then offered to help you, in a limited way."

Jo knew that the decision to inform MIA about the Pallas team must have been made at the highest levels. It was a tremendous risk, but now it might pay off. "How limited?" she asked

"First, we decided to steer our mutual adversary toward the horse farm for his mission, and away from Budapest. In this I think we have succeeded. This was to give your team a better chance against him than if he focused on the city."

"He tried to make an attempt here anyway," Jo said, "but we were able to stop him, although one of our people was seriously injured."

"We heard of the fight in the apartment building," Anna said. "Your man, he will be all right?"

"Yes," Jo said, "although he's out of commission now." She took a sip of her beer, forcing the image of Jennings' pained face out of her mind. "What else can you tell me about tomorrow?" she asked.

"As you saw today at the square, KGB is providing most of the front-line security for our guest. Our people are in a supporting role. It is similar to when your president is abroad, yes? Your Secret Service works with local security, but your people have the lead."

"How much support will your people be providing to KGB at the horse farm?"

"As little as possible, without being obvious about

it." When Jo raised her eyebrows, the woman added, "This tightrope I mentioned, it is very real. The next year, two years, will be critical to the future of our nation. What happens to our distinguished guest will decide Hungary's destiny for years to come. What will my country be in the twenty-first century? A thriving democracy, or a puppet on strings held by Moscow, as we have been for the last forty years?"

"If you desire the former course, I would think you would be going all-out to help KGB stop the man we seek," Jo said. "But perhaps, as you said, some of your leaders don't mind being controlled from another capital?"

"Even puppets can live pretty well, if they dance when they're told," Anna said with disdain. "Plus, they get to have puppets of their own."

Jo took another drink of her beer. "I believe I understand your situation," she said. "If we cannot count on your direct help tomorrow, what can you provide for us?"

The Hungarian withdrew a folded piece of paper from her clutch and slid it across the table to Jo. "That is a map of the horse farm, Bodor Major. The markings in red indicate where our guest is to make his tour. I am to be in the show as well, and I had an idea of how I might be able to assist you." She sketched out her plan. It was simple, but daring, and Jo thought it just might work.

"It is my opinion that the Wolf will strike when the target is most exposed, during the horsemanship show," Anna said as she sat back and took a sip of her drink.

Jo tilted her head in recognition. "You know our mutual friend by the same name we do."

"He is a legend among intelligence agencies in the Warsaw Pact," the MIA agent said. "A man of uncommon skill." With a tilt of her head and the slight raise of an eyebrow, she sent a signal Jo immediately understood.

"I can attest to his skill," she said, "although not in the area you are alluding to."

Anna smiled. "And you are still alive?" She raised her mug. "You are to be congratulated."

"It's a little early yet to hand out congratulations," Jo said. She drained the last of her beer. It really was quite good; too bad she was not in the mood to enjoy it.

"One last thing. You should know that tomorrow, KGB might very well be somewhat less than vigorous in its protection of their principal. We have information that the man in charge of the security at the horse farm is working for the same people as the Wolf."

Jo took a moment to consider that, then said, "But they will not do the deed themselves?"

"No, they would not be that obvious. And for reasons we've discussed, MIA will not be able to assist you, either, except perhaps to make it less difficult for you to escape than it would ordinarily be. If your original plan for extraction does not work, make your way to the lake between Gyór and Sopron, about a hundred twenty kilometers from the horse farm. The Austrians call it Neusiedler See. There is a small village on the Hungarian shore of the lake, Fertörákos. Inquire at the inn on the town square about the old Roman shrine just outside of town. There is a man in town who is an amateur archaeologist and he will help you get across the border to Austria. Use the code word 'Mithras.'"

"He's one of your people?"

“No, he is a smuggler. Retired now, mostly he putters around at the shrine but occasionally assists us.” She took one more sip of her beer and then stood. “I must go.”

“Thank you for your help,” Jo said. She really liked this woman. Perhaps someday they would work together again. “How sure are you about the Wolf taking the shot during the horsemanship show?”

“I’m the one who showed him the place,” Anna said. “I watched his eyes. He was planning his hunt.”

CHAPTER THIRTY-FOUR

KOMÁROM-ESZTERGOM COUNTY, HUNGARY
JUNE 20, 1987

When he was a boy, Grechko once asked his father if he ever had faced death during the war.

"Many times," his father said. They were at the dacha, splitting some logs for firewood. The autumn nights were getting colder. That night a fire would dance in the hearth and the dacha would be warm.

"Did you ever go on a mission and think you would not be coming back?"

The father paused and leaned on the axe, looking at his son. Then he looked off into the distance, and the boy knew he was thinking about his old comrades again. "Never," he finally said. "If you think that, when you go into battle you will not be bolstered by courage, but crippled with fear. And you will lose." He took another swing of the axe.

His father would have liked this place, Grechko thought as he walked through the stables. His Cossack heritage always came back to him when he was around horses, and these were magnificent animals. The Hungarians had been renowned horsemen for centuries, their cavalry both feared and respected. Like all cavalry units, the Hungarians had transitioned from the horse to the tank and truck during the Great Patriotic War. Grechko had to admit they had fought well against the Red Army, according to some of the more impartial histories he'd read in the West. In the end, though, valiant as they were, the Hungarians were defeated. It occurred to Grechko now that his mission, in effect, was to make sure they stayed defeated.

He stopped at the last stall. The horse, a beautiful Lipizzan, nuzzled his outstretched hand, then looked at him as if disappointed at not finding a carrot. Grechko stroked the animal's soft muzzle. "You care nothing of politics, do you?" Grechko said. "Your world is this warm, dry stall, running upon the plains, and a nice rubdown from your groom at day's end. Such a life you lead." For a moment, Grechko had a vision of saddling up this horse and riding away to the West. In a day, maybe less, he could be at the Austrian border, and then...

No. He forced himself to turn away. He had a mission to complete. The politics of the situation were not his concern. But even though he knew that, he'd also had time in the last several weeks to give some serious thought to the political question.

He was convinced that if Gorbachev lived, the Soviet Union would collapse, and soon. The communist system could not tolerate the freedoms he was proposing. What would replace it? Democracy? Russia had never known such a thing. The country had been ruled for a thousand years by strong men who brooked little if any dissent, and when the strong men of the Party were gone, other strong men would step in. The vassal states like Hungary, Poland, Czechoslovakia, they might be able to break free and align themselves with the West, but those states closer to Mother Russia herself would have a hard time. What would happen to Georgia, to Moldavia, the Baltics? To his beloved Ukraine? With an unruly and nuclear-armed Russian bear on her eastern frontier, how would Ukraine survive? The answer, he knew, was that she might very well not.

At the end of the stable, before stepping out into the morning sun, he checked his watch. He was slightly ahead of schedule. His last communication from Voloshin had told him where the gap in MIA's perimeter security screen would be, and sure enough, Grechko was able to hike the last two kilometers into the horse farm property without incident. The clothing had been cached exactly where it was supposed to be as well. Now, walking about in the traditional Hungarian rider's costume—black vest fitted over a blue shirt with billowing, gathered sleeves, blue pantaloons over high, black boots, topped with a black tricorn hat—he was hiding in plain sight. The riders, who would later put on the exhibition for his target, numbered about fifteen. From what Anna had told him, there would certainly be a few MIA and perhaps even KGB agents mingling among them today, dressed the same as the horsemen. His plan, audacious as it was, would succeed precisely because of its audacity.

Lightly strapped to his bicep, his weapon was carefully concealed under the loose sleeve that covered his left arm, accessible through a slit Grechko had created by pulling apart the seam of the garment. He had used a Makarov for years, and for a time had considered using a Walther PP for this mission, but in the end decided the Makarov's nine-millimeter cartridge gave him a more reasonable chance for success than the .22-caliber he would've used with the Walther. The Makarov had an eight-round magazine and he had two other mags concealed under the other sleeve. Strapped to his left hip inside the pants was his Kizlyar combat knife.

What had finally convinced him to stay with the Makarov was his decision to use the bullwhip demonstration as cover. He'd seen the horsemen practicing with them during his visit with Anna and the sound of the cracking whips would serve perfectly as cover for his shots. During one portion of the show, two men used their whips together, allowing him to take two shots, although he was confident he'd only need one.

His target's motorcade arrived right on time, and from a distance, careful not to be seen too far from some of the authentic horsemen, Grechko watched as the Soviet leader was greeted by the owner of the horse farm with the traditional Hungarian salty bread biscuit, *pogacsa,* and fruit brandy, *palinka.* Gorbachev tossed back the palinka with gusto, then appeared to cough. Two of the Hungarians near Grechko laughed. "That'll make his birthmark turn purple," one of them said.

The KGB presence here was somewhat lighter than what Grechko had expected. Well, Voloshin had told him the head of the detail today was one of the Committee's men, and so far that had been confirmed by everything Grechko had seen. Either that, or KGB had chosen a fool for this task. He doubted that; KGB was not known for fools.

Gorbachev went into the farm's main lodge, where he would sit down for a light luncheon. Then would come the horsemanship exhibition. The Hungarians began to walk back toward the barns, where they would ready their horses and equipment. Grechko kept pace with them, lagging just a pace behind. By staying with the men he avoided any possible contact with Anna, and in any event he had not yet seen her. So far, in fact, he had not seen anyone, either in costume or not, giving him any extra scrutiny. His luck only needed to hold for another hour.

***

Using her forged press credential from *Kommunist,* the pro-Soviet newspaper in Armenia, Jo had no trouble renting a car at the Budapest airport. The Lada she was given was serviceable but would've drawn laughter on an American highway. That is, if anybody had slowed down enough to laugh; the Lada's acceleration was a joke, less than half the rate of a comparable small American-made car. "You might have to get out and push," Harrison said when they finally made it onto the highway labeled E60.

"I make it about a hundred thirty kilometers to the horse farm," Jo said, looking at their CIA-supplied map.

"Just over an hour with an American car on the interstate back home," Harrison said, gripping the wheel tightly as the Lada's tiny four-cylinder engine whined. "With this heap, we'll be lucky to get there tomorrow."

Jo suppressed a sigh. Harrison's attitude had been

getting progressively worse since the failed attempt to stop the Wolf at the square the previous day. "We'll get there, Will," she said. "We have enough time." She estimated they'd arrive at the horse farm just before the arrival of G's motorcade, but they'd be deliberately cutting it close; showing up well in advance would only give the security detail more time to get suspicious of them.

They made it to Bodor Major with a half-hour to spare. The two-hour drive from Budapest had not been without tension. For one thing, neither one of them had any previous experience driving in rural Hungary, although the directions supplied by their CIA contact were not hard to follow. For another, Harrison's arm still clearly pained him, even though he denied it. Not only had his arm been injured the day before, so had his pride. Jo could only hope that Harrison's professionalism would keep his emotions under control this day. She couldn't afford to worry about him; her own fatigue and stress were eating away at her reserve of self-discipline. Her training and discipline had never failed her before, but she knew there was always a first time.

But not today. She would not allow it.

To her surprise, after they left the E60 and headed southwest along a two-lane road, there had been only two roadblocks, the first in the village of Környe, a second in the smaller hamlet of Dad, just before their turnoff to the horse farm. Both were manned by uniformed MIA troops who appeared less than enthused about their duty. They gave the Americans' false papers cursory looks and waved them on.

Now, they pulled the Lada into a small, gravel

parking area. Ahead of them was the large farmyard on the right with the main house, outbuildings and stables, along with outdoor pens for animals and birds. On the southern edge of the property was a small seating area for spectators, shaded by an awning and flanking the oval-shaped horse track. The uniformed police presence was not as heavy as they'd anticipated. "We need to reconnoiter the area," Jo said. She checked her watch. "G is due in about twenty-five minutes. Let's take different paths around the main farmhouse and meet back there. I think I see them setting up a press gallery."

"Got it. I'll circle around behind the track. Meet you in the gallery in about fifteen."

Carrying his camera to preserve his cover as a photographer, Harrison started off through the lot, heading for the track, where Jo could see some riders in native dress warming up their horses. In the track's small infield, one man was uncoiling a black bullwhip.

Jo's press credentials were checked twice, once by a uniformed Hungarian security officer, then by a man in plainclothes who was almost certainly KGB. Both times her Soviet passport and Russian language skills backed up the phony press credential. One of the agents also inspected her steno notebook; the first few pages were already filled with background notes she'd composed the night before. Jo exhaled slowly after the second encounter. No matter how many times she went undercover on a mission, these exchanges always brought tension that required all her discipline to control. One slip could result in arrest, prison, or a firing squad. Her training had always stressed that resisting arrest would be counterproductive. Stay calm and stick to the plan, help would come soon from the diplomatic side. That was the theory, anyway; Jo knew that in practice, things often didn't turn out that way. One more reason why she had long ago vowed that she would never be taken alive.

She joined a group of three journalists fussing over a miniature pony in one of the pens. A stout, thirtyish blonde woman scratched behind the pony's ears, then smiled at Jo. "Is she not beautiful?" the woman asked in Russian, with a distinct German accent.

"It is a he," Jo replied in German, smiling.

"Oh, my goodness," the woman said in the same tongue, blushing. "He's so small, I couldn't see from here."

Jo extended a hand. "Larisa Kocharian, from Armenia. And you?"

The woman took the hand with a firm grip. "Angela Merkel, from East Germany. Are you a journalist?"

"Yes," Jo said, "from *Kommunist,* in Yerevan. What paper are you with?"

"Oh, I'm not a reporter," Merkel said. "Actually, I'm with the Academy of Sciences in Berlin-Adlershoff. My gentleman friend, Alois, is with *Neues Deutschland*, out of East Berlin. He brought me along on this trip."

"I see," Jo said, noticing the tall man next to her. "Well, enjoy your visit."

Merkel touched her arm. "I will. I'm sure our friends from Moscow will as well." She nodded slightly to her right, raising an eyebrow. Jo followed with her eyes and saw a man with short-cropped brown hair, watching them from several feet away.

Jo looked back at the German and nodded ever so slightly.

Harrison caught up with her in the media section near the grandstand, designated by yellow tape and signs in Magyar, Russian and German. "I see the guest of honor is arriving," he said, gesturing toward the parking area where men were climbing out of two Zil limousines. They watched as Gorbachev, smiling broadly, shook hands with his hosts, then sampled the pogacsa and palinka. Photographers crowded for decent shots of the Soviet leader grimacing after downing the brandy.

"Our man isn't in that group," Jo said. She had already looked over each of the journalists and photographers carefully. None of them matched the description of the man she'd seen in Budapest yesterday.

"I didn't see him, either," Harrison said, "but remember, he could easily see us. We're not exactly in disguise, and he'll remember us from the square."

"If he does and it throws him off his game, all the better," Jo said. "We could be just enough deterrent to make him scrub the mission."

Harrison looked at her. "You don't believe that any more than I do," he said.

"You're right," Jo said. They watched Gorbachev and his party enter the farmhouse. "He'll be inside for thirty or forty minutes. When he comes out, he'll take a walk around the grounds to see the animals, and after that it's show time at the track."

"Where do you think our man will make his move?"

Jo looked back to the grandstand. A mounted horseman came thundering down the track. Beyond him in the infield, a man on foot stood with a bullwhip, focusing on an empty wine bottle fifteen feet in front of him. The man drew his arm back and then forward, the long black whip trailing behind and then coiling around like a living thing. The tip flicked against the bottle, cutting the neck like a knife through butter, the bottom half of the bottle barely moving. A split-second after the impact, Jo heard the supersonic crack of the whip.

"During the show," Jo said, "and I think I know how."

CHAPTER THIRTY-FIVE

KOMÁROM-ESZTERGOM COUNTY, HUNGARY JUNE 20, 1987

The dignitaries began settling onto the benches under the awning. They appeared to be in a good mood, Grechko observed as he joined several of the Hungarian horsemen and the two whip handlers in the infield. In the past hour he had been questioned by another man in costume, this one almost surely an MIA agent, but Grechko had been able to bluff his way through that by implying that he himself was KGB. That man would bear watching; he was back at the entrance to the track now, with the mounted horsemen, but if he made a move toward the security agents who were standing next to the spectators, Grechko knew he would have to act quickly or abort the mission.

The program called for six distinct exhibitions of horsemanship and weaponry, each one more spectacular than the one before. The bullwhip demonstration would be the next-to-last act on the program. The finale would be a Hungarian woman, in nineteenth century women's equestrienne dress, riding a truly magnificent Lipizzan, which she would guide through a form of dressage to demonstrate the horse's balance and intelligence. Grechko had watched her practice and was very impressed. It was too bad she would not get her chance to perform for their guest.

But where was Anna? She had told him that she would be in the program, but the only woman in costume was a brunette, taller than Anna, with glasses and a pronounced overbite. Perhaps Anna had been replaced by someone. Or perhaps she had simply been trying to impress him.

The horse farm owner introduced the program over a tinny public address system, and the first event began, two horsemen driving a four-wheel carriage, pulled by four black horses, thundering down the track. Right behind them was a one-man cart pulled by four white horses. The vehicles looked rather fragile to Grechko, but the horsemen handled their animals deftly and appeared to be as relaxed as gentlemen out on a Sunday ride.

As the next act began, involving four solo male riders displaying their archery skills, Grechko felt yet another whisper of doubt creeping past the barriers he'd erected in the back of his mind. These Hungarians, they were highly skilled, proud of their work and their country. Imagine what they could do if unfettered by politics.

He slammed the barrier down on the whispering and focused on the mission.

***

Will Harrison joined the other journalists in the press pool that was confined to a roped-off area, left of the shaded benches. About a dozen other men and women were in his group. His German was tested more than once as he responded to friendly hellos from some East Germans and Austrians. One reporter from Vienna's *Wiener Zeitung* clearly had doubts when Harrison said he was from *Wirtschafts Blatt,* Austria's leading financial and business paper.

A handful of photographers had gone across the track and set up in the infield so they could get straight-on shots of the spectators. Harrison wished he were over there, but Geary had insisted that he stay as close to G as possible. When she explained she was certain the Wolf would take his shot from the infield, Harrison was skeptical. It was highly doubtful their target had been able to smuggle a rifle onto the grounds, and a pistol shot from that distance–Harrison estimated it would be a good forty to fifty yards if the shooter used one of the two horse carts over there for cover–would be a superhuman shot indeed.

Then again, this guy had proven himself over and over to be somebody several grades above the average operative, so Harrison was willing to concede the possibility. Jo had hustled off somewhere to meet her MIA contact, and he didn't see her over there now. The only people in the infield were five of the Hungarian horsemen, all wearing their blue and black outfits and old-fashioned hats, plus two women in Victorian-era riding dress. They both had the "Sisi" look that Harrison had seen so often in Austrian media, recalling the Empress Elisabeth, who ruled the last great Habsburg dynasty alongside her husband Franz Josef. As he recalled, Elisabeth had been an athlete and equestrienne of some renown, so he wasn't surprised the Hungarians would put a woman in the show with Sisi-inspired skills.

He flexed his right arm, which was still sore from the shot he'd taken the day before. Damn, but that had pissed him off, and Jennings' attitude back at the safe house hadn't made him feel any better. Well, he'd always been considered the odd man out in Pallas Group, he knew that right from the start, but he was here now, one of only two agents they had left who could stop the Wolf. From the beginning, Geary had been the only team member who had made any real attempt to get to know him, and he respected the hell out of her for that. Of course her father was a spook himself, so he wasn't surprised. Harrison was sorry he'd been surly with her on the drive. If they made it out of here alive, he'd have to buy her a drink and apologize.

His job now, though, was to keep an eye out for the Wolf if he made an overt attempt on G from this side of the track. If the shot didn't come from the infield, it would have to be from here on this side, but that wouldn't be easy, either. Surrounding the group of eight dignitaries on three sides was a small phalanx of KGB security agents. The open side was facing the track. It made sense, though, to cover all possibilities. The major problem, as Harrison saw it, was that he and Jo were unarmed. They'd been carrying at the square yesterday, but that was one thing. Here, in a much more controlled environment, they simply couldn't take the chance of being searched by the security detail. No, if they were to move against the Wolf today, they would have to improvise weapons.

Harrison couldn't imagine a more hopeless

mission. They'd all been armed yesterday and they'd still failed to put down their target. That arrogant prick Jennings had the Wolf dead to rights and blew it. Now, just the two of them, unarmed... what chance did they have? Well, Geary seemed to think they had one, so he'd have to hang onto that. Just do your damn job, Will, he told himself. The colonel will do hers and maybe, between the two of you, you'll get lucky.

Could one of these journos be the Wolf in disguise? Harrison had looked all of the men over carefully and none of them bore much resemblance to the man he'd encountered in the square yesterday. He used his camera to take some shots of the crowd that filled the five rows of benches. The guy could be in there, maybe one or two of the men could be him, but none of them were within six feet of G.

Over in the infield, two of the Hungarians began uncoiling their long, wicked-looking bullwhips.

***

The last act before the bullwhip demonstration was wrapping up. Two horsemen, each with a harnessed team of four horses, rode down the track, standing on the bare backs of the two rear horses in each tandem. Each pass by the spectators came at a faster pace, until on the final one the horses were nearly at full gallop. The horsemen never wavered, displaying excellent balance and command of their steeds. The guest of honor was duly impressed, smiling broadly and applauding each act more vigorously than the one before.

Men began moving in the infield as the standing

horsemen jumped nimbly to the track and bowed to the spectators, drawing loud applause and cheers. As they led their horses away, the two bullwhip experts strode onto the track. Four other horsemen went ahead of them, two of them carrying small display stands, the others with boxes. As the first men placed the stands on the dirt, the others withdrew empty wine bottles from the boxes, placing one bottle on each stand. They lifted the boxes and scurried back to the infield as the announcer began to speak, first in Magyar and then in Russian, introducing the men with the whips.

***

The Hungarian woman reached over to adjust her companion's hat. "Do you see him?" she asked.

"I've got him," Jo said. She adjusted the small bustle underneath her skirt. She'd arranged it so that she could remove both quickly, but until then she'd have to put with the discomfort.

Anna saw Jo's expression and smiled, allowing her dental appliance to protrude in what would almost be comic if the situation weren't so serious. "At least my legs are bare, you're still in your jeans."

"I'll survive," Jo said. "Thanks again for your help."

"My colleague was not pleased that she was to be replaced by me today. I can't wait to get off these elevated boots, and these teeth are ridiculous. What we do for the cause, eh?" She smiled again, running her tongue along the edge of her appliance, but then turned serious again. "I wish I could do more, but I am not to interfere with our mutual friend. They should have allowed me to provide you with a weapon, not just these clothes."

"Don't worry," Jo said. "I'll make do with what I have."

"But you are unarmed," Anna said.

"I'm never unarmed."

Jo turned to face the infield. No, she was never unarmed. She always carried four weapons with her: two hands, two feet. But now she was about to confront one of the most dangerous, highly-trained men in the world. For the first time in her life, she feared that this time, her own four weapons would not be enough.

***

Grechko moved toward his pre-selected shooting position. There were two small horse-drawn carts in the infield, both now sitting alone without their horses or human attendants, and either one could've been used as a decent firing platform, but he'd ruled them out quickly. Both would require shots of longer range than he was comfortable with using a handgun, and neither provided the type of cover he'd need after the shots. Indeed, he now saw one of the Hungarian horsemen, the one Grechko had made already as the MIA agent, walking over to examine the carts.

The authentic horsemen, the ones not involved in whatever exhibition was going on at the moment, had positioned themselves along the edge of the infield grass, several meters away from the spot that would be directly across from the spectators. From here, Grechko would have an angle on the target of about forty-five degrees. The distance, he estimated, was now about twenty-five meters. Even better than he had hoped. As the bullwhip handlers began their demonstration, Grechko walked up behind the two Hungarians who stood watching the show. He chose the one on the left. One last glance over his shoulder showed the two women riders about fifteen meters away. One of them was adjusting the saddle on her horse, the other was fussing with her own skirt.

The first whip cracked, and the bottle nearer the spectators wobbled on its stand but stayed there, intact. The second whip followed three seconds later, neatly decapitating the bottle on the far stand. The crowd applauded as a horseman ran out to replace the bottle with a fresh target. Grechko knew that the program called for each of the bullwhip artists to do three bottles. As they prepared their second strikes, Grechko reached inside his left sleeve and removed his handgun.

***

Everyone else on this side of the track was watching the bullwhip handlers, and though Harrison had to take some photos to maintain his cover, he scanned the crowd carefully after each snap of his shutter. The journalists were busy scribbling in notebooks or snapping photos. The Austrian whom Harrison had met earlier, standing ahead of him to his left, leaned toward a woman next to him and said, “Real Indiana Jones guys!” The spectators were chatting among themselves, no doubt praising the skill of the Hungarians with the whips, although he did see a few of the security agents sitting silently, their eyes flicking between the crowd, the track and the journalists.

Harrison looked back across the track to the infield. The whips cracked through the air within split-seconds of each other and both bottles cracked in half, flying from the stand into the dirt. The crowd roared, and two horsemen with fresh bottles hustled out to the stands for the finale. Harrison had overheard two of the East Germans saying that there would be only three strikes.

Where in the hell was the Wolf? The CIA agent couldn't believe that the man would not be here. Perhaps he was going to wait until G made his way back to his limousine. No, that made no sense, the security detail would be tight around him then, much tighter than here. It had to be now.

In the infield, Harrison looked behind the whip handlers. Two Hungarian horsemen were standing on the edge of the infield, to the right of the handlers as Harrison looked at them. The geometry quickly materialized in Harrison's mind. He looked back at the security team around G and saw that one of them was eyeing those Hungarians, too.

Behind the two horsemen, another man came closer and Harrison saw him reach across his body to his left arm. Behind him, one of the Hungarian women in period dress was walking quickly toward the three men. Harrison saw her lift her skirt up slightly as she picked up the pace. On the track, the bullwhip handlers readied their whips, cracking them overhead, once, twice, as the PA announcer called for the final strike.

***

Grechko leaned close to the ear of the Hungarian

on the left. In German, he said, "State Security, comrade. Do not move." The other man looked over and his eyes went wide as he saw Grechko holding the Makarov, his wrist on the right shoulder of the horseman. On the track, the handlers brought their whips around and forward toward the bottles.

The whips cracked like rifle shots as the two bottles broke in half. Grechko sighted on his target and squeezed the trigger, a heartbeat after his arm was pulled down and to the side. His first shot went into the crowd, the second somewhere into the dirt of the track.

***

Harrison saw the pistol extend past the Hungarian's shoulder, almost completely disguised by the horseman's matching black vest. If he hadn't been looking right there, he would've missed it. *"Pistolet!"* he shouted in Russian. "Gun!" The Wolf's arm was pulled down as the first round fired, then the second. In the front row of spectators, a Russian screamed and fell backward, blood spurting from his leg. A KGB agent threw himself across Gorbachev, and the agent Harrison had seen watching the horsemen in the infield drew a pistol and fired three shots. One of the Hungarian's heads snapped back, his tricorner hat flying away.

Women screamed, men yelled, and a wave of terrified journalists and spectators surged against Harrison, pushing him away from the track as they stampeded. His last glimpse of the infield was of the woman in a long dress struggling with one of the horsemen.

CHAPTER THIRTY-SIX

**KOMÁROM-ESZTERGOM COUNTY,
HUNGARY
JUNE 20, 1987**

Grechko reacted immediately after his second shot, allowing his arm to go with the momentum of his unidentified opponent as he swiveled his body around to the right. The head of the Hungarian to his right suddenly snapped back as his hat flew off. Grechko saw the red hole in the man's forehead and knew someone in the security detachment was returning fire. The next round might find him instead of another innocent bystander.

He first saw his adversary's long dress and long-sleeved waistcoat, then the bonnet perched on top of black hair, and finally her eyes. Even as he recognized the American agent, his body continued its countermove, swinging his arm around to break her grip on his forearm. But she flowed with him and her grip did not loosen. He continued to swing his arm counter-clockwise, intending to bring his gun up into her abdomen and fire. His finger began to squeeze the trigger but something crashed into him from behind. He shouldered the woman aside as he went down, her grip finally broken. As he hit the ground he rolled onto his left side, dragging his new opponent with him. It was the first Hungarian, the man whose shoulder Grechko had intended to use as his firing platform. He was courageous, Grechko would give him that, but also untrained. He had failed to pin the Ukrainian's arms with his tackle, allowing Grechko to bring his right elbow around for a stunning blow to the man's head. Grechko scrambled to a crouch and saw the woman's booted foot swinging for his own head. He barely had time to bring his right arm up and redirect the kick, swinging her around to her left. He leaped to his feet and broke into a run.

***

The skirt's heavy fabric restricted Jo's movement and slowed her down, allowing her roundhouse kick to be deflected. As she pivoted on her left foot, the hem caught under her toe and pulled her off-balance. It took her only a second to recover, but that was enough time to allow the Wolf to get away. Jo saw him leap into the saddle of a horse, kick the horseman in the head and spur the animal into a gallop. From behind her, three shots rang out from the KGB protective detail. None of them found their mark on the Wolf or the horse. The powerful Lipizzan left the infield, crossed the track and raced through an open gate.

Armed men were running across the track to the infield. She saw one of the agents speak into a hand-held radio, holding his Makarov with the other hand. Another man grabbed her by the shoulder. "Who are you?" the man asked in Russian.

Jo didn't have time to waste. "State Security! Is Comrade Gorbachev all right?"

"I don't–"

"Then find out, you imbecile!" She ripped away the drawstring that held up her skirt and shoved the skirt and bustle down past her thighs. "Who is in command here?"

"Colonel Fetisov. But who–"

"Then report to the colonel immediately!" She shoved the skirt into the agent's hands and ran to the horse next to Anna, who had the animal ready. Jo grabbed the reins without a word and swung herself into the saddle, old memories coming back quickly. The last time she'd been on a horse had been, what, six years ago? Yes, at Mountain Home, the base in Idaho where she spent the summer on a training deployment. But a Hungarian horse responded just like its Idaho counterpart, and after a nod to Anna she was off in pursuit of the Wolf. He had a good start on her and was now disappearing into the forest.

Jo ripped the ridiculous hat from her head and her hair came loose and free. She could've stayed in the infield, but she surely would've been taken into custody by KGB, and God only knew when, or even if, she'd be allowed to return home. No, this was her best option. She would pursue the Wolf and bring him down, then make her way to Austria. As her horse vaulted the fence, she wondered briefly about Harrison, back there among the journalists. He was on his own now, but he was an experienced field operative and he'd find his way back to Budapest and the embassy.

***

Slowing the horse to a canter, Grechko guided it down the trail, the same one he and Anna had ridden just a week or so earlier. He shoved the memory of her away, focusing on the task at hand: escape from that devil of a woman and the security agents who were undoubtedly preparing their pursuit of him right now. The Committee's man in charge of the KGB detail would not be able to delay his response, now that shots had been fired and blood spilled.

He had planned this exfiltration route, although he had assumed he'd be on foot. The horse only made things easier. They topped a low hill and Grechko slowed his mount enough so that he could leap off, adding a slap to the animal's flank to speed it up again. As the horse followed the trail downward, Grechko found the intersection with the hiking trail that ran to the northeast along the crown of the ridge. He jogged at a healthy pace and, within a minute, he found the cache where he'd left his clothing and hiking boots wrapped in a plastic bag and stuffed into a rotted stump. As he changed quickly out of the Hungarian rider's costume, he heard the sounds of another horse along the first trail. So, someone had had the presence of mind to pursue him with the best means available, and he knew who that would be. He buckled his belt, tucked the Makarov into the small of his back and made a decision.

***

Jo brought the horse to a stop at the top of the hill and saw the trail ahead of her winding down the hillside. The horse snorted and stamped its front legs, frustrated at not being allowed to continue its run. Jo focused on the sounds from ahead of her, catching the rhythm of a horse, but it was intermittent. Within a few seconds the hoof beats stopped entirely. She rose in the stirrups and strained to look down through the trees. There! About three hundred yards ahead, the trees gave way to a small clearing and she could see the horse, but its saddle was empty. The Wolf was on foot now, but where?

She had to think like him. No doubt he'd scouted the terrain, planned his escape. It would have to involve stealth and deception, but no unnecessary delays. Somewhere nearby, probably within a mile or two, he would have a vehicle waiting. He had to know that once he took the shot the security teams would rally and move to seal off the area. This part of Hungary was heavily forested, but there were enough country roads to provide an experienced operator plenty of chances for a successful exfil.

He would not go thrashing about through the forest. He'd find a trail of some sort, not for horses but just for humans or even just a wildlife path. Jo had never hunted wild animals, but she'd hunted plenty of humans, both in training and on operations, and she'd been hunted herself. She dismounted, slapped the horse on its flank and sent it trotting away. Within seconds she discovered a path that looked like it would run along the ridgeline of these hills. Two feet down the path, she found a fern that had been pressed into the ground.

A hundred feet further she heard a twig snap and immediately crouched behind a tree. Ahead of her, the path twisted through the forest. The trail was no more than three feet wide, usually less, with the occasional plant rising from the dirt that had been trampled by generations of hikers. She attuned her hearing to the sounds of the forest around her, alert for anything out of the ordinary. There was nothing indicating pursuit by security forces. She was not surprised; it would take some time for the MIA to get organized and bring in local police to aid in the search. By now the KGB security detail would have hustled G back into his limo for a fast trip back to Budapest. No doubt his aircraft was being prepped at the airport right now, and once they got back to Moscow heads would roll. The detail's principal had not been harmed, at least as far as Jo could tell, but it had been a very close call and someone would have to answer for that.

There would be pursuit, of that there could be no doubt. She expected to hear helicopters any time now. During the mission prep back at MacDill, they'd been briefed about the disposition of Red Army units in country. There was a helicopter squadron south of Budapest, about a hundred twenty kilometers by air from her location. They could have a gunship over these trees in about thirty minutes. Within an hour there could be Spetsnaz troops all around them. She had to end this fast and make her way to the Austrian border.

But how? The Wolf was armed with his pistol, and she had nothing to counter it except her own skills. Against a highly-trained man with a gun, the odds were not in her favor. She looked around for something that might improve her odds, and some ten feet away she found it.

***

Grechko knew exactly what the Hungarian and Soviet authorities were doing right now. The initial confusion would quickly give way to order as someone took charge and began issuing commands. He knew the disposition of every Hungarian and Soviet military unit in the country, knew their strengths and weaknesses, and had taken it all into account in planning his escape. His best estimate was a window of thirty minutes, perhaps forty-five, before aircraft would be over these trees, searching for him, with troops not far behind. The Hungarian police, no slouches themselves, would also be very active. The route he'd planned over the back roads to the Austrian frontier would not be open for long.

Why, then, was he stopping now, waiting for the American woman? He could have easily maintained his head start and made it to his hidden car well before she could arrive. As supremely trained as she undoubtedly was, she was not superhuman. The smart thing to do, he knew, would be to make his escape. She had foiled what should have been his penultimate mission, but he would have other opportunities to make her pay.

His pride was making him wait for her. Don't be a fool, his trained mind told him, but some less-disciplined part of him demanded that he answer this challenge, and answer it right now. He had been a hunted man for weeks now and he was tired of being hunted. Very well, he would allow just a few more minutes. Ten at the most. Then he would move to the car and be gone. There would be another day. There always was.

***

Jo risked going another thirty feet down the trail. All logic told her the Wolf would be long gone by now, but instinct told her he wasn't, not yet. Not this one. He was up there, perhaps drawing a bead on her right now. She was already in mushin, and her training was in complete command. Her senses reached out and she heard every sound, felt the presence of birds, small mammals. A lizard skittered across the path behind her and she knew it was there without hearing it.

A faint deer path angled away from the hiking trail and she took the path without conscious thought. Moving without sound, her feet found their way without disturbing anything that would react to her presence. She kept low, using the trees as cover. Ninety-five seconds later the deer path curved back toward the trail, and she knew he was there, behind the trunk of a large oak tree only fifteen yards away. She gripped her weapon, feeling its weight, seeking the proper balance. She would have preferred her shuriken, but this would do.

***

Grechko took one last glance at his watch. Time was up. He'd heard the woman's horse come to a halt at the intersection with the hiking path, then gallop away. Once he thought he'd seen her on the path, but the shadow was gone in an instant. Perhaps a deer. No, it was her. But he could not wait any longer. Rising slowly, silently, he moved around the oak, his pistol at the ready. The trail was empty as far back as he could see. If she–

His ears barely registered the whisper of something

flying toward him, his eyes flicked just in time to see the stick as it tumbled end over end, but he could not move his gun hand fast enough. The stick struck the back of his hand and broke his grip. The pistol bounced off the oak and fell to the path. He made a move to reach it but he was too late. She was here.

CHAPTER THIRTY-SEVEN

KOMÁROM-ESZTERGOM COUNTY, HUNGARY JUNE 20, 1987

Jo was right behind her weapon, using the momentum of the throw to surge into her run. She was near her top speed as she crossed the path and ran up the trunk of the oak tree, two steps that turned her almost horizontal to the ground. At the peak she pivoted into a reflex kick, whipping her right leg around and driving her booted foot toward his head, catching him on the jaw with the ball of her foot. He'd been turning his head, but she'd given him her best shot. She landed on the path and spun around to face him.

No. He could not possibly be standing, not after that. But he was, staggering backward two steps, three, shaking his head. She went for him again, two steps to close the distance and then a chinning kick, launching off her left foot and then bringing her right nearly straight up, toward his vulnerable chin.

***

Yobany v rot! He saw stars as his optic nerve translated the intense pressure flowing through his head. If he had not turned it just enough... She was on him again! His reaction was sluggish, too slow, and he could only redirect the kick enough to just graze his jaw. The stars exploded again, but not so many this time. He had to rally, had to–

***

Her legs, she had to use her legs, they were her strength. If it came to hands she would lose, he was bigger and stronger. Men had always admired her legs, long for an Asian woman, supremely toned, but this Russian would not admire them, not after this. She came down from the chinning kick, regained her balance and pivoted into a turning side kick, giving it everything she had.

***

Through the lights he saw her turn, awesomely quick, such marvelous balance she had, truly an artist, but the lights were clearing fast and now he was almost back, able to flow with her kick, deflecting it enough to protect his solar plexus. Her heel crashed into his ribcage and he felt something crack, the pain searing through his side like fire. She came around again, a left roundhouse this time, aiming for the ribs. But now he brought his arm down as he'd been trained so long ago, crouching and twisting his body slightly, absorbing the impact on his upper arm, allowing the energy of her kick to flow through the arm and shoulder and around through the other shoulder and out in a punch, a jab that connected with the side of her head.

***

She stumbled back as she dealt with the pain and struggled to maintain her balance. Summoning up her *qigong* training, she kept her mind and body in balance, breathing steadily, her mind clear and focused, and the pain melted away. Instinctively she knew there was no serious damage. Her eyes focused on the Wolf, just in time to see him coming toward her. She surrendered herself completely to mushin and met his attack, flowing with him, redirecting his kick away from her knee, his punch from her face, but as she moved into a counterattack he suddenly dropped to the ground and swept her legs out from under her. She hit the ground hard but did not resist, allowing the energy to flow back through her as she rolled back onto her shoulders, chin tucked, knees brought in, and then arced herself into a kick-up that brought her back to her feet. She saw him moving again and brought her hands up, but not in time to stop the punch. The impact to her chest was like the explosion of an artillery shell.

***

His head clearing, he saw her go down. She would stay down, too. His ballistic punch had felled men, large men, and there was no way this woman could—

But she did. Dropping to her back, she tucked her head to the side and rolled backward, getting back to her feet, staggering back a couple steps to gather herself. She was breathing hard but her eyes were clear. He had seen eyes like that before. There was death in them. It was time to end this, while he still could.

***

The pain came close to overpowering Jo. The backward roll was instinctive, born of years of training, but even she had her limits, and she was getting dangerously close to them. As bad as her chest hurt now, she knew it would be worse later, assuming she would have a later. Right now that was in doubt.

She shook her head and forced the pain and fear away. No, there was no doubt. She would survive, she would triumph. Jo remembered what she'd heard in a dojo long ago. *Be like water.* Adapt. She could not overpower this man, but she could defeat him. Adapt to what he was doing, and bring it back onto him. Her sternum might be cracked, but her will was not.

He had a large combat knife in his right hand and was coming for her, waving the knife from side to side, trying to distract her. That wouldn't work. Her training against a knife-wielding opponent went back nineteen years, to a steamy dojo in Los Angeles where a charismatic young Chinese-American man was her instructor. The pain was like a flow of lava inside her chest. She pushed it back and let the Wolf get closer, closer, the knife moving less now as he got ready to strike.

***

He kept his breathing under control even as his mind marveled at this woman's resilience. That blow had hurt her badly, yet she was back on her feet. But the knife would tip the scales against her. Resilient she might be, but her flesh would still yield to his blade, her blood would pulse from the severed artery, just like it had from so many others. She made her move, aiming a finger thrust toward his face, and he brought the blade up to slice those deadly fingers, but as he did his left knee exploded in pain.

***

Jo's roundhouse kick to the Wolf's knee knocked him off balance and brought an agonized bellow. She stepped in and grabbed his wrist, brought her right hand inside his elbow and cranked, feeling his shoulder give way as he released the knife. Moving her hand up to his deltoid, she stepped behind his right leg, brought her hip behind his and levered him over her shoulder with a *hapkido* toss, slamming him to the ground. Swinging her legs around and over his chest, she pulled the arm back and used her thigh as a base to dislocate his elbow.

***

"Bozhiyey matyeri! Ya sdayoos'!" Grechko gasped. "Mother of God! I surrender!" The pain was like nothing he'd ever felt, overwhelming his defenses, his training. He could not redirect the pain out of his body through his breath because he could hardly breathe. His vision cleared slightly, enough to see the woman standing three feet away, aiming his pistol at his head. It took every bit of his will to calm himself, and even though he

could now breathe again, the pain was still there. It would not go away anytime soon, that much he knew. He also knew that his life was about to end. "Go ahead... finish it," he said in English.

She was panting and he could tell she was in pain, but instead of pulling the trigger, she asked, "Where is your vehicle?"

Grechko managed a barking laugh, which brought a jolt of pain from his ribcage, then more pain as he struggled to sit up. "You... will never find it," he said, as he assessed his injuries. They were numerous and debilitating. Either she would kill him now or the soldiers would find him, and his fate at that point might be worse. He could not count on protection from the Committee. No, that august body was finished. It would be the Lubyanka for them. He hoped Voloshin would be able to escape. He rather liked the Air Force general, although he could see now that the Committee's goal was foolish. History was against them, not to mention the Americans, who had sent this formidable woman to keep Gorbachev alive. His father would have been dumbfounded. The Americans, actually *defending* a Soviet leader? It was outlandish. Yet, here she was. He laughed again at the absurdity of it all.

"What's so funny?"

He shook his head. "It is not worth mentioning," he said. "So, shoot and be done with it. You do not have much time."

She pulled the pistol back, aiming it upward. "I'm not a murderer," she said. "Tell me where your car is."

A faint ray of hope pierced Grechko's pain. "I will make for you a deal," he said

Was that a grin twitching her lips? The side of her face was swelling from his punch, but still she was a vision of exotic beauty. No doubt there would soon be a large bruise on her chest, right in between the breasts that he assumed were perfectly formed, like the rest of her. He shook his head to clear the cobwebs. He had to think clearly here.

"You're not in any position to bargain," she said.

"Oh, but I am," he said. "You may find my car before the helicopters arrive, but probably not. I venture to say you do not know these back roads. I do. There will be roadblocks. I know where they will be." He pressed on his ribs and struggled to his feet, almost falling back down in the process. He could get up, but he would not be able to walk without assistance, and it was half a kilometer to the car.

"So, you take me to the car, guide us out of here to the border, and then what?"

Grechko looked at her, knowing that now he would have to do something he never thought he would do. But he did not want to die, and most especially he did not want to see the basement of the Lubyanka again. He'd seen it once from the good side of the iron bars and that was enough. He straightened to attention, as much as his battered body would allow. "I will turn myself in to your CIA," he said. "I will cooperate with your people, in exchange for asylum."

She leveled the gun at him again. "And how do I know you won't try something when we get to the car?"

"I will cooperate. You have my word as an officer in the *Sovetskaya Armiya*, the Army of the Soviet Union," Grechko said. "And I am a gentleman," he added. "I hope that still means something in your country."

She hesitated, then said, “It does.” She stepped off the path and picked up a long, sturdy stick. “Here,” she said, handing it to him. “Let’s go.”

CHAPTER THIRTY-EIGHT

VIENNA,
AUSTRIA
JUNE 22, 1987

Jo stood at the top of the Strudlhofstiege, looking at the intricate staircase, wondering if she should take the first step. She knew if she took the first, she would take the second, and the third, and when she found herself at the bottom she would keep walking and might never come back. A block from the bottom of the stairs, across a street, was the Liechtenstein Palace, fronted by a large park. She could lose herself in the halls of the palace, among the trees of the park...

A familiar voice broke her reverie. "Impressive, isn't it?"

Jo turned. Her father was standing there, a broad grin below his graying mustache. "Appa!" She threw herself into his arms and couldn't stop the sobs from coming. Allowing her iron-clad self-control to melt away, she didn't try to. Not even the pain in her chest was enough to keep her from hugging him.

He stroked her lustrous hair. "It's okay, JoJo. It's okay."

After a minute, she drew back, and he offered his handkerchief. As she dabbed her eyes and nose, she said, "I had no idea you were coming here."

"Neither did I until yesterday, when we got the word at Langley about you bringing our, ah, special guest to the embassy. I got in late last night."

"They sent you to escort him to Landstuhl?"

"That's right," Joseph said, putting his arm around his daughter. "Let's sit down, shall we? They said you were going for a walk, and I had to hustle to catch up. I'm not as young as I used to be, you know."

She had to laugh. "Daddy, you're in great shape and getting better." Still, she allowed him to lead her over to sit on a nearby bench. A few pedestrians walked by, coming up the ornate staircase from below, perhaps guests at the nearby hotel. The Alsergrund district of Vienna was relatively quiet, one reason the U.S. Embassy was here, on the nearby Boltzmangasse. CIA Station Vienna had been one of America's key listening posts for the past forty years, keeping an ear tuned to the goings-on behind the Iron Curtain, just forty kilometers away.

"Landstuhl is just the place for him," Jo said. "The best U.S. military hospital in Europe, and plenty of security." It would be a short flight from Vienna to the base in southwestern West Germany, one more leg on the Wolf's journey to... somewhere.

"He'll be there until we get his injuries treated, then I expect he'll be brought to the States."

"I suppose you can't tell me where," she said, knowing the answer.

"Nope, sorry," Joseph replied.

"Will you be doing any of the debrief?"

"Already started," he said. "I had breakfast with our guest. Some small talk with just a few preliminary questions, really. Enough to confirm some things we knew already, and I found out a few things we didn't."

Father and daughter were quiet for a full minute. Then Jo said, "He almost killed me, Daddy."

He nodded. "I read your report. You did well, honey. I'm real proud of you."

She hadn't felt this way in years, maybe since high school. Jo thought back to the time she'd been stood up by a young man. Her mother had comforted her as best she could, but she knew little about this strange American custom of teenage dating. Her father, though, had talked to her later that evening. She'd needed his strength then, and she needed it now. She took a breath, then said, "At the horse farm, I deflected his shots at Gorbachev. I tried to disarm him but it wasn't working, and if that Hungarian hadn't tackled him, he would've shot me, point blank."

He took her hand, helping to calm the shaking. "It didn't really hit me until just a while ago," she said softly.

"That's how it works sometimes. It just creeps up on you. Happens to the best of us."

She looked up at him. "To you?"

"Oh yeah. More than once. But you learn to deal with it."

"It's never been this bad," she said. "I–I'm not sure how to deal with it."

Joseph squeezed her hand, and she felt his strength. "You're doing a pretty good job right now." He switched hands, draping his right arm around her, pulling her close, and she rested her head on his shoulder.

"After that, when I chased him into the woods, I knew that if I found him I'd have to hit him with everything I had, or this time he'd finish me."

"From what I read, that's exactly what you did."

Jo felt herself calming down. Not enough, but it was a start. "Even then, it almost wasn't enough." She touched her chest gingerly. The bruise was deep and angry, but her sternum, miraculously, had not been cracked. It would be a few weeks before she could resume full training, but right now she just felt fortunate to have survived. "I've had close calls before, Daddy," she finally said. "On the beach in Argentina. Last year in North Korea."

"What was different this time?" he asked

She had thought about that, and finally the answer coalesced. "Those times, someone else bailed me out. In Argentina, it was Ian and his Marines. In North Korea, it was the SEAL team. This time... this time it was just me. Me against him. The toughest opponent I've ever faced."

"And you beat him." He squeezed her again. "Remember the very first taekwondo school we sent you to?"

"Yes, in Seoul. I was five. They didn't even call it taekwondo then."

"But you learned the Five Tenets there, didn't you?"

She smiled at the memory. "Yes. Courtesy, integrity, perseverance, self-control, and indomitable spirit."

"Well, I'd say this mission really brought out those last three, honey."

Jo was quiet for another half-minute as she felt her inner strength returning. "You're right, Daddy," she finally said. She sat up, taking a deep breath, but she kept hold of her father's hand. "Thanks for this talk. It really helped."

He gave her shoulder one more squeeze. "Jojo, I've known some of the greatest warriors this country has ever produced, and every one of them struggles with this sometime. You can't be afraid to talk to somebody when you need to. The Air Force has some great people for that. SOCOM will, too, and they'll need 'em, because there will be a lot of work for your people in the coming years."

"I'm sure there will be," Jo agreed. "And I suppose it's time to get started with it."

They stood up, and he smiled down at her. "That's my girl. And the first thing we'll do when we get back to the embassy is place a call back to Washington. There's someone there who wants to talk to you."

"Oh? Who's that?"

"The fellow who gave me this assignment in the first place. He'll want to hear all about the mission. He likes hearing about the things we do, especially when we get a win. And this was a big one."

EPILOGUE

DONETSK OBLAST, UKRAINE APRIL 2015

The men huddled around the antique wood-burning stove, trying to keep warm on the chilly spring evening. There were six of them, wearing combat fatigues and dark green berets, all devoid of unit patches. Four of the men carried the Fort-221 assault rifle, the standard weapon of Ukrainian Spetsnaz, although the two Regular Army men, from 25th Airborne, carried AK-74s. A month ago, when they first met and began training together for this mission, there had been some good-natured ribbing of the paratroopers for using weapons of Russian origin. The ribbing had stopped when the colonel used one of the AKs to outshoot every Spetsnaz operator on the range.

A pair of kerosene lanterns provided enough light for the men to eat. Each of them had cleaned out an American-supplied MRE packet, surprisingly filling and not without flavor. The food restored some of their energy, but they were still tired. The fatigue was apparent in the frustration one of the men displayed when he tossed his empty food packet to the floor. “I would trade twenty of these for one good American Javelin,” he said. The other men nodded. They’d all seen the Russian T-72s and T-80s, old and outmoded but still resistant to anything the Ukrainians could throw at them. They'd heard of the formidable antitank weapons used by the Americans, but nobody expected any of them to arrive in Kiev anytime soon.

Three of their comrades were out there on the perimeter, guarding the abandoned farmhouse. In the main room of the farmhouse were the unit's two officers and senior sergeant, plus the colonel. Also in the room was their prisoner. The men around the stove had not been able to hear anything from the room, save for an occasional thud that might have been something hard striking something not quite as hard, and each of those thuds had been followed immediately by a muffled scream. The last of these had been several minutes ago.

One of the paratroopers, a *starshina,* said, "Do you suppose they're done in there?"

"The colonel will tell us when they're done," another man said. He was from 3rd Separate Spetsnaz Detachment, one of the famous "Cyborgs" who had fought so fiercely in defense of Donetsk International Airport. His name was Anton. Everybody went by first name only; it was presumed, though, that the colonel knew their last names, in fact knew everything about them, as he had selected each one of them personally for this unit and this mission.

Everything had gone well so far, which had surprised the men, since everything had usually gone poorly for Ukraine in this war. The target was exactly where the colonel had said he'd be. Their tactical plan to eliminate the target's support unit was executed with a precision that showcased the experience and skill of the men, and most importantly the meticulous preparation and outstanding leadership of the colonel and his officers. The mission had gone so well, in fact, that the colonel had allowed them to stop here for a few hours' rest before proceeding westward with their prize. They ate more or less in silence, each man in his own thoughts, dissecting the mission, the firefight with the Russians, the growing prospects of their safe return to friendly lines. Each man also reflected on his own good fortune in being selected for this unit, and his deep desire to remain with his comrades, and especially the colonel, for as long as it would take to repel the invaders and bring peace and freedom to a land that had known precious little of either one.

The men conversed in Ukrainian, although each of them was fluent in Russian. Here in the Donbass region of eastern Ukraine, where the majority of people were ethnic Russians and spoke that language, the men never spoke Ukrainian except among themselves, and only then in locations that were at least somewhat secure, like this farmhouse.

They were behind the front lines, in an area controlled by the separatists, although one could never really be sure who was who until you started seeing more Russians, more of their tanks and artillery pieces, as you went east. The Russian frontier was only about sixty kilometers to the southeast. The city of Debaltseve was five kilometers to their south. Once it had been home to thirty thousand residents; now, barely three thousand remained. All of the men in this room had seen the lines of ethnic Ukrainian refugees heading west, something right out of grainy old films of the Great Patriotic War. Only this time the people were fleeing fascists coming from the east, not the west.

"When we get back to Kiev," Boris said, "I am going to have a long, hot bath. Then I am going to Chachapuri and have a big meal, and after that one of the waitresses will take me back to her flat, and then I will unlimber my artillery piece." He emphasized his point with a thrust of his pelvis. Boris was from Omega, the Ministry of Interior's counterterrorism Spetsnaz unit, and this little band's self-styled swordsman. Some of the other men chuckled. They had endured Boris's boasting for a month now, with not a shred of evidence to show the truth of his claims.

"Every girl in Kiev wants to take a veteran to bed," said Dmitry, from 73rd Marine Spetsnaz, the "Seals." Around the stove, heads nodded. All of the Ukrainians, although hardened combat veterans, were looking forward to being back in Kiev, safe from the Russians. So far, at least; none of them would be surprised to see Russian bombers over the city any day now. If that happened, they would be in deep shit, as the Americans said in their films. Well, maybe then the Americans would send something more substantial than MREs, although none of the men in the farmhouse had any illusions about U.S. or NATO troops coming to the rescue. In this fight, Ukraine was on its own.

Perhaps, though, if this mission succeeded, that horrible future could be avoided. The man in the other room, the prisoner, was one of the most important leaders of the so-called Donetsk People's Republic. He was the head of the Sparta Battalion, a Russian who used the *nom de guerre* of Leonidas, and he had personally boasted of having murdered fifteen Ukrainian prisoners. In a recording delivered to a Kiev radio station he bragged about the murders, openly challenging the Ukrainians to come after him.

His challenge had been accepted. Leonidas was not as smart as he thought he was. He was sure as hell not as smart as the colonel, who now had him trussed up in the next room, forcing him to spill his guts about what else the Sparta Battalion was up to. With that intelligence, the Kiev government, incompetent as it was, might actually be able to turn the tide of the war.

Denis, the starshina, spoke again to Anton. "Didn't you say you knew the colonel before the war?"

The men all looked at the Cyborg. "I worked with him once before," Anton said carefully.

Denis kept prodding. "What do you know of him?"

Anton brushed a non-existent crumb from his short beard. "He is SBU, and commands their Alpha unit." *Sluzhba Bezpeky Ukrayniy*, the Security Service of Ukraine, maintained its own paramilitary unit, very secretive and very efficient. "Before independence, he was KGB." Anton hesitated, then added, "It is said he failed his last mission for KGB and had to leave the country."

That brought a derisive snort from another man, Vitaly, from 10th Detachment, a Ministry of Defense Spetsnaz unit. Vitaly was a large man who was renowned as the best hand-to-hand fighter in the entire Ukrainian armed forces, yet in training he had been helpless against the colonel, even though he was thirty-five years younger. "The colonel, failing a mission? Impossible."

Anton shook his head. "I know. The stories we heard about him, well..." He hesitated, then said, "It is said in that mission, he was bested by a woman."

Some of the other men laughed. None of them believed that for a second. “Anton, you are so full of shit it is coming out your ears,” Boris said, smiling.

“I only relate what I heard,” Anton said. “She was an American woman. An ethnic Japanese, I think.”

“She was Korean,” a deep voice behind them said. Startled, the men leaped to their feet. “As you were,” the man said as he stepped into the light from the lanterns. Sitting on the only empty chair, the colonel held his hands out to the fire. “Anton, are there any of those MREs left?”

“Four, Comrade Colonel, not counting the ones we saved for the boys outside.” He pulled the four packets out of his ruck.

“I'll take a meat loaf,” the colonel said. Anton tossed it to him. The colonel opened the packet and prepared the meal with an expertise that had surprised the men when they'd first seen it happen on this mission. Nothing about the colonel surprised them anymore.

The men were respectfully silent for a few minutes as the colonel ate his meal. Like everything else he did, he ate efficiently. Finally, Boris could not hold his curiosity in check any longer. “Comrade Colonel, how did it go with the prisoner?”

“Very well,” the colonel said as he finished the meat loaf. “Arseniy Nikolayevich is a veritable fountain of information about the separatists. He was uncooperative at first, but after some discussion he began to see things in a different light.”

“You should've shot the Russian bastard!” Anton blurted. The colonel merely looked at him. The Cyborg blinked, then said, “Excuse me, Comrade Colonel, but I lost a lot of comrades at the airport.”

"I understand, Anton," the colonel said. He wiped his hands on a moist towel, which he stuffed in the MRE bag. Handing it back to the Cyborg, he said, "You will make sure all the garbage is properly buried?"

"Of course, sir." After a moment Anton asked, "We will not be burying the Russian as well?"

"Not today," the colonel said.

Anton shook his head. "The arrogant prick dishonors the name of a great hero who died defending his people. For that alone he should be executed." Some of the other men nodded agreement. They had recently seen the American movie *300*, about how Leonidas and his company of Spartans had sacrificed themselves to hold off the Persian invaders in 480 BC.

The colonel smile grimly. "I might agree with you, Anton, but I have my orders. Besides, if we can get him back to Kiev, he will undoubtedly provide us with even more information." He checked his watch, then stood, looking over at the starshina, who was the ranking non-commissioned officer in the unit. "We move out in ten minutes. Prepare the men. The ones on the perimeter will have to eat at our next stop."

"Very well, Comrade Colonel." The men began to gather their weapons and prepare their rucks.

The colonel stepped to the doorway of the farmhouse's main room. The door had opened and his executive officer, an SBU captain, stood there, watching the lieutenant prepare the prisoner for transport. "How is he doing, Kostyatyn Maksimovich?" the colonel asked in a low voice.

"He can travel, Comrade Colonel. I don't believe he will hold us back unnecessarily. It is fifteen kilometers to the rendezvous. Assuming we do not encounter any rebel patrols, we should be there in about three hours, maybe less. Skies are clear, and with the moon we have good visibility."

"Good." The colonel sighed. "A night march. I am getting too old for this, Kostya."

The captain grinned. "You will outlive us all, Comrade Colonel."

"Perhaps. We shall see what Comrade Director Nalyvaichenko wants us to do when we deliver our prize to him in Kiev. I am sure he will have more work for us."

The lieutenant pulled the prisoner to his feet. The man grunted, trying to wipe blood away from his lips with his bound hands. He muttered something to the lieutenant, who calmly reached for a certain point on the man's forearm and squeezed, exactly how the colonel had taught him. The prisoner gasped in pain and his knees buckled.

The colonel and his exec moved back into the kitchen, which the other men were now leaving through the back door of the farmhouse. The officers paused to warm themselves one last time by the wood stove, which was cooling now that the fire had been put out. The lieutenant shuffled the prisoner out into the night.

"Well, I suppose we should go, Kostya," the colonel said, regret in his voice.

"Comrade Colonel, may I ask a personal question?"

The older man looked at him, then nodded. "What do you want to know?"

"It is really true? About the Korean woman besting you?"

The colonel looked at the stove and rubbed his hands. His eyes seemed to be very far away for a moment. He rubbed his right shoulder and said, "Korean-American, to be precise, Kostya. And yes, it is true."

"She must have been an extremely formidable opponent."

"That she was, my friend, and she still is."

The young officer looked at his commander incredulously. "You mean, you know her still?"

"We have had the opportunity to work together, actually, once or twice since then." The colonel hefted his rifle. "Anything else before we move out, my inquisitive young friend? And no, I cannot tell you anything else about the American. Her work remains highly secretive. All you need know is that she is on our side."

"Well, that is good." The captain shouldered his pack and picked up his own rifle. He nodded toward the door. "Do you really think what we learned tonight will end this war?"

The older man was silent for a few seconds, then shook his head. "I hope it does, Kostya, but I fear it will not."

"Then the fight will continue," the captain said, and now his voice hardened. "It will continue until we do something to stop those damned Russians. Somebody should take out Putin. That would resolve the matter."

The colonel looked at his exec, and in the flickering light from the lanterns the captain thought he saw a gleam in the old warrior's eye.

AUTHOR'S NOTES

WISCONSIN
NOVEMBER 2015

I am a child of the Cold War. My father was serving in the U.S. Army in West Germany when I was born in Heidelberg, and for the first three months of my life we lived in an upstairs flat in nearby Karlsruhe, until my father was discharged and we returned to the States. My mother had joined him in Europe a year and half before my arrival. She told me years later that she always had to keep a suitcase packed, because if an alert was declared all U.S. military dependents would be evacuated immediately to England or America while the soldiers, including my father, would be sent east to the front lines.

Those front lines would not be very far away. Karlsruhe was only about a hundred fifty miles by road from the border with East Germany. NATO war planners expected that Warsaw Pact invaders, led by the Red Army, would come across the East German and Czech borders at several locations, utilizing West Germany's fine road system to speed their advance. Over the years the Soviets developed different plans for an invasion, keeping some of them on the shelf as late as 1987 or so.

Most of those plans anticipated the use of nuclear weapons by both sides, at least at the tactical level. One such plan, developed in 1979 and known as "Seven Days to the River Rhine," anticipated that the Soviets would have to use about 7.5 megatons of total nuclear power. Most of that tonnage would be in the form of tactical, or "battlefield," nuclear weapons with relatively small yields, designed to destroy specific NATO bases or troop concentrations. The "Seven Days" plan did anticipate that some cities in Austria, West Germany and Denmark would be targeted by 500-kiloton weapons, about twenty-five times more powerful than the bombs used to destroy Hiroshima and Nagasaki in 1945. I have visited Vienna, and it is truly sobering to think that for a long time the beautiful Austrian capital and many other cities were only minutes away from total destruction.

Although battlefield nuclear technology in the mid-fifties was not as sophisticated as it would be a quarter-century later, it is not hard to imagine that my mother probably would not have been able to escape the effects of Soviet nuclear strikes, even if Karlsruhe itself was not targeted. Certainly my father and his fellow soldiers would have been in great danger not just from nuclear weapons but from the massive armored and artillery divisions that the Warsaw Pact would have been able to deploy. I think it is unlikely my parents would have survived. Presumably, NATO would have been able to detect the buildup of forces the Warsaw Pact would need for an invasion, and would then have started the evacuation well before the first shot was fired. But maybe not.

It has now been thirty-seven years since the Berlin

Wall fell and Germany was reunited under one democratic government. The Soviet Union has been dead for almost as long, dissolved by the Russian people and replaced by what we all thought was going to be a democratic state that would start to bring freedom to a country that had never really known anything of the sort. But things haven't quite gone according to plan, which is why the real-life comrades of Sergey Grechko are fighting for their freedom in Ukraine as this is being written. Hardly a week goes by without more reports of Russian fighters and bombers buzzing NATO aircraft and lurking off the coasts of Great Britain and even the continental United States. Swedes and Finns are nervous as mysterious submarines are detected in their waters. The old hammer-and-sickle flag is long gone, but the threat it symbolized remains.

It was said that while the Soviet leadership wanted to rule the world, they did not want to rule a radioactive world, and so they kept their nuclear weapons in their silos and armories. We, of course, did the same, although there were a couple close calls, most notably in 1962. But most Americans living today have no memory of the Cuban Missile Crisis, and in fact one-third of our current population has no memory of the state known as the Soviet Union. Every day, the Cold War slips further into history. In a way, that's a good thing. After all, who wants to remember a time when we were all literally only an hour or so away from being atomized in a nuclear fireball?

Although the armed forces of the Soviet Union and United States never did meet on the battlefield, except for a very few clashes in Korea and Vietnam involving

Soviet advisers and pilots, the Cold War was definitely fought. Those battles occurred largely in the shadows, like the ones in which Sergey Grechko and Jo Ann Geary operated. The stakes were as high as they could be. For the individual operative, capture by the enemy meant certain imprisonment, perhaps even torture and execution. A successful mission might result only in the gathering of information, but that intelligence might be one more link in a chain that could eventually tip the balance of power to one side or the other. The men and women who did this work, on both sides, were for the most part dedicated patriots who wanted to serve their country. Many were idealists, to be sure, but very few were in position to influence the policies of their governments. Like the soldier in his tank or the pilot in his cockpit, the covert operative was a piece on a chessboard, and like most chess pieces, they were expendable. They all knew this, yet they served willingly and usually with a pretty fair degree of competence and honor, as their descendants do today.

Besides being born in Germany, I am of German extraction; my grandmothers were daughters of German immigrants, one of whom came to America to avoid service in Kaiser Wilhelm's army. I have a lot of pride in that heritage, and so I have always disliked the common portrayals of German soldiers from World War II, and to a lesser extent World War I, as strutting martinets intent on world domination. It's easy to understand why Germans are depicted in this way; history, after all, is written by the winners. But the average German soldier from those wars was just a young guy fighting for his country, and in many cases he was conscripted into service. In other words, he was a lot like the average American or British soldier. Similarly, I believe the average special operative employed by the Soviet Union during the Cold War was probably similar to Grechko in many ways. Perhaps not as highly skilled, and the same could be said for American operatives compared to Jo, but that's what fiction is for. It has been my intention with *The Red Wolf* to present these men and women as I believe most of them were.

Ultimately, our side was triumphant in the Cold War, although it was a close shave in many respects. Luck, at the very least, was on our side. Some would say a higher power might've had a say in the outcome, and while that thought might be comforting–at least for us on the winning side–I believe that God gives us a lot of latitude down here to make the best, or worst, of the world He gave us. In the case of the Cold War, thanks in large part to the real-life counterparts of Jo Ann Geary and her Pallas Group colleagues, we made the best of it.

For now.

ACKNOWLEDGEMENTS

This work would not have made it to your hands without the collaboration of several people. My critique group gave me biweekly input into the manuscript and was extremely helpful. My thanks go out to Donna White Glaser, Marjorie Swift Doering, Helen Block and Jodie Swanson, all of whom are fine writers in their own right. Check out their work on Amazon. Also, I owe a debt of gratitude to my beta readers, Carol Burnham and my brothers, Alan and Brian Tindell. Carol performs what I believe is one of modern civilization's most important duties: she is a librarian, in my wife's hometown of Chetek, up here in northwest Wisconsin. Alan is an attorney in Washington state, and Brian teaches American history at a high school in Phoenix. Although we live far away from each other, my brothers and I carry on a regular and lively correspondence, in which we regularly and somewhat irreverently solve the problems of the country.

It goes without saying that I have also been influenced by the work of other writers in this genre, a few of whom I have had the privilege to meet. Thanks to Brad Thor for showing the way and for his words of encouragement, to David Poyer and Stephen Hunter for showing how compelling protagonists should be drawn, and to now-departed writers Vince Flynn, Tom Clancy and Ian Fleming, for setting the bar high.

I must also thank these authors, whose works provided valuable research material: Dick Couch, *Chosen Soldier*; Howard Brinkley, *History of Soviet and Russian Spying*; Duane R. Clarridge and Digby Diehl, *A Spy for All Seasons*; Tom Clancy and John Gresham, *Special Forces: A Guided Tour of U.S. Army Special Forces*; Ray Hildreth and Charles W. Sasser, *Hill 488.* Special thanks to Ray, who provided insights into the Marines who fought to hold Hill 488, because he was one of them, and for his gracious permission to reference his unit's story in this work. If you're in the Tulsa area, look up Sifu Ray at his martial arts academy, www.tulsakungfu.com.

For insights into Ukrainian life, I thank Dima, a young gentleman from that country who has been traveling the world in recent years and took some time to correspond with me and offer his insights. Check out his blog at www.dimascorner.com.

Jo and Grechko are formidable martial artists, and I would never have been able to portray their skills with any sort of realism without the training I myself have had during my own martial arts journey. My taekwondo and karate instructors have been men and women of great skill and equally great patience: Duane Most, Eric Swan, Lloyd Brown, Peter Carbone, Brian and Stacy Swantz, and Jeff Gulczynski. A special thank-you goes out to my instructors in the fascinating Russian art of *Systema*: Vladimir Vasiliev, Konstantin Komarov and Col. Mikhail Ryabko. I've been privileged to spend many days training with these gentlemen and they are just that, albeit extremely lethal gentlemen. I have listed these folks' respective training centers and webpages below. For the reader who wants to begin his or her own martial arts journey, I urge you to find a training center in your area. It will take you awhile to get anywhere near the level of proficiency displayed by the characters in this book, and there will be some bumps and bruises along the way, but you won't regret it.

Finally, I have been fortunate beyond words to be able to travel to many of the places mentioned in *The Red Wolf*, and the thanks for that goes entirely to my wife, Susan Tindell. Not only does she provide honest critiques of my work, she takes me along with her on many of her travels. Being hitched to a travel agency owner has its perks, and although that's a good one, it's way down the list of the reasons why I married her.

LINKS

I invite you to visit my website, www.davidtindellauthor.com,

and my blog at www.djtindellauthor.com.

For social media aficionados, I'm on Facebook (www.facebook.com/DavidTindellAuthor),

Instagram (www.instagram.com/ djtindellauthor)

and Twitter (@DavidTindell1).

Thinking of traveling? Sue can send you anywhere in the world, because chances are she's been there and knows the ropes. Her company website is www.ricelakewi.vacation.travelleaders.com. Check out her travel blog at www.travelleadersyournextjourney.blogspot.com, and if you're especially interested in visiting the beautiful South Pacific islands of Tahiti (and who isn't), you can find out more through

www.facebook.com/Tahiti360.

Here are some links to martial arts centers and masters who have helped me on my own journey to the black belt and beyond:

www.ricelakemac.comwww.weaponsconnection.org
www.brownskarateacademy.comwww.russianmartialart.com

The next volume of the *White Vixen* series sends Jo to the top of Africa in *The Bronze Leopard.* Here's the opening chapter.

NORTHERN TANZANIA
SEPTEMBER 1989

The attack was sudden, fierce, and effective. The assault team went by the book and captured the objective inside of fifteen minutes. The problem was, the other side wasn't playing by the same book, and when some of them went off the page, the assault team didn't know what to do.

Jo Ann Geary's radio came alive. "Eagle One to Vixen, I see two bad guys getting through the perimeter, call it a hundred meters to your nine o'clock. They're heading for those two SUVs, over."

She keyed the transmit button. "Roger that. Any pursuit from our friends?"

"Negative on that, Vixen."

"Roger. We will pursue and engage." She holstered the radio and checked her M4 carbine. "Looks like it's up to us, people."

"ROE, Colonel," one of the men said. Lieutenant Barnes was her subordinate on this operation, but she always encouraged her people to speak their mind. Within reason. The two other Special Forces soldiers, both non-coms, waited patiently, but Jo knew they were ready to move. Since arriving in country they hadn't seen much action. That was about to change.

"Rules of engagement say we are to close with the enemy only if they threaten to overrun our position. I'd say if they get to a vehicle they could come back here after us."

Barnes grinned. "I like your way of thinking, ma'am." He nodded to the two sergeants. "Okay, gentlemen, let's get moving."

They cut through the bush along the trail they'd scouted earlier, down from the small knoll overlooking the terrorist camp. Technically they were here as advisers only, but Lt. Col. Jo Ann Geary, U.S. Air Force Special Operations, had quickly found that the local Tanzanian Army folks weren't entirely receptive to advice. For one thing, Colonel Njenga had decided against having a helicopter gunship provide cover for the assault. There were only three in his entire army and he said they couldn't be spared. Jo had been able to convince him to allow a single American UH-1 Iroquois, a Vietnam-era "Huey" on loan from the CIA, to monitor the mission. With one of her team members aboard, Jo had received a virtual play-by-play of the assault from the moment the helo emerged from behind the hills.

For another, she reflected as she hustled down the path at the head of her column, the Tanzanians certainly didn't want a woman telling them what to do, or even making suggestions. Well, she'd dealt with that in the U.S. military, although by now most American men were at least grudgingly receptive to having a female in command. She'd quickly discovered that wasn't the case over here.

But the locals needed help, whether it was offered by men or women. For nearly a year now, a shadowy terror group had been operating in the rural areas of northern Tanzania, destroying farms and burning an occasional village. The government was used to dealing with frontier bandits, but this outfit had stepped into the big time with its recent incursions into neighboring Kenya.

First was a raid against a border village, and then a bolder strike against the city of Kehancha. Close to a hundred heavily-armed men had attacked in two groups, one robbing three separate banks, the other storming a radio station and a nearby shopping plaza. Taking over the airwaves, the terrorist leader had identified the group as the *Chui* Brigade. "Chui" was the Swahili word for "leopard." The spokesman, who didn't identify himself but spoke Swahili with a distinct northern European accent, announced the formation of the People's Republic of Sekenke, and demanded recognition by the governments of Kenya and Tanzania. A manifesto left behind at the radio station declared that the breakaway nation's borders included large swaths of land along the southern and eastern shores of Lake Victoria, extending from the Tanzanian city of Mwanza all the way to Winam Gulf in Kenya, and inland to the middle of the Serengeti.

The Kenyans reacted quickly, chasing the terrorists

back into Tanzania and then closing the border, declaring that no remnants of the Leopard Brigade remained within their territory. But there were plenty of them in Tanzania, and the Kenyans demanded that their neighbors do something about them, or Nairobi would send its own men and tanks across the border to deal with the threat. The Tanzanian government in Dodoma, having fought a war against its northern neighbor Uganda just ten years earlier, wanted no part of another regional conflict, but quickly discovered that its small army was not quite up to the task. Someone had called Washington and asked for help, and the Pentagon delegated the mission to Special Operations Command.

Jo and five fellow operators were deployed by SOCOM to assist the Tanzanians, and within a month they'd been able to help the government isolate and kill, capture or scatter most of the Leopard Brigade. Finally they had located the last holdouts, including their mysterious leader, said to be a European. The rebel camp was surrounded and the Tanzanian soldiers moved in, with the Americans observing from their nearby hilltop and the helicopter. Colonel Njenga had assured them that his soldiers would now finish off the last of the Leopards.

Well, not quite.

***

What passed for the terrorists' motor pool was supposed to have been guarded by a squad of Njenga's men, but no Tanzanian soldiers were in sight when Jo and her troops emerged from the bush into the small clearing. Two dusty Land Rovers sat facing the crude road that had been hacked out of the bush. The closer of the two was empty, but the next one's engine turned over and revved high. The vehicle surged forward six feet and stalled.

"Barnes!" Jo shouted. "Take Carson and cover their rear. Saunders, you're with me." The Americans split into two pairs, weapons drawn, covering the twenty meters from the forest to surround the Land Rover.

The driver's door swung open and an African stepped out, holding a small object in his right hand. He reared back, preparing to throw.

"Grenade!" Saunders shouted. Jo sighted on the man with her M4 and fired a three-round burst, tattooing the African's chest. The grenade dropped to the ground and rolled under the engine block of the empty Land Rover.

Jo hit the ground onto her stomach, swinging her legs around so the heels of her boots faced the vehicle. Tucking her elbows to her sides, she covered her ears with her hands and opened her mouth. Behind her the grenade exploded with a loud thump, and she felt the shock wave rolling across her body. Bits of shrapnel hissed past her head, but she felt no impacts. She jumped to her feet and brought her weapon around.

The empty Land Rover was smoking, sitting off-kilter with its front wheels splayed outward. On the other side, the African's body slumped against the side of the stalled SUV, bleeding from the chest and legs. Jo and the sergeant approached cautiously, their weapons trained on the passenger seat. Through the dusty windshield she could see movement inside.

"You okay, Saunders?" she asked, without taking

her eyes off the vehicle.

"Good to go, ma'am. One tango still in the front seat."

"Roger that. Let's take him alive if we can."

Fifteen meters to her right, she saw Barnes and the other sergeant, both apparently unhurt, covering the vehicles from the rear. Jo used hand signals to tell them she was coming around to the passenger side.

The door swung open on rusty hinges as she cleared the front of the Land Rover. "You are surrounded!" she shouted in English. "Hands in the air!"

Nothing moved for three seconds, and Jo was almost at the door when a man burst from the interior of the vehicle. She caught a glimpse of dirty blonde hair and a camouflage-patterned jacket and pants as the man ran past her, heading for the edge of the clearing twenty meters away. Jo saw Barnes raising his rifle to shoot.

"Hold your fire!" she yelled. From a thigh pocket she took a *shuriken* and threw it backhanded at the fleeing terrorist. The metal star struck him in the left buttock, bringing a yell of pain. The man stumbled but kept his feet as he clawed at the star.

Jo closed the distance in three seconds, just as the man slashed his hand on a point of the star, bringing another yelp. *"Scheiss!"*

A German. Somehow she wasn't surprised. *"Hande hoch!"* Jo ordered, but instead of holding up his hands, he charged at her. Jo easily ducked his wild punch, side-stepped and drove a kick into his thigh. As he staggered, she flowed counter-clockwise and brought him down with a right roundhouse kick to the head.

The German collapsed to the ground, out cold.

"Nice job, Colonel," Barnes said as he walked up to her, keeping his weapon trained on the unconscious terrorist. "Looks like we have a European here."

"He spoke German, so my guess is he's Red Army Faction," Jo said.

"Why would a German terrorist be raising hell in the middle of Africa?"

"Your guess is as good as mine at this point, Ken. When we get him back to our base camp, maybe we can persuade our Tanzanian friends to let us spend a little time with him to get better acquainted." She retrieved her shuriken, wiped it on the German's pants, and returned it to the sheath in her pocket. "Tie this guy up, then take one of the sergeants and inform Njenga that we have a prisoner. I don't hear any more gunfire from over there, so he's probably getting his own prisoners set for transport."

Barnes gave her a knowing look. "Assuming they took any," he said.

***

The Tanzanians had actually taken four men alive in the raid on the Leopards' camp, all Africans. At the army's staging area, some fifteen kilometers from the target, Jo watched the prisoners being herded from a truck toward a hastily-constructed holding pen. Wrists bound with plastic zip ties, the captured men looked beaten to Jo, watching with her men from ten meters away. All of them, except the European; he was alert, and even though his jaw was starting to swell from Jo's kick, his eyes were clear and piercing as they took in his surroundings. For a long moment they fixed on the Americans.

"Something tells me you won't be getting a Christmas card from him, Colonel," Barnes said.

"He'll be lucky to be alive by Christmas," she said. "The Tanzanians are probably going to make an example of him."

"Do they still hang people down here?" Sgt. Saunders asked. Only twenty-five, Saunders had been in Special Forces for three years, and this was his first deployment to Africa.

"Hanging is probably the least of his worries right now," Barnes said.

Three heavily-armed Tanzanians took charge of the European, leading him away from his fellow prisoners toward another tent. "I'd better talk to Colonel Njenga about getting in a word with his new friend before he's taken away," Jo said. The distinct whup-whup of a helicopter heralded the arrival of the Huey, coming in from the west after searching for any terrorists who might've escaped the raid. Jo turned to the lieutenant and the two sergeants. "Why don't you guys see if the mess tent has anything going? When Major Reinecke checks in from the bird, I'll get on the sat phone back to the embassy in Dar es Salaam. I'd imagine we'll be heading home soon."

"We'll save some filet mignon for you," Barnes said with a grin.

The Huey came in for a deft landing in the clearing next to the base camp, and three seconds after the skids hit the ground, a lanky figure in woodland-patterned utilities jumped from the cabin and, head down, loped over to where Jo waited. When the figure straightened up, Jo caught the wide, toothy smile of Major Denise Reinecke, USMC, her longtime friend and comrade-in-arms. They'd met during the top-secret Diana Brigade training in '75 and had worked together several times since then. Two years ago they'd both joined Pallas Group, a small unit of special operators created by presidential order out of SOCOM.

"Nice job up there, Denise," Jo said.

"I saw the takedown, Jo. Any idea who he is?"

"We're about to find out. Let's go visit Colonel Njenga."

The Tanzanian officer was in his command tent, finishing up a radio call with his headquarters in Upanga, near Dar es Salaam. He waved the two Americans into the tent as he signed off the call in Swahili. Replacing the radio handset in its cradle, the tall officer broke out into a satisfied smile. "Colonel Geary, Major Reinecke," he said in English with a touch of British accent. "A pleasure, ladies, especially as we can now celebrate a successful mission."

"Your men performed well, Colonel," Jo said, and she meant it. The Tanzania People's Defense Force didn't have the best reputation in Africa, which meant it was several orders of magnitude below NATO-level efficiency in the quality of its soldiers and equipment, but they were willing to accept suggestions–at least from men–and displayed good spirit in the field. In a month of operations against the rebels, Njenga's force had lost only a dozen men in action. "My team will be returning to our embassy, if you have no further need of us," Jo said.

Njenga swept his hand toward the tents where the prisoners had been taken. "You have helped us a great deal. I am sure my president will be in communication with yours to express the thanks of our nation. As for now, I will be taking the prisoners back to Dar es

Salaam for interrogation."

"May we speak to the European first?"

Njenga shook his head. "I am afraid that is impossible. My orders are clear: the prisoners are to speak to no one until they are safely incarcerated in Upanga. I am sorry."

Jo hid her disappointment. "Perhaps some people from our embassy would be able to question the European. After your officers have done their own work, of course."

That drew a smile. "I will see what I can do." From out in the compound came the sound of truck engines starting up. "Ah, our transportation is here. Ladies, I must excuse myself. I am to accompany the prisoners personally. My second in command will strike the camp."

Njenga led the way out of the tent. He stopped, fists on hips, and drew in a deep breath. "I have always enjoyed being in the field with the men," he said. "Especially when we are defending our country."

"I know the feeling," Jo said. Denise just smiled.

"Tell me, Colonel," the Tanzanian said, looking down at her. "Will you be returning to America straight away? Perhaps you could stay a few days. Our country really has much to offer for our guests."

"We do have some leave coming," Denise said.

Jo gave her a surprised look. "I thought you wanted to go to Jamaica with Lionel."

The Marine major shrugged. "Change of plans. Got a 'Dear Denise' letter from him just before we moved out."

"What kind of letter is that?" Njenga asked.

Denise laughed. "The kind no lady wants to get from a man, Colonel. Let's just say if he goes to

Jamaica, it won't be with me."

"Oh. I am truly sorry."

"Don't be. He was a lousy–"

Knowing what was coming next, Jo interrupted. "Tell me, Colonel, if two ladies wanted to do something adventurous in your country that doesn't involve chasing rebels through the bush, what would you recommend?"

Njenga looked off into the distance to the south. "You cannot see it from here, but if you would like a challenge, I would suggest climbing Mount Kilimanjaro."

"How high is it?" Jo asked.

"Almost six thousand meters," Njenga said, "but the climb can be done without special mountaineering training. I myself have done so twice."

Jo did the calculations: nineteen thousand feet. She'd never climbed a mountain before, and she knew immediately she'd have to do it. She gave Denise a look and was rewarded with another dazzling smile. "Sounds like a trip," the Marine said.

Njenga's grin revealed teeth so white they were almost blinding. "Well, ladies, I am sure you will enjoy yourselves." He shook hands with the American women, and with one final nod he walked over to where the prisoners were being loaded into an old Bedford, the British version of the American deuce-and-a-half. This one looked old enough to have carried some of Montgomery's Tommies in Egypt nearly half a century before.

"So, no more Lionel," Jo said. "And you were so excited about him."

Denise shrugged her shoulders. "Let's just say he flunked his audition. Thought he was hot shit and I was just a Marine mattress." She gave Jo a sly look. "You've heard the phrase, 'Once you have black, you'll never go back'? Well, they never met Lionel."

"But, you said he sent a letter to you."

She shrugged. "Must've been upset that I laughed at him." She gestured at the departing Tanzanian colonel. "He was as tall as Njenga but Lionel used his height to intimidate people, especially women."

Jo nodded. "That's happened to me," she said.

Denise barked a harsh laugh. "Jo, my zoomie friend, there ain't a man tall enough to intimidate you."

***

The Africans were sloppy, but what else could one expect from them? Sitting in the back of the truck as it jolted along the road, Horst Wissmann waited patiently for his chance. The two Tanzanian soldiers riding back here with him were getting sleepy.

The side of his head where the American woman had kicked him would be swollen and bruised for the next few days, but nothing had been seriously harmed, with the exception of his pride. To have lost his command was bad enough, but be taken down by a *fraulein* was worse. Adding insult to injury was the apparent fact that she was Asian. Most likely of Japanese descent, considering her skills. Wissmann remembered his father talking of the Japanese officers he had met during the war. They were very cultured, the old SS *Obergruppenführer* had said, but in battle they could be savage.

Well, Wissmann thought, he was going to find out just how savage this particular Japanese woman could be.

Made in the USA
Columbia, SC
16 September 2021